"Our God and souldiers we alike adore,
Ev'n at the brink of danger; not before,
After deliverance, both are alike requited,
Our God's forgotten, and our souldiers slighted"
Francis Quarles – 1592 - 1644

PAPER, SCISSORS, STONE...

A Korean War Novel

R. N. CALLANDER

Paper, Scissors, Stone.
A Korean War Novel

First published in Australia by R. N. Callander 2024

A catalogue record for this
book is available from the
National Library of Australia

ISBN: 978-0-646-70091-5 (pbk)

Typesetting and design by Publicious Book Publishing
Published in collaboration with Publicious Book Publishing
www.publicious.com.au

Dedication: *All right you lot, fall in; you know the drill, tallest on the right, shortest on the left, don't mess about, I know you haven't seen each other for a while, but cut out the chat, this is a parade!*

You there – George Ball, Alan Beck, Ralph Bentley, Johnny Boiteau, Stanley Bombell, Jamie Bourke, David Bullock, Warwick (Jack) Callander, Algy Clark, Peter Cliff, 'Babe' Collins, 'Bing' Crosby, 'Doc' Doyle, George Engel, Ted Ersser, Patrick Forbes, Clarrie Frusher, 'Slim' Gargate, Eric Hayes, Richard Hetherington, Sid Hills, Graham Hodgson, Tom Huxtable, 'Chick' Jarman, 'Lofty' Jesse, Paddy Kent, Colin Khan, Paul Kim, Alan Laing, George Lang, Russ Lloyd, Neil McPhee, Len Montgomerie, Mick Moore, Tom Muggleton, Leon Murtagh, Douggie Nix, Dave Oldmeadow, Maurie Pears, Arthur Perks, Lou Perret, Norm Poole, Harry Pooley, Big Jim Prouten, Norman (Blue Leader) Ralph, Tan Roberts, Russ Roland, Bill Rodney, Ben Russell, Reg Saunders, Bobby Stewart, Ike Strain, John Sullivan, Les Taylor (Both Les Taylors), Alec Weaver, David Weir, 'Sleepy' Williams, Mike Yates. . . and you at the back…

You are not forgotten.

[The Author, 1951]

About the Title

'Paper-Scissors-Stone' *is an ancient Oriental hand game often used as a fair choosing method between players, something like flipping a coin to settle a dispute, or to reach a decision, such as 'who pays'. In Japan, the game is called stone-paper-scissors* (Jan-Ken-Pon), *in Korea, scissors-stone-cloth* (Kai-Bai-Bo), *and in China there are several regional variations, including in Mandarin: stone-scissors-paper* (Shi tou-Jian dao-Bu)

This book is fiction, and the characters are not intended to represent any real people living or dead. However, the Korean War did happen, and many of the incidents ascribed to Andrew, Jacob, Michael and other Australians in Korea, Japan, and at home, would be familiar to participants of that time and those places. However, the Preface about Korea's history "Hermit Kingdom", and each Year-Chapter Text-Box summary of annual events about real people, and the war, are factual.

[Some parts of this book have appeared previously as stories by the author, including "Blood On The Snow" (The Melbourne Age Literary Supplement, & 'Australian Short Stories'), "Vyosoká Sázka" (Czech journal Hlas Domova), and the anthology "MacArthur's Pyjamas and Other Stories" (Seaview Press)]

Author's Note

My own experience of the Korean War was insignificant, despite me being an Australian Regular Army officer in '*book-fook*' (BCFK - British Commonwealth Forces, Korea) – for three years; and later as Secretary of the Association of Queensland Korea Veterans. Of course, beginning as a teenager in the army from Puckapunyal, Australia in Summer Peacetime, to Tokchong, Korea in Winter Wartime, I was exposed to experiences and incidents which contributed to the stories and themes contained in this book. I am grateful for veteran friends like George Engel, Patrick Forbes, Mick Moore, and Maurie Pears who helped me to recall (at many years' distance) events of the 50s. I am also indebted to Korean friend Kong Sub Chang for details about the first invasion of Seoul, which I have fictionalised. However, neither he, nor any of my friends, is responsible for any errors committed, or (probably many) things which I have misinterpreted.

Acknowledgements

Some of the publications which have influenced me, and therefore this book, are: "Duntroon" by Chris Coulthard-Clark, "Korea Remembered" edited by Maurie Pears & Fred Kirkland, "The Forgotten War" by Peter Scott, "Korea: Land of the 38th Parallel" by Frank Gosfield & Bernhardt Hurwood, "Australia in the Korean War 1950 – 1953" (Vol 2 Combat Operations), by Robert O'Neill, "A Military History of Australia" by Jeffrey Grey, "The Korean War – A History" by Bruce Cumings, The UNSW "Australians At War Archive", "Wake Me If There's Trouble" by Denis Warner, "Bending Adversity: Japan & the Art of Survival" by David Pilling (Penguin), "The Korean War" by Max Hastings, "A Different Sort of War" by Richard Trembath, "Rifles & Small Arms" by Adam, Conolly & Wilkinson", "It's Cold In Pongo-Ni" by Edward Franklin, "Cold War Hot War" by Gavan McCormack, "The New Koreans" by Michael Breen, and an eternal classic "Why I Am Not A General" by army mate Alec Weaver.

Plus, of course, Private Google, who thinks he knows everything.

Caution

This book is about soldiers, and the language between them is often coarse and blasphemous. It is mostly not intended to be offensive, and is so common that soldiers often would not realise that they were using language that their mother might not like to hear, as it becomes so much a part of their normal speech. I have tried in this book to limit such use to the natural flow of conversation, without being precious.

This book also contains examples of derogatory terms in 1950s common army use which were no doubt racial, such as Jap, Wog, Boong, Abo, Nigger, Coolie, Chink, Chow, Gook, Canuck, Pommy, and Septic *(rhyming slang for septic-tank = Yank)*. These were mostly not intended to be offensive, and some of them even used in a friendly way among comrades. But, the usage was a fact of the times and recorded here as such. (Experienced travellers will be well aware that insulting or uncomplimentary names for foreigners and 'outsiders' have always existed in many languages, and still do. Such as *Gweilo, Yangnom, Faranj, Bulo*, etc.) It is what it is. It is gradually changing. During the Korean War, even the common use of the name 'Charlie' for the enemy, was mostly not used in hatred. After all, he was a soldier risking his life, too.

An Apology

Sorry: to all those Sailors, Airmen, Nurses, Padres, civilian ancillary workers and war correspondents who risked (and sometimes lost) their lives during the Korean War; sorry I did not feature you in this story. It was not in ignorance of your efforts and sacrifices.

Sorry too: (*Josong Hamnida!*), to you beautiful undeserving Korean people who suffered not only years of unwelcome Japanese domination, but also brutal Communist invasion and another long war which killed and displaced <u>millions</u> of your people. And then for being unthinkingly maligned by foreign soldiers as 'the arsehole of the world' when they saw only the ugliness inflicted on you, never having the opportunity to learn your culture, traditions, and family values.

You really are the forgotten people, of a forgotten war.

CONTENTS

Preface: Hermit Kingdom (Non Fiction)

You don't have to read this, but if you don't,
you might wonder how it all started,
and what the Korean War was all about.

Until the beginning of the 20th century, very few people in the Western world had heard of Korea (sometimes written 'Corea') – or if they had, assumed that it was another dirt-poor Asian province of China or Japan. And poor it was, a 70% impossibly-mountainous peninsula surrounded by thousands of islands, inflicted with savage tribal conflict and competing ancient 'kingdoms', at the same time as being restricted by an extreme climate varying from searing summers to below-freezing winters. And why would the outside world have heard of Korea? It had not become generally known (in Europe) as the site of any famous historical event; it did not produce anything of international interest, and was not renowned abroad as the unique origin of any outstanding civilisation, art, music, architecture or personage distinguishable from what was known of the Chinese or Japanese – (and anyway, they all looked the same, didn't they? Those inscrutable Orientals, whose scribbling languages were impossible, and written backwards.)

In fact, for much of its long history, Korea had managed to remain isolated from the outside world by choice, except for the acknowledged strong influences from the country's neighbouring 'elder brother' China, in whom it had a shared border, and shared history of Confucianism and Buddhism, with related historical traditions. But by 1904, Korea suddenly came to world notice when it was invaded by Japan with a strong military occupation as part of Japan's new era of expansionism, establishing Korea as a 'protectorate' - following the example of leading Western nations whose own forays into Colonialism Japan wanted to emulate, such as Britain's India, Burma, and Malaya, France's Indo-China, Netherland's Dutch East Indies, and America's Philippines. This was during a period when Japan, now emerging from years of its own isolation, was intent on joining "the big boys' club", marked significantly by Japan surprising Europe and America with brutal but successful wars against China in 1895 and Russia in 1905, proving her military capability.

Historically, Japan's governments had always regarded nearest-neighbour Korea with concern, fearing that foreign - possibly hostile - domination of Korea would be a dagger pointed at Japan's heart (for example; Russia's building a trans-Siberian railway with French finance - itself to counter British domination of Asian oceans with the Royal Navy). Back in 1894 Korea had appealed to Peking for help against local rebels, and China obligingly sent troops. Japan objected strongly to this incursion with its own military expedition, and when China naturally reacted to that, Japan destroyed China's army and fleet. China acknowledged defeat and ceded territory – Formosa (Taiwan), Pescadores, and the Liaotung Peninsula including Port Arthur (Lushun) — all this at a time when not just Russia, but also Japan, France, Britain & Germany were all claiming new spheres of influence in China via naval bases and railways into the vast hinterland. But Russia, alarmed at losing Pacific access, and the worrying possibility of Japan ruling China as well, participated in a 'Triple Intervention' joining Germany and France in 1895 to curb Japanese expansion – resulting in a humiliated Japan being forced to reluctantly return its mainland gains back to China. Russia achieved its goal by getting China to lease the Liaotung peninsula and Port Arthur, giving Russia naval access to the Pacific.

But in 1910, still-smarting Japan formally annexed Korea as a Colony. So what did Japan's colonisation mean to Korea? At first, major improvements in infrastructure and industrial development by the richer and more advanced neighbour were obvious – better roads, railways, telegraphic communication, improved sanitation, and education. Japan was intent to bring primitive and disunited Korea into the twentieth century after years of stagnation and political conflict, with the advantages to Japan of raw material access which Japan lacked. But Koreans protested at the shameful cost of losing Korea's existing traditions and language, so that there was widespread resistance to the occupation. Japan firmly put down rebellion, particularly from the threat of worker insurrection influenced by recent worldwide revolutionary example, which meant a fierce repression of any resistance through harsh imprisonment and even executions, but many groups including communists managed to escape retribution, remaining active in such a mountainous land difficult to adequately police, supported by exiled patriots in neighbouring and sympathetic countries. Japan not only controlled Korea's entire peninsula and many (more than 3,000) islands, but also large areas of adjacent Manchuria too, relying on those territories as an important source of manpower and materials, especially as her Pearl Harbour/Pacific War began and developed. [NB. By 1945, Korea was the second-most industrialised country in Asia, after Japan itself.]

From the 1930s, Japan's thorough policy of assimilation in Korea restricted schools to the use of Japanese language, and in homes, the adoption of Japanese family names instead of Korean. Geographical names were changed, the capital (Seoul) becoming Keijo. Korea was renamed Chosen. (This last was not completely new – Korea had already been named "Cho Sun" by ancient Chinese writer Guan Zhong – probably a variation of "Joseon", meaning morning brightness or morning calm, reflecting China's distant coastal views of Korea.) By 1945 when the Pacific War ended, the population of Japanese in Korea totalled over 1 million, a quarter of whom were in government. And don't forget that more than 100,000 Koreans served in the Japanese armed forces, many of them willing volunteers, including suicide pilots.

Division of Korea into North and South after the Japanese surrender was largely unplanned. At the end of the Pacific War following the atomic destruction of Hiroshima and Nagasaki, the tired Western allies (especially USA) faced the mammoth task of liberating all the Pacific territories which Japan had conquered, as well as their demilitarisation and reconstruction, the disarming and demobilisation of thousands of Japanese troops, plus the care, feeding, re-housing of refugees, and reorganisation of civil services everywhere in the West and South Pacific and SE Asia. So the de-colonisation of the Korean peninsula was something of a low priority for the allies, who really were war-exhausted and wanted to get their own surviving troops back home. They were content to "temporarily" divide Korea into Allied and Soviet liberation zones for postwar administration and wind-down. To assist in keeping things working, many Japanese, and Koreans who had worked for the Japanese, were re-employed, particularly in the South. The Allied and Soviet occupation zones divided the peninsula conveniently at the 38 degree parallel, roughly midway across Korea. Russia, which was then still a wartime ally of USA and conveniently a near territorial neighbour to Korea, was asked to assist by liberating the Northern half of the country from Japanese occupation (although Russia curiously had not been at war with Japan until the last week of the war), while the American Military Government was tasked with getting the rest of the country south of the 38th parallel, back on its feet. Many Koreans had long resisted Japanese occupation, and exiles had formed peoples' committees preparing for the Japanese defeat, but the U.S. leaders were concerned at the Leftist orientation of some of these Committees. Perhaps the most active resistance leader against the Japanese occupation had been Kim Ku (sometimes pronounced Gu) working mostly in China with the support of Nationalist leader Chiang Kai Chek. Kim Ku had always been a patriot, and had been imprisoned by both the former Korean government and the occupying Japanese. His first incarceration was in 1896 when he was accused of killing a suspected Japanese spy and was at first sentenced to death, later commuted to life imprisonment. But he escaped after two years and became a Buddhist priest until the Japanese invasion in 1905, when he joined action against the occupation, causing him to be imprisoned again in 1910 until released in 1913, when he fled to China to continue opposition. Immediately after Korea's liberation from Japan in 1945, Kim Ku returned to Seoul to meet other intending leaders including Syngman Rhee in the hope of forming a new national government. Syngman Rhee (original name Lee Seung Man) had lived and studied in exile in USA, and returned to Korea with American approval and support. In the Northern half of the country under Soviet occupation, not surprisingly the administration followed the Communist pattern, adopting a wartime anti-Japanese patriot Kim Il Sung as leader. There was still a somewhat fluid resettlement of freed Koreans North and South of the 'soft' border for family reasons, displaced by the long Japanese occupation. But in the North, many anti-communist missionaries and teachers and their families active against the Soviet regime were deported away to Siberia.

In the South, Syngman Rhee [NB: *Rhee, Ri, Li, Lee, are all variations of a common Korean surname*] put himself forward as the natural inheritor of democratic government, and relations between him and Kim Ku deteriorated. Kim Ku argued strongly against division of the country, while Syngman Rhee was prepared to support a separate South Korea if he was unable to convince Kim Il Sung to amalgamate - on Rhee's terms. By 1947, both new regimes claimed to represent all of Korea, and both sides imagined a return to unification *their* way. But North Korean leaders were supported by Moscow and Communist China both of whom were determined to avoid a total non-communist (and US-influenced) Korea on their land borders. Kim Ku pragmatically took a delegation to negotiate with North Korea about unification, against Rhee's wishes, who accused Kim of being weak on the Reds. And in June 1949, Kim Ku was assassinated (how convenient) leaving Rhee as the front-runner for leadership of the non-Communist South. Meanwhile in the North, Kim Il Sung secretly asked Stalin if he would support an invasion of the South. Stalin suggested Kim seek Communist China's agreement and help. Mao gave this his careful consideration.

UNCOK (UN Commission On Korea) had been formed by the United Nations in 1948 to supervise the withdrawal of occupation forces from both sides of the arbitrary border. Unfortunately, UNCOK was prevented from operating in North Korea by the Communist regime, and UNCOK's monitors on the Southern side were compromised by being 'embedded' with Rhee's Republic of Korea forces, and therefore reliant on them for interpretation, accommodation, transport and assistance. Not to mention analysis of reports, which tended to always reflect the Rhee anti-North viewpoint. When North Korean forces strongly invaded South Korea across the 38th parallel on 25 June 1950, there seemed no doubt that the Southern Republic was unprepared and undeserved of the massive and unexpected attack. It was a Sunday at 4 a.m. during heavy monsoon rain when relaxed ROK guards and their US Military Advisory Group were hit by the first wave of the 90,000 *Inmun Gun* (NK Peoples' Army) armed with 150 Soviet tanks and 200 aircraft forging South. Well-prepared by scouts and spies, they knew every ROK unit strongpoint and destroyed them first. News of the invasion reached Seoul within hours and rallied ROK forces into defensive action, attempting to block the Uijongbu corridor but they were outmanned.

Meanwhile word reached USA and UN HQ where it was still Saturday 24, and UN Secretary-General Trygvie Lie called a meeting of the Security Council which met without Russia, (whose boycott absence was due to the UN's refusal to allow Communist China a seat in place of the Nationalist Chinese island-nation of Taiwan) – and the SC immediately demanded ceasefire and withdrawal – which was predictably ignored by North Korea, so that the Security Council called for UN Member countries to assist South Korea in repelling the invaders. Amongst these was Australia, which urgently assembled an infantry battalion, units of the RAAF, and vessels of the RAN, from occupation duties in Japan, to become some of the earliest respondents to the call for help. Gradually, troops from Belgium, Canada, Columbia, Ethiopia, France, Greece, Luxembourg, Netherlands, New Zealand, the Philippines, Thailand, Turkey, and the United Kingdom joined the South Korean and US forces, plus a fighter squadron from South Africa, and medical units from Denmark, Italy, India, Norway and Sweden. USA brought troops from garrison duties in Japan to the support of South Korea, whose defences had tumbled under the strong Northern assault as the North's momentum drove the defenders, battle after battle, all the way down the peninsula to a desperate perimeter around the Southern port of Pusan. But reinforcement by fresh US troops swung the balance to halt the North Korean aura of invincibility which hid their over-stretched lines of communication and a serious loss of men. US President Truman made it clear that this UN force would not involve any warlike action against the Peoples' Republic of China, or the Soviet Union. At the same time, General MacArthur, who commanded the UN Forces, planned an audacious flanking attack in force at Inchon up near the 38th parallel, cutting the North Korean supply column and recapturing Seoul. By October the tables had turned against North Korea, and MacArthur planned the destruction of the NK military forces and the surrender of Kim Il Sung's government. But the neighbouring Chinese Peoples' Republic announced that if US or UN forces crossed the 38th parallel, China would come to North Korea's aid – however China would not act if only South Korean forces crossed the parallel, limiting the war to conflicting Korean ideologies.

In many peoples' minds, the military defeat of the North Korean forces' invasion would be achieved when they were driven back over the 38th parallel, but as the Americans (and Australia's PM Menzies) pointed out, "It will be of no use to go to the 38th parallel and leave an armed enemy on the other side of the border quite intact, and then withdraw, because that would mean that we could have another aggression the next day" – however the opposite view (taken by many including Chifley, former PM of Australia) was that "if UN forces continue beyond the 38th parallel, then *they* will become the aggressors". Both of them were right. On 1st October 1950, South Korean forces advanced into North Korea, and the UN General Assembly voted on a resolution authorising an advance by UN forces.

MacArthur mistakenly judged that despite their threats, the Chinese would not dare to intervene against combined UN/International forces, and he ordered continuation of advances far into North Korea as the winter became severe, claiming that the war was almost won, and UN troops 'could be home for Christmas 1950'. Unsurprisingly, USSR and her satellites opposed the UN resolution; some neutral nations abstained, and the UN forces under American direction advanced, almost to the Chinese border at the Yalu River, triggering the threatened massive Chinese entry to support North Korea. Chinese General Lin Piao's battle-hardened veterans poured across the border into North Korea and began a second offensive which forced the US/South Korean/UN armies to retreat all the way back to below capital Seoul, which changed hands again. Another major counter-offensive took place in January 1951, enabling the recapture of Seoul and a hard fight to drive the Chinese and North Koreans back across the 38th parallel once more. So by March 1951, the front line was close to where it had been at the outbreak of war the previous June, and President Truman was ready to reach a negotiated settlement, but MacArthur was aggressively determined to threaten China with destruction if they continued to interfere – hinting at nuclear warfare - causing US allies to question what was US policy, and what was the MacArthur's personal attitude. President Truman, after several instances of MacArthur conflicting with Washington (and UN) policy over confrontation with China, relieved MacArthur of his command in April, replacing him with General Ridgeway. This was followed by a series of fierce offensives above and below the 38th parallel during that 1951 hot summer, leading UN Soviet Delegate Jacob Malik to reconsider the Communist situation (with heavy losses) and propose that negotiations should begin for a cease-fire along the border between North and South. Truman instructed General Ridgeway to begin truce talks, and this infuriated 75-year-old Syngman Rhee, who still considered his 'Republic of Korea' to include the whole peninsula, and who had meanwhile turned South Korea into a repressive police state where few dared to oppose him.

His rule, however, was completely dependent upon US support for economic and military aid.

In July 1951, the first of several meetings was held between representatives of the combatants – first at the village of Kaesong just inside North Korea, and later at a specially constructed "Peace Village" of Panmunjom in no-man's-land, to determine a ceasefire line, the return of captured prisoners, and many other agenda items, often in an atmosphere of petulant hostility. By October 1951, battle lines between North and South Korea and their allies were almost restricted to deeply-entrenched opposing positions in an area of precipitous, rugged mountains across the peninsula from coast to coast, where bitterly fought battles continued over months for minor territorial advantage on either side. Meanwhile, Syngman Rhee relied upon questionable evidence of regional communist actions to declare martial law in the South, which permitted him to defeat opposition to his increasing one-man dictatorship. In USA, the election of President Dwight Eisenhower in January 1953 had affected the truce talks, where China and North Korea waited to hear the new president's position on Korea, which was ambiguous, despite his public promise 'to end the Korean War'. Truce talks had stalled over the repatriation of prisoners-of-war, because roughly one third of the 132,000 captured North Koreans did not want to return home, which the Communist delegates insisted on, as part of the negotiation. Eisenhower's position was firm however, and hinted that USA could use nuclear arms if necessary to bring the war to an end. Stalin's death in March 1953 and heavy battlefield losses were strong influences on North Korea and China to agree to most items on the agenda, and – after 158 frustrating meetings over two years – at 9.57 a.m. on 27 July 1953, the two chief delegates, North Korean General Nam Il, and U.S. General William Harrison sat down to sign the Armistice document. The procedure took 15 minutes.

And an uneasy peace began.

"Do you know what a soldier is, laddie?
He's the chap who makes it possible
for civilised folk to despise war."
Allan Massie

PART 1. *PAPER. . .*

1947

Top Songs:
All Of Me (Frankie Lane)
Open The Door Richard (Count Basie)
Zippety Doodah (James Baskett)
April Showers (Al Jolson)
Anything You Can Do (Andrews Sisters)

- Truman is President of USA, Atlee PM of Britain, Chifley PM of Australia

- India & Pakistan gain independence from Britain but amid widespread deadly ethnic violence.

- Communists seize power in Hungary.

- Capt. Chuck Yaeger USAF breaks sound barrier

- UK Royal Wedding: Princess Elizabeth & Prince Philip

- UN recognizes independent state of Israel

- ***UN resolution calls for withdrawal of all foreign troops in postwar Korea, with free elections, and the formation of a UN Commission to unite the divided peninsula-*** *(What could possibly go wrong?)*

- Thor Heyerdahl's Kontiki expedition crosses Pacific on a sailing raft from Peru.

- Tubeless Tyres are developed in USA.

- US Secretary of State George Marshall proposes post-war European recovery – "Marshall Plan"

- North America & Europe experience severe winters.

- The "New Look" is a female fashion of long full skirts.

ndrew, the tall gangly teenager with a mass of curly blond hair stood awkwardly in his school uniform (for which he was getting too big) in front of his father's desk in the Canberra study, hands linked behind him, one bare knee slightly trembling above the long school uniform socks as he endured another angry tirade from the man seated before him, who slammed his hand on the desk. "You *will* go back and do it again, and you *will* get it right this time. You will keep doing the exercise until you get it word-perfect. No excuses. When you attend that entrance interview, you will have nothing but excellent passes in every subject, and you *will* be accepted by Royal Military College."

"But I don't want to go to military college," Andrew dared to challenge.

"Don't be insolent! What <u>you</u> want and don't want has nothing to do with it. You are just a kid, and you will do what you are told! You are going to Duntroon whether you like it or not. I have had to pull all sorts of strings to ensure you get selected as long as you pass your school examinations, and that is what will happen. You *will* pass all the examinations! You will go to RMC! Now get back to your room and go over those old exam papers again!"

(So do you wonder why I hate him, and everything he stands for? And in my room, flinging myself down onto the narrow bed, I choked up. I almost wanted to cry in frustration, the hot tears welling up but I managed to control them. He knows he can still make me cry, even at my age, even without that humiliating trip to the woodshed and another whipping, but I'll be damned if I will give him the satisfaction this time. The one thing he can't control is the level of my academic work, my results, so if I crash the exams and fail the RMC selection, that's it – I will have destroyed his ambition to get me a commission in the army, just because he wants to show off to his colleagues in his department, so he can just stick that up his arse. I do not want to be a bloody soldier. I will not be a bloody soldier. I will run away, this time, I will. I will. But where will I go?)

There was a small knock on my bedroom door, and I knew it would be my stupid little sister Elizabeth, interfering as usual, so

I called back angrily "Get lost!" The last thing I wanted was her infantile remarks, whatever they are, or even her sympathy. It has been bad enough when she wanted to commiserate with me after those beatings as I came back to my room wet-faced, and I know she means well, but I don't want her sympathy. But no, it was my mother's soft voice. "Andrew" "Go away" I said, but quietly and more civilly this time. "Andrew Dear, let me talk to you for a minute." So I gathered myself up a bit and wiped my eyes as she opened the door and came in. "Look, Andrew, I know you are not getting along with your father at the moment, and I hate to see you hurting like this. But Darling, I'm on your side, really I am, and there is one thing you might not have thought about." I was sort of half-listening to her, but not looking at her as she sat on the edge of the single bed next to me. I was staring at the floor, or some depth beneath it where I would like to bury myself at the moment. "Look," she said. "I know you don't want to be bullied by him into attending Duntroon just because it is what <u>he</u> wants because of his position or some ambition, but look at it this way – it would get you completely away from him for four years. He wouldn't be able to bully you in there! It would make you your own person, and – just maybe – you might find you can enjoy it - no; really, think about it - in the company of other young men the same age, very much like you, growing up away from home. And anyway, apart from an army career, which I know is the last thing you want, it would give you such a wonderful start at university level, so that as a man, you would be able to make your own choices with something to back you up. Think about it. And" – she hesitated – "By the time you graduate, you would be a man and able to make your own way."

And now I understood something else, because there was a slight unsteadiness in her voice, and she said "I don't know why I am saying all this, because if you listen to me and take my advice; if you go, I will miss you terribly, and yet I know it is the right thing for you, to get away from … him. To make your own way."

So there was another way of looking at it. Escape. Independence. Just maybe…

3

As far away from the house as he could get, past the vegetable plots and rose gardens so carefully tended by Mr Patterson the gardener and his apprentice, down to the gully which was rough and lined with original eucalypts and black wattle, where the dog Simba uselessly chases rabbits without ever catching one. Andrew now slides down the gravel bank and sits with his arms around his knees, knowing that he is out of sight of the house, feeling miserable. The golden Labrador, Simba, which had followed Andrew from the house, now tried to attract his attention, wagging its tail and pushing Andrew with its muzzle. The boy tried to be annoyed by the persistent dog, saying "Piss off, will you, Simba! Can't you see I'm not in the frigging mood." But the dog broke his mood by pushing past Andrew's hands and slobbered at his face, making the boy splutter, shaking his curly head, laughing despite himself. "You stupid dog." Andrew relented, and picked up a stick at his feet, making the dog instantly alert, prancing, anticipating the game. "God, it doesn't take much to make you happy, does it?" But there's no way a responsive friendly dog can allow you to stay miserable, is there? Andrew feinted twice, then threw the stick downhill as far as he could, and the dog galloped off in a swirl of dust, skidding to retrieve the stick, and then, bringing it back, pretended to be reluctant to give it back, yet realising that to get Andrew to throw it again, it was necessary to let it go. Andrew shook his head, laughing, and threw he stick over and over again, to his, and the dog's delight.

My name's Michael Whan, and I'm a Corporal in the Australian Regular Army. I know, some people don't understand why anyone would want to be a soldier in peacetime, and it would take a smarter man than me to explain the philosophy behind that. If I look back to my own voluntary enlistment, the answer is easy – Terry, my brother-in-law, who was just my sister's boyfriend back then when I first met him, was a Corporal in the Army, and I really admired him. Part of that was because he is a great person, everybody likes him, and what kid wouldn't want to emulate him? Plus, back then I was, I suppose, very young and impressionable, and he looked terrific as a returned warrior in his jungle greens and with his bearing and campaign ribbons, and that was an image I wanted to copy, if I could. Plus, of course, his stories about wartime Army life in the islands, and the mates he had, and how they connected. Some of those mates of his we met from time to time, and they were all in the same mould – clean, fit, smart, polite, respectful to parents – I guess they were just the kind of people a young man could look up to. Anyway, as I approached school-leaving age, I had no idea what I wanted to do as an occupation, despite my Dad wanting me to go into the shop with him, and when I casually mentioned my indecision to Terry, he gave me further incentive to join up. "Listen" he said, "There are hundreds of different jobs in the Army – I mean technical jobs - and you have the advantage that the army will train you with the most skilled instructors you could get while at the same time they will house you, clothe you, feed you, and pay you – and the pay's not bad compared to civvy jobs. Plus, the Army has every sport you can name with number-one facilities and expert coaches. Not to mention the great friends you make, and the fun you can have. What more could a young bloke ask for? And if you ever get sick of soldiering, there are employers out there who are always looking for skilled and experienced craftsmen, tradesmen, who are well trained with qualifications. So it can also be a long-term consideration." I reckon Terry should be on the recruiting panel. So, I guess my decision to enlist was simple.

The Section – my army unit is called a Section, a small 'Band of Brothers': Just to put you in the picture, a Platoon is a basic semi-independent Army fighting unit of around 35-40 men led by a Sergeant or Lieutenant. And then each Platoon is made up of normally three Sections of around a Dozen men each led by a Corporal, and that too, is a semi-independent unit which can operate on its own if it has to. Let me tell you a bit more about our mob, my Section, that I am in charge of. People out there never seem to understand how a unit like ours (and ours is just like all the others) becomes a close-knit group of men who are more of a "family" than their own *family*-family. Not so hard to understand really, when we spend more time over the months and years with together and get to know each other probably closer than members of a family ever did. You kind of grow up with each other. Part of that is because you train as soldiers together, learning together, sometimes suffering together, becoming men together under all sorts of conditions and stresses. Oh, I know we sling off at each other, and often have some reservations about individuals who piss you off from time to time, but that is normal, right? Even in a homogenised collection like us, basically everybody's different. Things some of them say or do get up your nose from time to time just like in any group, any family, but you know – it is really moulded into you – that you are a soldier, part of a solid unit in which everybody helps everyone else and works together. You know, you don't have to be told, that you won't ever have to look over your shoulder to see if you are being backed up. And you know that whatever happens when it comes to the crunch in real wartime action, if you go down, that you won't get left behind like a shag on a rock. That always there will be one of your mob or maybe more than one, who will concern themselves that you are down, and will do everything in their power to help you, to rescue you, to patch you up and get you back where you can be fixed – sometimes at great risk to themselves. That's something which doesn't have to be engraved in stone, not just a nice intention or feel-good motto for the civilian newspapers on Anzac Day; it is something you can bank your house, your wife and your dog on. It just **is**. And it is therefore something instilled in your own soldier character, the surety, the no-question obligation, that if one of your unit needs it, you will fight to protect him, and no matter what, you will do everything you can to help him back, even if it means carrying him, even if it means shouldering his and your own gun while the bastards continue to fire bullets zipping around your ears, plucking at your clothing and equipment, kicking up dirt to sting your face. We've all heard of that Shakespeare quotation "We Band of Brothers" even if we don't know what story it is from or the whole sentence, the actual words – but we know better than anyone, the sentiment, the meaning of it all, and we know that it has always been like that for soldiers like us in every war that there ever was, real or fictional (and you can soon tell if the fictional one was written by someone who was there, right?) Mates? Brothers? Yeah, but more than brothers. Like patiently showing him over and over how to do something technical when he hasn't quite grasped the detail, bringing him up to speed, so that he is as good as the rest of you, and the whole group is better for it. Like helping someone get through a hard time when his girlfriend has given him the flick, patiently listening to him, letting him get it all off his chest. Like fronting up at the Seymour Police Station, carefully going to bat with the weary desk Sergeant for your army mate when he has been locked up for something trivial like being 'tired and emotional' and maybe too loud at closing time in the front bar of the Wheatsheaf; by politely talking his case and hopefully getting him back out. Like helping a mate when he has over-indulged and needs not only someone to calm him down and ensure he gets home to barracks by *23.59*, but also needs a brother to guide him safely past officious MPs at the gates, even putting the sorry bastard to bed. Like making excuses for him when he is late for parade, because you know he would do the same for you. Anyway, there is a lot to tell you about the army, but we've got plenty of time.

I'll tell you a bit more later, if you're interested.

J akob arrived at Victoria Barracks at the appointed time, after an unfamiliar journey by train and tram through Sydney, and was directed by a smart Corporal from the guardhouse to where the interviews were being held. He was ushered into waiting corridor by another efficient NCO, this time a smartly-uniformed Sergeant, and shown to a long bench seat where other nervous applicants waited. For the first time, he was suddenly aware of what the army looked like, close up. And being Victoria Barracks, there were no slackers in sight – everything was sharp, disciplined. Nobody walked here, everybody marched; they all seemed to have a purpose. There was a lot of saluting; well, you would expect that, with a lot of officers around, wouldn't you? In the busy echoing sandstone passage, there were five other boys – or young men – seemingly in the same situation as Jakob, all in various stages of expectation as they sat waiting for their call. All of them were dressed in their best Sunday suit or – as in Jakob's case, tie, sport jacket and slacks. All of them 'clean, bright, and slightly oiled' in the timeworn parlance, shoes clean and polished. One of them was even dressed in the uniform of a boarding-school cadet lieutenant, and Jakob wondered if that gave him an edge in the competitive interviews, although he too looked as nervous any everybody else.

The interviews were conducted in a room by three senior army officers seated behind a long table on which there were several bulky files, no doubt containing the collected personal details of the applicants, with additional notes taken as the enquiries proceeded. Another less senior officer, a Captain, sat on a straight chair to the side of the interviewing panel with a clip-board, and it was he who accompanied each delegate into and out of the room, coming back into the corridor to consult his notes and asking the next youth by name to come with him into the boardroom. When Jakob's turn came, he was impressed by the seated top brass on the panel, all smartly uniformed with polished brass buttons, Sam Browne belts crossing their chests, rows of campaign ribbons, serious faces, and bristle moustaches.

They were all tanned and healthy-looking. "Been raised in a top paddock" Jakob's grandfather Aleksi would have said. It was the centre officer who addressed Jakob first when he arrived, and despite the formality of the set-up, he seemed to have kindly eyes. "Sit down, Mr. er, Blask. We would just like to find out a bit more about you. I am Colonel Jamieson, and I'm the Commandant of the Royal Military College which you have applied to enter. On my left is Colonel Atkinson, from Army Headquarters Personnel Section, and on my right is Colonel Devine, from Victoria Barracks Melbourne, Training and Appointments Wing. You have already met Captain Banks, my Adjutant, who has brought you in just now. I know this process is a bit daunting, but please relax and give us your best answers to our questions, to help us in our selection. To start with, can we clarify your correct name, which seems to have variations. "Yes, sir. As written on my application, my name is Blask, B L A S K. My family is Polish, and the original name was Blaszczyk, which is hard to pronounce or spell, so we changed it for Australian convenience." The officers all smiled, nodding. "Understandable. Thank you for that. Now, first of all, may I call you Jakob?" "Yes sir." "Now, Jakob, obviously we have looked into your application and the references you supplied, and we have naturally made enquiries about you at school and elsewhere, to help us make up our minds. Can I ask you first, why you want to become an army officer?" Jakob tried to suppress the smile at his eyes, but the Colonel picked up on it straight away. "Are you smiling? Did I say something amusing?" Jakob hastened to answer seriously "Oh no, I'm sorry sir, I apologise. It's just that in my preparation planning for this interview, I made a sort of bet with myself, that probably the first question would be: 'why do you want to become an army officer?' and here it is." Jamieson laughed, and the officers next to him echoed it. "So you won a bet with yourself, Jakob. I like your anticipation. Well done. But it also means that you should have an answer prepared. What is it?" "Yes sir. I'm sorry if I sounded like a Smart Alec, but it was the kind of question *I* would ask, if I was in your position. So; to answer that question, there are several reasons why I would like to become an army officer. Firstly, for the status. I think it is an important position which attracts respect in the community, as well as in the services. I believe that it is a career which provides security, satisfaction, a good living, and prospects for advancement for someone who applies himself and is prepared to work hard. It might also offer opportunities for travel and promotion, and there is always the possibility of excitement through action. I like the environment of working with men with similar aims, and because I am a keen sportsman, I like the idea of an organization where sports and fitness are encouraged."

Well that's my best shot, thought Jakob.

The panel members seemed to approve his answer. There was a bit of nodding and exchanging glances, a note or two on the pads in front of them. The commandant was still half-smiling from their exchange, and looked at the others before addressing Jakob himself again. "So, Jakob, you correctly anticipated my first question which you have answered very well; and... I wonder, did you also guess what my <u>next</u> question would be?" The other panel members laughed at this. Jakob smiled and said "Sir, it would really be impertinent, for me to attempt to predict your thoughts... But, if I was the interviewer instead of the applicant, I might ask if there was an alternative plan – in other words, what would the applicant do if he was <u>unsuccessful</u>?" This time, the Commandant and his fellow interviewers all laughed heartily. The Commandant said "OK, Jakob, that was indeed *one* of my thoughts, and the fact that you have considered alternatives is encouraging. One of the things which we teach trainee officers at RMC, is always to work out available options to every decision and evaluate them before action. So. <u>*Do*</u> you have alternative plans?" "Well sir, I always try to prepare myself for other outcomes, and in this case, I made enquiries about a career in the NSW Police as an officer cadet, which has some of the same career possibilities as the army, on a much smaller scale." The panel members took that in, exchanging looks, but

Jakob continued: "However, I admit that the second option was just that, a second choice." "Is it the uniform that attracts you, either army or police?" "No sir, I didn't think of that – in fact, in the case of the police, there is a strong possibility of plain-clothes service. But in both cases, I do relate to a disciplined, well organized service." That also seemed to gain approval from the brass seated at the table. Jakob started to feel more confident. Was he winning? He couldn't relax yet. The Commandant continued "Jakob, we have your quite good academic record and your answers to written questions, but there is a lot about you we don't know. For example, what are your hobbies?" "Well sir, I really don't have any hobbies. You know my situation – my father is dead, and my mother in hospital. Since I am largely looking after myself, I manage a couple of part-time jobs after school out of necessity, and any spare time, I play sport." One of the other panelists asked "What sports do you play?" And Jakob answered "In summer, cricket of course, and in winter, Football." "What code of football?" "Rugby League, sir." That animated the officers on the panel, and the Melbourne officer, Devine, shook his head sadly and mumbled "Mobile wrestling" so that the others laughed at him. The Commandant said "The army game is Rugby *Union*, Jakob, which I'm sure you would easily convert to, but we also plan an Australian Rules football team in the local ACT competition soon." Colonel Atkinson, the other panel member snorted "Aerial ping-pong." And the others laughed at him. It was obviously a favorite point of contention between States. Colonel Devine asked Jakob "What books do you read, Jakob?" And Jakob shook his head regretfully. "Sorry sir, but I don't do much reading outside of study subjects at the moment. When I have more time perhaps." They seemed to accept this. The Commandant took over again. "Jakob, I have to say that you are not the typical applicant we get from the Greater Public Schools, and your background is" – he paused – "different..." (Jakob thought to himself, *yes, you could say that – parents Polish immigrants and the father killed himself drunk in a road crash, mother wasting away in a nursing home, grandfather a raving ratbag permanently at war with local authorities about building and other regulations – yeah, not your usual blue plate officer candidate.*) "...But we are encouraged by your top academic results, your confidence, and your sporting teamwork, and it has been interesting to meet you today." The Commandant conferred with the other members of the panel, asking them if they had any further questions, to which they shook their heads, and then he nodded to the adjutant, who stood up. "Thank you, Jakob. You will be advised of the army's decision in due course." Jakob didn't know whether to bow, salute, or make an attempt to shake any hands. But he compromised. He nodded to each of the three senior officers. "Thank you sir, sirs, for your time. Good afternoon." It seemed the best he could do.

After Jakob left, the three officers of the board discussed him before calling in the next applicant. One of the officers commented "Compared with the previous young men, I have to say that he," (he referred to his notes) "Jakob, was different; not what I would have automatically considered 'officer material' – was I wrong?" The Commandant smiled "You are certainly right about him being different; from basic State School and his non-British family background. But the reason he was included this far as a candidate, is his intelligence and academic level, plus his independence and initiative – as evidenced by hard work without parental direction – not to mention his obvious success in team sports." He smiled at them "As you know we look for vital character traits, such as Initiative, Leadership Potential, Team Player, Clear Thinker... I know, we don't teach them <u>what</u> to think, only *how* to think. But Jakob impressed me as a strong candidate with those attributes. And David, 'officer material'? You might be right. But if we accept him, we've got four years to polish that aspect, don't you think? Isn't that what we're for? However, early days; we have the rest of the candidates to consider, so we just have to list him where we think he should be."

"Alright, Stanley, who's next?" "The next candidate's name is Andrew Turner, up from ACT." "Ah yes, Burgess Turner's boy." "Who's that?" "Burgess Turner? You would know him, from the Defence Department in Canberra." "Oh, *that* Turner?" "Yes, I'm afraid he's a bit pushy, but this is the son we're considering, not his father." He looked at his papers. "Anyway, the son came up well on his own merit, good academic background and references. Let's see what he's made of as an applicant."

When the petrol station closed for the day out on the Emu Plains Road, Jakob cleaned down the fascias of the bowsers, wheeled the rack of engine-oil bottles inside the workshop, swept the concrete apron and then connected the entrance chain and 'Closed' sign across the driveway from the dirt road, while he heard Danny the mechanic petrol-scrubbing his hands and talking over his shoulder to Mr. French, the disabled owner, who was in his office. Mr. French slid open his window hatch and called to Jakob "Will you put the demos away too, Jake?" Jakob was used to driving and putting away the new clean grey Ferguson tractor that Mr. French was agent for, and the new demonstration Standard Vanguard sedan, before he pulled down the wide screeching roller door and padlocked it, twice. When he came back inside and hung the keys on the board, Jakob joined Danny and Mr. French in the office, where as their knocking-off ritual they were just opening a tall bottle of Resch's from the ice-box, and where, every time, they invited him to join them in a closing time drink, but each time, Jakob would politely decline the offer. "A small one for the road, Jake?" Mr. French smiled, and Jakob thanked him but said no. He still had to visit his invalid mother on the way home, and there was still some packing-up to do in his rooms before he could leave. Besides, he was riding his motorbike.

Mr.French rolled his wheelchair backwards over towards his worn antique pigeonholed desk and reached for an envelope, which he removed and held out to Jakob. "This's yours. We're sorry to lose you, son, and I've given you a bit extra for doing a good job. There's always a place for you here if you want it." "Thanks, Mr.French." "So you're going to join the army, eh? Always thought with your good marks at school, you'd be going on to Uni or something. Anyway, don't you have to be eighteen or more for the army? How old are you now?" Jakob seemed embarrassed to admit, "Sixteen, nearly seventeen. I'm going to Duntroon, the military college, I've passed their selection, and start down there at the beginning of the year." Danny put in his sixpence worth: "Now, as an old soldier meself, can I give you a bit of advice Jake, when you're in the army – don't volunteer for anything. Take it from me. Never volunteer."

"I didn't know you were in the army, Danny?" "Yes mate, more than a year Caterpillering in the islands making airstrips and getting shot at by Jap snipers in the palmtrees, the bastards."

Mr.French took a sip of his beer and laughed. "Anyway, Danny, no use telling him not to volunteer for anything, when he has already signed up to join the army."

Danny grinned at him over his beer, shaking his head as if in wonder. "Military College, hey? Isn't that a bit posh, like for officers and that?" And Jakob, self-conscious, nodded. "Sort of. It's four years of hard work and study though, down at Canberra." "Canberra? Jeez. You'll freeze down there in the winter, mate." "Used to be three years, but now they've upped it to four." "And what does your mother think about you going, Jake?" Mr. French asked. "Well, I had to get her permission. She wasn't too keen on it, but she signed the papers anyway." "And how is she these days, your Mum?" "She's not bad. They look after her well at Aquinas House, but I'm afraid..." He hesitated. "Well, I don't think she'll be getting any better, really." He shook his head, looking at his feet. Mr. French said "Sorry to hear that. You give her my regards when you see her, son, that's if she remembers us." "Thank you, I will." "What about your place in West Street – that's where you're still living isn't it; will it be up for sale?" "No Mr. French, it's only a rental, so when I go, that's it." "And the rest of your family, is it just your Grandad; where's he? Out in the bush somewhere isn't he?" "Not too far. He lives up near Kurrajong. I'll go and stay with him when I'm on leave."

Jakob was awkward in saying goodbye, but he reached across and shook hands with both of the men. "I'm off then; cheerio Danny, Mr. French." Even though Danny had petrol- and Solvol-scrubbed his mechanic's hands when he knocked off, he now wiped his right hand on the front of his flannel check shirt before offering it, saying "Mind how you go mate. All the best." And Mr. French just nodded "You look after yourself, Jake. Come and see us again if you're back up this way. If you get time."

15

And after the boy had gone and the clatter of his motorbike had faded away, Danny drank half of his beer and said "Well, how about that? What d'you reckon?" "About what?" "About Jake, how d'you reckon he'll go?" "Oh, he'll do fine at whatever he does, he's a hard worker, and top of his class from what I hear." Mr. French took another sip of his beer. "And a great five eighths – did you see or read about the game here last Saturday? Jake scored and converted two tries against Windsor Seconds. Richmond are gonna miss him." He pondered. "Yes, a good kid. A hard worker. Apart from us here, he's always had a couple of other jobs, cleaning shop windows, and delivering for Mario's fruit shop in town. If I'd had a boy, I hope he would have been like Jake."

"Is he a Jew?" "Who, Jake? Dunno, why?" "Just the name, Jakob, and 'Blask' - sort of sounds Jewish and with all these foreigners Arthur Calwell is bringing in since the war, thought he might be." "Well he could be. Jewish I mean, but he's Australian. I know he was born here, so he's no immigrant, just that his parents were from somewhere – Russian or Polish, I think. That's where the name Blask comes from – I think it's short for Blaskovich, or Blaskovinski or something just as foreign." "Do you know his Dad?" "No, never met him, he's dead. I met his Mum, but never met his Dad, but I know his dad killed himself in a road crash out Windsor way, pissed out of his mind, and young Jake has been looking after his sick Mum ever since." Danny drank and thought about it for a minute. "But about this 'populate or perish' immigrant scheme of Calwell's, what d'you reckon?" "Well Calwell might be right, the war was a bit of a wake-up for us, too far away from Britain for us to rely on them for support like we used to; and it's too big a country for our piddly seven and a half million – there are too many over-populated countries nearby who would like to get their foot in the door, so if we bring in European workers, we can choose the kind of people we take. People more like us." Danny considered this for a bit, and added "But I think the unions are right, we don't want any Asians or blackies taking our jobs for half the proper pay, like." "Well I think Chifley and Calwell have got it worked out that there are thousands of white men in Europe displaced with that war, and want to get away from the wreckage of Europe to start a new life." "Yeah, well we're gonna need a lot of them by the sound of things, if they ever get this Snowy Mountains idea up and running, down south." "Yeah, I think you're right, but it sounds like a pipe dream to me, tunneling through the mountains to change which way the river flows. Wouldn't be surprised if it all come to nothing." "Typical politicians. All piss and wind like the barber's cat." "Yeah. I'd like to see one of them with the guts to stop petrol rationing and give us garage owners a fair go."

A t her nursing home, Jakob's mother had been frail and breathless on the chair next to her bed wearing a chenille robe. She let him kiss each pale cheek in the old way, but there was only the one chair, hers, so Jake sat awkwardly on the edge of her high bed in the small room with its crucifix and picture of the sacred heart, whatever that was.

"You should go see your Dziadziu before you go off to war."

"Mama, I keep telling you that I am not going off to war; just to military school."

"Then they will send you to war, that is what military schools is for" Her hands upturned, her red-rimmed sad eyes challenging him to dispute her logic.

"Mama, I will be at RMC for years. Years. The war is over; there <u>is</u> no war; there will be no war. RMC is a school. For me it is just another school, like going to university, except maybe wearing uniform, but getting accommodation and an allowance instead of having to pay." "In a university, there will be not people shooting bombs at you, trying to kill you. That is the reason for armies, for soldiers. Anyway you know what I think about soldiers, I can't say it more. If Karol was still here, he..." She choked on it. (Not, Jakob thought; 'if Karol was still here he would be proud of me getting selected for officer school' – no, that was too much to expect.) *She went on "But you should go again and see your Gro'papa before you go off to the military like I wrote him, now he is on his own; you know he loves you. Anyway, you haven't seen him a long while, and he gets old."* He protested. *"Mama, I went to see him two weeks ago, remember? When he made me that tripe soup."* He grimaced. *"Flaki,"* she rebuked him. *"You know he loves that, and to him it was a special treat for him to make you." "Anyway Mama, like I said, you forgot, I am going already after seeing you, I planned that, like I told you. To see you first, then Dziadzia." "Good boy, Jakub."* So that the next hour was easier, more relaxed, as long as he didn't mention anything to do with soldiering. She was even appreciative of the flowers which he brought her. One of the nuns came in with a vase to put them in.

At Kurrajong when Jakob arrived, the old man came out front of the scattering of structures which he called home, grinning as usual, to meet him as he parked the motorbike and hauled it back onto its stand, the old BSA engine ticking as it cooled. His grandfather looking much the same as he always did, but every time a bit more stooped in his huge frame, as usual smelling of strong tobacco and carbolic soap, and now embracing Jakob roughly slapping his leather jacket and hauling him towards the doorway of the main building. Aleksi said: "Hey, 'Kuba, new system here now. You don't have to sleep out back any more. You sleep in the front room this time and I will sleep in the annexe." (He calls Jakob 'Kuba, diminutive of Jakub, like they did when he was little; Blask supposing that was the old man's way of trying to keep him as a grandchild, even though he is now a young man, and matching his grandfather's size.)

"No, *Dziadzia*," Jakob said. "That has always been my room; I can't sleep anywhere else, I am not a sook." The old man roared laughing. He pulled Jakob into the kitchen. "Sook. Sook. I love that word. So you come to say goodbye? Kati writes you will be a soldier. A *professional* soldier. Tell me about that. I thought you were so good in school and maybe go to university somethings. Doctor, Professor, Teacher, what?"

"Nothing to tell. That was then, this is now. Last year I applied to go to Royal Military College, and they just advised me, I have been accepted." Jakob shrugged. "It is a bit like a university anyhow, but the difference they feed me, clothe me and pay me an allowance." His grandfather smiled broadly, nodding. Is he now going to make some joke about it, take the mickey? But no, he just repeated the words, as if rolling them around his mouth to feel the importance of them. "Royal. Military. College. *Royal?*" Raising eyebrows and nodding wisely at that word, pushing his bottom lip out as if impressed. "Royal? Is it then an officer school, 'Kuba?" "Yes, *Dziadzia*." Still waiting for him to tease, to make fun of it. But the old man reached his big calloused hand across and sort of gripped Jakob open-cupped behind the neck; a kind of caress. Now the old man's voice lowered and he was gentle.

"Good. Good. You will do good, I know it, better than the English. You always workink hard like I am teach you. You will be a General. Special. Now we have a little drink to celebrate." And he went inside that small side room where Jakob knew he kept his dusty bottles of *Slivovitz, Egri Bikaver,* and home-made vodka, and Jakob recognized that it will now be impossible to stop him. Even if he wanted to. The old man brought out two not exactly squeaky clean glasses from another cupboard pinched between his thick scarred fingers, glug glug pouring and then facing Jakob, grinning, formally clinking successive toasts raised; to his grandson, to the College, the Australian army, the Swiss Navy, anything. Who needed a reason for a toast? And after each toast, the empty glass raised to eye level in salute. Jakob knew that there is a fair chance that there will be no meal that night, and he will probably have to help the old man off to bed, but it wouldn't be the first time.

1948

Top Songs:
   Ballerina (Vaughn Monroe)
   I'm Looking Over A 4-Leafed Clover (Art Mooney)
   Mañana is Soon Enough For Me (Peggy Lee)
   Nature Boy (Nat King Cole)
   Woody Woodpecker Song (Kay Kyser).

Australia's Prime Minister Ben Chifley and Immigration Minister Arthur Calwell plan a goal of 70,000 European Immigrants per year to boost Australian population. Chifley unveils Snowy Mountains Scheme to reverse the river and provide hydroelectricity plus irrigation. GMHolden begins producing Australian cars.

- Stalin orders a Blockade of Berlin to starve out allied occupation – The Allies respond with an 'Airbridge' to air supply the besieged city.

- A Communist Coup takes over Czechoslovakia, and Winston Churchill warns: 'From Stettin in the Baltic to Trieste in the Adriatic, an Iron Curtain has descended across the continent.'

- ***In South Korea, a vote confirms Syngman Rhee President of the divided peninsula. He claims to represent all Korea.***

- ***In North Korea, The Democratic Peoples' Republic is declared by PM Kim Il Sung as the legitimate government of all Korea.***

- A Communist insurgency in British Malaya begins.

- Olympic Games held in London.

- Famous cricketer Australian Donald Bradman is bowled for a duck by Eric Hollies at Lords.

- Mahatma Gandhi is murdered by a Hindu extremist.

- The National Health Service is created in U.K.

- Harry S Truman is re-elected President in USA

- World Health Organization is formed by UN

As the train left Sydney, the self-conscious young candidates in civilian clothes in the separate compartment allocated by the RTO, settled in and finished racking their bags or suitcases. They were naturally comparing notes; some reserved, some chatty, some competitive. "Are you part of the Duntroon intake?" "Yes. I think we all are, aren't we?"

"Where are you from?" "Parramatta. You?" "Emu Plains." "*Emu Plains?* (laughing.) *Where the hell is that?*" Another chipped in: "I'm from Richmond, not far from you at Emu Plains, I thought you were part of the Richmond Footy team?" "Yeah, I've been playing for their Seconds." "I thought so." "Do you play too?" "Nah, I just go and barrack – or at least I used to until now. I've seen you play a few times." The Richmond candidate nodded at the duffle bag "Is that all of your stuff?" "Yes, why?" Laughing, "Travelling light, eh?" "Well, I figured we are all going to get issued with uniforms, kit and everything aren't we? So we shouldn't need much." "Hang on, didn't you get that paperwork list of what we're supposed to bring?" "Yes, amongst all the other ton of bumf they sent me – didn't read all of it." "Jesus, you take things easy don't you?" "Well, to be honest, I didn't have much to bring anyway, certainly nothing of value." Jakob swung his duffle up onto the compartment luggage rack and sat in one corner. The Richmond barracker asked: "What's your name anyway?" "Blask. What's yours?" "Clark. What's yours again, I didn't catch it?" "Blask." He spelled it. "*B L A S K.*" As he always had to. It was easier than trying to explain, and spell, Blaszczyk. When Jakob had first become aware of the family name change as a schoolboy, he had asked his granddad about it. The old man had laughed. 'It's they Aussies, 'Kuba, they not too smart, hey? A simple name like Blaszczyk, they can't handle it. But okay, no problem, we just take out a couple of *Zets*, one Ce, one *Igrek*, and it makes Blask, a pretty good new name, no?' Jakob smiled at the memory of his grandfather.

"Blask." Jake said, now. "It's Polish." He noticed one of the other candidates smirk on one side.

On arrival, as they collected their luggage and filed out of the Canberra Railway Station entrance, they discovered a drab khaki bus parked on the kerb, and a very smart erect Sergeant-Major in uniform as well as an army Corporal, both of them spick and span with shining brass and gleaming boots. The Sergeant-Major's military efficiency was tinged with uncharacteristic friendliness (unlikely to be repeated during their course, but they didn't know that yet). "Right *gentlemen*, fall in, line up here please, I need to get your particulars before we get going, so give the corporal your names if you will, one at a time and then get on the bus. We'll soon be on our way."

And then a shiny Dodge sedan pulled in, despite a railways employee calling "You can't park there" – ignored by the driver, a tall balding man in a pinstripe suit, while another probable Cadet candidate, a tall youth in sports coat and slacks alighted from the back seat. He had a generous mop of curly blond hair which he continued to brush back in place with his hand. A little girl in pigtails and a school uniform appeared in the Dodge's rear window kneeling, watching. One of the earlier arrived cadets from the train said "Jesus, some people," as the Dodge driver called officiously "Would someone lend a hand with this luggage?" And surprisingly, the young man from the train, Blask, who was 'travelling light', moved across to take one of the three pieces of luggage which the tall young blond sports coat youth was removing from the boot of the Dodge, watched impatiently by the driver in the suit. His father? The youth in the sports coat acknowledged Blask's help while the Sergeant-Major chivvied him to join the embussing group, but the young man in the sports coat went back to briefly embrace the elegant lady in the passenger seat (his mother?), almost ignoring the pinstriped driver. So maybe it wasn't his father after all. The Dodge drove off from the dusty Station forecourt, with the pigtailed little schoolgirl kneeling on the back seat still watching out the rear window.

At the College Staff Sergeants' Mess, relaxing after a frustrating day trying to herd the new cadets into some kind of military order.

"Gawd what a shower; don't tell me every intake is getting worse. Some of them must have two left feet, and no bloody coordination. They'll never become soldiers."

"Ah, we'll eventually get them beaten into shape, the little bastards, if I've got anything to do with it." "What about your lot, Tony; years of hard work?" "I don't know. They're not much different from usual, the little Sirs. A bit wet behind the ears, especially those from boarding schools, but we'll make men out of 'em yet with a bit of luck. And anyway, you can bet the Corps of Staff Cadets will sort them out -- or send them running home to mummy."

The chaos of the first couple of days, finding our way around, endlessly shouted at, endlessly at-the-double, endlessly getting things wrong. No longer part of our old life, but not yet part of the new; always it seemed that others were better at everything than you, and there was so much to learn about the new environment. The collection of army kit at the Quartermaster's Store, when the pile of new clothes and accessories grew higher on the bench than the cadet collecting it. Summer Uniforms, Winter Uniforms, Fatigues, Sporting Gear, Number Ones; You wouldn't believe the range of uniforms and strange equipment. Someone humorously enquired in a squeaky voice "Where are my jockstraps and spurs?" When we stagger back to our individual rooms from the QM Store with toppling armloads of uniforms and equipment, in some cases excited about the generosity of free accoutrements, (can't wait to try it all on in front of the mirror) all of the clothing smelling of warehouse newness and stiff with sizing, but also warning that the issue boots are wooden-stiff and dull and have to be promptly converted to supple gleaming polish, and the many brass buckles, hooks, keepers and badges are not just dull but almost green with oxidisation, and you wonder how in hell you are supposed to raise a shine on them. Tins of polish available, but elbow grease, time and effort you have to provide yourself.

Next, it was the issue of books and notes, being handed out to each desk in the junior classroom by a staff Corporal supervised by a Sergeant Instructor, whose sharp voice cut through the amazed comment among the cadets as the unbelievable stack of books and leaflets grew in front of each cadet. The heavy and thick volumes of MML (Manual of Military Law); AMR&O (Australian Military Regulations and Orders); Staff Duties In The Field; Stacks of Roneoed sheets stapled uniformly in one top left corner - RMC Standing Orders; Class Duty Schedules; Platoon Tactics and Administration; Specifications Use and Care of Automatic Weapons, Inspection Maintenance and Care of Army Vehicles (Wheeled); etc etc, on and on, piles of textbooks and printed sheets. Endless. The sitting students were soon walled in by the towers of print material.

"Don't think" the Sergeant's sharp voice interrupted a babble of talk, which quickly dwindled down to silence; "Don't think, that all you have to do is read every page of every text that you receive as part of your instruction, inwardly digest, understand, apply and memorise it for your examinations. Oh no, gentlemen. The first task that you are obliged to complete, is to note the many included slips of amendments and updates accompanying these volumes, for you in your spare time to locate the superceded sections, correct them, and where necessary replace them with cut and paste amendments which you will initial and date, so that when your books are inspected (which they will be at any time – mark my words) they will be found complete and accurately updated. Do I make myself clear?" (A mumble) "I didn't hear that. Do I make myself clear?" (loudly and in unison, **Yes! Sergeant!**) And then an anticlimax as someone knocked his tower of books, pamphlets and Leaflets in a thundering slippery cascade of paper onto the floor, causing a burst of nervous laughter.

They assembled again as ordered in another classroom (once they had located it), in which smartly-uniformed non-commissioned instructors stood at various posts around the walls, waiting. Some cadets recognised the Sergeant-Major who had met them at the railway station and had helpfully inducted them on arrival. But was this the same friendly father-figure? Stern – no, not just stern, glowering – but now uniformed like a model for the part; upright, brisk, nothing out of place, boots shining like glass, every part of his uniform starched and ironed and creased where it should be, cap peak eye level and badges sparkling, belt and gaiters clean and blancoed, and a deep disciplined voice. He waited stony-faced in front of the class, and until everyone stood still and silent, which they rapidly were, in awe of this advertisement for military bearing. "At ease. Sit down Gentlemen. (Which they promptly and quietly did.) My name is Sunderland. I am your RSM, which for those who are new to the army, means Regimental Sergeant-Major, and I want to talk to you about Standing Orders which regulate your daily life here. If anyone has any questions, please wait until I am finished, when you may stand up, and when I address you, announce your name, and speak – but not before. I will not be interrupted."

"Now gentlemen" he said evenly, (with a hint of emphasis on the word *gentlemen*), "Standing Orders. Standing, as in Permanent. Orders, as in Commands and Regulations which you will obey. Each of you will find that even in your own barrack room, there are requirements which reflect the propriety and discipline of the school. You will fold and place each article of your uniform and clothing in the drawers of your regulation furniture exactly as detailed in this Roneoed summary which is now given to you as a hand-out. This," he said slapping a thick stapled sheaf of paper, "is a copy of the aforesaid Standing Orders, with which each of you has been supplied, and which you will know by heart. The requirement for your clothes and equipment is always related to the shape and dimensions of 'Standing Orders' – this document. For Example. This laundered uniform shirt which I am holding, has been correctly starched ironed and folded as you will immediately learn to do - to match the width and length of Standing Orders. Similarly, each other reserve clean piece of your uniform clothing will conform to this size/shape requirement. Each item of your clothing, including even underclothes, will be folded exactly to the size of Standing Orders, so that you will find that every two items will lie side by side in the space of each drawer. Note; your rooms are subject to regular and random inspection, and any variation from Standing Orders will result in the awarding of Extra Drills, Confinement to Barracks or other fatigue punishments with no excuse or exception. Your beds will be made up before you leave your clean room on time every morning, with straight bedclothes and hospital corners to RMC standard. The top sheet will be turned down at the head of the bed straight, level, and exactly to the width of Standing Orders. In the wardrobe hanging space, you will hang each item in the order listed on this schedule so that it faces to the Left, with the hook of the clothes hanger facing towards the rear, and your footwear will be placed together clean and polished in pairs, toes foremost with the laces closed and loose ends tucked inside the shoe or boot in exact line." And so it went on. And on. And on.

"I can't fucking believe it," said Cadet Peters when the NCOs had gone, and the class sat dazed. "Our bloody clothes folded to some idiot dimensions – is this real, or are we in fairyland?" "You better believe it," laughed Cadet Spencer. "*This is the army Mister Jones*" he sang. "And we have signed up to this and many other types of idiocy and torture. Much of which, I believe, is just to see if we can take the pressure. Sort out the sheep from the goats. Which is why apparently 10 percent of us will either quit or get sacked before the first year is out." "You're kidding?" "Uh-uh, it's true."

"Sunderland," Cadet Heath quoted, "RSM Sunderland. Also known as 'Thunderbum'. But never, needless to say, within his hearing. Thunderbum." Other cadets laughed as Heath went on "And his sacred office, down near the Orderly Room, is naturally called the 'Bummery'. And only an idiot will find himself within sight or sound of the Bummery if he knows what is good for him. Go miles to avoid it. If he sees you, he'll find something to pick on you."

'*Only an idiot*' – and yet, how was one to avoid it? Because, to reach the canteen store, it was necessary to go up the main Street

- naturally called Gallipoli - and cross over within view of the RSM's holy of holies, and from which - even though you couldn't see him - he could always see you, and that voice could demand: "That man! That man!" – and you knew that Thunderbum had spotted some irregularity or slackness which was about to be rewarded with punishment. Was it worth it? Well, if you wanted basics like toothpaste, tobacco (Cigarettes were only for those rich enough to afford them, the rest rolled their own) and polish, there was no other opportunity for purchase. Not to mention luxuries like chocolate or sweets, which the RSM contemptuously referred to as "Isotopes for children". Heath continued "One of the Third Class told me that, within a week of arrival, old Thunderbum knows the name of every new cadet by sight. Nobody knows how he does it." "Probably has a photo of every cadet in his room as a dart-board" They laughed. But they knew that they had been in the presence of God. A presence which they would come to know well in the coming weeks, months, and years. (Wait; did you say years? *Years? Christ.*)

Jakob sat on the step outside his barrack room which was next to Andrew's, rubbing, rubbing, rubbing, with Brasso and a blackened rag. Andrew, returning from the tennis courts, watched him for a second shaking his head, and then said "Fck this." He went back to his room briefly, and then came back to Blask. "Give us your belt buckles." "What are you doing?" "There's always more than one way of skinning a cat. Give us your brass." Andrew showed him his own collection of brass accoutrements, which he returned to his shorts pocket. "Where are you off to?" "Official. Well sort of. Cross country run. Training, as required by the Sports Sergeant if anyone asks; plus a bit of reconnaissance if they don't ask. I've got an idea."

Which worked. Didn't even work up a sweat. At the near shopping street beyond the College, there was a boot repairer, and Andrew entered in his singlet, shorts and runners, wishing the workman (who was black-painting a repaired lady's shoe heel) a good afternoon. "Look mate, I've got a couple of bits of army brass as dull as lead, can I put them on your buffer for a sec?" He indicated the humming machinery behind the counter, which included a Sanding strip, Trimmer, Combined Finisher, and Polishing Belt. The man in his stained leather apron, glasses pushed up on his forehead showing specks of debris, ingrained dirt on his hands, laughed "You from the College?" "Afraid so." "If you leave them with me, I'll do them for you when I've got a minute." "Sorry, can't leave them, got to go straight back. Bloody orders." So the bootmaker agreed laughing, and showed Andrew how to operate the bank of machines, and Andrew made short work of buffing the brass pieces up to a nice gleam. At least it was the basis for eventually bringing them up to a real polish. "Appreciate that. What do I owe you?" Andrew quickly added, "I've only got ten bob, will that do?" The bootmaker grinned "Keep your money, son, just don't tell your fellow cadets about it, I don't want half the college queuing up here to polish their brass, I've got a business to run." "Thanks mate." Andrew waved and jogged back out of the shop towards the school, smiling.

When he gave Jakob his pieces back, now gleaming, Blask laughed "You're a genius, mate, thanks."

And yes; there was the Corps of Staff Cadets – the next most Senior Class, 'Third Year', able and ever keen to discipline the new boys, imposing all kinds of initiation penalties; 'tradition' they called it, but it was basically bastardry, like public-school prefect bullying. Just when you need it least, when you are trying to find your feet in strange surroundings away from home, millions of rules to learn and remember, there were elements of this upper class relishing the opportunity of using their seniority and privilege in harassing those junior to them in every pecking order. Not all of them fortunately, some were even helpful, having been through it all themselves. But there were a few who enjoyed bullying – not a good example for junior leaders hoping to graduate as commissioned officers – but then don't forget, the Directing Staff of the college were watching and noting everything, weren't they? Besides, it didn't last long, only until after the 'official' initiation night when you got put through the mill. Childish, really, but no harm done.

Initiation Day. It was about a month after induction. Just us new boys, the Fourth Class. (Stupid isn't it, we were actually in our first year, but called fourth class. Third was the one above us, and so on. The First Class was the real old-timers who had done it all, and were now graduating as men and officers. So, about the Fourth Class Initiation. They (we) had to strip naked in the Gym, bad enough, then were blindfolded and supposed to be exposed to stepping in boiling water treatment (it was a block of ice which gave a similar effect, intended to be linked to an low electric charge to give you a shock, but somehow that didn't always work properly) and then we all ended up forced down a chute getting dumped into a canvas bath of muck and kitchen slops, followed by a cold shower and a wielded stiff brush. Depending on the new boy's sense of humour, it could be a lot of laughs, or embarrassing humiliation. Most of the new cadets, groaning, laughed it off together with their tormentors. Those that didn't, and took it to heart, suffered. One boy even cried. And it seemed to satisfy the Corps of Staff Cadets, a group which (don't forget) we would aspire to become next year.

Tradition? Stupid when you think about it. And there was a lot more where that came from, particularly for the ones who resisted it, like having to learn and recite the obituary on General Bridge's grave before being allowed to sit down at the mess table for lunch. Like having to list the specifications (weight, calibre, measurements, rate of fire etc) of the Vickers Gun before you could eat. Or like some obscure Duntroon history event which you were expected to learn and remember from somewhere. Like getting the seniors' names right, even when they obscured their name badges, the bastards. With various punishments for failure.

And in between times, you realised that you were the lowest of the low, that there were three more senior classes who had been through it all, had progressed towards their graduation and commissioning, while you still had everything to learn. You realised that it was only the beginning, that you had to put up with all this for days, weeks, months, years; forever it seemed.

But there were compensations – especially sport, if you were a sporting type. Competitive friendships. Fitness. Slowly becoming adept at what you were being trained, thus gaining a sense of success, a satisfaction from being recognised by your trainers for minor achievements. It doesn't take much encouragement to make you feel you are getting somewhere.

I t's me again, Michael Whan, Corporal; remember? I was saying how we soldiers became welded together into a close unit of mates. Of course in an army unit like anywhere else, you sometimes get dealt a no-hoper, although the recruitment scheme and basic training schedule generally weeds out the deadbeats. But there have always been men who are failed husbands, failed fathers, failed *everythings*, just looking for a way to escape their old life, looking for a new start, a new chance, and if that is the case, the army certainly provides the opportunity – and most of the time, converts the failure into more of a success. It is not ever a hideaway or rest home, or an escape hatch for a useless jerk looking to hide from responsibility. Army life immediately presents you with responsibility – to begin with, responsibility to yourself to keep up – like personal hygiene, dress, bearing, fitness, behaviour. And gradually, as you learn your soldiering skills, you automatically assume important responsibilities like safety, acting like a team member, and (I keep on coming back to) meshing with, and looking after your mates. You are never alone.

An army unit can be a cross-section of the country. You know, in our Company we have got men who have been farmers, sailors, builders, boundary-riders, miners, shopkeepers, panel-beaters, teachers, students – anything you can think of. We even had a trainee-priest for a while, until they moved him to army education – he was too smart for a foot-slogger. Over time, we all share in each other's wide experiences as we yak over a couple of drinks or just boots-off in barracks, or around a campfire. We have men from all over the country, able to fill us in on places and conditions they have encountered, so we also become really well educated in general by listening to other peoples' experiences. Wouldn't miss it for quids.

And Nicknames? Of course most have nicknames, some of which stick. Particularly when we first got together and you didn't remember everyone's real name. But their origins, such as Sand-gropers, Banana-benders, Cornstalks, Crow-eaters, and so on, depending which State they had come from. Then there were references to physical characteristics, like Shorty, Lofty, Desert-head, Bluey, Stallion (you can guess what that's for, can't you?). His real name is Edwards. They laugh about Stallion and his conquests. "Would do a brown dog on a chain" or "Would root a fence-post if it smiled at him" or "Would fck a snake if it had hips." But really Edwards is shy and polite, maybe that's why he is popular with the girls. And OK, he is well-stacked in the showers, as well. Another with an enviable reputation too is Wombat (yeah, the usual: 'eats, roots, and leaves'). Other tags, like Gannet, Toxic; or related to surnames, e.g. Private Bonsell became 'Bonza'. And there was 'Albert' – not his real name, which was Dave, but his surname is Ross, so he became 'Albert Ross', *albatross*, get it? (Yeah, I know, pathetic.) There is Private Mackenzie, and of course he is "DoctorMac" after that wireless serial on 2GB, advertising Doctor Mackenzie's Menthoid pills (whatever they are), where the episode always starts with a phone ringing, and this Scots voice saying "Aye, it's me, Doctor Mac". For a while there, Mackenzie used to play it up at roll call when his name was called, saying in an imitation Scottish accent "*Aye, it's me, Doctorr Mac*", but that joke ran a bit stale after a while. I can't remember how Peachy got his nickname. And then there is the Prof, who seems to know everything, when he is not being called Specs or Four-Eyes because of his glasses. And me, my family name is Whan, which name is originally from Ireland, 'Whan' rhymes with 'John' – but you can imagine the variations I get with that, such as 'When', or idiots thinking I was lisping and my name was 'Ron'. When I was in recruit training, our drill Sergeant at rollcall demanded to know: "Whan? What kind of a fkn name is that? Chinese or something?" And I tried to explain, but he wasn't interested, just considered me to be some kind of foreigner, and admittedly we've got a few of those too, haven't we? And later, when I became an NCO, I became "Corp One" which was a bit of a joke ('Corporal Whan = Corp One', see?) until you got sick of it.

Some members of a unit come and go as people are selected for differing duties and transferred, or promoted – but then a base core of troops become well known to each other through close-quarter training - living and working, and begin to develop an esprit which is sometimes competitive, but mostly cooperative, striving to show each other how good they can be and take pride in their ability. Even in something as basic as arms drill, there was a great satisfaction in doing everything well, smartly, so that others outside the unit would take notice and even admire. And the military skills of weapon handling, accurate marksmanship on the range, turnout, marching, were things which made you realise that you were becoming part of an efficient military force, not just 'playing soldiers'. Of course there was always a lot of laughing, mucking about, chiacking, playing practical jokes and enjoying life – even if it resulted in defaulters punishments, kitchen fatigue duty, confinement to barracks, and other penalties early on, worn like badges of honour. But even that brought people closer together, so that years later (and even at army reunions) people might say "Remember that time when the Provosts chased us up Flinders Street and that lady let us in the back door of her shop..." And so on. And that was only when we were training – we became even closer after we went overseas, and when we went into action. Yeah, fighting for your life, and for other peoples' lives, certainly makes a difference. I'll tell you about that later.

When we were at Puckapunyal Base, we discovered that one of the boys in our unit, Olley (remember Olley? Who transferred to Engineers, and got a dream posting to the Aussie base at Antarctica?), Well Olley told us that he had an elder sister married to a farmer not far away from camp at Benalla, and one weekend when we were at a loose end, we decided to all go there in someone's car and visit that Sunday, we were all on our best behaviour, well dressed, no bad language, and Olley's sister treated us all like family, made us welcome and turned on a batch of fresh scones with a gallon of tea; and she let slip how her husband Roger – a nice bloke - had a bad heart and wasn't able to do some heavy jobs, such as renew the sliprails on his dairy yard. And how we all decided there and then to give him a hand; in fact made him sit and tell us how to do it, direct us properly, as we got stuck into the work of cutting and replacing redgum posts and poles until we made sure he had a finished job which would last forever. He was rapt, and so were we. More than satisfaction. I think they call it bonding. And I was grateful when three of my section got leave and came to my Dad's funeral; I know my Mum appreciated it. We were all in uniform, and wore black armbands. This is what I mean about us sticking together for each other. Makes you proud.

And then there was Private Calabria's wedding. Tony Calabria was popular and a great sportsman – we reckon he could have been snapped up by the VFL he was such a good kick, and tall enough to dominate any ruck, but he was quite happy to represent us as a unit at forces level. He came from a very big Italian family somewhere up in the Riverina (Well, all Italian families are big, right, you don't have to say). When we first knew him, he had this girlfriend Maria he used to write to up in Griffith somewhere, and spent ages on the phone at the barracks post office until the queue behind him would complain (*Oh for Christ sake Tony, tell her you love her and get off the fkn phone, there's other people waiting*). So it was no surprise to anyone when they planned this wedding; but what surprised us was when he decided to invite us, his Section, if we could all get leave together. Yes, all of our section, his mates. Because Calabria said that we were 'his other family'. I don't know whose idea it was to provide a wedding guard of honour – it certainly wasn't Tony's - but when we discussed it in barracks, we all wanted to be part of it. When we talked about it, everyone agreed that it had to be done properly – you know, no arseing about; all in dress uniforms, polished brass and Blanco, smart drill movements etc. So that naturally meant practise, to get it right. I mean, this was going to be part of someone's wedding picture on their mantelpiece for years, so it was really important to them. I think it was Peachy who suggested forming a guard of honour outside the church with an arch of long bayonets. Should have been swords, but that kind of thing is like only for officers, right? and there's no established procedure for an arch of bayonets, but when we argued about it, the consensus was – why don't we start our own tradition, create our own piece of drill? And that's what happened, and they put me in charge of it. I had only just become a Lance-Corporal back then. At first there was a lot of confused arguing, everyone had his own idea, but I persuaded them that it had to be done so everyone could be proud of it – proud of <u>us</u> – especially Tony himself, so I did what any professional soldier would do, I worked out a drill for it, and demonstrated it in our barracks. At first we were a bit self-conscious as we tried it out, but it soon evolved into an understandable procedure like so many of our armed drill movements, so that we knew it like the back of our hands, and were proud of it. At the church we were nearly snookered when one of the church officials said that we could not wear bayonets into the church – a place of peace - but I overruled him and said it was part of the wedding ceremony, and that was that.

[Just like we actually wrote it: (polished bayonet scabbards on blancoed belt LHS just to rear of hip) All of us Guard of Honour sat together just inside the doors, alerted to move before end of service when bridal party about to leave; divided into two equal files, march smartly out to either side of church entrance below the steps, halt, to the front, face, attention. All commands given quietly spoken by me, no shouting. 1. "Guard of Honour, Bayonets!" First movement: Right Hand across body to grasp bayonet grip thumb down. Left hand holds/steadies bayonet scabbard, fingers together. 2. "Guard of Honour, Draw!" Second movement: bayonets withdrawn vertically clear of scabbard, pause, then on command: 3. "Guard of Honour, Pree-sent!" Right Hand turns bayonet vertical and crosses body with forearm horizontal, elbow beside waist. Finally, 4. "Guard of Honour, Bayonets arch!" Right arms - hands gripping bayonets – raised at 45 degree angle from shoulder, blades flat, pointing to an imaginary centre arch high above the bridal party approaching down the church steps. Hold that pose until wedding party passes, allow photographs. 5. (And after complete wedding party passes under arch) "Guard of Honour, Bayonets pree-sent!" Arms lower with hands gripping bayonets vertical again, elbows to waist, forearms horizontal. 6. "Guard of Honour, Sheath Bayonets!"

Right Hand gripping bayonet returns across body turning bayonet point down to opening of scabbard, blade inserted, leaving half-inch clear for final movement. Left hand holds bayonet scabbard, fingers together. 7. "Guard of Honour, Atten – shun!" Right hands complete return bayonet into scabbard with an audible click, both Left and Right hands return to stand at attention position.]

It worked as we had practised it, it was mighty. There were even pictures of us in their local paper. And the new bridegroom, our mate Tony Calabria who didn't know what we had planned, was dead chuffed, speechless with surprise. He just shook his head in admiration, saying "You blokes. You fkn blokes." And you should have seen the attention we got from the families – and the bridesmaids. Oh yes, those lovely Italian girls. Their boyfriends were jealous of the attention, and didn't we love that? But we managed to stay out of any fights that night. Well, mostly. There was a lot of wine.

Some civilians say we soldiers are cannon fodder, just following orders. They don't understand. Of course we follow orders. We give, and follow, orders. You have to, don't you? If you expect men to risk their lives. This is providing a united front to achieve success in battle, everyone knowing his part (OK, call it duty) and doing what has to be done, without a committee meeting and twenty different opinions. That would be like herding cats. We're Organised. Why? Simple really. Such a vast body as an Army has to be controlled in detail, or collapse into chaos. Everyone is listed, numbered, classified and remembered. Each unit, each force and location has a 'Strength' – in other words, a theoretical number of servicemen of various ranks and skills required to efficiently operate its function. And because of leave, sickness, shortage through assignment and transit, each unit has an Actual (rather than theoretical) strength – which of course records the number of bodies able to operate, and needed to be housed and fed at any given time.

So, if – for example - you thought that the daily roll call was a tedious stupid waste of time, it was always more than that – it was a summary of who was present, and its recording, and later processing by the Army clerk in the Orderly Room (and his collation and submission to next more senior authority, on and on) provided the basis for the Army to know how many men were available on any one day for service, and how many mouths had to be fed or equipped, and where they were. The fact that orders possibly requiring soldier 'A' to be transferred to unit 'B' were authorized and issued, resulted in the deduction of one body from Unit 'A's strength to be added to Unit 'B', and would generate a Movement Order which notified an appropriate Transport system (Wheels, Trains, Planes, and Boats) of Soldier 'X's number, rank, name and movement (Origin and Destination) plus dates/times. The order also advised Unit 'B' of Soldier 'X's incoming details, transit and estimated arrival, so that he would be expected, picked up, and then accommodated, fed, and introduced to his new duties. As I said, simple. Once upon a time, armies were just assembled from some Royal demand of lords of the manor to gather as many men and weapons as possible from his domain, and those poor 'soldiers' whether fighters or not, were generally burdened with bringing their own weapons and rations, which usually had to be continually resupplied from the countryside they travelled through, which often resulted in pillaging and robbing. Haphazard, unreliable, and a burden on the populace. These days after you sign up, I suppose the army owns you. And therefore looks after you, lock stock and barrel. Restrictive? No. Reassuring, really, when you get used to it.

(Letter from Jakob to his mother-from RMC):

Mrs. K. Blaszczyk, St.Thomas Aquinas Hospital, River Road, Emu Plains, NSW.

<Dear Mama – sorry I didn't write last week, but we had many work projects to complete, and I ran out of time. I hope that you are still doing OK, and that they are looking after you well. You will know by now that we both had a letter from Mr. Davidson last week about the settlement and the insurance. I hope it will be a relief to you, as it is to me, that everything has been settled and we don't have to worry about money for the hospital any more. After Mr Davidson's letter, I also had another one from Sister Benedict bringing me up to date with your treatment and how you are helping her with some of the other patients. That sounds good. Maybe you should have been a nurse? That was very kind of Sister Benedict, wasn't it? I wrote and thanked her. It seems some way off, but I get leave not too far away and I'll be able to come up and see you, and tell you all about the school and how things are going. With much love, Jakob>

We're getting near leave time at RMC (which we all call 'Clink'), and everyone is looking forward to a break, a getaway from the strict discipline, the endless routine, the drill, the continual exams. Andrew said "What are your leave plans, Jake? Will you be going to your granddad's place?" "Yes, I guess so. He lives up in the bush up near Kurrajong. I hadn't really planned ahead. What about you? You live here locally, don't you?" "Yeah, Belconnen." Andrew was having difficulty explaining. "Haven't decided yet. Can't ... Don't want to go home, it will only end up with a series of rows with my father." He shook his head. "He and I don't get on. No, that's an understatement, I hate the bastard, and he hates me. He used to beat me when I was a kid. But – I am expected to go home this first leave, especially my mother wants me to. I'm older now, I should be able to handle it. If he ever goes to lay a hand on me again, I'll deck him. One thing occurred to me – a possible solution - but what I was thinking – well, it would be different if I conned someone into coming home with me for the leave, or part of it at least. It would be a totally different atmosphere with a guest at the house." Blask puzzled "Are you thinking of me?" "Well yeah, but like I said, it would be such a great favour, even for a mate, but I couldn't ask – I mean – No, forget I mentioned it. I'll work something else out." Jakob smiled. "Is this an invitation? If it is, it's a bit cack-handed, even for a jerk like you." Andrew laughed too, "You're right, I didn't really sugar-coat it, did I? But it <u>could</u> be fun. I mean, it's a nice big house, and there are plenty of things we could do, and if I keep away from the old man, I shouldn't put you into any discomfort."

"Sounds OK, but I'll need to go and visit my mother in her nursing home too this leave, if you don't mind me doing a hit and run. Or I should say, if your parents don't mind."

They had to stop on the way, when Jakob insisted on buying flowers for Andrew's mother. "You're crazy, she's got a whole acre of flower gardens." "It's not that, it's - what, a gesture of thanks. Anyway, I'm doing it." And he did. The taxi driver hesitated at the grand gateway "Is this the one?" "That's it" said Andrew, "just drive in." "Jesus, you didn't say it was a castle" Jakob muttered, and Andrew laughed "I've asked all the servants to line up in the drive to welcome you." But when the taxi stopped in the circular gravel driveway in front of the entrance stairs of the big house, there was no line of servants, just a skinny little schoolgirl plus a bounding golden Labrador. Then Andrew and Jakob argued briefly about paying the taxi driver but Andrew won, and then as they unloaded their luggage from the trunk, the little girl tried to take Andrew's suitcase. "Leave that, Twerp." And to Jakob, "This pest is my little sister Lizzie, but hopefully you won't have to put up with her much." Just then, Andrew's mother hurried down the steps wiping her hands on her apron, saying "And this must be Jakob. Welcome Jakob, we've heard such a lot about you." "Not from me, you haven't" Andrew mumbled. Mrs Turner accepted the flowers from Blask, and said "What a nice thing to do; thank you, Jakob." She shook Jakob's hand, and then put her arms out and around Andrew who looked embarrassed, wriggling out of the motherly embrace while she said "Oh Andrew, just look at you; how are you, darling? My, you have put on some weight". "Cut it out, Mum" he said uncomfortably. The schoolgirl said to Jakob "I'm Elizabeth. I remember you. You are the one who helped Andrew with his luggage at the railway station that time". But Jakob didn't know what she was referring to. The dog, with its bushy tail sweeping, was still trying to get Andrew's attention, so he put his suitcase down and hugged the dog which raised its forepaws to around his waist. "And this is Simba, who seems to have remembered me." Mrs Turner hurried back up the entry stairs, saying "You show Jakob the guest room Andrew, while I put the kettle on. We'll have a cup of tea on the terrace. Elizabeth, you can give me a hand, will you, dear." As they went through the front door into a wide hall which led to an internal staircase, Elizabeth said proudly to Jakob "We've got six bedrooms, and three bathrooms. And there's an extra toilet downstairs as well." Mrs Turner hurried her away "There's no need for that, Elizabeth, Andrew will show Jakob everything when he's settled in properly."

41

They had finished their tea and fresh buttered scones on the rear flagged terrace overlooking a wide lawn and rose garden when Mr Turner's Dodge crunched up the gravel drive, and Andrew's father came through, dressed for the city office complete with bulging briefcase which he dumped on a chair, and strode across to shake hands with Jakob, before nodding to Andrew and pecking his wife on the cheek, ignoring Elizabeth. "Well Jakob, nice to meet you. My friends on the RMC staff speak highly of you. I hope some of it will rub off on our son; he needs a bit of positive influence. Now, if you'll excuse me, I'll take a shower before we have a drink and a chat." He turned back briefly "Oh, and both of you, I've booked you – us - in for a round of golf at eight thirty, 18 holes at the club. Mr Haig will make up the four - so don't make any other plans for the morning will you?" Andrew looked at Jakob as if to say Sorry Mate, whatever you thought we might do is taken out of our hands.

They had a brief walk around the garden perimeter past a tennis court before meeting Mr Turner again in the – what was it? Library? Lounge? Drawing Room? What did people living in a palatial home like this called their rooms? It was a warmly comfortable room with dark wooden bookshelves, several original oil paintings, relaxed furniture, a side table supplied with liquor bottles and an ice bucket. Turner smiled "I know you lads are not yet officially of drinking age, but a glass of sherry wouldn't do you any harm, *mm?*" Andrew and Jakob glanced at each other, reading each other's mind, both reflecting on the illegal after-hours drinking at RMC, the sports-field excursion (cross-country runs) excuses to dash into a pub for a half-bottle of scotch or rum easily concealed and shared back in the school. So they both acted the part of shy young teetotallers accepting this generous adult favour of a mickey-mouse glass of dry sherry. "Can I have one too please, Daddy?" Elizabeth asked, coming into the room. "I don't think so, darling; you wouldn't like it, but you can have a sip of mine," her father said smiling. And as if also playing a part, the little girl tasted her father's glass and (real or pretended?) made a face as if she was soured by the spirit. She went out to the kitchen to get a glass of milk. "Now

Jakob," Andrew's father said, handing out the delicate engraved sherry glasses, "how are you managing? You look fit enough." "I think we're both fit as fiddles," Jakob said, "lots of exercise, plenty of good food, and – I don't know about you Andrew – but I sleep like a log – except, never get enough of it." "Yeah, me too, mostly exhausted by lights-out." But Jakob noticed that Andrew's father seemed to ignore his son, instead, making Jakob the focus of his questions about the school and the course. "And I hear that you have all been doing your bit helping fight the local bushfires." Which was true. And why not, when you have a few hundred fit and disciplined young men available for local emergency service. And the army organisation able to make an example of it all, as though it were part of the curriculum.

"And what about hectoring, hazing, whatever they call it? Is it a problem?" "Not for tough-guy Jakob it isn't" Andrew offered, but Mr Turner was waiting for Jakob's answer. "It's no great problem," Jakob smiled, "just some juvenile pranks and sort of teasing, like boarding-school initiation (not that I've been to boarding school); but if you put up with it in good humour, they leave you alone."

All right for some, Andrew thought, remembering some vicious incidents (Here's the little rich boy, make him sing for his supper. You know his daddy is some big cheese at the Defence Department, so we'll have to give him special treatment, won't we, chaps?) There was one mean senior cadet in particular, Holbrook, who seemed to resent Andrew and regularly made it tough for him, especially in the mess hall. Made him stand on the seat and recite the Obituary from General Bridges' grave, made Andrew go through the childish 'square meal' routine – which was a comic robot imitation of lifting the fork or spoon in jerky vertical and horizontal mechanical actions, out-up-in-down-back while the rest of the table juniors as well as seniors laughed, but when Holbrook subsequently ordered Jakob to do it too, the prank came unstuck when a loaded half-spoonful of food somehow 'accidentally' flicked off from Blask's utensil onto Holbrook's uniform. Holbrook was furious, red-faced, getting to his feet, but when Jakob (smiling while the rest of the table laughed) stood up to his full height too, and the men measured off face to face, Holbrook suddenly realised that tough muscular Blask was no willing foil for his meanness and not a good idea to be pushed too far. "Sooo sorry" Jakob had said, "I do apologise, Mr Holbrook, a silly accident of course, but it was all in good traditional fun, wasn't it?" And then someone else of the seniors, grinning, flicked a spoonful of food at the person opposite him, and then it was on, bits of food flying about amid shrieks of laughter until a stern Captain staff supervisor demanded order and clean-up ensuring that the incident passed without further ado (except defaulter punishments). But it seemed to mark a point with the senior class: you don't mess about with Cadet Blask, he'll give as good as he gets - he's a bit of a punchy, too, one of the new stars of the rugby and boxing teams as well.

The talk was polite enquiry. "Have you got any sisters, Jakob?" "No." "Lucky chap," Andrew put in, and Elizabeth tried to elbow him in return. "No sisters or brothers, I'm afraid." "And Andrew said your mother is in hospital?" "Well, not exactly hospital, she is an invalid in a nursing home." "And your father?" "I'm afraid my father is dead; he died a few years ago when I was young" – he shrugged – "I guess about Elizabeth's age. In a traffic accident." (Jakob didn't have to tell them how Karol killed himself riding his motorbike and sidecar at speed into the back of an unlit parked truck in Windsor while he was drunk. They said he was decapitated by the tray of the truck, and would never have known what hit him. But thank God he didn't kill someone else.)

At the dinner table, Elizabeth was setting the places – "I want to sit next to Jakob" and nobody seemed to mind, and later after the meal was served, when there was a gap in the conversation, Elizabeth made it her duty to interrogate Blask. "What do you actually do all day at Duntroon, just march about?" "Don't ask silly questions, Elizabeth". Her father asked her to just concentrate on her food, which she was slowly eating, but Blask took her seriously. "No, Elizabeth, there's a lot more to it than marching about; Andrew will tell you, it is really a college, with classrooms and lectures and exams for university subjects as well as military subjects." "Like...?" "Well, like

engineering, and science, and maths and English and History."
"Let Jakob finish his dinner, darling." "No, it's OK, Mrs Turner,
I believe the best way people learn is through asking questions."
Elizabeth seemed to appreciate being listened to. "Well, what did
you mean Military Subjects?"

"Well, Elizabeth, there is so much to learn about becoming an
army officer – for instance, all the strategy and tactics of fighting
an enemy. Apart from fighting with weapons, there is all the boring
stuff like training and motivating soldiers. ." "What is motivating?"
"It means leading men to do what has to be done, leading them so
that everybody knows what to do, and does it properly, together."
Mr Turner interrupted "Elizabeth, let Jakob get on with his
dinner." "Oh all right," she said, "it's just I wish I could go into
the army." Jakob smiled "Sorry Elizabeth, it's not for girls." "Why
not?" "There are just some things, Elizabeth, which are gender-
specific, and the army is one of them." She screwed up her nose
"What is that; gender-*spiffysomething?*" "Gender-specific – it means
only for one sex – for example, like Boxing, or Football, or... It's
just for men only." "But why?" "It is just the way it is, Elizabeth,
don't ask me. Just like men can't be mothers." Again, Mr Turner
broke in "Elizabeth, you're being tiresome. Let someone else have
a conversation, for a change." Which they did, for a while, and Mrs
Turner managed to get Elizabeth to help clear the dishes into the
kitchen, but the little girl was grumpy when she sat down again,
sighing, to nobody in particular "I wish I could have a new name,
I hate Elizabeth." "But it is a lovely name darling," her mother said.
"I don't like it, it's too ordinary." "But you can have many options
of how Elizabeths are called; for example, Liz, or Beth, or Betty"
"Or Lizard Breath" offered Andrew. Jakob joined in "Or Liza, or
Ellie..." She said to herself "Ellie. That's a nice one. I like Ellie" But
her father grumped from his chair, ending the discussion. "That's
enough nonsense Elizabeth. "You're Elizabeth, and that's all." And
even though the small girl pushed out her bottom lip, she just as
quickly changed her mood again. "Let's play Monopoly after dinner.
Can we play Monopoly, *pleeease?*"

So they played Monopoly, but only four of them, Mr Turner saying that he had office work to do, and he retired to his study. During the game, at one stage when Elizabeth left the room temporarily, Mrs Turner said, fondly "Don't mind her, Jakob. Elizabeth always wanted to be a boy. In fact when she was very young, she honestly believed that it was just another stage of growing up – that everyone started off as girls, and later turned into boys. I think she was genuinely disappointed when she found that she was female for life." They laughed "Poor girl" Mrs Turner added wistfully, "there's no escape".

After the game, Elizabeth pleaded for another, but her mother was firm. "No, Elizabeth dear, it's already past your bed-time, and you've got school tomorrow. Did you finish all your homework?" Elizabeth grumbled and dawdled. "Yes, Mum. Will you still be here tomorrow, Jakob?" "Yes, Elizabeth." He grinned, "Yes - Ellie." And she laughed. Goodnight, Jakob." but giving her mother a kiss.

After Elizabeth left, they talked and listened to music from the record-player, Andrew's mother explaining what a couple of pieces were, but it was not a late night, and both Andrew and Jakob were glad to get to bed.

Jakob slept soundly, and woke with the sun streaming between curtains, so that for a minute he wondered where he was. It was a quiet house. He managed to use the guest bathroom without running into anyone. Somewhere downstairs someone was playing – or practising – a piano, scales, then a nice melody, halting to repeat a phrase, getting it right then going back to include it in a fluid piece. Again. And again.

When Jakob joined the breakfast table, only Elizabeth and her mother were sitting, and Mrs Turner went to the kitchen to get Jakob fresh coffee. Jakob asked the little girl "Was that you, playing the piano?" Elizabeth screwed up her face, groaning "Yes, sorry, it was terrible I know, but I have to practise every morning." "No, it was not terrible, it was a beautiful piece of music, what is it?" "It's Beethoven, *Für Elise*." "Sorry. Say again?" "*Für Elise* – it's German; it means 'For Elise'. (Whoever she was) It's one of my class set pieces." Mrs Turner returned. "Do you like music Jakob?" "Well yes, listening, but not playing any instrument." "What do you like?" He seemed a bit embarrassed. "I like Country music." That was when Andrew joined them and sat down. "Country music? You mean like your wife ran away with your best friend and your dog died?" Andrew taunted. Jakob corrected "My horse, not my dog." They laughed. "Don't let them tease you, Jakob," Mrs Turner said, but Jakob admitted "I know some of it is really ordinary, but I like pieces like Tennessee Waltz. Sorry, I don't really know any *proper* music – serious music." "Then we shall have to teach Jakob, won't we, Liz? We've got heaps of records, and we'll find something to interest you."

Andrew's father appeared, returning newspapers to the table where he had obviously finished breakfast already. "All right you boys, don't forget our golf date this morning at 8.30 at the club, we'll need to leave here by eight." Jakob said "I'm a bit embarrassed, Mr Turner, I haven't got any proper golf shoes or anything..." "No problem Jakob, we'll fit you out at the Pro Shop."

The 18 holes was not a complete disaster – in fact Jakob took to it like a duck to water, although he hadn't played before, and Mr Turner was fulsome in his praise of good straight drives. Jakob tried to congratulate Andrew on his many good shots – particular the tight accurate putting – but Andrew's father seemed to choose to ignore his son's efforts. This man is an arsehole, Blask said to himself, no wonder Andrew has a big problem. It was time he cut his father adrift and regained his confidence. Blask determined to help him do that. When they got back to Clink.

The next day at Kurrajong with Jakob's grandad was in fine form, but then Jakob suggested that they phone before going to visit his mother. Blask's grandad grimaced "No, I'll leave you visit Kati alone this time. She was a bit" (he held out a flat hand and wobbled it) "vague? Is the right word, vague? last time; so I think she might is better with just you, not me." Jakob wondered if it had been his mother's criticism again of her father's ratbag lifestyle of which she didn't approve; especially his drinking and wildness.

When he arrived at the small nursing home on the banks of the Nepean, the smiling Nun at the reception desk hesitated, and said "Before you go in Mr Blask, Doctor Vincent asked to have a word with you. If you give me those flowers, I'll put them in a vase for Katie." So he handed them over, and waited outside the Doctor's office. Jakob wondered if it was a financial problem, or a medical one. It wasn't for long, although Doctor Vincent always seemed to have a nurse or two walking with him from his rounds, noting instructions, before he was able to speak to Blask. "Oh, Jakob, isn't it? Good man, come in and take a seat. I sort of expected you to be in uniform." "My mother doesn't like to be reminded that I am in the army, doctor" And the doctor nodded. "Oh. I understand. Now, Jakob, what I wanted to talk to you about. Have you heard from your mother lately?" "Well yes, by mail, we exchange letters every few weeks. I haven't been the best correspondent, but. ." "Katie's fine; it's just, Jakob, that we have recorded some changes in your mother's behaviour lately, and I wanted to prepare you, in case you were unaware, in case she is different this time. Now don't worry, medically Katie is her usual self, still doing OK, but like a lot of us, she is losing her memory." "You mean she's getting a bit 'vague' ?" (He remembered his grandfather) "Well yes, you could call it that." "My grandfather warned me." "Right. Yes, I remember him saying that she rambled on a bit strangely. Sister Benedict has got her doing a few small chores and chatting to some of the older patients, which is good for them, and for her." Doctor Vincent stood up from his desk "I'll let you get on with your visit, Jakob, but don't be alarmed if Katie's mind is not working as fast as she used to. There's been a bit of deterioration in the last few weeks, but we're keeping an eye on it." He walked Blask to the door. "Remember, Jakob, we have Katie's welfare at heart all the time, and we're always available if you want to phone us up and have a chat." He offered his hand. "By the way, I should have asked. Is everything going alright with you at your studies?" "Yes, fine, thank you, Doctor."

Jakob didn't find his mother at first, and when he asked, he was directed to a group of ambulant patients on garden benches outside, leading down to the Nepean River. He smiled as he greeted her "Hello Mama, enjoying a bit of sunshine?" The lady patient next to Katie laughed, responding "Katie is keeping us amused with stories about the old days when you were a little boy." But Katie didn't seem to recognise him straight away, frowning "That's the question." Jakob tried to give her a cheek-kiss, but she turned aside. "What question, Ma?" But she looked strangely at him, and said "Banny should have been here hours ago" (Who's Banny? Or was it Manny?) "Who's that, Ma?" She stared at him as if she didn't recognize him. "It's me, Jakob, Mama, *Kuba*. It's me." And then she seemed to come out of a daze. "Carmel said you were coming, but I thought you had been." "Ma, I wouldn't have left without seeing you, you know that. *Dziadziu* was sorry he couldn't come this time." She humphed. The lady patient next to Katie said "Maybe I'd better leave you to it." But Jakob protested "No, stay here; don't let me disturb you. Are you Carmel?" She laughed, "No, dear, Carmel is Sister Benedict, your mother's friend." Jakob continued to try and make conversation with Katie, but it was strained, and he had a fixed smile after half an hour. It was the other patient, (her name was Mrs Maitland he discovered), who created most of the conversation. At one stage, Jakob's mother said a couple of times, "That's the question" and he realized that it didn't mean anything, it was just a useless expression of hers. After asking about her health, and the routine, and even the food, he was running out of topics to which his mother was not offering any elaboration. He knew that he shouldn't raise the subject of the army, and his training.

Eventually, he said "I'd better have a word with Dr Vincent and Sister Benedict before I go. I've brought you some lovely flowers for your room, Mama." Again he tried to kiss her farewell, but she was awkward, and she said "Tell Carmel – tell Sister Benedict..." but it seemed she had forgotten what she was going to say, although he waited. "Goodbye, Mama. *Kocham Cię*" He blew her a kiss, and waved to Mrs Maitland as he left. He didn't know why, but he was terribly sad. He felt he had not really connected with her. Had he abandoned her by going into the army? He wished... There was no answer. Maybe next time would be better.

1949

Top Songs:
   All I Want For Christmas Is My Two Front Teeth (Spike Jones)
   Buttons and Bows (Dinah Shore),
   A Little Bird Told Me (Evelyn Knight),
   Cruising Down The River (Blue Barron),
   Ghost Riders In The Sky (Vaughn Monroe),
   Some Enchanted Evening (Perry Como).

- Heavy snowfall in Canberra.

- Soviets detonate Atom Bomb "Joe One".

- Berlin Blockade is lifted.

- Communist-led miners' strike in Australia cripples industry and power. PM Chifley reluctantly sends in army to operate open cut mines, with rail unions cooperating.

- December Election: Menzies wins landslide, but his attempt to outlaw Communist Party of Australia is unsuccessful.

- Communists gain power in China defeating Nationalists, who flee to Taiwan (formerly Formosa)

- South Africa introduces Apartheid ('Separate Development')

- NATO established.

- Indonesia becomes independent from Netherlands

ichael. Like I was saying, when I joined as a private, we did our recruit training at 'Pucka' – that is, the vast army base at Puckapunyal, near Seymour in Victoria. Now, even at this stage, in 1949, Pucka is still a bit of a mash-up of post-war units, some of them trying to form separate Corps training schools competing for limited facilities, and at the same time trying to deal with remnants of wartime demobilization. Yes, hard to believe, but there are still returning soldiers from World War Two needing to get quit of their uniforms and obligations. Some poor blighters were still being repatriated from overseas. I think we were lucky, that our Platoon Sergeant is one of those, an experienced infantryman from the islands, one of those who battled down the Malay Peninsula until their depleted unit was overwhelmed by the Japs and then surrendered by their officers to be imprisoned like slaves for the rest of the war. He, Sergeant Stagg, spent time in severe camps and mines in Changi and Thailand, and then fronted at the War Crimes Trials before being repatriated. But to us, he was just a real soldier from whom we were able to believe everything that he was teaching us – someone who had done it, not just learned it in a manual. He taught us a lot, sometimes even when we were off duty. And one of the most important things he taught us, was that we relied on one another, and had that obligation to look after each other. This, he kept on emphasizing.

Of course at basic training there was a lot of drill, masses of it, until we knew everything there was to know about all our personal weapons and manoeuvres, but we also fell into the hundreds of jobs created by a still-disbanding wartime army, including collection, transport and disposal of military materiel 'no longer required' – so that sometimes you would have thought we were storemen, delivery drivers, and stocktakers. At other times we were drafted in to repairing and rebuilding army facilities; carpentering and painting, plumbing and roofing. A bit of variety which did none of us any harm, in fact we often enjoyed the change. And in between times, discovering that our Section and Platoon were just small cogs in the total defence wheel, uniting with other sub-units to form Companies and Battalions. And did I tell you about us acting as aid to the civil authorities when the rivers in Central Victoria flooded, and we worked together tirelessly for days evacuating farming properties and helping to rescue livestock. The farmers were really appreciative.

We also had to assist with the annual training camps for school cadets. Cadets from schools all over the State. Still hard to comprehend, that school cadet corps taught kids to be soldiers four years after the war's end, and had them taking home their 303 rifles and bayonets between weekly drill days. Mind you, a lot of Australian kids already owned pea-rifles, 22s, or shotguns in the wardrobe, anyway, for hunting rabbits. And nobody locked their doors. Remarkable that there were so few (almost no) gun accidents or crime. Some of our squad – especially Walshy – turned up their nose at the school cadets "playing soldiers" calling them Wednesday Warriors – but I had to remind the sneerers that the kids were doing their training in their own time, for no pay, and would be one step ahead if they were ever called up. Every chance I got, I tried to commend and encourage the cadets and their teachers. To me, they were part of us, the army.

Mainly, we were training, training, training. We got it all down to a fine art, second nature. Drill, tactics, manoeuvres, weaponry, all types of combat, and always fitness – route marches, climbing, races, football, competitive sport of every kind. Some of it – a lot of it, most of it, was fun.

----

igid. Not a move, as the college RSM – starched and crisp and polished – his heavy varnished pace stick balanced under a wing like a badge of office – cap peak not far off touching his nose – head so erect that the fine shorn bristles at the nape of his neck were almost a straight vertical line from his ramrod back – moved silently despite the studs on the soles of his gleaming boots – and suddenly you knew he was immediately behind you, you felt his presence, his body heat, the faintest hint of what-was-it some old-fashioned Bay Rum hair tonic, and waited for the fault you knew he was always able to find somewhere, hoping it was not you, hoping it was Thomson or Davies on each side of you. Who was behind you? Can't remember. "Cadet Wilson." Thank God it's not me, poor Wilson. "Sir!" Still rigid, facing the front, heavy rifle still gripped tight waiting for the order, whatever it would be. But no, a polite caring voice. "Mister Wilson; am I hurting you?" *What?* What is he on about? "No sir?" Then the voice resumed its usual thunder behind you. "Then I should be, I am standing on your hair; *GET IT CUT!*" "Sir!" "And you, Cadet Turner, what are you smiling at?" "Sorry sir, thought you were making a joke." "Oh no, Mister Turner, I don't make jokes on parade. But for smiling on my parade, You, Mister, take an extra drill." "Sir!" "I can't hear you boy." "SIR!" "Better." Poor Andy. And now, the RSM has moved in front of Jakob, who is, like everybody, rigidly at attention eyes front. The RSM is only inches away, eye to eye, staring at Jakob, both of them motionless. Is it a game?

Jakob wills himself not to blink, barely breathe. The RSM's eyes opposite his are grey, or is it green? No matter. The RSM has an old scar high across the bridge of his nose. Is he daring me to smile or say something? How long is he going to keep this up? Is it a *who-blinks-first* competition? I can outlast him. Perhaps I should purse my lips, pretend to blow him a kiss. (Don't even think that, you silly bugger, it could make your eyes smile and bring down hell on you.) Every cadet is rigid, gripping those heavy old 8 ½ Pound sweat-slippery wooden-framed .303 Short Lee-Enfield rifles with almost numb fingers, knowing that to drop a rifle on parade would be committing cadet suicide, and as if the thought also occurred to the RSM, he growled at the assembled cadets "Don't move. Don't even think of moving. No-one moves on my parade unless I say so. No one wavers or faints on my parade unless they are dying. And then, they will be grateful that they are dead, Clear?" And he has to repeat it: "*Clear?*" The Class echo this time is in unison in that young male voice-breaking chorus which is so simultaneous, it could have been rehearsed: "**Clear, Sir!**"

Then Vickery with a weekend's soft blond growth on his upper lip gets attention. "You, Cadet Vickery, you are on my parade, and you have remnants of your breakfast on your top lip. Fall out and wash your face!" "But Sir..." "Yes man, what is it?" (but knowing full well what is coming) "Sir, not breakfast; I'm growing a moustache, sir." "Oh, is that what it is? Tut-tut. I thought it was some pollen fallen off the pansies. Anyway, you should know that here, you have to ask permission to grow a moustache. (Brief Pause) And, before you ask, the answer to that is, no. N. O. Permission refused." "But sir..." "Mister Vickery, are you deaf? The answer is No. Nan Oboe, No. That is cadet kindergarten bum-fluff on your face, and you will wipe it off or shave. And if you are determined to try again, wait until your Christmas leave when you might have a few weeks start to grow more than four hairs, and let me take another look at it when you come back. That is all!" None of us dare smile. Anyway, like Vickery, we are all aware that we are practically still kids, and can't grow up fast enough, some of us only just needing to shave (which is compulsory here anyway), all of us when off duty looking around at each other comparing notes and wondering when we will become men. We notice Cadet Campbell off duty smoking a pipe (or trying to) and looking distinctively self-conscious, probably practises it in front of a mirror so that he doesn't choke on it in public. Of course quite a lot of us smoke cigarettes, about the same proportion as the general population I guess, but because of being permanently broke, most of us roll-our-owns for smoking when we are permitted – (generous roll-'ems early in the fortnight, and as our tobacco pouches dwindle flat towards payday our smokes becoming race-horse thin, or we cadge a smoke off a mate, or do without. Doing without is character-building, no?)

We are allocated "Buddies" in the system; conveniently for me and Andrew, as we are next-door neighbours. The greatest advantage of Buddies is that of helping one another to survive the Extra Drills, preferably when one of the pair was given the punishment, the other was able to hastily help assemble the ordered kit for that particular session (because every extra drill dress and accoutrement could be different), and check the correctness of the victim on his breathless way past, making sure (well, it was never sure, was it?) that there was no pathetic reason for the drill instructor to nit-pick about a button unsecured or some other stupid excuse to award the cadet further drills on top of the one being expunged. And then there was always the advantage of the Buddy system that one could help the other to hear and memorise definitions, decode mathematical formulae, explain something vague and possibly misheard from a recent class; even just be a physical presence of someone who cared – who at least knew what you were going through, and who sympathised. Mind you, if people groaned or complained, the others said "I feel for you, but from where I'm standing, I can't quite reach you." Or, "The padre's office is past the Orderly Room, tell him."

The classrooms study detailed campaigns from El Alamein to the River Sangro, Kokoda, Operation Overlord, Nijmegen, Irrawaddi. TEWTS (Tactical Exercises Without Troops) are held on the big sand-tray and later on the rolling fields of ACT, drill drill drill square-bashing on that sunbaked parade ground (and in the rain, and shivering in that freezing July alpine snow-wind too), mathematical calculations of artillery trajectory and ballistics, w/t radio and battery technicalities, physical exertions across punishing obstacle courses and teamwork exercises in crossing the Molonglo River. Football games and compulsory boxing matches, visits off base to specialist units for experience in armoured vehicles with deafening shellfire. One minute soaked and filthy digging foxholes (and filling them in again); the next minute poncing about in Number One dress uniform at an officers' mess dinner pretending to be gentlemen soldiers of the King. Tradition. Practising your parade ground voice shouting commands as each officer cadet takes turns in directing juniors, or the remainder of his class. And the exams, exams, always the exams, and then – there but for the grace of God, you notice the absence in class, an emptied room where a colleague has been "let go" – or even someone who decided that he couldn't take it any more, - and you realise that it all has a serious purpose of assessment and selection, and not everybody makes it, or wants to.

Like Andrew, who at one stage of infantry tactics training, where he and Blask had crawled 50 metres across knuckle-skinning rocky gravel from cover to cover towards the target dugout, managing somehow to avoid the Directing Staff referee who had officially "killed" several other cadets but had not yet seen Andrew and Jakob. They lay there exhausted, heavy breathing from their physical exertion and tension, looking each other in the eyes, and Blask was inclined to grin at their predicament, that they were the last remaining 'live' soldiers in the unit, but he suddenly realised that Andrew was beat. Really beat. "Fuck this", Andrew said. "I never wanted to be here in the first place, and I've had enough. I'm going to chuck it in. The whole damn thing." Jakob laughed, but then realised that Andrew was serious. "Oh no mate, you can't do that, because we're tied together like Siamese twins, and if you go, I have to go too. You are my buddy and I can't survive this fucking paradise without you. And if we both go, yeah, I can see us washing greasy dishes in some sleazy Sydney dive for peanuts and getting drunk on metho in a brown paper bag, and lining up at Ozanam House for soup and a bed with bugs, and hairy-arsed drunks trying to climb into your blanket with you. Oh no, Turner, even surviving Thunderbum here is better than us becoming downhill derelicts with no future. You support me through this, and I'll support you. You've got to. I need you. We need each other." Andrew slumped, about to say something, but the exercise referee Captain had tuned in on their voices, and discovered them, making notes on his clip-board. "Well done you two. You are the only survivors of Section Ten. Congratulations. Fall back in."

Another day, a Regular Corporal conducted their weapon parade, but in the distance they saw Drill Sergeant Kelly approaching, no, not just approaching – *marching* as he always did, Kelly the immaculate, smart, erect, poker-faced. Maybe he had smiled once, but no-one had ever seen it. And everyone knew that something serious was happening, and hoped that it was not, this time, for him. The Corporal conducting the parade, whose name was Brereton, could see that Sgt Kelly was a man with a mission, and called the squad to attention. Even Cpl Brereton was hoping that Kelly would not find anything about him to criticize. The squad stood straight, straining to be anyone but the person Kelly was going to pick out for some misdemeanor, wondering: what have I done wrong now? But Kelly had only one cadet in mind, and his parade-ground voice was sharp. "Cadet Heath, fall out!" But as if the Sergeant immediately recognized that that was too vague an order, he amended it. "Cadet Heath; one pace forward: March! Remain at attention. The rest of the squad, Squad! Stand at - Ease! Corporal Brereton, take over! Mister Heath, you are wanted at the Adjutant's Office, give your rifle to Corporal Brereton and come with me!"

And everybody knew that a command to the Adjutant's Office was Heap Big Trouble. This rare command was something which they knew had occurred before where a fellow cadet was never seen or heard from again, and this time was no exception. Drill Sergeant Kelly halted Heath at the edge of the parade ground and inspected him front and back, nit-picking a couple of uniform adjustments, and then marched Heath off beside him, nagging him "Keep in step man, head up, back straight," and the pair of them disappeared out of sight. When the day's classes and duties were complete, at that echoing mess hall, there were only rumours, with very few details added. "When we got back to quarters at the end of the day, Heath had gone, packed; all his personal gear, and an orderly was returning most of his equipment to the Q Store. His room was bare empty" "Did you ask what had happened?" "I did, but they all clammed up, not a word, other than he had apparently been sacked." "Jesus." "Poor bloody Heath, wonder what he did wrong?"

It was not for a couple of days that the story filtered through. "You hear about Heath?" "No, what?" "He got kicked out. 'Conduct Unbecoming', got some town girl up the duff" "What d'you mean?" "You know, a bun in the oven; up the duff." "Which girl, do you know?" "Dunno, some local chick he met." "Poor bugger." "Or maybe, lucky bugger, getting his leg over." Laughter, then "Not lucky, if it got him sacked. And on top of that, he'll now have to do the right thing and marry the girl." A fate worse than death, apparently. "Poor bastard." And later still, the word got around that she was, you know, that flirtatious one, the girl they saw Heath with that Sunday in the hired Molonglo River rowboat, down past the Golf Club, you know the girl, the one always giving cadets the eye at church parades, the girl who used to smoke those Balkan Sobranis." "Jesus, I wonder where they managed to do it." "Not likely in that hired rowing boat" (They laughed at the thought) "No problem finding somewhere to bloody do it; the problem is finding some girl who'll let you." "Well you can understand why now, can't you? I'm sure she wouldn't have wanted to get pregnant, any more than Heath did." "Silly bugger for not taking precautions. Both of them. Easy enough to buy Frangers." "Yes, but you know about 'heat of the moment' opportunity, right? A standing prick has no conscience."

But another surprise eventually leaked out a couple of weeks later, that Old Thunderbum the RSM put in a word for Heath, about what a waste of two years' strenuous military training, and as a soldier Heath had been doing well, so they somehow arranged for him to be discharged, then re-enlisted as a Private and sent to a Junior Leader's course at Sydney's North Head, which if he passed, would make him a Corporal and maybe even entitled to a married quarter in a training battalion somewhere when the girl had the baby. Good old Thunderbum, so he actually had a heart in the right place.

We are all fitter than we'll ever be again, and not surprising, when you consider the amount of physical exercise we get every day. Plus, I guess, we started off in top condition anyway, when we were medically examined as part of our entry – they tended to reject any candidates who were less than A-one, and we have been building on that ever since. The school has a strong emphasis on PT and sport, and we all play everything, as well as choose to specialise in sports we are comfortable or experienced in. A good example is Jakob, who was welcomed to rugby and cricket like a pro, and has already shown himself to be a competitive star in both, but then he was sports-oriented to begin with. My sports preference is, in general, athletics in which I have shown some natural skill, particularly long-distance running and the high jump. I also play tennis and hockey, like a lot of my classmates.

Boxing is a compulsory sport here for everyone, and again, Jakob excels, and has already been selected to box competitively for the school. 'The Noble Art' they reckon, dating from before ancient Greece or something, engraved on the pyramids etc. Thuggery, if you ask me, two men belting one another until one of them falls down, or time is called. It is not my 'thing', but like everybody, I do my best when I have to, and take my regular punishment in the ring. One day, jogging together with Jakob, I hesitantly asked him if he would give me a few boxing tips, maybe to reduce the amount of punishment I was getting. "Cut it out, Andy, I'm not an expert, you know." But when I persisted, pointing out the number of bouts he won easily, he reluctantly agreed, and we went to the gym, to the boxing ring, one weekend afternoon in our rare spare time. There were a few cadets doing various bits of PT with the gym equipment, who were curious about our session, but I decided it had to be done and ignored their curiosity. Jakob and I gloved up and got into the ring. He said "Listen, I'm not a boxing instructor, so all I can do is pass on what works for me, OK? The first thing", Jakob said, "is to get your guard right. You can prevent and deflect a lot of punishment if you have a solid guard." He set me up with better stance, with my body aligned, my chin tucked in, my feet stabilised for solid balance, and my arms raised so that the gloves in front of my face and the position of my elbows better protected me from body punches. "Yes, like that," he said, "so for now, for a start, don't try to throw punches, just concentrate on your protective position and your balance. Just move around like that while I throw punches at you." He joked, "only kidding, I'll try not to kill you, but if you get that defence part of it right, you'll put yourself in a prime position from which to launch your attack." "Me? Attack?" I laughed. "It's all I can do to keep off the floor."

After a bit of sparring, I began to see what he was getting at, and already I felt more comfortable, more confident. Time and again he made me correct my stance so that I could move forward, sideways or even back without compromising balance. We boxed around for a bit, and then Jakob gave me a tip. "Do you want to know a trick which I use?" "You mean the secrets of your success?" I hoped. "Sort of, but wasted on an idiot like you. Because you're a dozy bastard and don't pay any attention to our lecturers, you will have missed one of the key principles of warfare. Do you remember anything you've learned about first principles?" "You mean, like concealment and camouflage?" I asked, laughing, but he whacked me one. "No, you dope, pay attention. I mean, like Old Bob taught us, One: the element of surprise, plus overwhelming force, plus speed of attack, and above all, confidence. You watch most of the cadets here when they face off in the boxing ring – a bunch of sad sacks, they adopt their pose and they dance around, watching their opponent, waiting for an opportunity or a weakness, sparring, feinting, farting about. Some guys, they can swan around for minutes and no blow is struck while they size up their opponent. Well, I want you to try a different approach – and believe me, it works. When the bell rings and the round starts, don't faff around sizing up your opponent, Attack!" I laughed at him, but he was serious. "Really?" "Yes, bloody really. Your opponent will have expected you to square up to him to spar and bob and weave about like they do. Like everyone else does. But if you go fast straight across the ring at him, whack him, the first blow, the flurry of blows, which he will not have expected, will do three things to your advantage – One, it will scare the hell out of him and make him realise that he has to defend himself against a fighter. A fighter. Two, it will give you the benefit of being the aggressor, in control, and that is an enormous psychological plus. Three, it will make you feel good, because you are already in his territory and in a position to maintain the attack. He won't have time to remember all the classic guards and protections he thought he had planned, because you have already broken through that and put him on the back foot (if not on the floor). All you need is determination and belief in yourself, and that is what you need more of, and what I am going to extract from you." I am still bemused "You're right that is what I lack. I can't do that, sail into the attack Jakob, it's not <u>me</u>." He leaned forward and glared at me "You can, and you will, if you want me to help you perform better in the ring. Look Andy, no-one here is going to expect you to come out blazing in your next fight, so if you do, you will be a winner, believe me. Now let's practise that. I want you to come straight across the ring swinging. No; say again, not swinging, straight punching. A straight left and an unexpected immediate hook with the same left, like this. It's one of Dave Sands's winning specials. Of course, I'm going to defend myself from your attack, but because of the surprise element and your momentum, I'm going to be struggling to keep you off. So let's practise that, OK?" And we did. Over and over. "Anyway, who's Dave Sands?" "God you're hopeless Andy, I don't know why I bother with you as a mate." He cuffed me lightly over the ear, smiling. And then he gave me a second secret weapon – expression. "Listen, your opponent is watching you, looking for your weaknesses. Don't give him one by looking worried or frightened. Give <u>him</u> something to worry about, by grinning at him. He doesn't know why, but you do – it is because you are super-confident, and you are enjoying this, and you are going to beat the shit out of him. OK? Now try this. Hit me, and grin. And if he falters, or has to go backwards, or trips or falls, laugh. You have got the upper hand, right? And if by chance he manages to land a lucky punch on you, grin at him. Let him know that he was lucky that time, but he's going to get his coming."

I got the hang of it. And surprisingly, it worked. And the first time I tried it all out on someone else (Cadet Mackie later that week in our regular boxing sessions) I saw what Jakob was talking about; I saw the momentary panic in Mackie's eyes, and I recognised my advantage and pressed it for the next three minutes, grinning, and knew that I had won. Both that particular fight, and the psychological war. And that win did even more for me as I observed the look that some of the other cadets gave me afterwards. A new respect. Thanks, Jake.

Well, you can get used to anything, can't you. Like the frog in the kettle, who doesn't notice the water getting gradually hotter until it kills him. We are so regimented it is like being in a machine, but in a way that is a help, you can just surrender to the system, the routine, and let it carry you along with its irresistible flow, while you are studying, studying. Sure, you make mistakes, and get punished, and try to keep alert ahead of the game, but there is also a sense of inevitability about it, sleepwalking at a high level of awareness, if there can be such a thing. Christ, you never knew there were so many hours in a day, or a week could be so long. But at the same time, there was never enough time to get things done, but the days weeks and months seem to speed past.

This is our second year. Does it feel like we are old hands? Not quite, not yet; but at least we can now look at the newly inducted class behind us and, seeing what green kids they are, we can realise what green kids we were ourselves (not too long ago). In the new year, we have to vacate and move to other rooms, for some obscure reason. We have got the measure of all our own classmates by now. Most of them are much alike in their attitudes and reactions – after all, we are all here for the same reasons. And when you think of it, we were selected with the same criteria, from most of the same ingredients, so it is only when one of us reacts weirdly or violently that you notice a character trait which maybe you didn't notice before. So most of them you get along with, because you recognise yourself in them, and it is only the oddball or rebel who stands out like a sore thumb.

At least we are proudly aware that we have a little seniority, now that a new intake of gremlins has arrived and been inducted. It doesn't seem long since we too were a batch of schoolboys being shouted at by everybody, discovering that we were the lowest of the low with four years of torture facing us. And now we realise that we have chalked off a quarter of our sentence, and that maybe – just maybe – we might be able to see our eventual graduation as officers somewhere away in the foggy future. We might even, if we have a minute, spare a second's pity for those incoming poor Fourth Year babies just getting their initiation. There are even some of us, a few miserable bastards, who want to take sadistic pleasure in tormenting the new class with hazing like we received in our first months; but most of us remember what it felt like, and take it easy on the new boys. For one thing, we are not so far advanced ourselves, and secondly, there are more important things to think about. We have got every second of every minute packed with duties and responsibilities, including the onerous extra drills to put up with. Oh no, we haven't escaped the punishment schedules, but with a bit of experience, we can now avoid many of them, and when they happen handle them.

Apart from the academic classes and exams, and the endless necessary military subjects, there is a ton of ceremonial to prepare for, and take part in, such as the annual Anzac Day and Remembrance Day parades, and the huge Graduation Day Parade for the finishing senior class (in which every other class participates), all of which are occasions of precision and detail which the RSM is never quite satisfied with. But we try. Getting better at it all the time.

Among the staff, we all have our favourites and *bêtes-noirs*. There are some good guys and some absolute drips. A couple of them we sincerely hate; enough to do them serious harm, those who make our lives sheer hell unnecessarily. And there are a couple of the staff just going through the motions, seeing out their time. But the majority are efficient, some super-efficient. I think most of us relate to Captain Whitton. He is an infantry weapons specialist who knows his subject with a confidence and ease you know comes from experience, and he looks good so that many of us would like to emulate him if we could. He is always smart. His uniforms always fit perfectly (Wilson says that Capt Whitton has his shirts tailored to fit slim rather than baggy at the waist) and whoever his Batman is, he does a great job on the Captain's webbing and brass. And his cap, field service, slightly folded down at the sides; or if he is wearing *hat khaki fur felt*, it has a desirable 'bash' to be envied and attempted to copy in private. Whitton is a fine figure of a man, well-built, good-looking, serious-eyed, permanently marked by that unmistakeable purple scar down from his left eye which adds to his masculine aura. We know – although no-one knows how we know – that he was taken by the Japanese in Malaya and imprisoned in a coalmine on one of their home islands, staying on after the war to testify at several war-crime trials. But he also has a reputation that he is a skilled hand-to-hand fighter, a man you wouldn't mess with. And we know from those bloody boring church parades that he turns up with his attractive young wife and two small children who obviously adore him, and everybody wants to be like him.

Oh yes, those church parades. Remember the RSM Thunderbum last year, saying reasonably in answer to an innocent question, "No son, Sunday church parades are not compulsory; no no, not at all. But cadets who do not attend church parades may – because they find themselves <u>available</u> - thus *accidentally* find themselves being awarded alternative duties instead, just to keep their minds above their navel, so do not be tempted to avoid improving your godliness." And it was true, that those stupid enough to opt out of church parades (Which were allocated C of E, R.C., or catch-all OPD – 'other protestant denomination') attendance, found themselves enslaved in fatigues, or generally unpleasant duties.

Anyway, church parades were a way to meet chicks, even at a distance – those lovely scented girls in their silk dresses, gloves, hats and stockings. (All the women and girls always wore gloves and hats). If you sat behind the girls, them safely protected with their supervising parents and junior siblings, you could inhale their beautiful perfume and deliciously, achingly, watch their feminine movements as they stand or sit or kneel, all the time suffering their distance, their inaccessibility, yet occasionally receiving a demure sidelong almost-smile of politeness as they passed your pew on their way out at service end. *Sooo* lucky if you got an introduction to one of them chatting below the church steps; luckier still if you got a family invitation to Sunday afternoon tea, or a game of tennis next weekend, or some other way to get a foot in the door, even if supervised by a girl's father who knew how predatory a boy could be. Still, you could always dream, couldn't you? If you had time.

Marching, marching everywhere. Not just on parade as a unit marching, but marching solo or in a group whenever it was necessary to 'walk' anywhere – that's just it, walking did not exist anymore. And not just walking. Strolling. Ambling. That's what civilians did 'out there' in another life. In order to 'proceed' anywhere on foot within the sacred territory of the School, one marched. Straight, erect, eyes front, chest out, shoulders back, chin in, arms swung high, purposeful. Oh yes, there was one other exception to this – Doubling. And there was a lot of that, mostly as punishment. With the appropriate weapons and kit, of course.

Reading, studying, was one thing, a permanent thing, but having to think things through, sometimes racking your brain for the right way to express yourself with convincing logic, might take time – and there was never enough time. You were not allowed to leave your room during study time from seven-thirty, and you were not allowed to study after *Lights Out* (although some crammed subjects with a torch under the bedclothes hoping not to be discovered by a roving Screw and suitably punished, because it was forbidden), so you didn't have the luxury of being able to compare notes with colleagues during study times. At nine-thirty you could go down for supper: tea and a biscuit and then it was Lights Out at ten fifteen, and everybody had, like yourself, studied each night – Academic subjects and Military subjects - not just studying set texts, but writing commentaries and projects which had to be handed in the next day or presented verbally in front of class, subject to analysis and criticism on content and presentation. Lights Out – you had to be back in your room by then, and even though you wanted, desperately needed to study that last couple of pages, you also badly needed that sleep as well, because you were knackered. Always exhausted.

Reveille was at six o'clock, which was when defaulters punishment drills began, which you had to be ready for on the parade ground, ready <u>and</u> correct, reporting to the duty Sergeant. So that if you were late, that attracted another defaulter drill added to your punishment schedule. Not to mention any deficiency in your dress, weapon or behavior which could be punished in addition. There was also another period of extra drills conducted after classes at four in the afternoon, while everyone else was enjoying afternoon tea and a piece, at the end of an arduous day, before organized sporting fixtures.

Being called out to go under escort to the adjutant's office was ominous, and now it was Jakob's turn. Everybody knew that it was the precursor to some disaster, some serious disciplinary action, not just the usual extra drill meted out by the staff and NCOs for minor (sometimes *very* minor) infringements. Jakob handed over his rifle to the drill NCO and accompanied the escort. As they marched towards the admin block, he asked the escorting Corporal what it was about. "Do you know what I am supposed to have done?" And the stern Corporal, tight-lipped, said "Not for me to say. Keep in step." And the anticipation was worse when Jakob recognized from a distance that the RSM was there too. Everyone was serious, but then he saw his Grandfather, standing awkwardly in rough working clothes amongst this array of smart uniforms and military protocol. As Jakob arrived, it was his grandfather who spoke first, reaching for him, groaning in a hoarse whisper, "Oh 'Kuba, 'Kuba, *bardzo przepraszam!* And he knew then it was about Katie, his mother. His grandfather reverted to English, "'Kuba; Kati die yesterday. Funeral tomorrow." He submitted to the rough bear-hug from his Grandfather, and at the same time, the RSM and the adjutant both expressed their condolences. "So sorry about your mother, Blask," Captain Banks said (the man who never showed emotion), and the RSM sort of put a hand on Jakob's shoulder. The Adjutant said "Take a few days off, unless you want to take your mid-year leave early and catch up with classes and everything later?" "No sir, a couple of days should do it. I need to get back for my exams. I'll go now with my Grandfather, if that's OK." "That's fine. When you're ready to come back, I'll make sure there'll be a rail warrant for you at Sydney Central RTO, and someone from here will pick you up at the railway station, if you let us know which train. Get the RTO to signal us." When Jakob collected his duffle, they went back through the school, and despite the sadness, *Dziadziu* was suitably impressed, smiling and nodding to every squad they passed, the cadets marching, jogging, parading, or sitting intent in their classrooms with their civilian university lecturers. The old man's dilapidated truck was parked by the guardroom, and Jakob climbed into the bench seat (avoiding that one memorable wayward spring from piercing his back), knowing it would be a long and uncomfortable journey back home, as well as a sad one. "What happened?" Jakob asked, and his grandfather only shrugged "Kati died." As he repeatedly started the temperamental engine until it caught, the old man sighed, and Jakob said "That's terrible." His grandfather heaved a long shuddering breath, and said "It is, it is." There wasn't much to say on the long clattering drive back, but conversation was impossible anyway for the truck noise.

At the undertaker's, although Jakob didn't really want to see his mother's dead body, it was apparently expected as part of the funeral tradition, and he looked at that immobile pale face which still, in death, managed to wear the same old frown furrow between her closed eyes, as if she was embarrassed to be here on show, or, as Jakob remembered, annoyed at something he had done, or not done - so often in the past. She looked asleep, framed by the white satin lining in the varnished coffin, at the funeral parlour.. "Poor Mama," he whispered, "*Cześć* - Goodbye," wanting to get away, glad that she could not see him now in his uniform. They didn't go back to the grandfather's place at Kurrajong for the night, but stayed at a Penrith hotel, 'The Red Cow' next to the railway station, where they shared one of the few noisy rooms, where Jakob did not sleep well, full of thoughts and memories, not helped by the old man's thunderous snoring from the other bed, and the goods trains shunting nearby.

Next day the cemetery was a desolate place. Depressing and empty. Surrounded by tall aged pine trees, which soughed in the wind. 'Soughing' What a strange word he thought, a bit like sighing, wasn't it. Plenty to sigh about here. Such a pitiful small group gathered at the freshly dug gravesite. Jakob was pleased to recognize Sister Benedict from his mother's hospital, and he was surprised to see his former employer Mr. French in his wheelchair, helped to negotiate the gravel paths by Danny from the service station. There was a tall thin priest in black, whom he didn't know (but then, come to think of it, he didn't know many priests). The solemn funeral parlour people of course, whom he had met at the viewing, and his grandfather Aleksi talking quietly to a middle-aged couple, the man in a worn-shiny suit, but with a tie-less shirt closed at the neck. The woman (the man's wife?) was all in black, like a nun, black shoes and stockings, plain black dress, and a black headscarf. They spoke in Polish to Jakob. *'Prosze przyjać moje kondolencje'*, but *Dziadzia*, whose eyes were full of tears, said "Sorry, he not speak much *Polsku*. 'Kuba, this my friends Viktor and Anja." He pronounced it *Wiktor*. They shook hands. The priest came over too, and spoke to Jakob, saying something that sounded like *'Movees popolskoo?'* But Jakob was already shaking his head, and the priest changed to English. "You are Jakob, no? Very sorry, my son. God be with your mother, and God be with you," crossing himself. And then he was called away by one of the men from the funeral parlour, and Sister Benedict, who came over shyly, tried to comfort Jakob. "Katie is now at peace, Jakob, she will have no more pain." He said "Is the priest from your parish?" "No, he is Polish, from I think, Redfern. Somewhere in the city. I didn't meet him before. Doctor Vincent sends his condolences by the way, and the nurses. Everyone loved Katie. Your mother was a favourite patient, and a great help to me." "What was it? What did she die from?" "It was very sudden, Jakob. Poor Katie had been having some breathing problems two days back, but we thought she would recover again like she always did, which is why we didn't bother you or your grandfather. During the night, she had a severe coughing fit and collapsed. We put her into intensive care, and on a ventilator, but she didn't respond. Dr Vincent said pneumonia. Your grandfather has the certificate." He nodded. What difference did it make? He remembered how frail his mother was. Sister Benedict said "There are not many of Katie's things left, Jakob, will we give them to you, or your grandfather?" He shook his head, thinking of her few clothes and toiletries, she wouldn't have much, better to leave it for the church, or a charity... But the Sister added "There are a few photos, and she kept all your letters, you'd want those. Mr O'Brien from the undertakers has her wedding ring and rosary, for you, or your grandfather." "Thank you, Sister."

Jakob went across to Mr. French and Danny, and shook hands with them both. "I really appreciate you coming, both of you." Mr. French said "I remember Katie, Jakob, she was a lovely girl, and we're very sorry." "Thank you." Danny asked "Hey Jake, how's it going down there, are you still at that military college?" "Yes, Danny It's OK. Harder than I thought, but I'll get the hang of it. I'm still in my second year, and there's a long way to go, but..." He shrugged. Have you met my grandfather? I'll bring him over." And *Dziadzia*, his face still streaked with tears, was cheered up and pleased to meet these friends of Jakob. "I know that place," he said (meaning the petrol station), "I been there yes with my truck. That's good on you come say goodbye to Kati. You know Kati?" Mr. French nodded "When Karol was killed, Katie got a job at Meldrum's café. I used to eat there sometimes." And Jakob also remembered the café, because after work at the petrol station it was easier to get something to eat there than to go back to the rented rooms which always seemed to smell of cabbage from another guest's kitchen efforts. He remembered big bearded Meldrum, Katie's boss at the café, and the long painted sign above the blackboard price lists: '*Man can live without love; what is passion but pining – but where is the man who can live without dining?*' "Is Meldrum still there?" Jakob asked. "No mate, it's a real estate agent's now. Meldrum moved to Sydney a while back." Times changed. It didn't take long.

The service commenced, and the small group gathered together. The very shiny closed coffin was supported on two wooden bearers at the top of the grave, and at some agreed signal, the undertakers manipulated slings as the bearers were removed, and they lowered Kati's coffin into the grave, the priest bowing and talking in Polish, repeatedly crossing himself, which was echoed by *Dziadzia*, the Polish couple, and Sister Benedict. Jakob remained silent, head bowed. The priest took a handful of earth from the pile at graveside, and scattered it thudding on top of the coffin, saying "*Z prochu powstałeś I w proch się obrócisz*", which the other Poles repeated, each of them scattering a handful of earth on Kati's coffin. It was a terrible hollow sound. The priest then spoke in English, still crossing himself "We are all dust. And from dust, we return to dust." The funeral director said something, and two workmen (were they gravediggers?) took over filling the grave, as the director moved around the group, saying that they should now move to the nearby kiosk, where some refreshments were prepared. It seemed wrong, that that was all the ceremony there was, but it was better than staying to watch the grave slowly fill with fresh earth, over the top of Katie in her coffin. Jakob, still dry-eyed, bowed his head at the grave, standing for a minute longer with his thoughts, and let himself be shown across to the circular kiosk in the centre of the cemetery. It was more like a band-stand, open-sided with wooden seating around the inner perimeter, and in the middle, a trestle table laid with cups and saucers, a tea urn, and plates of what? *Pierogi*, sandwiches, and those things rolled up with toothpicks which his mother used to make, *Sliwki w boczku?* Something like that. Prunes wrapped in bacon – isn't there another name for them? Something on horseback. Plus, of course, a vodka bottle with some glasses. The couple, Anja and Viktor, seemed to have provided the refreshments, and helped people to serve themselves. Viktor was offering the vodka around, but Jakob shook his head. Sister Benedict said she would get tea, would he like one? He nodded thanks.

Mr. French wheeled himself over to Jakob. "I'm really sorry, Jake. About your Mum. Will you be staying long?" "No, Mr. French. I'll get a train back down tomorrow from Sydney, I've got exams next week. I'll stay tonight with granddad up at Kurrajong." French nodded, and accepted a sandwich from the plate offered him by one of the funeral parlour people, thanking him. To Jakob, he said ""I'm a bit puzzled about one thing, Jakob. I always wanted to ask." "Which is?" "Your name is Blask, OK?" "Well, yes; short for Blaszczyk." "Blaszcyzk,, right. That's Katie's, your mother's name, and your Grandfather's name. But it wasn't your father's name, was it? – how did that happen?" Jakob smiled slightly. "OK, yeah - well my mother's maiden name was also Blaskzcyzk – until she got married. But my father's name was Karol Stettin, and my

mother said that's a German name, and dug her heels in against it.
"No thanks, I won't have a German name", so she decided that she
(and then, me) would take *her* original name, i.e. Granddad's name,
which is Blaszcyzk, shortened to Blask. OK?" "OK. That makes
sense. Sort of. So your dad was German?" "No. Polish. His family
must have originally come from Stettin, that's how a lot of families
got their name way back, of where they came from; but Stettin
is a Polish city, and its Polish name is Szczecin (sounds much the
same), but the Germans called it Stettin, so that's why my mother
was so against it. She refused the name. She was against anything
German, like a lot of Poles." He shrugged, "Sometimes when I have
to explain Blask, or spell Blaszcyzk, I think Stettin would have been
a damn sight easier." They laughed.

The funeral lasted a short while, not because of tradition, or
the few mourners, but because there was another funeral booked to
follow, so that the "wake", or whatever that refreshment was in the
kiosk, was not long drawn-out. Aleksi, Jakob's grandfather, invited
everyone to adjourn, to follow on to his place at Kurrajong, but the
only takers were his friends Anja and Viktor, who seemed to know
their way. They offered the left-over food to Sister Benedict, the
funeral staff, and the men from the petrol station, but it was only
the Nun who shyly accepted, saying her patients would be grateful.
Jakob noticed that Viktor slipped the part-empty vodka bottle
into a coat pocket as the group broke up. More handshakes, more
murmurs of condolence, more religious crossing breasts. He was
so tired, he wished he could go somewhere to lie down, but that
wouldn't come for a while.

You would arrive at the old man's house on the dirt road,
and wonder what it was. Permanently half-built, changing
its appearance every time the old man had another creative
inspiration, or found / bought another odd amount of (mostly
used) building materials from someone or somewhere. Best not to
ask too many questions, some of the acquisitions were decidedly
dodgy. The rambling home was semi-built on one level against
the steep rocky hillside, so that one part 'extension' was actually

74

tunnelled metres into the hill. Jakob remembered once helping his grandfather to excavate a kind of underground store or workshop, but it had gone well past that. During a previous visit, Jakob wondered if *Dziadziu* was trying to prospect for something, or even build a primitive cave. (A fallout shelter? a bushfire refuge?) It was surrounded by bush, and Jakob remembered as a boy waking in the night to hear loud possum noises – screeching, hissing, growling and grunting somewhere close above his bed, probably in the sagging roof space which the animals had taken over as their own. There were always wandering chickens, and at least one mongrel dog each time he came, rescued from somewhere, and then let go as they wandered off. Grandfather was continually fighting with the local building inspector, Mr. Jessup, whose rulings and threat of fines forced *Dziadziu* to abandon (and sometimes tear down) adventurous constructions. Once, when Jakob was about 12, his grandfather took him to court with him for support, (maybe to help with his English) to fight one of the prosecutions – it was an earlier inspector, Mr. Sinclair (whom *Dziadziu* insisted on calling Mr Zinkler) – and he had appealed to the magistrate that a man's home was his castle. The smiling magistrate was gentle with the old man, and waived the prospective heavy fine, *'providing Mr. Blaszcyzk removed all of the unauthorised extensions to the original dwelling, within thirty days'*. *Dziadziu* wanted to debate that, but finally listened to his grandson as Jakob somehow convinced him it was the best deal he could get. Even at his young age, Jakob knew that his grandfather would suffer badly from imprisonment in lieu of what might be an impossible fine. Later, when Mr. Sinclair retired, Jakob had smiled, wondering if most of that inspector's grey hairs came from dealing with his grandfather. He was sure that Mr Sinclair would have warned his replacement, Mr Jessup, about the Polish madman that he would have to deal with, up in the bush at Kurrajong.

When they arrived 'home' after the funeral, Jakob slung his duffle into the 'annexe' where he had usually slept (this time finding half the room occupied with stacks of lichen-covered used roofing tiles and a startled hen) — at least there was still a bed in there somewhere, while his Grandfather ushered Viktor and Anja into the 'front' room with its miss-matched chairs and long scarred table. Jakob changed out of uniform and joined them. Of course the funeral vodka bottle came out, supplemented with another bottle from the old man's pantry. The lady, Anja, insisted on washing up some dishes which the old man had accumulated in the sink. Jakob let Viktor pour him a glass of vodka, but he toyed with it, not intending to drink just now. He wanted to help his grandfather mourn the loss of Katie, but the whole situation was too alien to him; he who had just buried his mother. The only thing which felt regular to him now, strangely enough, was that other strange new life, his barrack routine back at Duntroon, to which he would return tomorrow, needing to return and hide himself in routine. Here, he just let things flow around him. There was too much on his mind. The lady, Anja, came and sat next to him, trying to cheer him. She had washed and stacked the dishes, and now asked Viktor to pour her a glass. "Jakub?" she said, "we too, have also a Jakub, already." She calculated "Already is twenty years, our Jakub, is mining at Marblebar. You know Marblebar?" "Marble Bar? Yes, I know about it. Opal mines?" "Yes" she crowed, "Opals!" And she delved fingers into the high neckline of her severe black dress to retrieve a hidden chain, on the end of which was a nice opal, which she showed him, and then tucked it back out of sight. Jakob was awkward with calling her Anja, and asked "Excuse me. What is your name? Your family name? Mrs-?" So that she laughed. "Ni ko lo va." Introducing herself formally: Mrs Nikolova, Mr. Blaszcyzk - Mister Blask, OK? Him, Wiktor Novak, me Anja Nikolova." Jakob was confused by the W/V interchange. He assumed that they were 'a couple', but maybe not formally married.

The Polish priest arrived not long after (he complained about the vague directions he had been given), and it became a Polish old home week with four of them yabbering away in the old language, with frequent translations for Jakob, whether he wanted them or not. He found himself with a fixed smile on his face, trying to be polite.

(Poor Mama, he thought, you would be uncomfortable too with this loud conversation, almost like a celebration; it hadn't been your style at all. Karol's perhaps, but not yours. You were always uncomfortable amongst drinkers, or was that only because of Karol's fondness for the bottle?) Soon Dziadziu was roaring with laughter at some comment, and brought out another bottle from the pantry. Loud voices in due course as they farewelled the Priest, who joked about not being able to find his way back to the main road, manouvering his car between trees, piles of timber, and scattered bricks, helped (or hindered) by numerous shouted driving directions "Left hand down!". Back inside, loud voices and laughter as the lady, Mrs Nikolova, insisted on cooking something for them to eat, complaining about the scarcity of ingredients in the old man's larder, but boasting that anyway, 'any Polish woman could make a meal of even one potato and an egg'. They opened yet another bottle.

Don't try to keep up, Jakob knew, impossible to keep up anyway as it got later, one of them had to keep sane and sober, so watched his grandfather refill his own glass several times in the gathering night as he told stories (some of which Jakob has heard before, but what the hell), laughing, singing, occasionally lapsing back into Polish Jakob can't understand, writing himself off again, letting an empty bottle roll off the table. It didn't take long – not as long as it used to. Soon bleary, spilling some as he poured from a new bottle, eyes watering, sometimes Jakob not sure if his Dziadziu was still aware of his guests, waving his arms now as he sang the Dobrowski Mazurka Anthem, which the Novak/Nikolova couple joined, beating time on the table: '*Dla ojczyzny ratowania / Wrócim się przez morze / Marsz! Marsz!*', [yes, march-march forever saving the homeland from across the sea].

And as so many times before, it ended up with Aleksi – this ancient battered giant - crying, tears trickling down his weathered and bristly cheeks past that broken nose. What for? He never explains. For the beloved homeland he escaped before it was invaded by Nazis one side, and the Ivans the other? For his mates in the brave overwhelmed Polish Army which fought alone (without him) for over a month until annihilated? For the 22 thousand (without him) who were massacred by the Ivans in the Katyn forest? *O Dziadzia*. And as it is his duty, Jakob eventually managed to say goodnight to the Polish couple. God knows how they managed to get home, although he noticed at least that Mrs Nikolova had taken over the car keys. Jakob succeeded to get his grandfather into the bedroom and heavily onto the high bed, still singing, so that he could remove the boots, partly undress him, lay him horizontal below the hand-tinted photo portrait above the bed-head of that lovely smiling lady Grandma with her coiled plaits of greyed fair hair; and this big strong hulking man, hairy-armed with faded sailor tattoos, weak with alcohol and age, allowed himself to be covered with the faded tartan rug, mumbling in Polish, and then saying clearly: "*To jest życie*, 'Kuba, *takie jest życie*." Whatever that meant. In five minutes, he was snoring loudly, and Jakob retreated to the 'annexe', collapsing until a pre-daylight rooster woke him. The old man was already in the kitchen singing, stoking up the wood stove and stripping the rind off bacon. "'Kuba! Good morning. Kettle soon." Jakob smiled to himself; Aleksi was back to his usual cheerful form. How could he rebound so fully from such a grog session? And from such a sad day, burying his daughter, his only child?

Back at the college, Blask quickly inserted himself into the current timetable and the intricacies of human anatomy and first aid. Despite his absence, he didn't seem to have missed much, if anything, and after the first day back, nobody made any reference or allowance for his bereavement. Just back on duty.

"You! Spell your name, phonetically." "Tare Uncle Roger Nan Easy Roger; Turner, Sergeant." "And *Where* are we? Spell it." "Charlie Love Item Nan King. Sergeant." Because we all call the school 'Clink', and this risky move raised hilarious laughter from the group – even a reluctant half-smile from the otherwise serious Signals Sergeant, trying to maintain order. But he let it go this time. "Very droll, Mister Turner. Try again, with the proper name this time." "Dog Uncle Nan Tare Roger Oboe Oboe Nan – Duntroon, Sergeant." "Much better. Now you, Mister Wilson, spell the word artillery." "Able Roger Tare Item Love Love" (He stumbles) "Easy Roger Yoke - Artillery, Sergeant." "Not bad. Practice it until it becomes second nature, until you can say your prayers in it. And judging by your test results, you'll need all your prayers to get through this course, Mister Wilson."

In army terms, our class is a Company, and for instruction convenience, we are divided into Platoons, a manageable sized group, and allocated an instructor for most military skills. We are so lucky, that our allocated instructor is Captain Whitton. It could just as easily have been Captain Milne, who we had once for a few subjects, and who is a bit useless, maybe knowing his stuff (you would think he had to pass some standard to become an instructor, wouldn't you) but never really passing much on. Maybe he is lazy, but he never remembers anyone's name, and you get the impression that he skips over subjects of which he has little experience. But our man Whitton is the full quid. We pay attention to him. Captain Whitton takes us for fieldcraft topography, and takes us away into the bush with compasses and maps with talc overlays, and gets us 'hull down' as he calls it, lying on the dirt in an arc while he explains the strategic potential of the empty scrub in front of us, pointing out the features which we recognize from the field maps, but instead of squiggles and contour lines, he makes the surface come alive to planned movement and concealment options. "Remember," he advises wryly, "What you might have played cowboys and Indians with when you were a kid, now becomes really serious, deadly serious. The careless man who sticks his head up gets a bullet in it. And these will be your best men, and you need every man Jack of them, so you <u>will</u> protect them.."

Whitton also takes us for the class described as Ethics, which you can imagine some of those long-hairs at civilian university laughing at (*a soldier with ethics?* Ho-ho, pull the other one!) and Whitton instills in us a sense of responsibility which we might never have had. The Geneva Convention, and the Rules of Engagement, and it seems ironic, doesn't it, that many of the principles which he is impressing on us, are the very things which he, and other prisoners of war of the Japanese, were never able to expect in their inhuman treatment. He never mentions it, but we know. And we know what is acceptable behavior even on the battlefield, and what is not. What the expectations of us as Australian army officers to abide by, to live up to, even in anger.

"We sleep peaceably in our beds at night
only because rough men stand ready
to do violence on our behalf."-
George Orwell

PART 2. *SCISSORS. . .*

1950

Top Records:
   Mona Lisa (Nat King Cole),
   The Third Man Theme (Anton Karas),
   Tennessee Waltz (Patti Page),
   Music, Music, Music (Teresa Brewer),
   Goodnight Irene (Gordon Jenkins).

- **June 30 - North Korea troops invade South, occupy Seoul, push ROK and US defenders down to Pusan perimeter. UN Security Council calls on members to join forces to oppose NK invasion. Australia commits Navy, Airforce, and newly-formed 3rd Battalion RAR, to join UN forces. In September – MacArthur launches successful Inchon flank attack, invades North Korea, provoking China to enter war in October, driving UN forces back below 38 Parallel.**

- ANZUS Treaty is signed.

- UK conducts nuclear tests at Monte Bello islands off West Australia coast.

- Australia plans National Service Scheme to strengthen depleted armed forces, putting pressure on permanent defence staff.

- USA – Senator Joseph McCarthy claims that over 200 Communists are working for Government, incl in the State Department. (but never actually names them)

- China invades Tibet, ignoring international protests

- UK Labour Government wins general election

- Truman authorizes H-Bomb production in USA

- Australia Ends Petrol Rationing.

- Israel appoints Jerusalem as nation's capital

- Ho Chi Minh begins offensive against French in Indo-China

Michael: Our Section has got a barrack-room on the Eastern edge of the Victorian army base, an old unlined corrugated-iron building with a raised wooden floor at the end of a row of similar buildings in the dustbowl of the area. These buildings date from the '40s, and there is a rumour that the defence department is going to build new modern barracks up near Armoured Corps, when they can get the building materials. Number Four Section from our same Platoon is one side of us, and Six Section the other side, in identical huts. Nothing grows between the huts, which is not surprising, because of the massive indiscriminate foot traffic round about. All you see is the regulation clotheslines with towels and stuff (at regulation times), and the obligatory fire buckets, some filled with sand. Not exactly beautiful suburbia, is it? We are six buildings away from the ablutions block where our Company toilets, showers and washrooms are, which is inconvenient when it is raining. Same in the middle of the night, but early on, I put a stop to lazy men from my unit taking a short-cut after lights-out and peeing at the back of our building; partly because of the stink, and besides, it is unhygienic and another way for men to let their standards go. Not many of them go feral, but there's always one who wasn't brought up with high personal principles. I remember when Charlie Brooks (they call him Toxic) joined us, he was a bit lax in the personal hygiene department, and after a few warnings, the men gave him a boot-polishing. I knew something was going on, but don't interfere in barrack discipline. Boot-polishing involves several people catching and holding the victim down, stripping him, and administering boot polish to his privates. Mostly painless, but embarrassing and undignifying, and of course requiring significant (and uncomfortable) scrubbing to remove traces of his shame. An extreme case. Mostly, after recruit training, you find that men are already well-trained hygienically, even if they didn't come into the army like that. The one thing I insist on in the unit is that my men are clean, fit, and stick to proper standards, no letting themselves go just because we are encamped or out of sight of the public. A couple of the men don't like my rules, but since I am Section Corporal, they have to get used to it. The barrack-room is long and wide, but is divided off at one end into a separate small room which is mine. A bit of NCO (Non Commissioned Officer) privilege and privacy, just a bunk, locker, a side table and a chair, but it is my home and 'office'. Of course I can hear some of what's going on through the wall in the main barrack room, but I don't interfere or try to eavesdrop on the section's doings – that's their business when they are off duty. They see enough of me enforcing them during the day so they don't want to be bothered with me after hours – although, I have made it crystal clear, that I am available if anyone wants to see me about personal problems or whinges. If it is a matter of complaints about another member of the section, then what I do is take the 'complainer' with me for a walk so that he can get it off his chest as we pace around the huts. And sometimes I might have to sort out a fight between members of the section in the hut, but that is extremely rare. They know I can handle any of them myself, so I don't get too many challenges.

The camp has a recorded bugle-call Reveille played over the intercom at Six, but I am always awake before it, and properly dressed when I disturb their sleep-in with the traditional NCO shouted greetings: "OK you lot, on your feet, wakey wakey, hit the deck and smile at the dawn, hands off cocks, on with socks, let's have you, out of those fart-sacks, another lovely day for being heroes" and so on. (The same thing happened to me, and will probably still happen when one of these Digs is an NCO in years to come, so I suppose it is army tradition.) Anyway, it is the same routine in all of the nearby huts, so nobody is getting more than their fair share – any resistance and I rip the bedclothes off, so they stumble out of those lovely warm army blankets into the crisp freezing corrugated iron shed we call home in their bare feet. I can make roll-call as fast as they like, or if they give me trouble I can delay their discomfort; and I wouldn't want to do that, would I? I then dismiss them for ablutions, where there is no privacy in a row of toilets and open group showers, and a line of wash-basins and discoloured wall mirrors which you have to share with elbowing fellow shavers in a hurry to get to breakfast. The ablution block is an echo-chamber. There are always people singing soldier songs which you wouldn't sing in front of the padre, plus laughter, and horseplay. And surprisingly, you might even sometimes get men not singing but declaiming poetry; you know the kind of thing you learned at school, like "The Man From Snowy River", or other bush ballads. What's that one about 'a thumbnail dipped in tar?'

Our Platoon Sergeant, McVitty, doesn't bother us much, he knows I keep my section up to scratch without interference. He just checks with me each morning on the Platoon parade for the day's timetable. You know, like, Eleven Hundred, a lecture. Fifteen Hundred, a full Company Parade. O800 tomorrow, rifle range, grenade practise. When we first came here, we had a Lieutenant as Platoon Commander, Bob Campbell; he was a really nice guy. Maybe a bit old to be a Lieutenant, he had been field-commissioned up in the islands from Sergeant, never likely to get much further he said, even though he was a good soldier. It was Lt Campbell who put me up for Corporal, he said I had the makings of a 30-year man, teasing me. He came down to my room a couple of times just before he was discharged, shutting the door and pulling out a half-bottle of whisky to share – even though grog was supposed to be off-limits in the barracks. "Give us your glass. Not Scotch," he apologised, "*C.O.R. Ten*" (Corio brand, get it? and C.O.R. also meant Commonwealth Oil Refineries) but despite the pun the whisky was good, nothing to complain about. "Where will you go, Boss?" I asked him, and he laughed. "Life on the ranch. I came from Beaudesert up in Queensland, and last leave I bought a little farm nearby in the hills at Boonah. Just big enough for a couple of cows, a couple of sheep, a couple of chooks, plus me and the dog. All a man needs. Apart from this," he joked, indicating the bottle. I hesitated, "I thought you were married." He smiled. "Yeah, so did I, but she got a better offer while I was in New Guinea. Dear John letter." "I'm sorry." "Don't be sorry, Mike, better to find out these things early. We got married too young anyway, the excitement of embarkation leave, going off to war and all that, back then."

It makes you think about how war stuffs peoples' lives up. Stuffs everything up, I suppose. Anyway, Bob Campbell's gone, McVitty has been in charge of the Platoon since, but then he tells me last week that we are going to get a new Platoon Commander, another officer. McVitty sneers "Some wet-behind-the-ears fkn baby lieutenant fresh out of Duntroon, to tell us how to suck eggs. Due to arrive next month, so enjoy the peace while we got it."

There's this one morning when, after breakfast, as part of PT, I am leading the section in a regular circuit double for half an hour, boots and trousers but just singlets, no rifles, bare-headed, clenched fists at chests, past the point of everyone getting their second wind, well exerted and sweating but keeping easy time with boots crunching on gravel, watched by some of the other sections who recognize that we are the fittest section in the Company and proud with it; we could keep this up for hours if we needed to, sometimes chanting the beat (we have some deadly rhymes), sometimes saving our breath, as we run at double-time up the main road hill which connects the outside of the camp with the administration centre, not minding who sees us. *Hoping* people see us – there are plenty about. And this time, as we approach Admin on the run, there is this young woman, a girl civilian worker on a bike, probably a typist or something, on the same wide road. Smartly dressed for the office in a dress or skirt, and you know how it is somehow inevitable that the action of pedalling a bike reveals a girl's legs, and even an unintentional flash of thigh, or white - you know, private clothing - and of course there are a couple of my section who whistle or call 'Hello Darling' as we pass before I can sharply pull them back to control. And then we are already past her, and down past the ball courts and the tank harbour. Along a brief section of paved road, past the mess-halls and canteen. Later, when we are paused, catching our breath, I give them a lecture about how the girl on the bike could object to our behaviour, and one of them says 'But Corp, it's a compliment, init, to show a man's appreciation" and I try to explain how it might be unwanted, and what if it was one of their, you know, girlfriend or sister, who may not want it. A matter of respect. But I don't think I won that one completely. Maybe I'm old-fashioned about women. So we start again and continue, along the high wired-in barrier around the base hospital and nurses' quarters. Always some comments as we run past the hospital – "That high fence is to stop Matron Temby from getting out and raping all of us in the night" sort of thing. Matron (Captain) Temby is the severe dragon in charge, who enjoys giving brave soldiers big injections. Poor lady has bristles on her chin. She takes no nonsense from either nurses or soldiers. Or officers, come to that.

Call me an idiot, but that afternoon I made sure my uniform was all correct, and I marched down to Admin and sure enough, located her – the bike girl – behind a desk at the Regimental Post Office. Anyway, the Staff Sergeant in charge there asked to know what I wanted, and I said I wanted to speak to the lady privately, and it was a bit embarrassing because the rest of the office staff were hanging in on every word, but I bit the bullet and said to her "Miss, I'm Corporal Whan, and it was my Section which whistled at you this morning while we were on exercise, and I apologise for their behaviour. It won't happen again." Everyone was sort of smiling like it might be a joke, but the girl was pleasantly polite, and she said seriously "Thank you, Corporal. Appreciate it." And it was then that I noticed that she was beautiful. The Staff Sergeant walked out with me, and said "Where are you from?" I told him, and he went on, laughing, with a head nod back at the office "You'll be right there, son; that's the Major's daughter." "Who?" "Vicky, the girl you just spoke to. Daughter of Major Sutton, your company commander." So, without trying, I had established who she was, her name, and that I couldn't wait for an excuse to see her again. But a Major's daughter? I must be crazy.

Kim Seo-Jin, (Seoul, Korea)
There had been rumours, always rumours. But even so, the dawn attack over our border by Communist forces at Kaesung on June 25 was a shock when we had it confirmed over the wireless. They had also invaded our territory at several other places at the same time. Of course we trusted our own brave Korean National Army to take care of that and throw the Reds back. We obsessively listened to the news over the next days that our army was counter-attacking, and in Seoul we felt confident, despite the streams of refugees from the border areas already filling the streets over the next two days. Oddly, some people were going both ways, causing some confusion. We heard that the Reds were about 10 miles away, and more of our soldiers in trucks and Jeeps poured out of the city as bystanders and children cheered them on with flags. We were glued to radio sets, even if the news was often conflicting. At first, it was reported that our Government would move to Suwon for safety, but then, after a brief military success at Uijongbu, it reported that the Government would remain in Seoul "to the death", but no doubt that was bravado. You know what politicians are like. My wife Park Su-Ah and I discussed whether we should flee, but there were too many complications. We had no vehicle, not even a hand-cart, and we had Su-Ah's mother who was old and needed care, as well as our small six year old daughter. Also, there was the thought of leaving our tiny house empty and vulnerable to squatters; anyway, where would we go? When we thought about it, that was the worst part: where to? We had seen how desperate and aimless the refugees were, wouldn't we be the same if we left our familiar home? Besides, my boss at the shipping office, where I am a junior clerk, said that we were important to the nation and should remain at work. It was a difficult time, an impossible time. By the evening of the 27th, we could even hear the terrifying loud sounds of artillery, seemingly coming closer, and the steady rain all night accentuated the dismal plight of the streams of refugees past our small house, even in back streets. "Should we

offer them shelter?" My wife was concerned for all of them, but I tried to be practical. "How can we? There are hundreds of them, maybe even thousands, and no end in sight." But I was more worried about how the gunfire seemed to be getting louder, closer, convincing me that I should stay home from work. By noon, there was an unofficial announcement that Communist tanks had surrounded the Capitol at daybreak; for everyone to stay home, and stay down. Of course I was frightened. We all were. I knew the invaders were Koreans similar to us, but would the North soldiers rampage and attack everyone who was not one of them? Were our womenfolk safe from violation? At my age, how could I protect them? As the incoming Red troops swarmed into suburbs of Seoul, I thought it was ironic to see the same people and children who had cheered <u>our</u> soldiers, now welcoming the Communists with home-made red flags. I worried at what might lie ahead. It didn't take long. On the second morning, a gang of rude young men with guns came into our yard and called me out. My darling wife sobbed. I guessed that I was going to be taken to a 'Peoples' Trial' where some South Korean citizens were already being accused and shot dead for various crimes according to popular (i.e. mob) resolution. Frequently we had heard the ominous gunshot sound of these political public murders. But this time, the youths only demanded to examine our rice jars, from which they expropriated half, which seemed to satisfy them. (But this happened several times with different gangs, until our rice supply was empty.) They didn't bother with our small vegetable garden at that stage. Incidentally, I recognised some of the young men as being former 'loyal' members of the Republic Youth Corps – perhaps they were being pragmatic and 'reconsidering their allegiances'. Excuse my cynicism. Within a few tense days, the invaders – through their mobile loud-speaker announcements and public meetings (they seemed to like public meetings) - ordered businesses to reopen, including many companies now under new Red management. Everybody was ordered to be at work by 8.00 a.m. When I didn't go the first day, local officials eventually came to the house and interrogated me, and I told them I was reluctant to leave my wife, daughter, and mother-in-law unprotected, but they scolded me and said Communist soldiers were disciplined and trustworthy, so I changed my tune and said that it was not them, but because of the masses of unknown civilian refugees wandering around, and this viewpoint was accepted. But when I turned up at work, I was told my office was closed indefinitely, as the company, because of its foreign relationships, had been disbanded. So, no work, meaning no income, and we had almost no savings. Also, we were unable to get access to our small bank deposit. All bank accounts had been 'frozen'. There was another rumour that the banks had been looted anyway.

We, and everyone else were soon short of food. Nothing in the shops was worth buying. Rice, if you could find it, went from 3,000 to 10,000 Won per mal. Meals soon needed to consist of 30% or less of rice, and 70% barley, millet or any grain. We ate every green thing we had. Seoul citizens went out to surrounding countryside to barter with anything for grains, potatoes, etc., but they/we were competing with the tide of refugees doing the same thing. We had to sell anything we could - sewing machine, shoes, clothes - to get food. After two weeks of occupation chaos, we started to worry that we would starve. Darling and I made sure that Mother and little Gong-Ju-Nim were fed first, and I could always tighten my belt a couple of notches. Three organizations had been set up to control us, the city being divided into 9 sections, again sub-divided into blocks. There was a Block Committee, the Red Youth Corps, and the Communist Party all in charge; apart from the ever-present Police and OGPU, and it seemed that many frightening actions were intent on settling old scores (or new ones), as well as seeking out 'reactionaries' and political criminals. At first there seemed to be some tolerance towards what they called 'middle of the road' citizens, persuading them/us through public meetings to change their thinking, but soon this attitude hardened. Anyone who was wealthy or spoke English was an immediate target, and I made sure that nobody knew that I spoke English. I secretly destroyed my four or five English books (Goodbye Shakespeare, I never managed to understand you), and made sure that I wore only my old clothes. As they were recruiting soldiers in their campaign at the obligatory public meetings, I also used my mother-in-law's walking stick and developed a convincing limp. It was shameful for me to act like this, but it worked, ingratiating myself, in the hope of winning some food access. Some of the meetings gave out a few rations to new loyalists. At the recruiting meetings, I hobbled up and shouted "Take me, teach me to shoot Americans!" but they laughed and said "Go home old man, and dig your garden." But my act worked, and at one stage they gave me a ration-subsidised job pasting up posters on walls, of 'Comrade Stalin and Beloved Leader Kim Il-Sung', and as I glued them, I satisfied myself by pretending that I was wetting them with cowshit. It enabled me to smile as though I was enjoying my work. At least it gave me access to some of the hand-outs. There were many compulsory gatherings and assemblies, always similar speeches agitating young men and women to join up and smash the American Puppet forces of the South. This became more common as the southern fighting got more difficult for the Reds, who were getting bogged down. Meantime, we were frequently raided at home – always, alarmingly, at midnight – by Ogpu and others searching for hidden weapons, short-wave radios, escapees and wanted criminals. Sometimes I was taken away to be interrogated for hours – always without sense. "Do you speak foreign languages?" They asked. "Of course. I speak Japanese, we all do. Don't you?" Had they forgotten the years when we were occupied by Japan, and it was compulsory to learn *Nihongo*? We even had Japanese names. Short memories. Fortunately they didn't take away our little radio so that we could secretly switch to NHK and get true news from Japan instead of continual Red propaganda from Pyongyang. It was from Japan radio that we learned in early July that UN forces had been mobilised from several countries to help us, under the leadership of General "I Shall Return" MacArthur. This was encouraging. It was sad to see American prisoners of war being paraded in Seoul to show how the 'Wall Street Capitalist

Running Dogs' had started all this. Some of them were forced to make statements apologising for being misled into interfering in the political aspirations of Korea. The poor prisoners spoke only English, and the Reds asked if anyone could translate, but I didn't fall into that trap, just shook my head like others.

When the UN air raids began here on military targets in July, we knew the tide was changing. The Han River bridge was destroyed several times after being repaired. Were the Reds retreating? They seemed to be short of transport and fuel, so that citizens were forced to help carry loads and to start digging trenches at night. Then it was air-raid shelters, and I was conscripted to help build them. I made sure that the first one I built was conveniently available for my small family. The UN air-raids made the Communists edgy, and many of us were interrogated more frequently. Always an unknown person in a hat would approach and say "My chief wants to see you" "Who, and where?" But you could never get an answer. You would be marched to this office or that, sometimes kept waiting for hours, and then, hopefully, released. All the time, you knew that it might be your last march, that it might be to some vacant block, where they would make you kneel and: Goodnight. And everyone knew that it was dangerous for family members even to go and take a victim's body away for proper burial, because it marked them too, as reactionaries. Every time I was able to return exhausted to my sobbing wife, we would both bow to the sun or moon, mountain or tree, in bewildered gratitude. We tried to hide this terrifying insecurity from the old lady or our little girl.

On September 17 according to Tokyo radio, a massive UN force invasion had landed at Inchon, cutting off the Reds' supply line, and the battle to rescue South Korea had moved into gear. But it was dangerous to show signs of pleasure or relief amid the increased air-raids which added danger and destruction to the retreating Red soldiers who were setting fire to buildings as a demonstration that they would not leave Seoul to new rescuers. There were more house raids, and more executions. Many people just disappeared. Smoke darkened the sky for days, and in the distance we heard the sounds of battle again as UN Forces were rumoured to be only a few miles from Seoul. News spread on the 25th that South Korean and UN forces were now in the West Gate area, minutes away, and public announcements warned everyone to stay home and stay down to avoid becoming unintentional victims of the rescue. We obliged, even though it was around noon on the 28th when gunfire ended around our area, and we cautiously emerged. I went downtown on the morning of September the 29th, surrounded by happy people embracing, laughing, talking, shaking hands. I couldn't believe that we had survived. It was a time for offering up thanks to our family and household gods.

My office was still closed when I got access to the building to inquire, and while I was light-heartedly coming back, a stranger in a suit and dark hat stopped me, calling me by name. "So, you don't need that walking stick anymore" he mocked. I could see that he wore a gun on his belt. And then he attempted to copy my formerly pretended voice, in a falsetto whine *"Please teach me to shoot Americans"*. (Was that really how I had sounded?) I trembled. "Come on," he said tersely. "My boss wants to talk to you about your eager collaboration, helping the Reds, even pasting up their propaganda."

And then I knew it was all over.

At the whistle blast, our officer cadet unit collapses on the slope where we have been on manoeuvres, everyone exhausted, out of breath, our sweat-lined faces covered with dirt converting the streaks to mud, almost unable to raise a word of complaint. Except Raymond, who shook his head weakly and gasped "God bless our little souls." Mackey grunted "Arseholes" so that Raymond, laugh-panting, amended "OK, God bless our little *arse*holes." Individuals slowly recovered their strength, almost too tired to joke, too tired to get up from lying in the dust, and Blask sighed "Can someone please tell me why I signed up for this?" Ardley offered "I think it is supposed to be something to do with becoming an ossifer in the army, whatever that is." Wilson, ever helpful, reminded them "Never mind chaps, only two more years to go" and we all groaned. It reminds me, I never wanted to come here in the first place; never wanted to become a soldier, and particularly never wanted to become a bloody officer.

(But there's only this year and next, and we're already well into this year, so it's not really two more years – think of it that way, it's better. There is a reminder in the Cadets' Mess – the "*Days To Go*" board, which is changed every day at 18.30 hrs by the youngest member of the Third Class. It doesn't bear looking at - how many days still to survive)

We've done all the engineering constructions and artillery ballistic calculations. We know how to assess accurately the width of a river and the height of a tree, and we are continually set diabolical mathematical problems to solve. Andrew is great at these, and at any mental arithmetic puzzle. Jakob is slower, but perseveres and seems to eventually get the right answer. Some cadets come near to tearing their hair out. And of course, no slide-rules or calculators like an abacus are permitted during exams.

Weapons training, first the familiar old Lee-Enfield .303 rifle with which we constantly drill, then the Bren LMG (Light Machine Gun – *Light?* Whoever called the fkn thing Light?), the Vickers Machine Gun, The Mortars, the Owen submachine gun, the

95

Thompson, the Grenades, all the Mines, the anti-tank 'Bazooka', the fuses. Someone asked "When are we going to train on the officers' revolver too, Sir?" Captain Whitton, the infantry weapons supervisor smiled sardonically, "Can't resist it, some of you cowboys; you too, Fitzpatrick? Want to play with six-guns. Well, let me tell you a couple of things about pistols revolver. First, how useless they are, unless you want to put one in your ear and end it all, goodbye cruel world. Probably the only reason they were ever issued as an officer's weapon was back in Lord Fauntleroy's First World War instead of his sword, so he could shoot any common soldier who advanced backwards, lack of moral fibre, instead of going over the top as ordered by his lordship to almost certain death. Revolvers? Useless as an offensive weapon against an enemy, you wouldn't hit the side of a barn with one, you might as well throw the bloody pistol at your enemy if that's all you've got left. Second, the fact that you carry it or wear it, immediately marks you as an officer <u>target</u>, you silly bastard, like pasting a bullseye on your uniform, marked *'shoot this idiot first'*. No, Fitzpatrick, if you are issued with Pistols Revolver Smith & Wesson Point Three Eight O, if and when you reach the sharp end, get rid of the damn thing and get hold of a proper military weapon to fight with, that's my advice to you all. Preferably one with a large magazine."

The next class schedule this time just said "Field Exercise 0800 – Dress: Fatigues/AFVs, no weapons, take notebooks. Embus front of Orderly Room 0800", so they assumed it was another outdoor lecture, maybe a Tactical Exercise Without Troops, maybe a large scale 'sandpit' instruction, a replay of some battle correcting some general's mistake, the hindsight analysis of what German Field Marshal von Schlieffen *should* have done... But no, they were ordered to board the one worn khaki bus and the overflow ones who didn't fit, clambered aboard the 2½ ton GMC Troop Carrier to sit uncomfortably side-by-side along the fold-down benches, with Senior Instructor Major Collier (Old Bob) in front with the driver. And no idea of the destination, none of the usual, looked like they were headed out on the

Goulburn Road, but who cared, it was a beautiful sunny day away from the College classrooms and the shouting parade grounds, and the GMC's tyres buzzed evenly on the hot tarmac, with the high-revving Army bus following. Then after half an hour as they slowed, the cadets in the truck tried to see where they were heading, and probably didn't catch sight of the peeling painted wooden signboard high above the wire gates, although they would have heard (and maybe smelled) the stockyards at each side of the entrance. Surprisingly – or maybe not so surprisingly, knowing 'Old Bob' - Maj. Collier – even though he was a senior officer, he got down and opened the wide wire gate for the vehicles to enter, and then closed the gate after them, as if he was the driver's turn-boy apprentice. The high painted signboard had said: **McLaren Abattoir and Rendering Works**, and as the cadets debussed in front of the steaming rusty corrugated iron high wide buildings at Maj. Collier's order, they could already smell the sickly-sweet boiling fat, the open-guts stench of ruptured bowels, and the metallic odour of blood, and the ever-present fresh stockyard manure. Several of the platoon were now showing signs of unease, but this is what happens, isn't it? Unease at the unknown. Why the abattoir? What's Old Bob up to? Lined up in threes, stood at ease, the cadets waited for their instructions as the vehicles parked over in what little shade there was beside some peppercorn trees, and an abattoir worker – or as it turned out the manager - a haggard man in rubber boots, a loose bloodstained grey dustcoat, and a dented felt hat with a sweat-blackened band, came to wait for Collier to finish addressing the squad.

"Right, now pay attention and listen in. Don't be worried, Mister Gower, you are not going to be knackered, although you probably deserve it." (Laughter) "This – he indicated the buildings beyond them with his worn swagger-stick – is an abattoir. *Abattoir*, from the French '*Abatre*' = to put down, or to kill; yes, as you have guessed, an abattoir is a slaughterhouse. Some of you, particularly you lucky country blokes, will know all about them, but for most of you, this is part of your general education. This is where farm animals are brought to be converted into meat, food and other by-products, as hygienically, safely, and humanely as possibly. And this is the Abattoir Manager, Jack McLaren, who is kindly allowing us to interrupt his business by looking over his company's process this morning to teach us about how things are done." (The abattoir manager nodded and smiled at them, revealing yellowing teeth, if you could take your eyes away from the spectacular bunches of hairs growing out of his ears.) 'Old Bob' continued. "Now keep up, stay together and watch and learn. The bright ones amongst you will be aware that I am deliberately bringing you into an environment where living creatures are routinely killed, bled, skinned, butchered, and dismembered. To some of you, this might be the first time you have seen an animal killed, and been exposed to the close-up sight of death, blood and guts. But as you are intelligent army officer cadets, it will no doubt have occurred to you (and if it hasn't I will bring it to your attention) that eventually, maybe even soon, in the course of your chosen careers as volunteer professional soldiers, you will be exposed to the sight and unpleasant experience of people – people; human beings – being killed; shot, blown apart, decapitated, eviscerated and dismembered – some of them your own men, some your familiar mates - an experience which you will never get used to, but which you should understand is part of our wartime profession which you must take on board, and, most importantly, which you must not let interfere with your military objectives and care of your men. So consider this as an exercise in familiarity and desensitisation, so that you will be able to look at blood and sudden death without fainting, throwing up, or losing control of your main purpose. Now. If this exercise affects you adversely; if you don't feel well, take a step outside and get some fresh air, but treat it like another obstacle course, and handle it like the men you are. OK? Let's go."

And there was a bit of uneasiness, nervous smiles, looking at one another wondering how it would affect them, and where I was standing next to Blask, turning up my nose a bit at the smells, saying "Yuk. This is gross." But as they went through the guided process, watching the wide-eyed terrified animals following each other along the chute, and when singled out, the unannounced bolt to the head, the sudden heavy lifeless drop and from then on it was a mechanised chain-progressed production line of hoist, slippery bleeding, blue-white guts disembowelment, skinning and conversion of an animal to red-gleaming butchered meat. The manager, McLaren, spoke all the time describing the processes like a tour guide (he had to shout hoarsely above the noise of the cattle, the generator and the machinery), but Andrew noticed that the Chief Instructor, Old Bob, was not watching the procedures – maybe he had seen it all before - but was watching each cadet's face carefully for their reaction, ready to take someone aside if it needed to be done. And who knows? Maybe assessing each man's ability to handle what might be a confronting experience. You never knew with Old Bob, did you?

ajor Robert Collier brushed his hands briefly down over the front of his battledress as if ensuring all front button flaps were closed, and automatically, he stamped his boots on the pavement below the front step to shake any dust off them, as well as to settle the neat overhang of his trousers over the webbing ankle gaiters. Although he and the Commandant were old colleagues - and indeed fellow graduates of the College, he acted formally, nodding to Beryl at her secretarial desk in the ante-room before entering the holy of holies, wedging his short leather-bound swagger-stick under the left arm, coming to attention in front of the Commandant's desk, and saluting in his old-fashioned way, longest way up, shortest way down. But the Commandant was terse. "Shut the door behind you." Most unusual, and he was obviously upset, even before Major Collier had turned from closing the office door, the Colonel was pacing up and down across the space beyond the neat desk, beneath the wall portraits. No invitation to sit. His low voice was anguished. "Bob, I can't *believe* the report I have just received, that you changed the company schedule and took a class to an abattoir today - to a damned abattoir! - without warning, without discussion. Tell me it's not true. I can't believe you would *do* something so thoughtless!" He was obviously irate, his hands waving alongside his reddened face, not yet looking the major in the eye. "Jesus, man. Apart from the Board. Apart from the Defence Department. Apart from the bloody parents of our little Sirs. Can you imagine what will happen if the bloody newspapers or the bloody wireless gets hold of this? They are always looking for an excuse to criticize us, our so-called 'elite' training. Christ, I'll be on the mat, hung out to dry - I mean, these are only cadets – not much more than schoolboys, and all our usual critics - the outsiders – the damned civilians - will be saying we are blooding them into a killing frame of mind." Still striding about, still angry faced, and Major Collier trying to speak, to somehow

100

begin apologising. Surprisingly, these two officers were almost mirror-images of each other, except for their rank. Both about the same size and weight, both weathered complexions with similar clipped mustache bristles, both in khaki new-pattern battledress uniforms where, in faded ribbons above the left pocket, they both showed their similarity in service: 39-45 Star, Africa Star, Pacific Star, Italy Star, Defence Medal, War Medal, both of them wearing the oak leaf ribbon decoration for a mention in despatches for meritorious action in the face of the enemy. Only the Commandant's Military Cross for bravery from that frenzied action against the suicidal Japanese on Isavura, made a difference.

Major Collier started formally "Sir, I'm sorry. I'll let you have my resignation immediately..." "Oh Bob, Bob, Bob." The commandant, still walking, found himself back behind his desk space, and sank onto his swivel chair, rubbing his face. "Sit down, man, sit. No, of course I don't want your resignation. Apart from losing my best instructor and friend, that would just accentuate the situation, which I would prefer disappeared out of sight." The two men sat in silence for a moment, one wanting to speak, to somehow apologise, the other maybe regretting his first outburst. The Commandant spoke first, and his voice was back to normal, quiet. "Oh, Bob. What we can't teach them. What nobody can teach them – what nobody could teach us – is the reality of war, what they call combat these days. None of us ever knows what to expect, and there is no possible way to teach, to prepare young men for what they have to face; when they have to see men die, get blown to bits, and to kill men themselves. I know what you did was with that in mind, as we always have that in the back of our minds. Sometimes I wish that this school was just a military academy, just bullshit and brass, but we know only too well, that it ain't so. That's not what we are all about, is it? We are always preparing our boys for another war. For fighting. For killing. For being killed. Oh, Bob." He continued to shake his head. "Christ Bob, I just wish you had talked to me about it; I would have advised against it. And on top of everything, there is now this situation in Godforsaken Korea, where we will probably have to send some of our boys."

[Did you hear about Old Bob? Apparently the Commandant didn't authorise that abattoir thing, and hauled him over the coals for it. Cameron, who was on sweepers defaulter duty at HQ, said the old man tore strips off him; poor old Bob.]

Michael was nervous. Dry mouth. Didn't want to do this, but it was Vicky's idea. "It's about time my parents met the man I'm going out with," she said. And I stupidly said "Is that right? Are we going out together?" And she gave me one of those looks she does, where her mouth is straight-serious, but with crinkled laughing eyes, as if she is trying not to laugh. I love that look. I love *her*. <u>Are</u> we going out together? I suppose so. It began with me all those weeks ago after I apologized for the squad; psyching myself up over several days, and eventually "accidentally" meeting her after work one day as she came out the side of the Regimental Post Office wheeling her bike, and I asked if I could walk her home. She gave me one of those serious-smiling looks with pursed mouth and laughing eyes and indicated the bike "Well I don't think I can give you a double-dink on this," and we laughed. That was the beginning of many walks home – not always possible because of duty, and when we reached her home in the married quarters I remember seeing the twitch of curtains at one stage suggesting I was being sussed out at her family end. I couldn't tell you now what we talked about all those times, nothing of consequence, just getting to know one another, and we could never know enough about each other; it was like a bottomless well we had to fill up. And even those intimate silences were satisfying, thrilling. Of course we talked about growing up, schooldays, places we had been, people we knew. She told me all about working in her office, and the characters she came across. I told her all about the men in my section, and the way we had sort of matured together, and which ones were the idiots to laugh about. I was cautious about her father the Major, but she was relaxed "He's really very nice you know, you'll like him when you get to know him." As if I was going to get to know him one day. Of course I knew **who** he was, and I had seen him quite a few times in his regimental capacity as the Company Commander, but most of the time I had seen him, had been on formal duty, where you are not likely ever to get to know anyone. It was soon obvious from what she said, that she was Daddy's girl, which means any man who was going out with her was going to be put under the microscope, even if he wasn't a corporal, so I was not looking forward to any meeting with Major daddy.

Apart from the walks home from work, we went to the camp cinema twice. Don't ask me what we saw, I probably didn't register any of the films with my high state of intoxication from being so close to her. There were some of my platoon at the cinema, and that put a bit of a damper on the occasions. I knew that they were going to take the mickey out of me either directly or behind my back. Not that I cared, but I was careful to be on my best public behavior. Both times, I picked up Vicky in a car I borrowed from one of the other platoon corporals, Jamie, and delivered her home properly – you know – no snogging up the road or anything. But I have to tell you that the second time, in the cinema, Vicky somehow let her hand between us on the armrest touch mine, and then move to hold my hand, interlocking our fingers gently, turning to smile at me, and my heart flipped like a fish out of water, and I thought I would implode.

So now, no excuses, I have been invited home to lunch on Sunday to meet the family, which is why I am so nervous. "They won't bite you" she smiled, "they are really very nice people" and why would I doubt that, being the family which produced her. I decided to wear civilian clothes ('smart casual' they call it, don't they?) on purpose, to lessen the distinction of me, a humble corporal, being in the home of a senior officer, but as soon as I was introduced at the front door, I knew that I shouldn't have worried. They really were as nice as she is, and made me feel welcome. Straight off, her father said: "Right, listen; here's the drill – in this house, there's no Sir, no Mister and Missus, we're Vicky's parents Jean and Reg, and you're Michael, is that clear? Welcome, Michael." And Vicky said proudly, as she sort of hugged my arm, "There, didn't I tell you? They are the best parents in the world. Come in and sit down."

It was a wonderful Sunday lunch, (mind you anything would beat canteen meals), and Reg poured me out a drink without asking me. It was Cider (which I'd never had before in my life), in an anodized aluminium beaker (had never seen one of those before either) and he said "Try this Michael, it is very cool and refreshing. You'll like it" And it was, and I did.

And we talked and laughed about everything. At one stage, relaxed, the major (Reg) says to me "What do you make of this Korea thing, Michael, with the Commos invading the South? Think it could involve us?" And I said, off the top of my head, "I suppose it depends if the Americans get into it and ask others like us to back them up, doesn't it?" The major nodded. "I wouldn't be surprised if the Yanks join the South Koreans and drive the Commos back; could be over in a month or two, with MacArthur in charge up there. I just hope Russia doesn't decide to get stuck in as well, they live next door."

None of us thought that we would be up there soon. Very soon.

The Greek Café was one of those few places where Duntroon cadets were able – in their controlled, rare, spare time - to socialize with local girls, as also happened within limits at church and the tennis club, but at the Greek café more casual, more relaxed, maybe feeling under less supervision, even though such meetings were public, and even infrequent because of RMC timetables. For the town teenagers and early twenties, and RMC cadets, it was not so much a dining place, as a place to briefly hang out, listen to latest popular music, and have a few laughs. There were two Greek cafés this side of town – the other one being The Paragon, across the corner from the Imperial Hotel, and that was especially busy when the pub closed after the Six o'clock closing rush, when many pub drinkers went across to the Paragon for food. 'Our' Greek Café was formally named 'The White Rose of Athens', although nobody ever called it that, and no one seemed to know what the name symbolized. If you asked Con, the proprietor, he would only shrug and say that the White Rose was "some sort of revolutionary love song, you know?" But we didn't know what he was talking about – and we wondered if he did anyway, being a born and bred Aussie himself, just with Greek parentage.

It was a spacious restaurant, with a counter or serving bar down one long side, tables and chairs down the middle, and shoulder-height divided booths along the other long side, plus a large Wurlitzer 1015 model juke box at the end of the room in the middle between the tastefully screened-off Ladies and Gentlemen washrooms. The White Rose did a steady trade in breakfasts, morning teas, lunches (particularly for country people in town for their weekly shop on market days) and suppers, with other busy periods during cinema intervals serving ice creams, drinks, and hot chips.

Con was the manager, and seemed to be always there, opening early enough to make and serve breakfasts to some of the local workers; and incredibly, Con was still there at night, not closing until his last customers were ready to go home. High on the end wall were matching framed pictures of English King George VI and the late King George II of Greece (even though George II had already died and was succeeded by his young brother Paul who hadn't yet made his mark in turbulent postwar Greece.) On the walls there were also faded remnants of Christmas decorations from last year. Apart from Con, the smiling elderly couple (who didn't appear to speak much, if any, English) were usually behind the counter or in the kitchen. Were they Con's parents? Possibly. There was also a very pregnant young woman (Con's wife? Probably) with another small skirt-holding child, and a varying couple of local high-school girl waitresses working shifts, serving tables.

It was not only young people who used the café as a meeting place. It also did a regular trade in meals – particularly lunches, with some of Con's specials, such as his Mixed Grill, and late breakfasts of bacon and eggs, sausages, toast, and of course, chips. Chips with everything. Because of their permanent shortage of money, the RMC cadets usually had to restrict themselves to milkshakes or weak stewed coffee from the permanent urn; better still, a pot of tea which they could manage to make last out by a refill of hot water. Con didn't seem to mind. It is hard to believe, but Con's soda fountain even had an iced water spigot, and he had no reluctance to serving a free glass of cold water if asked.

The modern Jukebox kept up with the latest in popular songs and film music such as *Ghost Riders In The Sky* (Vaughn Monroe), *The Harry Lime Theme* (Anton Karas on his Zither), *Mule Train* (Frankie Lane), or *La Vie En Rose* (Edith Piaf). Often the meeting up of girls and boys was a chance arrangement, and friendships overlapped without many close commitments. Blask and Andrew arrived to join a group where two other cadets (Nicholson and Swift) were talking to three girls, who were raving about some film that was on in town, arguing which they preferred (It was between *The Third Man, She Wore a Yellow Ribbon*, and *12 o'clock High*). The cast of *The Third Man*, also currently showing (Joseph Cotton, Trevor Howard, or Orson Welles) did not seem to attract as much admiration as John Wayne or Gregory Peck, but everyone seemed to be attracted to the unusual Zither theme of *The Third Man*, played often on the café juke box. There were a few other tables or booths occupied with customers unknown to the group, including a group of young men sporting the latest bodgie Hollywood haircuts, who were loud and showing off to attract the attention of any girls.

As Andy and Jakob arrived and exchanged greetings around, there was already much laughter and shushing and whispering. "What's going on?" "What?" "Rita is teaching us some Italian swearwords." "*I am not!*" "But you just said--" "That's not a swearword; not exactly, just maybe rude." Rita was a lovely vivacious girl in her late teens whom the cadets saw at regular church parades with her family – her father was a prosperous local building contractor, and a friend to some of the school staff. "What was it?" Andrew asked, "I won't tell anyone, promise." '*Porca Miseria!*' Rita says quietly, still laughing, and they all laughed with her. It's not what she said, it's the way she said it, the accent, the expression – everyone then has a go, complete with copied hand gestures – *Porca Miseria!* "Anyway what's it mean?" "It is like kind of Damn and Blast." Rita said. "You say it to let off steam. It actually means 'Sad Pig!'" That sets them off. Shrieks of laughter from the girls, "is that <u>all</u>? 'Sad Pig'? I thought you said it was something rude." Everyone laughs at that. "Tell us again, Rita." But when she tries to say it, can't talk for laughing, which sets them all off again. "*Porca Miseria!*" One of the RMC cadets says "That's got to be our new expression when Thunderbum gives us hell." Practising, in a supposed stern male voice: "You, son, take two extra drills! Oh shit, porca miseria!" Continual laughter. 'One girl asks "What's that, who's Thunderbum?" They all laugh at the nickname. "He's the RSM – the Regimental Sergeant-Major" "He's the bane of our existence, and we're the Sad Pigs." More laughter. "What else Rita? Teach us some more Italian." Nicholson says "I've heard someone say some swear words, sounds like *Va Fon Kool* – what's that? Have I got it nearly right? What does it mean?" Rita shushes, embarrassed. Laughing, not quite but... "No", Rita says, blush-frowning prettily, shaking her head vigorously, "that's <u>very</u>

bad, really really bad, you don't say that". "Why? What's it mean?" She waves her hand in front of her face. "It is – I think what you maybe heard is – it's <u>really</u> bad - what they were saying "(She whispers, head down" '*Va 'afare in culo*', but don't say it; it means Up Your Arse, even worse.") More shrieks of laughter. Someone tries it out, with what they think is Italian accent and expressive hands, causing more laughter. But Rita doesn't want any of it, waving her hand in front of her face again.

Two of the young Bodgies from the far end booth come, attracted both by the presence of girls and the laughter and animated conversation, wishing they were part of such a happy group enjoying themselves – One of them, with elaborate Brylcremed hairstyle, cheeky, a real mug lair, sleeves exaggeratedly tightly rolled up high above his biceps , shirt collar turned up. "Hey, you not talk bad language in here. We Italian don't like you insulting". One of the girls says "we're not insulting anyone." Rita says something to him, and the young man speaks back to her in Italian, but she answers him in English, saying 'We're not speaking Italian here. Anyway, this is private conversation, nothing to do with you," turning away. Andrew thinks: cool it Rita, this could get ugly. And then it does get ugly, because the Italian youth, having felt put down by a girl, sneers "So you won't speak some Italian boy, you only talk your toy soldier boyfriends. OK, I can be toy soldier too" (and grabs one of the cadet's caps and puts it on, tilted jauntily, pretending a mock salute copied from some American movie he'd seen) He turns back showing off to his remaining friends in the rear booth grinning, and tries it again louder – "I can be a toy soldier now". Jakob rises in his seat, smiling calmly "OK, joke over, let's have the cap back now please". But the Italian boy has made his mates laugh, has performed in front of these girls whom he wants to impress, and has to build on the moment. "Hey, I think I can be a Colonel-Captain OK", and he makes another attempt at (what he thinks is) saluting. You can see that already Con had recognized that a 'situation' might be brewing when the Italian boy first came down from the end booth, and Con had wiped his hands on a tea-towel coming out from behind the counter, not wanting to inhibit fun, but not sure which way this is going; whether he should intervene or not. But Jakob, still semi-smiling but serious, now out of the booth, reaching for the army cap to put an end to the horseplay, as the youth sneers, and violently pushes Jakob away, heel of his hand jarring Blask's shoulder hard, now aggressively challenging "Hey toy soldier, you want to make something?" And his push having caught Blask a bit off balance making him stagger, almost having to sit on Rita's lap until he corrects himself, causing the other boy to laugh; but what Jakob then did surprised everyone, even the Italian youth, because Blask seemed to turn away, but it was part of a powerful gathering of strength, a swivelling turn like a coiled spring, coming back so that his brick-hard fist caught the Italian boy's face squarely, and the boy staggered back buckling as Blask reached across and took the cap from where it fell, saying quietly – "That's enough, or do you want some more?" Cadet Nicholson, sitting alongside the girls, alarmed, said "Jesus, Jake!", while Andrew had risen to confront the Italian boy's mate who hurried towards them from the rear booths, so that the two faced off – Andrew grinning "Do you want some too?" and two of the girls had already risen shocked and started leaving towards the front entrance not wanting any part of this male rivalry, or the escalated fierce violence which Jakob used, while Con had arrived reaching the booth with both arms extended, and the Italian boy slumped across the empty next booth seat, choke-gasping, eyes watering, blood from his nose running down over his shirt. Two other nearby disapproving adult customers had risen from their seats frowning, but the second youth from the rear had already said to Andrew "No trouble, no trouble, let me help my mate," half-raising his hands. Andrew said to Jakob, "Enough mate, we better go. Sorry girls, sorry Con, but we didn't start it, OK." But Con was more concerned with placating the adult customers who had risen, saying "Everything fine now, no trouble."

On the way back to barracks, Jakob hesitated shaking his bruised knuckles and said "Maybe I should go back, should have made sure he was OK, I think I might have broken his nose." But

Andrew hurried him along, saying "He asked for it mate, and he has friends there to help him." Jakob, still concerned, went on, "I wonder if news of it will get back to the Clink. I could be in big trouble with Thunderbum" And he was.

Not with Thunderbum, but the Adjutant, where Jakob was summoned soon after they had arrived back. New travels fast in a small community. The staff Corporal who escorted Jakob was serious "I think you've really done it, Blask. They've got a thing about fighting in public." Jakob said "But it wasn't fighting," and yet he realized that it was. And the Adjutant, Captain Banks, always serious, was not in any doubt, making Blask stand at attention in front of his desk in the small office next to the orderly room. "You know why you're here, Mr Blask. The school has a strict policy about getting into any public brawls. You're sacked. You will clear out your room, stack your gear, and wait at the guardhouse in civilian clothes for transport. I will write you a travel voucher for the 1800 train to Sydney, and when you get there, you will be officially discharged at Marrickville Personnel Depot and paid out any allowance owing. There is not much more to say, is there?" And Jakob said "No, Sir." Pause, then he saluted and about-turned correctly. Force of habit, everything done properly.

But back at Jakob's room, Andrew came along from his room fuming, not accepting the way it turned out. Jakob shook his head and said "Let it go, Andy, I clearly did the wrong thing, and it is what it is." He stripped the bed and began to fold up his blankets and sheets. There was a lot to organize, a lot to rearrange; from the pile of books at the study desk, to the wardrobe and chest full of uniforms and equipment. Andrew watched, anguished, for a moment, his head turning this way and that, and then stormed out. (Cadet Swift said later, you should have seen Turner, steam coming out his ears, and we had thought he was a pussycat). Andrew marched smartly down to the admin area and at the Bummery, banged loudly on the door. The RSM at ease in his braces, feet up, boots off, and not expecting company, opened his door, amazed at who could possibly be suicidal enough to do this, and for a second, they both spoke loudly over each other at the same time, the RSM gaining the control. "Mister Turner, what the devil!" And angry Andrew: "Sir, sorry, but I need your help to correct something very wrong. You're the only one who can do this." I guess this was one way to get the RSM's attention. It was certainly an unusual situation. No-one had ever heard of a cadet being invited into the Bummery and asked to sit down and pour out their troubles behind closed doors like going to the padre. No-one knows exactly what went on, but we think it went something like this. Surely the RSM would have let Andrew get it off his chest, then said something like: "Rules are rules, son. There is no excuse for getting into a public fight in town, and that's that." But, as we know Andrew, he would have said something like: "So, if a cadet is attacked – *attacked* – in public by a town bodgie, he should be unable to defend himself?" "Well, no..." "And if the attack includes insulting this college by calling us all 'Toy Soldiers'? And if defending himself to that unprovoked attack includes trying to protect young civilian females, as an honourable cadet should? Wouldn't that be considered a cadet's duty?" Something like that. And maybe even: "Besides, I was there, and can provide several witnesses to the true facts of the event, including the proprietor Mr. Michaelides, who would not want Cadet Blask to be punished for doing the honorable thing in his café..." Anyway, apparently Andrew managed somehow to persuade Thunderbum to come with him to the Adjutant and plead Jakob's case. And somehow they got the Adj to reverse his decision (don't ask me how, despite the fact that the Adjutant had already set several official things in motion, and it was like trying to halt a steam locomotive to unscramble them). It took half an hour. On their way back to tell Jakob the news, that he had been exonerated (marching smartly all the way, of course), Thunderbum had snarled aside to Andrew "You took a big risk, Mister Turner." And Andrew said "I had to, sir. I was involved too. If Jake hadn't hit the bodgie sir, I would have, and then I'd be sacked too." But all the RSM said tersely in return was "Don't make a habit of this." But we don't know if he meant the café fight, or involving him, the RSM.

When they reached the quarters, Blask was still assembling gear to return to the QM Store watched by a couple of hopeful cadets, who quickly scarpered when they saw Thunderbum coming.

When Jakob heard the news, he sort of sagged to sit on the edge of his bed, head in his hands. Typically, the RSM thundered "Come on man, get up, get this room back in order, it's like a gypsy camp! I'll be inspecting this in ten minutes!" So that Jakob and Andrew looked at each other, and almost smiled. Almost. Finally, leaving, Thunderbum turned and had the last quiet word. "Mister Blask, you really owe him one." Nodding towards Andrew. That was not all. A second time, leaving but not leaving, Thunderbum turned again and this time his voice was back to the normal official voice. "You, both, are confined to barracks for a month, and you are banned from the Greek restaurant for good. Totally. Hear me?" "*Sir!*" In unison. Good timing. Now they could hazard a smile at each other.

1951

Top Songs:

Too Young – (Nat King Cole)
Because of You – (Tony Bennett)
How High The Moon – (Les Paul, Mary Ford)
Come-on-a My House – (Rosemary Clooney)
Be My Love – (Mario Lanza)

- **In Korea, UN Forces recapture Seoul. General MacArthur is sacked by President Truman for disobedience, replaced by General Ridgeway. Chinese launched major offensive, stalled by British 1st Bn Glostershire Regiment despite heavy losses. Gen.Van Fleet orders counter offensive taking town of Kansong, Chorwon and Kumwha. In April, Australian troops battle to hold Kapyong (successfully) against desperate Chinese and North Korean attempts to ecapture Seoul.**

- Sept. Japan Peace Treaty is signed.

- Anzus Treaty comes into force.

- Record prices for Wool as result of KWar demand.

- Introduction of National Service in Australia for all males 18 : 176 days training (99 days recruit camp, then 2 yrs Citizen Military Force part-time soldiering)

- Festival of Britain opens at Royal Festival Hall

- Iran nationalizes its oilfields despite world protests

- In UK, Winston Churchill becomes PM again, replacing Clement Atlee

Michael

Very soon, the powers that be decided that we – our platoons, our company - were next in line for making up numbers for the new Battalions, for the war in Korea. Or the 'Police Action' as it was being called by some newspapers. Sergeant Stagg said "Police Action? Yeah, right, that's probably the Defence Department calling it that, so that they can weasel out of paying active service entitlements." But remember, there was no argument about our original enlistment papers in which we voluntarily signed up for overseas service if required, and we didn't question being told what inoculations we had to have on account of health risks in some Asian countries. They explained it as being because our bodies were used to a certain lifestyle, and how a sudden change to something totally different could introduce us to new bugs. So we all fronted up for the routine of all the needles we had to get – and it is amazing, that some big tough fighting soldiers would turn into sooks when the nurse produced a hypodermic. It makes you smile and shake your head.

As Sgt Stagg had predicted, we were introduced to our newly-appointed Platoon Commander, a Lieutenant fresh out of Duntroon. He sure was – as they say - bright-eyed and bushy-tailed and keen as mustard. His name was Boland, and boy, was he trying hard to please, especially with us NCOs. Not really trying to be one of the boys, which was impossible, but you could he was straining to become accepted as our Lieutenant, and it was an uphill climb, because he had nothing except his newly appointed rank to work from. Sure, he knew all the drills, the orders, and the procedures, but he was well aware – we were all aware, that he was starting from scratch. He had this habit of reinforcing his position by asking the squad after some procedure or manoeuvre "Are you with me?" And if the response was anything but enthusiastic (which was generally the case, because none of us was used to being asked such a stupid question) – he would repeat it, until he got the unanimous platoon reply he wanted: **Yes Sir!** He used to say "You're either with me or agin me. So are you with me?" Now I ask you, who in a unit as a private soldier is going to be stupid enough to say to a new officer "I'm agin you." A couple of the digs said to me later "Who *is* this peanut, Corp?" pretending to mimic him in a comic voice ("Are you with me, or agin me?") "Jesus where do they get 'em from?" and I calmed them down, telling them Boland was a lot better than some of the brand-new officers we had seen floating around, trying out their new authority. Besides, he wouldn't be with us forever.

The engagement was not Michael's idea. Nor the engagement party. Probably both were Vicky's mother's idea – she was like that. In a way, Michael thought, Vicky's mother Jean almost seemed to be reliving her own teenage years through her daughter. Don't forget, Reg the Major used to be an NCO himself, years back. Anyway, the party was sort of a farewell too, with Michael's Company being shipped off to join other units building up the new Battalions in either Sydney or Brisbane. Vicky's father Reg was frustrated, that he was not going too. It was Vicky who brought up the subject of the engagement, one night when they were canoodling in the borrowed car out on the fringe of the armoured vehicle testing range. It had become an occasion which Michael looked forward to, if he could borrow his mate Jamie's car again. Jamie teased him, saying "OK Mike, but I don't want to see any high heel marks on the ceiling of the car, or stains on the upholstery". Jamie knew despite the teasing, that there was not much chance of sex taking place in his car, even if it was borrowed at night, and even in such a remote part of the barracks. His mate Michael was such a straight up-and-down bloke, it was impossible to imagine him having sex with anyone before getting married. And Vicky was, after all, a Major's daughter, even though she often jokingly referred to herself as an army brat. 'Watching the sunset' was one way they described their kissing and cuddling in Jamie's car at the extremity of the camp. They usually tuned the car radio in to one of the commercial stations played softly, and often just talked, as well as caressing. The 'sex' never progressed very far, although Vicky had permitted Michael to slide his hand inside her dress and fondle her breast, which she seemed to enjoy. When he had tried to move his hand under her dress between her legs, she had drawn the line at that and warned him off. Similarly, he had not been able to interest her in touching his yearning equipment, which was always at attention during their sessions. Ah well.

At one stage, Vicky had broached the subject innocently. "Darling, do you ever think about getting married?" He played up to it by saying "Well yeah, I did propose, but Matron Temby turned me down." Vicky punched him on the arm, "You beast. Be serious for once." Which he did, saying "Of course I think about it, love, but with this overseas posting, it's probably not the most sensible time to make plans like that." "I didn't mean immediately, but what about later, when you come back. Would it be part of our future, you and me, do you think?" Michael thought about it. The idea of marriage brought one immediate image to mind, and that was the two of them in a big double bed. A barracks married quarter? Maybe one of those identical Defence Department bungalows with a lawn to mow, some playground equipment in the yard like swings, a nursery; Whoa! Slow down boy. One thing at a time. "Yeah, that could be the way to go, especially if I manage to get some more stripes up." "So," she invited shyly, "do you think we could get engaged? Like, we would promise to wait for each other, and make a few plans for when we could get together again?" And Michael didn't really feel pressured, just that it was probably a logical progression, if you thought about it, the way things happened, wasn't it? And it did head towards that double bed, didn't it?

Of course Michael invited all of his Section, his special 'band of brothers', but only five of the ten made it. For a start, an engagement party at a Major's house in the barracks married quarter was not exactly on top of every soldier's best idea of spending a Saturday night. The five who went were understandably ill-at-ease; not exactly shy, but you know, on their best behaviour and not wanting to spoil things for Corporal Whan, who was, after all, a really good bloke. So they sat on the edge of their chairs to start with, super-polite to Vicky's mother and almost reverential to Reg, the Major, until the ice was broken and people began to enjoy themselves. Vicky had invited four of her girlfriends from the base, which helped, especially when they crowded around to admire the engagement ring, and there was nice music and food, as well as drink to smooth the sharp edges, as long as you didn't let go and get sozzled and spoil things. Furniture had been moved back to provide space for some restricted dancing. There was also a special event as they stayed tuned to the local wireless station's Request Hour, and everybody shushed each other as the time came for the expected announcement *"And a special cheerio to a wonderful couple in Puckapunyal celebrating their engagement tonight, Vicky and Michael!"* followed by cheering and playing 'For They Are Jolly Good Fellows'. More cheering in the house as Michael and Vicky performed the obligatory chaste public kiss. That served as the farewell party too.

'Are You With Me?' Boland was with us for less than a month, when we were transferred to Ingleburn in N.S.W. for pre-embarkation drills, and the news that we were off to Korea "very soon". We left Lieutenant Boland behind, being told that he was remaining to train fresh troops, possibly national servicemen, when that system got going properly. (Poor suckers) Similarly we lost Sergeant Stagg to another training unit, and we were advised that we would get a new Platoon Sergeant and Officer when we arrived "Up There", as they put it. But before we left, there were some farewells. Our original Company was reorganized completely, losing some men, and gaining others from the newly recruited force of experienced soldiers who had volunteered for "K Force". That was a mixed blessing. A few of them were hard-boiled ex-digs who had served in WWII, as well as some who were recruited overseas – mainly in Britain – with previous war service. When I say a mixed blessing, I mean that some of them looked down on us who had no previous war service, while many others of the old brigade were a pleasure to serve with, because they knew the ropes and didn't need spoon-feeding, and realistically understood that you've got to start somewhere. This last lot were also a help and inspiration to a recently promoted NCO like me.

When the time came, there was no departure ceremony, and almost no farewells – although somehow a few privileged family members somehow got to attend the departure of our flight from Mascot, to say goodbye to their son/husband/boyfriend. We were in uniform, but unarmed. Most of us had never been outside Australia before, and some of us had never been on a plane before, so it was a bit of an adventure. The Draft Conducting Officer in charge was an unfriendly Ordnance Major not attached to any of us, and he wasn't having any nonsense. While we were assembling in the departure lounge, he made a small terse speech to the assembled troops, and let it be known that if there was any misbehavior in transit, he would have the plane met by Military Police, and any miscreants would be marched off to the glasshouse. He needn't have worried. It was a three-day flight, and after the first leg (and the men's discovery that they could get free beer from the stewardess), they settled down, and then a lot of them slept most of the way. We refueled at Darwin, after which it was almost a boring flight to Manila. High and nothing to see. At Manila, we were all a bit surprised by the massive American presence, especially around the airport where we landed. We were each given five U.S. Dollars (which everybody mocked, even the officers) and shown to the U.S. Forces' Canteen at the airport, but the Australians were such a novelty to the Yank troops and the fact that we were joining their fight as allies in Korea, meant that their welcome was genuine and generous, and most of our draft came away still with their original Greenback Fiver. Not to mention a few sore heads, even if the American beer was "weak as nanny-goat's piss" according to Peter, the bald private everybody called Nude-Nut. Again, a long flight over the sea with nothing to look at except clouds below, and then the approach to, and landing at Iwakuni, Japan, which was obviously another huge operational airbase in a foreign country. This is where you realize that you are out of your comfort zone, that you don't know your way around and have to be identified and counted and instructed, and you are surrounded by efficient service personnel doing their regular duty in which you just have to fit in.

It was late and everyone was tired from the long journey, and the day had not finished by a long shot. There was a train trip to the small city of Kure (pronounced Koo-ray), where buses were waiting to take us all out to our new barracks at Hiro (pronounced Hee-ro), through fascinating Japanese civilian traffic and scenery. But the best of all was what we found waiting for us – comfortable clean barracks in pleasant surroundings, and a meal waiting for us in a well-appointed mess (more like a restaurant) served on china plates by neat Japanese female waitresses – (none of your usual hairy-arsed army cooks slopping food onto your dixie as you queued at the cook-station). Heaven.

And then we were back in our hard-working comfort zone of familiar drill and weapon training, even if it was in an unfamiliar setting in a foreign country.

Jakob

At the College there was finally the announcement of post-graduate Corps allocations. Because in a few days after graduation, everyone was going to be sent to post-graduate training schools for specialist instruction and practice in their new tasks as regimental officers, Lieutenants. Months ago, during the course, the senior class had all filled in forms giving their personal preferences for post-graduate posting, being warned "You may not get what you would like, but your preferences will be taken into account". And since the demands of the new war in Korea ('a platoon commanders' war', someone important had said), and the even greater demands of setting up and operating the huge new Australian National Service scheme needing hundreds of new officers and NCOs to train and administer those recruits, there was no doubt – even no hint of a *shadow* of a reason for doubt – that Jakob would be appointed to Infantry, which he had requested. And still smiling in anticipation at the posted official lists, running his eyes down the names beneath Royal Australian Infantry (past the familiar names, even past Andrew's) no, he must have missed it, maybe 'Blask' miss-spelled, go back to the top and read again, more slowly, and then, as he was aware of a couple of his fellow graduates watching him; no, it wasn't there. Perhaps it was just a clerical omission, surely – unless (please God no) he was listed elsewhere... *Oh no, surely not.* And as the possibility of massive disappointment dawned on him, he read further down to the shorter lists, of Armoured Corps (No) – Artillery (No) – Engineers (No) – Signals (No) – Ordnance (No) – and then there he was, listed under Royal Australian Army Service Corps, with two other fellow graduate names. He was stunned. *Service Corps,* supply and transport? Not even a combat corps. Jesus. He felt like he was kicked in the guts. But *why?* He had graduated high in his class, excellent exam results, sporting prizes, no really bad discipline conflicts... Certainly, there was that business at Con's Café, but that had been settled, surely? And OK, he had received many extra drills for minor infringements, but everybody had. Sure, he had kicked against discipline a bit and queried a few decisions over the years, but had always accepted the Staff verdict and got on with the job. He retreated to his barrack room, dudded.

Andrew tapped on his door, which was part open. Jakob was sitting on his bed, just looking blankly at the window. Andrew could see, could almost feel, Jakob's disappointment, and said "Oh Jake, I'm so sorry. If only I could change places with you; you know I don't want to be a *Ra-Ra-Up and At 'Em* Infanteer. It's not fair." Jakob shook his head, "No mate, it's not fair. I don't know what I did wrong." "Can't you appeal, or something?" "I don't know. But I'll have to try. At least I'll have to try."

Surprisingly, Thunderbum was sitting relaxed on a chair in the sun outside his office trimming his stubby fingernails and looked up at the interruption and put away the small scissors as if discovered performing something unmilitary. Brusquely – "What is it, Mister Blask?" "Sir, I want an appointment to see the Commandant; I tried the Adjutant just now, but he is off site." "What for? Stand easy man." (An explanation is the hard part, thought Jakob, swallowing.) "To discuss my post-graduate posting, my Corps allocation, sir." "Go on, tell me about it first." "I want to ask for reallocation, sir, to Infantry." "Where have they got you?" "Service Corps." Hint of a smile. "I can well understand your preference for God's own regiment of course; but can I just tell you kindly" (slightly shaking his grizzled head) "it won't do you any good, son. Corps allocations have been made ages ago and post-graduate selections and training schedules long drawn up at the specialist schools where you have all been slotted in. Done and dusted. Yes; I can, of course, arrange for you to see the Old Man, but I can tell you now, that you won't be changing your Corps appointment. Sorry, but it won't happen; never *hatchi*." "I'd still like give it my best shot, sir, if it's OK with you. I have to try." The RSM shook his head slowly, saying "Blask, Blask, Blask." He sighed. "You never give up, do you. Wait here." Closed door, but Jakob could hear the respectful murmur of the RSM's voice. And after the private phone call inside the closed door of the Bummery, and after the re-emerged RSM sternly inspecting Jakob again for correct boots belt buttons and straight cap, he marched him up along the inner road side by side to the Commandant's Office unable to stop himself from almost whispering under his breath the step timing Hep Hep Hep as they marched together, both of them chests out, heads back, chins in, arms straight, and the RSM's low-voiced 'Halt, Wait Here' as he went boot-crashing, stiff-saluting ahead of Jakob as he was delivered into God's Presence. Thunderbum came back out and ordered. "March in, Mister Blask." He added, quietly "Come and see me when you are finished here."

Inside, past the civilian lady secretary in the ante-room, after saluting, the Commandant stood him at ease, and then came from behind his desk to straighten (or pretend to) one of several group photos of men in uniform on the wall, before leaning his backside against the broad table which was his neat – and almost empty - desk. He seemed almost in a philosophical mood, gazing at his ceiling, maybe half listening to the distant shouting of a drill squad somewhere not too far away. Which was the permanent sound-track of the college, as it was of every training unit. "Mister Blask" the Colonel said gently. "We have you men for four years and watch you as you struggle and progress and develop from schoolboys into men, into soldiers and officers; and after all the work, exams and graduation, as we push you out into the real world, we often feel we still don't really know you, and sometimes we feel guilty that we have never spent enough time with each of you, did you know that?" But it was a question which Jakob knew didn't require an answer, as the Commandant's eyes came back to his. The Colonel half-turned to tap a bulky file on his desk; no doubt brought out to remind him who Blask was. "And you, Blask, you've done well, you should know that, way above average for your Class. And not only academically, we're going to miss you badly on the sports field; but I'm sure you are aware of that." And then he waved a hand aside, as if realizing that Jakob was not here to listen to soft soap. "So; you are disappointed with your Corps posting – but surely you must know that we make these allocations ages ago, well ahead of Graduation, and we make them from a dozen different criteria, not least of which is that the Army demands a certain number of selected new officers to each of the various arms and services, and wants the best men for the job. You see that, don't you?" He paused, so that Jakob felt it was his opportunity. "I do see that, sir, but with the new demands of this war in Korea and an increased need for Infantry officers which may not have been obvious during the Corps allocations, I wanted to make every effort..." But already he could see the big man slowly shaking his head sadly, and he knew that it was too late, too late, there was no use. And they both heard a nearer junior squad quick-marching along the lower road with crunching boots on gravel, their NCO counting off the beat well aware of his squad's proximity to headquarters and God, *both* Gods, with RSM Thunderbum in full view waiting outside the office no doubt severely frowning, watching them. The Commandant waited until the noisy squad passed before adding, smiling, "There they go, bright-eyed and bushy-tailed, just like you did, every man a keen soldier, and every man naturally wanting to become an Infantry platoon leader, a hero at the sharp end where the action is, but we both know that not all of them will be able to get there. The army needs other officers, Mr Blask, with other skills, in other duties." He paused. "You probably know – I'm sure everybody knows – that I am an old 'dropshort', a loyal artillery man." He spread his hands. "But here I am, running a military college – 'the Clink'. And you know that in a year or two when I am posted from here, I could be running a national service battalion, or driving a procurement desk in a stuffy office in Canberra. I don't know." He shrugged. "It's the army, Blask. We do what we are told. It's what the army expects. It's what it *demands* of us. We take the King's Shilling, and we are obliged to follow his orders. And you, being one of my best officers, that is what you must do, too. It is what you <u>will</u> do."

124

Andrew

If you take a broad view, the whole point of the last four years in RMC of extreme discipline and hard work, was to produce qualified commissioned officers for the Army, who could take anything the world handed out. Not only our army, but we had also two keen cadets from India, and four from New Zealand (although only two of them finished the course.) Jakob and I had become firm friends during the course – probably the best friend I had ever had. I was so lucky that we hit it off; and he had almost become one of the family, coming with me on leave to our place several times, where he was so much at home, that we joked about the guestroom, calling it 'Jakob's Room'. My father had always been impressed with Jakob, I suppose wishing that he had had a son like Jakob instead of me; and sometimes I wished that I was more like Jakob – but not because of wanting to please my father – anyway, there are some things you can't change. My mother sort of adopted Jakob, especially after Jakob's mother died, and even my little pest of a sister got on well with him, and Jake was very patient with her. I was even amused by Jakob getting patient instruction by my mother about our collection of classical music records, and I used to tease him about her civilizing him.

Anyway, here we were, finally surviving, after those interminable examinations – (some at the college, and some at a central hall with invigilators), and heading up to the end graduations. I suppose that our Graduation was something of an anti-climax when it happened. For a start, there were the three previous graduations that we had attended of earlier senior classes, being part of their parades which were always the second Tuesday in December, acting as guides and ushers and dogsbodies for other peoples' guests during their ceremonies, taking over the graduates' empty rooms in the annual shift. And now for ours, there were the hours of preparation, rehearsals for the big parade, inspections, corrections, the selections and announcements of prize-giving, the arrangements for families – after a while, I think that most of our class were just wishing it was all over. Let's get out there.

The graduation parade was massive, really massive. Everyone knew what to do because of the preparations and rehearsals. As usual, press and newsreel cameramen were there to record the event, with the colourful Eastern Command Band parading and playing. The classes were inspected by the Governor-General, the Prime Minister, and the Chief of General Staff. We marched past in slow and quick time, and advanced in review order, always commanded - not by Thunderbum - but by the senior cadet, Mainwaring, the Battalion Sergeant-Major. It was totally our show. As we, the graduating class marched off following the Colours, the remainder classes presented arms saluting us, and the band played "Auld Lang Syne". I know; a lot of bullshit, but it was moving to be part of it; it made your scalp prickle, even in someone like me, who didn't take the army seriously. Well, I didn't use to, but I was surprised at how I was being converted. After the parade, the presentation of diplomas and prizes followed by a garden party Canberra's weather was at its finest, and the school's gardens were magnificent.

Most cadets had someone from family (sometimes whole family groups and girlfriends) coming to attend the parade and the evening's graduation ball, where it is traditional for the graduate's partners to pin on their 'Pips' at midnight. Those who had partners. Quite a few had parents, and it in some cases it would be the graduate's mother who would do the honours, 'badging' him. The 'Pips' are junior officers' badges of rank, like stars – in the case of Lieutenants, two on each epaulette. They are really *Stars of the Knight Grand Cross of the Military Division of the Most Honorable Order of the Bath*' from British army tradition, bearing the motto 'Tria Juncta In Uno' relating to the union of England, Scotland and Ireland, if you want to get technical. I knew that my mother and father would be there; I wasn't sure about Elizabeth, who was in high school now, but still a kid and probably had kid's things to do.

In Jakob's case, his family consisted only of his granddad, and Jakob had the usual worry about whether the old man would (a) stay sober, and (b), behave himself. But he need not have worried, Aleksi was at his best. When he insisted that he would attend Jakob's graduation, there was the matter of accommodation, and the few Canberra hotel rooms were already fully booked well ahead, but the old man was cheerful – "No worries, maybe I find a friendly widow who will give me a bed for the night" (and Jakob never did find out where the old man stayed – he wondered if his *Dziadziu* slept in that battered old truck, but then...) "You never know your luck in a big city" the old man had chuckled, nudging him.

At the trophy presentations in the packed hall, of which Jakob won two awards, for Rugby and Boxing, he was self-conscious to be called out in front of the rows of temporary seating full of families, marching smartly forward receiving his prizes, then marching back, embarrassed by the applause from the huge audience of well-dressed civilians whom he didn't know, except in the middle of the crowd, he recognized Andrew's mother and young sister Elizabeth smiling and waving to him as he returned to his seat. No sign of Andrew's father with them, but no doubt he was hobnobbing (or *'hobsnobbing'* as Andrew would have it, with senior officers and officials somewhere). When Jakob's name was announced and rose from his seat to go and receive the first of the engraved cups, amidst the polite clapping, there was the unmistakable hoarse voice of his grandfather calling *"Dobry chlopak!* (good boy) *Brawo!"*, and for Jakob's second prize, another rough shout *"Gratulacje, 'Kuba!"* As Jakob returned to his seat in front among the prize-winners, he searched and located his grandfather's beaming proud and scrubbed-shining face back in the crowd, and he raised a prize cup in each hand to the old man. His family. But soon it was the seemingly endless presentation of certificates, and the super-prize, the King's Commission, signed by H.E. the Governor-General, Viscount Slim, representing The King.

Then at the traditional Ball, the presence of so many formally-dressed women and girls in long dresses and styled hair added a softness to the military scene, just as the subtle emanations of their feminine perfume enhanced the atmosphere. The Commandant and most of the staff in their best bib and tucker uniforms circulated to speak to as many of the families as possible, and it just happened that Jakob and Andrew were talking to Jakob's grandfather when the Colonel came up. Aleksi was in a (borrowed? rented?) dinner suit which seemed a bit tight, and everything about him needed a bit of an iron, but the old man's shoes were polished to a glass shine, and his white shirt sparkled white despite one collar peak needing some discipline. Pity about the odd socks when they showed. His face was beaming and his remaining hair was brilliantined to keep it in order. Jakob said "Sir, this is my grandfather, Aleksi Blask." The Commandant offered his firm hand and spoke clearly, unsure about how much English the old man had, "Pleased to meet you, sir. You must be very proud, your grandson has done well, and will make a fine officer." Aleksi said "I know, you must be proud too, you did a good job with him." They laughed. "I had good material to start with," the Commandant said, and Jakob thought – there are some people who always know the right thing to say, looking at the Colonel with renewed respect.

And then there was Andrew's mother and sister Elizabeth coming to claim Andrew. Young schoolgirl Elizabeth impulsively hugged Jakob's arm. "Now, you haven't got a partner to pin on your Pips at midnight, so I am going to do it, while Mummy does Andrew's. That's settled, so no argument." The Commandant, smiling, excused himself to continue circulating, and Jakob's grandfather raised his eyebrows. "So, who is this I haven't met, so beautiful?" He bowed, actually formally bowed, and took Elizabeth's hand as if he would kiss it, but didn't, just held it gently an inch below his bowed head, introducing himself "*Aleksi Blask. Jestem do twoich uslug.*" (At your service) "Wow," blushed Elizabeth, "What a gentleman." Jakob laughed at them, addressing his grandfather "You old smoothie. This is Andrew's mother Mrs Turner, and this is Andrew's sister Elizabeth." To them he explained "This is my grandfather Aleksi. He <u>can</u> speak English." He was interrupted by a loudspeaker announcing the 'Trooping of Casey', to which many of the audience had looked forward, having heard about it. Another long-standing RMC tradition, consisting of a uniformed human skeleton ('Cadet Casey') mounted on 'Invader', the skeleton of a racehorse, which was paraded around the centre of the ballroom just prior to midnight, to applause, much photography, and continuous laughter.

The orchestra played a chord, announcing the Graduation Waltz. Elizabeth claimed Jakob, leading him onto the crowded dance floor. Speaking so softly he had to bend his head to hear her above the noise and laughter, she said "You look very smart in your uniform, Jakob." "Thank you, Ellie. You look very smart too in..." He hesitated, and she laughed at him "It is called a dress, Jakob, a dress. You need more female company." Laughing, he said "That's true. Here in clink, it's a bit like a monastery." He apologized for stumbling "I'm sorry Ellie, I'm no dancer." They danced for a minute being squashed and bumped by the crowd, then she continued, seriously "But now we'll never see you again, you being posted everywhere like Andrew" and Jakob was going to make some light remark, but suddenly realized Elizabeth's eyes looked full of tears, and she tried to turn her head away. "Oh Liz. Ellie; of course we'll keep in touch. I could write to you." She struggled to say "Promise?" Jakob stopped, fumbled for his clean handkerchief to offer her, but the embarrassed girl had turned and gone, disappearing through the crowded dance floor of excited laughing couples. He didn't see her again that night. What a strange little girl.

So that's it. Packed up and cleared. Equipment audited, returned and signed off. Rooms emptied cleaned and inspected. Dispersing graduates in high spirits - but chivvied by stern staff (and thundering Thunderbum himself) that 'You men may not have noticed, but there is a functioning college of hundreds of military students to run - which is not to be interrupted by idle departing officers suddenly released from restrictions like schoolboys let out of class (So behave yourselves and keep your voices down!). Some graduates have left already, straight after last night's graduation ceremonies, others were picked up by families or representatives at the gates, presumably for leave before being taken to their next postings. New Staff Corps officers (smart in their uniforms proudly bearing new badges of rank) have been issued their travel warrants by the Orderly Room to new duties all over the country with appropriate movement orders, most new jobs being additional training in specialist courses – more schools? – yes, sorry, schools - just when they thought they were finished being new boys with lectures and studies and examinations. God, will this never end? This included Andrew and Jakob, joining several others for Victorian postings whose means of transport was to be a well-worn local civilian plane due to leave Canberra Airport at 1800 hours for Melbourne.

Andrew said "Look, come home with me. The TAA flight's not until eighteen hundred. We've got all day, basically. Dad's away interstate at present, so come and have a relaxed lunch at our place, we can have a game of tennis or something. Besides, we probably won't see each other again for ages and we can have a talk. There are one or two things I have to do before I leave home, anyway. Then Mum will drop us at the airport in time for our plane. Come with me, Jakob, please." So naturally, Jakob agreed. It was, he figured, the last time he would visit the Turner mansion, and it had always been pleasant. The Turner family had, in a way, given him a view of family life – well, what some people would consider normal family life. Not, he smiled to himself, the kind of family life with his Dziadziu at Kurrajong.

They had a simple yet delicious lunch prepared by busy housekeeper Mrs Wilkins, who herself seemed excited to welcome Andrew and Jakob for the day, knowing they were going away for their new careers. Elizabeth, home from school, wanting to be included in every conversation, and again insisting on sitting with them at the big table. Even Mrs Turner, who must be sad at the prospect of Andrew going away again – this time even further - was acting bright and cheerful, and planned to do some shopping while taking Andrew into town for the few chores that he said he had. "Is there anything that you need at the shops, Jakob?" "No, thanks. Liz tells me that I have to beat her again at tennis before I go; she's a tiger for punishment." "You wait!" Elizabeth crowed "I have vastly improved since you last played me, so watch out, Jakob. I've been getting coached by Lindsay Hassett." They all laughed, and Mrs Turner reminded Elizabeth, "Lindsay Hassett is a cricketer, Liz, not a tennis player." "Oh well" she shrugged, "never mind, I'm going to beat Jakob anyway." It was a beautiful day, sunny but with a nice cooling breeze, and the surrounding garden trees were full of birdsong. It couldn't have been a better day to finish up at Belconnen, and with such enjoyable company.

Jakob served again, and again it was just out, and 14 year old Elizabeth triumphed "Double Fault!" laughing. "Serve you right, you were trying to bully me with fast serves, and it went out again." Blask shook his head ruefully, knowing she was right, he *was* trying to Ace her, and it went against him. "I'll get you next time. Love Forty." Elizabeth laughed, "Not if you keep on slamming them down like that." So he reconsidered, and served again, this time more gently and accurately, and Elizabeth returned it evenly, to the far corner of his court, so that he had to scramble to get it back. Again she returned it, to the other extreme corner, so that he had to run once more to reach it. "You rascal, that's not fair, making an old man run." "You soldiers are supposed to be fit," she replied. He slammed the ball back to Elizabeth's empty corner, but again he misjudged, and the ball went out. He groaned, and Elizabeth cheered "Hooray! That's Game, and I won. Will we play another one?" "Sorry Ellie, but if Andrew's picking me up soon, I have to shower and get ready. My time's nearly gone. I'll take you on again next time I come, and I'll whip the socks off you." "Maybe we won't be able to play here again. Daddy said he's going to rip up the court and put in a swimming pool. So if we want to play next time, we'll have to go down to the church courts in town next time." "Will you miss it, this court?" He asked as they walked back. "Yes, I really will, but then I suppose I will really love having a pool instead. Do you like swimming, Jakob?" "Yes, doesn't everyone?" They walked back up toward the house, and Elizabeth said "Give me that, I'll put the tennis gear away."

After his shower, dressed and repacked, Jakob looked around the familiar guestroom ensuring that he had left it tidied as much as possible. There was a knock on the doorframe, and it was Elizabeth standing in the open doorway. She had changed from her tennis gear into a cotton summer dress. "Jakob, can I ask you something?" She asked seriously. "Of course, Ellie." He smiled at how much she had changed since that day all those years ago at the beginning of RMC when, he had first met her as little kid in pigtails in her school uniform. Was she now what they called a bobby-soxer? Still long-legged and skinny, but gradually growing up. That's what girls do, he reminded himself. In a very few years she will be a young woman. "What is it?" "Jakob, will you do something for me?" She said awkwardly. "Sure. You know I will, if I can." She looked down at her feet, hesitating, and then as if challenging herself, looked up again, earnestly direct, serious, in a low voice. "Jakob, will you fuck me?" He was stunned. "*Whaat?*" Concentrate. Perhaps he had miss-heard. Surely.

"I said, will you fuck me? I know _what_ it is, I sort of know a bit about it, but I want to know what it is _like_, what it is actually like." Jakob had to pause, lost for words, wearily shaking his head. She stood just inside the door, swaying shyly, not quite meeting his eyes. "Oh Ellie," he said softly, "Oh sweetie. No; I can't do that, I'm sorry." Now, she looked up frowning directly at him. "Why not?" It reminded him of when she was so much younger, wanting to know why a girl couldn't be a soldier. "Well, in the first place, you're under the Age of Consent, which means you are not legally old enough to… to do it. It would be illegal, and I could go to jail if I… If we… Flustered, he shook his head in anguish "But that's not the main reason. Jesus, Ellie, you shouldn't ask _any_ man such a thing. That's not the way it works. Anyway. The main reason is, _my_ main reason is, you are family to me, like you are my sister; you know that." He shrugged, "In a way – I guess I should be honoured that you should ask me, of all people, but oh God – Ellie, I would do anything for you, babe, but that is one thing I couldn't. I can't. I won't. Anyway, that **word**, that language, that's not how it happens. The way it happens is when you love someone and someone loves you and you both want to make love together, that's when it happens, like when you get married. Making Love. Making **Love**. Not" He hesitated to use the word softly, shaking his head, "not 'fuck' – that's what dogs do in the street, random, animal, no love, no mutual feeling." She looked at her feet. "So you don't love me?" He shook his head sadly "Oh Ellie, oh yes, I do love you, very much. But not like that. Oh God no." And he knew there was more he needed to say, more he wanted to try to explain, but the young girl turned head down and hurried out of the room and he heard her fast steps down the stairs and out the back somewhere. He could hear her calling the dog outside. Jakob shook his head as if to clear it. Should he go and find her, to try and explain more clearly? (But how could he explain any clearer than he had?) Problem Solving was something they taught you at the college – but how could anyone prepare you for this? If only...

Thank God nothing had happened between them, because he now heard the crunch of gravel on the drive as the Dodge returned, and as he carried his duffle out to the top of the stairs, Andrew and Mrs.Turner came in the front door. Andrew was carrying a large square carton printed Drake & Newstead, and grinning. "No time to tart this up with ribbons, this is yours, a present for you, to help you become civilised down there in that Rasky jungle." Mrs. Turner was laughing at them. "We decided to help you with your culture appreciation, Jakob. It's a small record player." Jakob didn't know what to say, or think. Andrew enthused, "Just plug in and play, and we've started you off with a couple of favourite records to begin your big collection." But while he was explaining something about the records, Jakob protested "But hey no, I can't accept that. No, really, it's too much. No, please." Mrs.Turner said "Where's Elizabeth, she'll love this. We've got you a classical record which has got Chopin one side, and Beethoven the other, including *Für*

Elise." Andrew added "And to keep you sane, the other – my choice – the second record, is of Hank Snow, *'The Singin' Ranger and his Rainbow Ranch Boys'.* That was my idea; a bit of Western to balance the Culture. Especially as Hank Snow's record is called *'I'm Movin' On'.* Appropriate, hey? No argument mate, this is what we want to give you as a farewell gift, and (teasing him, Blask's favourite expression) 'it is what it is'. Where is Lizzie, by the way; did you play tennis?" Jakob hesitated – there was no-one he could talk to about that strange episode at the guestroom door. Had it really happened? Had he imagined it? No; no-one could imagine such a thing, even about as wild a child as Elizabeth. But tennis, yes, he brought his mind back. "Yes, we played tennis and she beat me, of course. I think she's taken Simba for a walk." He thought, I wonder if she's all right, after my rejection. I hope I didn't hurt her. I wish I could explain (but then I did that, didn't I?). Andrew went on, "Then she'll miss the fun about the records, because we've got to go, if we expect to catch that plane South we're booked on. You'll just have to write to her and tell her about *Furry Elisa".* They looked around for Elizabeth and Simba, but they were nowhere to be seen. "Please tell her I'm sorry I missed her," Jakob told Mrs Turner.

Mrs Turner clung to Andrew at the airport, her eyes wet. "I know you hate writing letters, Andrew, but please, please write a few lines, won't you, please darling." And he was embarrassed and noncommittal. Jakob went to shake hands with Mrs Turner, but she enveloped him in her arms. "Oh Jakob, it's been so good to have you with us each time. Please keep in touch, won't you. You know there's always a welcome for you here." Oddly enough, Jakob himself felt his eyes moisten. "You've been so good to me; thank you, thank you." Apart from the tannoy announcement, the plane ran up each of its propellers in turn briefly, and taxied closer to the gate. The boys joined the line of passengers walking to the plane, some of whom turned at the top of the stairs to wave back at the departure building.

"Well goodbye Canberra, goodbye Clink. I wish I could say sorry to be leaving" Andrew said as they located their seats in the half-empty plane. Blask added, "The surprising thing to me, was Thunderbum coming to the guardroom to say goodbye and shake hands when we left." "Not so surprising, I think he had a soft spot for you." "Yeah? Well, he had a funny way of showing it, making my life hell for four years." "Not really. Don't forget, he stopped you from getting booted out that time, over the Greek cafe business." "I don't forget. And that was you, who saved me. And like he said, I owe you enormously for that." "Anyway, what you said about making your life hell for four years, join the queue. That wasn't just you, that was every man Jack of us. And he's probably doing the same now for the next lot of poor bastards." They laughed, and the stewardess asked them to please secure their seatbelts. Andrew seemed excited "So mate – now on to our new adventures?" But Jakob was thinking again about poor Ellie, and having to leave her without – without what? Explaining? Consoling her? He wished he could have given her a comforting hug. But even that might have been unwise.

The Platoon

At the Reinforcement Holding Unit in the Japanese town of Hiro, the olive-green army bus with its white star sat outside the orderly room with its engine idling. Already several soldiers with leave passes had chosen seats inside while others were still assembling, when Platoon Sergeant Mason appeared, shouting: "Alright you lot, everybody out and fall in". There was a chorus of groans, and somebody complained: "Sarge, the bus is ready to go". But he countered: "The bus will go when I say so, and *if* I say so, so shift your arses and get fell in". And when a few of the soldiers inside the bus seemed reluctant to give up their preselected seats, he added: "And the longer you take to fall in, the longer you hold everybody else up, so move it!" The men de-bussed, fell into line and automatically corrected straight dressing. When all were present (including a latecomer, Adams, who ran from the barracks still getting dressed), the sergeant scanned them for defaults and continued his parade-ground voice: "Right. What a useless shower you are, stand up straight! Now get this. The Kure bus - *This bus* – on its return back here, will leave the corner of Nakadori where it drops you off, at twenty-three hundred hours exactly – got that? Nakadori is a main street. 2300 hours on the dot – at the corner of Nakadori where it drops you off. When you get out, remember where it is. That's where you have to be at twenty-three hundred. No later. Do not be tempted to miss it, because you will be on jankers for 30 days after the MPs find you, beat you up, put you in the slammer, and hand you over to me for real punishment. Do not come back in any unfit condition – yes, you listen especially, Peach – because tomorrow, are you listening, McKenzie? Tomorrow, you will all be route-marching in full battle gear to the top of Mount Yoshimatsu and back, and you will need all your strength without hangovers and needing to spew on the way. Goes without saying, you will behave yourselves tonight like true soldiers of my platoon and not lose control, get paralytic, or involved in punch-ups with Americans, Vandoos, Provosts, or any other low forms of pond-life". (A few laughs) "You will look after each other. You will

136

watch out for your mates. If you are lucky enough to have intimate congress with a Japanese of the female variety, you will take suitable precautions with your Blue-Light Outfit the army has so kindly equipped you with, otherwise you will probably cop a painful dose, and after you spend an agonising week in BCGH Urology Ward pissing fish-hooks and razorblades, you will have missed your draft with your mates, plus you will front the Colonel here and get heavily fined for self-inflicted, and have VD listed on your AB83 so that no decent female will be game to have anything to do with you, and your mother will be disgusted; right, Corporal Whan?" "True, Sarge." "And even worse, you would miss the Korea draft and wind up in another platoon with useless no-hopers you don't know, and who don't know you and love you like we do. He pretended to cross himself like a priest: "So bless you my sons, dismiss." But he added to Corporal Whan, "And if you go near the Flemington Bar, tell my mate Matsunaga that I expect him to do the right thing and look after my men."

And on their way towards Kure city centre, there was a shared sense of high excitement as the bus rolled down the main road from Hiro, lots of laughter and loud talk. "You've been here before, Macka, what's it like?" (Macka had been a Corporal in the Occupation Force, but had re-enlisted as a Private for Korea) "*Ichi-ban*, son, number one, better than any leave town you been in. Hundreds of bars and beer halls, lots of souvenir shops to relieve you of your hard-earned." "What about girls?" "Oh yes, I think there are one or two girls, as well, if you look hard." They laughed, knowing that the city was filled with good-time Japanese girls looking to make a few Yen. The ones who identified themselves as "*Mo-ga*" an abbreviation of '*modan garu*' (modern girl), the ones who spoke a few phrases of English, who dressed and made-up in the American style, who understood what soldiers wanted, and were prepared to negotiate to supply it.

"Barnsey says that they will do anything for you, the Jap girls; is that right?" "Yes mate, they are very willing, whether it's a cuppa tea, a massage and a Turkish bath, or if it's a Round-The-World-Everything for five thousand Yen." "What's that, Macka?" "What; Round the World? Well, imagine everything you ever dreamed of a girl doing to you, or letting you do to her, that sort of covers it." "Jesus, for five thousand yen; what's that, only five quid?" And Macka, being a man of the world and knowing that whether it was five hundred Yen or five thousand, once a man had shot his bolt it made no difference – it was all in the mind; that greatest sex organ of all, and whether it was worth it, depended on the anticipation, the memory, and the tale to tell everyone for ages afterwards, big-noting it.

The youngest soldier, Timmy, fresh-faced like a schoolboy, hanging on every word from the seat behind, asks: "But Mike, what about the Red Cross Leave Centre up at the Hospital where Sarge told me I should go?" "Well it's alright son, yeah, if that's where he wants you to go, I think you should do what he says; he knows best. You get free tea, coffee, Cokes, and stuff to eat, and lots of games; you know – table tennis, billiards, card-games, magazines, all that, and the Red Cross dames are nice and friendly, even write letters home for you, but there's no alcohol, mind, so, well it can be a bit quiet." Peachy pipes up: "What about the white dames, you know, the British nurses and that, up at BCGH?" [Brit Com General Hospital]. Nude-Nut laughs, "You mean the round-eyed chicks?" Macka replies "Off limits, mate, don't waste your breath. Lookee but no touchee. Anyway, most times they won't talk to anything lower than a Captain, the stuck-up bitches. Not worth the effort. If you want female company, better off with a Jap sheila, at least they are democratic." Crowe asks: "But about what Sarge said, have they all got VD?" "I dunno, mate, most of them are clean – at least I think they probably are – they look after themselves - but you have to be careful, like he said. Keep the muzzle of your weapon covered and you should be alright." And the subject turned to other army towns, and the action on Saturday leave nights. "Back at Kapooka, when we went to town in Wagga Saturday nights, we used to call the nurses' quarters there the "Bulk Store" – always in with a chance there." "Yeah, but that was back there in Oz, not up here.

The army protects their nurses up here; has to, you can imagine how the poor bloody nurses get propositioned here all the time, with a new reinforcement group turning up every coupla weeks, and the soldiers all trying to get a bit. Not worth the effort mate, stick with the *musumés*." And Crowe sighed: "Yeah I hear what you're saying Macka, but sometimes I would just like to meet some <u>nice</u> girls, for a change; you know the kind of girls I mean." Macka laughed "Son, you are dreaming. You are a character in the wrong book. Don't forget you are just a fkn soldier, and nice girls don't have anything to do with us soldiers. OK? Simple reason? As far as females are concerned, soldiers are only after one thing. True. Fact of life, init? Second; soldiers are here today and gone tomorrow, which is why soldiers are only after one thing. Third; soldiers are only meant for digging holes and getting shot at, not providing a home and family, and mowing the grass, which is what nice girls think about. So thank your lucky stars that we are in a great leave town full of friendly willing girls, cheap beer and music, and you got money in your kick." Then Peachy asked, pretend-seriously, frowning: "Macka, is it true what they say, that Jap pussy is not up-and-down, but side-to-side?' And the group roared with laughter, until the old-timer said: "I wouldn't know, son, me cherry-boy." More laughter - 'cherry' means virgin in army speak. Macka continued: "But I do know one thing; this is an army town, and soldiers like us have been dipping their wicks here from Nakadori to *Ju-san-chome* since 1945, so if there is a cherry girl in this town, she is still in her pram." More laughter.

"Hey Corp; where is this Flemington Bar that Sarge always raves about?" "I'll show you – that's where I'm headed anyway. It's as good as any of them, and the Jap boss, Sarge's mate Matsunaga, will give us a good price, otherwise in some joints you'll be paying two hundred yen for a bottle of Kirin, and your money will soon be gone."

Andrew

You would think, wouldn't you, that after graduation as a newly commissioned officer, your first regimental posting would be an exciting, reasonably enjoyable time? Especially if you, like me, were looking forward to actually being a professional army officer with all its perks and rewards; and in my case, getting away from that Canberra web where there was always the looming influential shadow of my father working in the nearby defence department, who even seemed to have connections with senior staff at the College. Back at Clink, there was always the thought that he was able to keep an eye on my behaviour and progress, however much I determined not to let it interfere with my life, and my relationship with my colleagues.

Well, that was the expectation. But as soon as I, and others of my fellow graduates, arrived at the recruit training battalion, we woke up to the shock of being barely-tolerated, inexperienced, despised, junior members of that officers' mess, treated with undisguised contempt by our new CO, Lt Colonel Badger. We, (and there were six of us fresh out of Duntroon – Peters, Spencer, Vickery, Clark, Nicholson and me – all Infantry graduates) found ourselves given the status of inexperienced new boys, to be chivvied, criticised, sneered at, and generally given the worst of any situation Badger controlled. This meant that even while we were trying to gain our spurs as platoon commanders hoping to influence recruits, we were constantly being undermined and harassed in front of the other ranks we tried to lead. At first, I thought it might be because of me – that Badger had had some departmental experience of my father which then reflected on me, and he did in the early stages of my arrival make some reference to me 'having connections' – but then it soon became evident that it was a common attitude to each of us new graduates, and he had just decided to make our lives hell as much as possible. A bit like the first year of hazing bastardry we all endured by the Senior Class when we first arrived at Clink, and similar to that, we found that other, more senior subalterns in the new mess tended to fall in with Badger's bullying and showed us no sympathy. Although we were serving officers, we were made aware that we had a long way to go to be accepted by Badger and some of his staff. Inescapable drill, route marches, frequent duty officer appointments, even the disappointment of sharing between two of us of a batman, when we expected a batman each. At least we had our own individual rooms in the officers' barracks.

Batman, *batmen*. I know, the appointment of an officer's 'batman' was an archaic privilege, a left-over from the British Army when officers were already from a supposedly upper class who brought their personal servants with them into the army, to forage for them, attend to their horse, look after the officer's elaborate uniforms and equipment, decant their wine. We learned about this in Clink, when Old Bob took us for a class in mess procedure and tradition. "Batmen," he said, "are a dying institution, probably long overdue for revision or extinction. No doubt one day soon, the provision of a batman for an officer will be officially discontinued, except for senior ranks as a sort of aide-de-camp/cum/secretary. No good reason for you young poodle-fakers to be given the services of a military servant, just because it was done for years over in Blighty. We follow a lot of British military tradition, but fortunately we tend to be a bit more republican this side of the water. However, if your Commanding Officer decides to award you the privilege of a batman, here are the ground-rules.

One: you are <u>not</u> being given a servant. Servants do not exist in this man's army. Two. You may be given the assistance of a batman in order to redirect your time to properly running a unit (which is a fulltime job anyway), saving you from wasting time over polishing brass and boots. In most cases, your batman would be selected from a group of volunteers, chosen for their skill at maintaining uniforms and equipment at a high level, i.e. brass and bullshit. Your batman – if you are fortunate enough to get one – will be first and foremost, always a regular serving soldier able to take the place of any fighting man at a moment's notice. Your batman may be your driver, if you have one. Or your bodyguard, if you need one, or your messenger in the field. Three. If you <u>get</u> a batman, you will not abuse the privilege by treating him badly. You will not become *Matey-matey* with him like your best friend, but your relationship with him will be professional and military, so that there is nothing for anyone to criticise or complain about."

So; if we had already had any imaginary expectations of being brought a nice whisky-soda while our route-march feet were soaking in a welcome hot tub provided by our attentive bearer, nice though that might have been, it was not going to happen. There were other things to worry about at Badger's hands. At one stage we six new officers had a 'secret' meeting to discuss the situation (at a weekend pub in the countryside away from camp – where, with the stupid State drinking laws, we had to sign in as bona-fide travellers) – at which we let off a lot of steam, but decided eventually that we were mature adults who could handle any adversity including the juvenile behaviour of this so-called senior officer. After all, we agreed, it can't be forever, and if we could survive four years of Thunderbum's discipline, we could handle anything. In my case, I could only shake my head sadly and envy Jakob's posting at the RAASC School not so far away from the School of Inf, where it sounded as if he was a popular welcome member of their officers' mess, and was busy learning the important techniques of army transport and supply in a more leisurely pace than we were. Jakob and I managed to meet up a few times to compare notes, and he commiserated with us on our bad luck getting 'Badgered'. But he agreed that the only thing to do was persevere.

Jakob

Jakob's batman, Private Shrubsell, was eager to please. He realized early that being appointed batman to an officer at the Supply & Transport School was a nice job, which is why he volunteered for it, instead of being an ordinary driver. A way to manipulate the system, as long as he was careful to always satisfy the officer to whom he was allocated. It enabled Shrubsell to avoid many fatigues and parades, always explaining – if he had to - that his special duties were such that he was forced to march to a different drum. The duties were really not onerous. All he really had to do was basically 'housekeep' for his appointed officer, which was a piece of cake. Lieutenant Blask was a tidy man, so that he was not hard to look after. By the time Blask had showered, shaved, and gone to breakfast, Shrubsell was able to make his boss's bed, tidy the room, and take the usual small amount of laundry to the washroom with his own gear. And in the evenings when Blask returned to quarters, Shrubsell would meet him with clean ironed laundry, and relieve him of his boots and belt for polishing and blancoing ready for the next day. Not much else. In the afternoons when Shrubsell would normally have to be doing squad drill or manoeuvres, he could explain to his NCO that, sorry, he had to starch and iron more officer's gear in the laundry – which was a great excuse, not always true, and a nice place to listen to the radio and the cricket, or the races. Particularly the races. Shrubsell was a punter.

There was no reason why he should personally intercept Blask's mail from the officers' mess anteroom where it was delivered, but to Shrubsell, there were three good reasons for him to intervene – one, it enabled him to show Lieutenant Blask that he was on the ball and proactive in anticipating duties, even those which were not totally required; and two, it made the mess staff think that Blask himself had asked Shrubsell to do it (because batmen were normally not given access to the officers' mess); and three, it enabled Shrubsell to quickly assess what kind of mail Blask was receiving, sometimes in the form of those official khaki departmental circular memo envelopes which carried a list of recipients who would sign against their name and forward to the next on the list; and which were helpfully unsealed, so that a quick private peek could reveal to even a humble Private like Shrubsell, what was going on, of which he would normally not be aware, and could sometimes be of value. Information could always be useful. Any information. You never knew what could come in handy.

One of the pieces of Blask's mail this day was a private letter addressed in neat handwriting. No return address on the back, no indication of its origin, except the Australian stamp. Shrubsell couldn't read the postmark. A girl, perhaps, by the handwriting. Maybe family? Nobody knew anything about Lieutenant Blask's family. Probably foreign with a name like that, although Blask himself was as Aussie as you can get. He never said much, and didn't seem to have any special friends in the mess. Shrubsell wished that he could develop some sort of closer relationship with his officer other than The Duty, but he was not given any encouragement to do it. Jakob Blask was a serious and private person, and very keen on fitness. He was always up very early, going to the gym or for long runs before his shower, and someone said that he had won prizes at Duntroon for rugby, or was it boxing? Maybe both. He was certainly built for it. Shrubsell hoped that someday, Lieutenant Blask might need a favour which Shrubsell could provide, and that might give him an edge. You know, 'you scratch my back, and I'll scratch yours', sort of thing.

The letter, when Jakob came to open it, he recognized immediately being from Elizabeth, Andrew's little sister, and he was smiling to himself in perplexed memory of the girl as he began reading it.

<'Dear Jakob' he read, 'Please hear me out before you tear this up. I am so, so sorry. You know why. I am terribly embarrassed, and know that you will despise me for my behavior back at Belconnen that day you left. Oh God I could shrivel up. Please forgive me. I am particularly sorry because it was your last day here (I dread to think your last day here ever?) and I did not then get a chance

144

to say goodbye, and I am afraid I might not ever see you again. I know what I did or said was probably unforgivable, but I am pleading with you to forgive me anyway as a stupid 14 year old kid. What you did and said was right, of course. Please can we wipe the slate clean and start again as the friends we were before that? I sincerely hope that this address reaches you, and I don't deserve it, but I wish you might write back to me sometime. Please. Yours affectionately, "Ellie".'>

Shrubsell did read the letter later, when Blask was out on an air supply exercise at Mangalore airstrip, (loading and unloading a battered DC3 which they called the 'bully beef bomber'. Shrubsell, snooping, found the letter still in its opened envelope tucked into Blask's leather compendium in the desk drawer, and when he read it (and re-read it) he wondered if he had discovered something. It was obviously from a girl, 'Ellie', who was – or had been – 14 years old during some kind of relationship with Blask. But wasn't that illegal? You know; age of consent and all that? And why did the girl sign her name with inverted commas; was that not her real name? After memorizing the details, Shrubsell made sure that the letter was folded the way he found it and returned carefully back inside the compendium exactly as before. He smiled, wondering if he had discovered something valuable. File that away. You never know, do you?

"Dining-In Night". One of those formal Officers' Mess dinners when everybody – even non-residents - is supposed to front up. All dressed up, Number Ones, the mess dining room lit up like a Christmas tree with gleaming silverware and candles, places set with more cutlery than you can poke a stick at, polished brass, leather shining, hand-calligraphed menus, mess orderlies in those pre-Federation uniforms someone dug up from the Corps museum. Lots of loud conversations and smoke in the Mess bar-room first, glasses in hand during the 1930 for 1800 'meet & greet', when everyone checks the printed seating plan to see where they will be placed (and maybe whom they will be stuck next to). Then – where did they borrow him from? – a fully-rigged Scots piper, tuned up and marching in from the dining room to escort the Colonel and PMC in to – what was that traditional tune? '*Wait For The Wagons*', of course, what else, the Regimental march; and the rest of the officers in turn by rank (some hastily finishing their drink because it might be a while until the next one) and the slow settling of places at the table by recognition of place-cards. They all stand by their chairs obediently waiting until the occupants of the head table sit, and for the formal timing of the event. Yes, event, because it is not just a dinner; it is a parade. And compulsory for all the mess members, whether they normally eat dinner in the mess or not. (For many of them live in married quarters and only frequent the mess at midday or after work.) Despite the planning and worried efforts of the catering manager and kitchen staff, the actual food (which is excellent and beautifully presented) takes second place to the formality, the speeches, the toasts, the guests responding to their introductions. Each course accompanied by the matched wine, each course served with practised timing and flourish, each speech announced by the usual spoon on glass to achieve silence, and as part of the tradition Blask, being the mess junior and hence "Mr Vice", required to propose the toast to the King.

Back in the mess proper after the dinner, the CRASC sought him out. "Jakob, there's someone I want you to meet." The Colonel was a jovial large man, with a hint that his dress uniform was fighting to cover a recent expansion. Blask had been introduced to him before the dinner, at the School Chief Instructor's office to which he had been summoned, when the Colonel had officially welcomed him to the Corps. "Jakob," he had said, "we are all aware that this so-called war up in Korea might fizzle out at any time, and I would like you to get what experience there is out of it while it lasts. So I hope you will not object to a posting to BCFK." Jakob glowed "Certainly not, sir. I was really

146

hoping there might be a chance to get up there." "Well, your specialist school course here is about finished, so I'll get Major Harris to set that in motion. Now, most of the S and T up there is handled by the British and the Yanks, but we still have a few units operating, so you should get the experience you need. Most of our chaps up there have been in the Occupation Force in Japan, which means most of them went directly up there from war service in the Pacific Islands. Very few of our officers have benefitted from RMC training like yours, but they have a wealth of experience of war transport and supply, so I'm hoping that both you and they will get the best out of each other's background when you work together." Anyway, tonight, I want you to meet Bernie Rogers, Captain Rogers. He has not long come back from BCOF, and will be able to put you in the picture." The Colonel looked over heads around him. "Here he is, another old Balikpapan Boy like me. Bernie! Bernie, over here, I want you to meet Jakob. (Jakob, how do you spell your name again?)" "Blask, sir." He spelled it (again). The Colonel introduced him to a big sandy-haired man. "Bernie, this is the young chap I told you about, Jakob Blask. He's going to be up there in BCOF next month, and I want you to put him in the picture, a bit of background OK?" The room was loud with after-dinner laughter and conversation, and the sandy-haired Captain pulled Jakob aside. "Listen, we'll never hear one another in this shambles, and they'll get rowdier by the minute if I'm any judge; let's grab a drink and get away. Are your quarters nearby?" "Sure, next building. What are you drinking, sir?" "Cut out the sir for a start, I'm Bernie. And it's Scotch, thanks. See if Archie will let us have a bottle; save a few trips" They sorted out the drinks and took them to Jakob's room, where they relaxed in comparative quiet. Bernie looked around, nodding. "Nice place. Army barracks are getting better every time I come here. Did Jimmy say where he's posting you?" "Who?" "Jimmy, the colonel." "Not really. He mentioned the 119 Transport Platoon, but he said I'll probably be moving around a bit." "Good unit, One-One-Nine, that'll be in Area 5, Kure, Japan. Nice post. You'll find Japan's wonderful, but Korea's the pits. Amazing contrast – Korea, one minute you're in a war zone, worst poorest country in the world, ration packs, shocking climate from one extreme to the other, have to keep your head down with bastards trying to kill you; next thing you're in Japan, wonderful place, peace and prosperity, wine women and song, everything going like clockwork. I'd go back up there in a flash. Mind you, wasn't always like that. When the war first broke out in Korea, and Australia decided to get involved, a bunch of us in BCOF had to prep things over there before we could send our newly organized battalion over. We had to form a base unit to solve the problems of working within such a mixed army of Koreans, Yanks, Brits and every Tom Dick and Harry with different weapons and supplies and systems. We all spoke English" He laughed, "well sort of – anyway, we managed somehow. There were only about 60 of us. We were called "AUSTFIKMA" – 'Australian Formation In Korea Maintenance Area' – and our first task was to set up a location in the Pusan perimeter, holding out on the port. It was chaos. Pusan was crammed with vehicles, personnel, war equipment, refugees, and remnants of troops who had retreated from the Reds' invasion, even deserters. We were the odd ones out, but we persevered, commandeering a site, getting workers, constructing buildings, security fences, transport, connecting power, water, rail and port connection, you know, the whole caboodle. Fortunately, a lot of us had been doing much the same sort of thing in the other war – yeah, the second world war – so we knew what worked and what didn't. Everyone thought we were going to have to evacuate, like Dunkirk. There were no trains to begin with. Pusan docks were chock-a-block with all sorts of craft, and the inadequate local airstrip was a left-over from Japanese days, cracking under the strain of heavy supply planes coming in, and being patched up by civilians with baskets of rocks between aircraft landings – it was bedlam. Somehow we arranged assembly of items not common to the U.S. – our-calibre ammo, ordnance, spare parts, miscellaneous 'A' Services, a million things that nobody thought of. Even bloody tea. Imagine Aussie soldiers fighting without a brew. Amazing what you can do with goodwill and co-operation, plus the three B's; 'Bullshit Baffles Brains'. We charged some things up to Ned Kelly – the poor bloody Yanks were run off their feet. By the time our 3rd Battalion arrived in Korea, we were able to get them well set up and railed to Taegu in the new counter-attack, while we arranged catch-up convoys of 2½ ton 6x6s towing 17 pounder anti-tank guns 120 miles in groups of 25, over primitive dirt roads, sometimes subject to ambush, heading into a war."

Jakob shook his head. "Crikey, never knew any of this." "Son, that was only the beginning – it would have been easier if the war had been static – but MacArthur cut the North Koreans off at the pass, and then we chased them all the way back up the peninsula to the Yalu river, with us trying to keep up with the bloody supplies." He laughed. "Front lines were a bit fluid in those days. We even drove one truckload of stuff into the midst of the enemy at one stage, and fortunately, the North Koreans were baffled by the uniforms and thought we were their friendly Russian allies, so our boys managed to get away with it and escape. But soon the bloody Chinese came into the war, and buggered things up."

Blask was astounded. "They don't teach you any of this stuff – either at Clink, or here at the school." "Well that's why I'm here, isn't it, to put you in the picture a bit." Jakob asked, "OK, and what's this 'old Balikpapan Boys' stuff? Was that New Guinea?" Bernie smiled, shaking his head a bit. "Yeah, Jimmy and I were there, he was a Captain then, and I was just a baggy-arsed Sergeant. No, not New Guinea, although that's where we started, from Morotai. But no, Balikpapan was Borneo. Our last battle of the Pacific war, the 7th Divvy did the fighting, we just landed them there, moved them, armed them, fed and watered them, supplied them, kept them going as they cleared about 5 thousand fanatical Japs from well-defended jungle fortresses, tunnels, and bunkers over a couple of weeks. Mad bastards those Japs. Knew the war was finished, but determined to die for their emperor. We had to keep our heads down."

"In Japan, did you ever get to Hiroshima or Nagasaki?" Blask asked. "Hiroshima, yes. And you will too, it's just up the road a bit from our base in Kure." Bernie shook his head again. "When we first saw it, it was cactus, flattened, wiped out for miles. Mind you, a lot of Kure was too, it had been a leading naval base and navy school in Hiroshima Prefecture, so it got a lot of pasting in bombing raids. But Hiroshima City was different. Stopped the war, no doubt about it. The Yanks had been relentlessly fire-bombing Japan for weeks, without result, until then. But Hiroshima woke Japan, and the world, up with a jolt. Just imagine; One plane. One bomb. One city. Shocked everyone. The war couldn't go on, at that rate. They had to chuck in their cards."

The nightclub in Melbourne was a poky, dark little basement place downstairs from a wool and grain merchants office at the fringe of the CBD, its entry semi-lit by an obscure neon sign announcing "Pietro's". Probably the darkness was intentional, to hide the shabbiness. It would be perfect if you were making a film about an American speak-easy way back in the 30s, although this time there was no identifying peephole in the door; you just went in to a cloakroom attendant, up to a lectern where the maitre-d' checked your reservation or directed you to a table.. It was intimate, with only about 20 small tables, each with an electric candle in a glass holder in centre, not to lighten the place up, more for atmosphere. The tables, most of which were occupied, faced a small dance floor, which was overlooked by a band alcove, where a male trio played Blues under subdued spotlights.

Jakob had trouble finding the place, and when he arrived, he had to apologise to Andrew and the two ladies sitting with him, for being late. "Sorry mate, the taxi driver had never heard of it, either that, or he just wanted a bigger fare by driving around for a while until I managed to spot the sign." They shook hands as Andrew stood up. "Jake, this is Rita, remember her from Canberra?" Jakob's eyes lit up "Of course. Rita, how nice to see you again! What a wonderful surprise. How are you?" "I'm fine, Jakob. And this is my friend Claire. Claire, this is Jakob, an army colleague of Andy's." Jakob shook hands with the second girl, and asked "Are you from Canberra too, Claire?" She laughed "No, I'm a Melbourne girl. Rita and I work together at the Tiv." Rita explained "Jakob, we are both dancers at the Tivoli." Andrew was trying to gain the attention of a waiter, and the band ended its set with a flourish, and applause. Blask laughed, addressing himself again to Rita "What; dancers at the Tivoli? That's great. I sure wouldn't have expected that from knowing you back then, Rita." "No, and nobody else would have, either. When I came to Melbourne, it was supposed to be to learn short-hand and typing at business school, but I sort of had a change of mind. Had to persuade my Daddy. Do you remember him? When I was a kid, I always wanted to be a ballet dancer, and this is ... well, it's dancing of a kind, to music, in front of an audience, so..." Andrew meanwhile, had attracted a waiter, and was taking orders, "What's everybody having? Will I get a bottle of wine?" "Could I have a G and T?" Rita asked. "Me too," said Claire. "What about you, Jake?" Andrew asked. "A Scotch would be nice." "Rocks?" "Great." "That'll do me too. We'll start with that." When Andrew finished with the waiter, Jakob accused him "You didn't tell me about Rita; that's a nice surprise. I didn't even know you kept in touch, you two." Rita laughed "There's a lot you don't know, Jakob." And she exchanged a look with Andrew which spoke volumes. Jakob apologized to Claire "Sorry Claire, of course you are a pleasant surprise too, not just Rita." Claire said "When Rita said you were a couple of army officers, I was expecting you to be in uniform." Jakob said "Are you disappointed? I could go back and change." They laughed. Andrew added "I'll let you into a secret. If we were in uniform, they would automatically load the prices another 50%. That's another reason we wear mufti when we socialize, and it keeps us out of a few arguments too." Jakob continued "Dancers at the Tivoli, eh? That's probably hard work. Lots of training, rehearsals?" "Yeah, all of the above" Rita replied.

"Plus a manager who likes to be difficult. That's why Claire and I look forward to our days off. At the moment we're on two days free, and then it's back to the grind for another fortnight." Jakob asked "Are you an escapee from typing and business school too, Claire?" She laughed. "No, I'm an escapee from University. First year Arts. Taking a year off to grow up and travel."

"What's it like; dancing at the Tiv?" "Well, sometimes it's fun. We're called the *'Dancing Debonnaires'* – there are six of us. We have a manager, who keeps on promising us to put us on a gig with the singers, to Hong Kong and Macau, but he won't be pinned down on it." Their dinner arrived, and their drinks.

While they were eating their dinner, the band leader at the mike introduced a comedian named Billy Bristow. He was a short man wearing a loud check suit, and a matching trilby with an upturned front brim. "Hello folks. Don't let me disturb your meal," he began. "They always put me on during dinner on purpose. If the meal is good, you won't notice how bad I am, and if the food is lousy, I'll take your mind off it, so everybody wins, OK?" The drummer, who had remained on the dais with him, rewarded every joke with a *'boom tish'*. The comedian got some applause, and continued on with his patter. "At least he's different," Rita said. "We have to put up with our resident comedian whose routine we know off by heart, every one of his corny jokes, plus you have to keep away from his wandering hands, backstage." Claire said "Unfortunately, he is supposed to be the best part of our current show, according to the critics. The last newspaper review said: *'A clever, relaxed American comedian named Sammy Star, and a bright Chinese troupe of juggling acrobats saved the new Tivoli revue from mediocrity last night.'* Well, that's his opinion." Rita added "Not to mention the most brilliant dance troupe this side of Paris, how could the reviewer fail to mention that? He must have left before we came on."

The comedian continued in the background. It didn't matter what he said, there was always someone laughing at everything. The routine was not that funny. "There are these two Russian Colonels. Now before I go on, I don't want to offend anyone, so are there any Russian Colonels in the audience? Good, I hoped so. Right, so these two Russian colonels have been drinking away in their barracks, and decide to go outside for a wee-wee in the garden. It's night time, OK, and it's cold. And one Russian colonel says to the other: "Comrade Colonel, I wonder." The comedian puts on his stage Russian accent, full of rolling 'r's. "Vy is it, zat ven I pee, it sounds like the roaring Volga River flooding to fertilize the black plains below. But Comrade Colonel, ven <u>you</u> pee, it sounds like the gentle breeze across the city of Moscow? (Pause – but of course there is always someone laughing anyway, anticipating...) "And the other Colonel says; Comrade Colonel, maybe it is because I am pissing on your fur coat." *Boom tish.* There is one lady, all peroxide hair and jewelry and a too-short skirt at a table of six, whose laughter is like a squeal of delight, and the comedian loved it, of course, and played up to that. Rita says "He'll just about get his routine past the vice squad boys. I'm sure they're here as usual." The comedian continues "It's all relative. Talking about relatives, take my mother-in-law for example. Yes, please take her, someone!" (Laughter. And then some mother-in-law jokes). They finished their dinner, and the girls excused themselves to go and freshen up. Both men stood up, and then when the girls had gone, Andrew said "50/50 OK with you, Jake? Rita always wants to pay her way, but..." "No, that's fine, I expected that. Let me give you something now, what, a century?" "No mate. Let me settle up, and I'll tell you how much you owe me when we're back at camp." "You sure?" "Sure, that's fine. Anything happening at your school? "The usual. Although they are sending a few specialists up North. I keep trying, but no luck so far. What about your mob?" "Yeah, likewise. Two companies have gone up to Ingleburn to integrate with another battalion, otherwise, it looks like I'll be training new recruits here, unless I can somehow escape from The Badger – Korea sounds like a terrible place, what I've heard, but it might be my way out. By the way, where are you staying tonight?" "The YMCA as usual. Where are you...?" He caught Andrew's smirk "Don't tell me, you - and Rita? Jesus, you're a dark horse." Andrew looked pleased with himself, which he was. "Anyway Jake, what do you think of Claire for a blind date?" "Yeah, nice lady." But before they could enlarge on that, the ladies returned. The band had taken over from the comedian again, and were playing. Jakob remained standing from getting up when the ladies returned. "Claire, I'd like to ask you to dance, which always comes with a warning. And now that I know you are a *professional* dancer, it comes with a double warning – I can't dance." She laughed "Everyone can dance." "No, really." "Well, I'll show you. Come on." She rose and held out her hand to Blask. "Look, the floor is crowded, so this is going to be easy. The answer is, don't try to stride about. Try this. Just stand in one place and let your body move to the music. Feel the groove. Here, let me show you. Hold me like this." She returned his extended 'ballroom' hand and arm back to him. They moved closer together, her cheek near to his, his one hand holding her small hand at his chest, his other hand on her waist, her soft hip. He tried not to think too much about that soft hip. She continued "Now, just feel the music, the beat. You don't have to go anywhere, just sway, just. ." Jakob got the picture. He gulped. It wasn't the music, or her movements, it was the closeness of a woman, the scent of her, the softness of her hair brushing his face, the swaying of her dress against him. God, this was so sensual, wasn't it? She pulled her head back a little to look up at him. "See? That's not hard, is it?" (And the wicked thought crossed his mind, if I don't watch out, 'it' *will* become hard. Concentrate. Behave yourself.) "Claire laughed at him "See what I mean? You're a great dancer, Jakob. I don't know what you were complaining about."

"Can I see you safely home Claire?" Blask had said. She smiled at the formality of it. "Thank you Jakob, that's kind of you. It's not far," Claire said, "We could walk." Jakob had first suggested hailing a taxi, but she said "It's really quite close." "OK," he said, "that's fine, I'd like a walk, the club was a bit smoky." "I share an apartment with some others about five blocks away," she said.

Well, that made one thing clear, he was unlikely to get invited in, not that he had banked on it. "Other dancers?" He asked, smiling. "No, other students. Or at least some of them are, or were. We're all a bit uncertain about our careers." A well-lit but mostly empty green tram passed them, its wheels screeching metal at a curve, and the trolley pole flashed sparks as it negotiated a join on the electric overhead cable. "Where are you from originally," Claire asked. "Near Sydney. A place called Emu Plains, not that anyone has seen an emu there – at least not in living memory." They laughed. "What about you?" "Another little place nobody ever heard of," Claire said, "up in Western Victoria, called Wycheproof, where the wheat trains run up the middle of the main street." "That sounds like the kind of place a famous dancer might come from, in a publicity article." They laughed. "What's with the train down the main street?" "Well, the story goes, that the authorities would not pay for the extra land needed for a rail line, and they had a wide street big enough for bullock wagons to turn around in, so..." "Sounds logical." "And don't laugh, but the main street is called Broadway." He did laugh. "That sounds like the kind of place I should visit someday." "Well, it's not hard to find, at the edge of the Mallee, where the wheat silos stand out against those miles and miles of flat farmland. And every now and then, there's a huge dust-storm so that the sky is black, and the topsoil moves from one farm to the next." They walked easily now, laughing at everything, their footsteps echoing on the near-empty street. He didn't know when it began, but he realized that they were holding hands loosely as they walked.

Claire said "Do you mind if I ask you a personal question, Jakob?" "Sure, what is it?" "Well, hearing you and Andy talk about the possibility of maybe getting sent to Korea, to that war, and I've never met a soldier before to talk to, and you sound so casual about it, about the risk. The risk of being killed. I mean, why do soldiers die?" Jakob sort of smiled at the question, a bit puzzled. "Soldiers die, because enemy soldiers kill them." Claire shook her head, "No no, that's not what I mean. I mean why do soldiers join up? Why do they put themselves in that position, where someone would kill them? Or is it, that *they* don't put themselves in that position, but are ordered to; and they blindly follow their General's orders?" Now Jakob really smiled. "I don't think you know soldiers – at least Australian soldiers – they, we, don't ever just blindly follow orders. I mean, of course we follow orders, - we have to, that's our job - and sometimes we even question orders, to ensure that we understand the reason for them. But we all sign up to serve our country, that's what we are all for; and in the end we do what we are directed to do, and sometimes that requires us to face our country's enemies, which might mean that we could get killed." Claire shook her head, still not understanding "But don't you...? I mean, do you... do soldiers <u>want</u> to die?" "No, of course not. Nobody wants to die. I don't think any soldier makes that decision: '*Here I go, death or glory*'. I think it's more like the old car-smash principle where we always assume, we know it's not going to happen to me, is it? It's always the other person, in our case, the soldier next to me."

"I just can't get used to the idea of anyone, especially someone like you, or like Andy, signing up to be a soldier, whose main purpose is to kill someone"

Jakob was suddenly reminded of his mother, ages ago, dear Katie, objecting to him joining up, saying "*In a university, there will be not people shooting bombs at you, trying to kill you. That is the reason for armies, for soldiers.* Oh Mama. And yes, he couldn't argue, that he had just spent four years learning the most efficient ways to kill people, and not be killed himself. He shrugged "No argument, Claire. I am a soldier. A regular soldier, and that is what we are trained to do; to kill people if we have to, before they kill us, or kill you. That is what armies are for. To defend our country." "But," she floundered, "what has defending Australia, got to do with killing people away in a foreign place like Korea?" Frustrated, he scratched his head, searching for inspiration in the night sky. "Claire, the only way I can explain that, is to quote the Government's Forward Defence Policy – in other words, defending freedom and democracy everywhere, defeating aggression in our region, before it occurs here on our doorstep. Coming to the aid

156

of neighbours and allied nations who are in trouble – in the hope that they would aid us if we needed help. In the case of Korea, defending South Korea when they were invaded by the North." "Oh, Jakob, you sound like a Government spokesperson, that's just all government propaganda." "Do you think so? Maybe I'm not good at explaining." He paused, then went on. "Most of the soldiers I know, don't really want to fight to the death, but they can, and they will if they have to, because they know that's our purpose, what we're paid for, what we're trained for, and because we don't want you to have to defend yourself." "Me?" she queried, "I couldn't be a soldier. I couldn't kill anyone." "No, not you personally, but you; the Australian civilian population."

She persisted. "Anyway, what I was trying to say, is, if there weren't any soldiers, there wouldn't be any wars." "Ah, Claire, if only that were so. Soldiers do not start wars; they are only sent to fight them, and hopefully finish them." She seemed to think about that, but already Jakob wanted to get out of this subject. "Look Claire, let's not talk about it, please. I'm uncomfortable with this conversation. I was just enjoying the night and your wonderful company, and suddenly I'm deep into the philosophy of war and life and God knows what else. Can we try this some other time? That is, if I haven't turned you against me." "No it's me, Jakob, me and my university questioning and rebellion. Sorry. I didn't mean to put you on the griller. And yes, I would like to see you again, if you can bear it. I had a great evening, and thank you. I hope I haven't spoiled it." They had stopped at the entrance to an old rooming house with worn-hollow bluestone steps leading up to a stained-glass door. "This is it, Jakob." And Claire quickly stood on tiptoe and kissed him briefly on the cheek. "Goodnight, soldier." Jakob walked back to the city centre, much of it with a smile on his face, and it wasn't until he reached the YMCA, that he suddenly realized that he had no way of contacting Claire – he had forgotten to ask for her phone number or address. He laughed at himself. Idiot.

Andrew

After enjoying sex on the bed in Rita's St.Kilda flat, Andrew and Rita lay naked close together on their backs contentedly holding hands, facing the ceiling, coming back to reality. The room was dimly lit by a shaded lamp, and around the wall hung several of Rita's colourful revue costumes. His clothes were folded neatly on a chair, while hers were scattered on the floor, suggesting their hasty removal. Andrew said, musing "I wonder how Jake got on, with Claire." Rita turned her head towards him, reflecting his smile with one of her own "You mean; you wonder if he took her to bed?" "Well, sort of. They seemed to be getting along fine on the dance floor, and he did suggest escorting her home. Do you think Claire would have invited him in?" She tutted. "Dearest Andy, you are amazing. Here, you have just made love to me a minute ago, and already you are imagining other peoples' romantic lives. Aren't you satisfied with your own?" He laughed, "*Touché*. Sorry Rita, I didn't mean to insult you. You were wonderful. You are <u>always</u> wonderful. I thought the last fifteen minutes would have proved that." "Oh yes, you did, my lovely lover. No complaints there. In fact that was so good, I don't want to think about anything or anybody else for a while." They were each silent with their own thoughts for a second, then Rita mused "Anyway, about Claire. I don't think Jakob would be moving in; Claire shares her flat with three others – it's a bit crowded at times. Poor Claire. I didn't tell you before, but Claire has had a run of men who have treated her badly. A bunch of rats. Perhaps it's about time she met someone honorable like Jakob." Andrew grunted a short laugh. "Honorable? Jake would love that description. You know, he's a very modest person. He's quite shy, you know?" "I'm not surprised." Rita says "Back when you were at Clink, we all used to think Jakob was terrific; all the girls thought he was a dreamboat." "Until he bashed that idiot at the café that time and we got banned." She shook her head "No, not at all, we knew he was a super jockstrap at Duntroon, good at any sports, we assumed he was a tough guy, that was just another part of his image; that didn't really affect our opinion of him." "But...?" "Yeah, there was a 'But'. He didn't seem to be interested in girls, any of us girls, and between us, we assumed it might be because he was One of Them, you know." Andy laughed. "You mean...?" He wagged his head. "Yeah; well, if a man isn't interested in girls, it usually means one thing, doesn't it? That he is Homo." "You mean a horse's hoof?" "A what?" "A horse's hoof; a poof." "That is a terrible word, Andy. No. Yeah, anyway, that is basically what we thought." She paused. "*Is* he? One of them?" Andrew laughed, his hands spread "How would I know?" "Well, you're supposed to be his best friend; wouldn't you know?" "Oh, you mean – has he propositioned me?" Rita jabbed him with her elbow in affected annoyance "No, you idiot. But wouldn't a man's best friend know, if his mate was, you know, one of Them?" "I don't know" Andrew said seriously, "never really thought about it. Someone once said that they are about 10% of the male population, so it's theoretically possible that a tenth of the blokes at Clink were Poof-- sorry, Homosexual. But on the other hand, we were all selected as potential regular soldiers, so probably that might tilt the percentage more the other way. Anyway, let's face it, we were so stressed out all the time, as cadets we never had a spare minute to even think about sexual thoughts, so it would have been unlikely to come up." Rita giggled at him. Andrew queried "What? What now?" "What you said – something to *come up*." Andrew turned and wrestled with her, so that she squealed and twisted on the bed. "You're a naughty girl with a dirty mind, and I ought to spank you." The two naked young bodies played lovingly on the bed as they pretended wrestling, and suddenly Rita said "God. What is *That!*" pulling away slightly as she noticed his recovered swelling between them. "Oops, sorry miss," he laughed, "You must have disturbed him. '*Something came up*'." He attempted to hide it, push it down, but it sprang back, stiffening more. Rita was solicitous "Poor little chap. It would be a pity to ignore him now he's here again." And she twisted her body to climb over Andrew – still on his back - until she was kneeling upright either side of his waist, poised above "the little chap", which wasn't so little, now. She was looking down at Andrew with love in her eyes as she reached below her and grasped the object of her attention, guiding it to where she wanted it as she lowered herself slowly onto it, groaning, until she was totally impaled, swooning closed-eyes as she released her hold on it, rocking gently to obtain the depth and total sensation of feeling she wanted. "Oh Andy," she moaned softly. "Oh Andy." Andrew reached up from where he lay beneath her and held both of her breasts gently in his spread fingers as he moved his hips slightly to match Rita's rocking. "Oh God, Rita."

Letter from Blask to Andrew at School of Infantry:
<Dear Andy – Here's my cheque. That was a good night, wasn't it, and I enjoyed meeting Claire. I hope to see her again sometime, but I will have to get her phone or address details from you next time you see Rita. As I told you on the phone, the CRASC is arranging to send me up to BCFK (they call it "book-fook" here at the school) and I have been getting a brief on what might be involved with my posting. I have already had my first inoculations. Remember when I said this school was going to be a piece of cake, just expanding what I knew about vehicles from working at Mr. French's garage, plus what we did at Clink on all kinds of military transport, but I was surprised at how much we missed out on, and what was involved in it all. Last week, we spent a lot of time getting intimate with the "Tractor 30-ton GS 6x4" which is, to you useless infanteers, a beautiful 27 foot Thornycroft Antar tank transporter – a six-wheeler with a Rolls Royce Meteorite V8 engine. Admittedly, they didn't yet let me drive a Centurion onto the trailer, but they did let me play with a Matilda tank down at the Dysart Siding. God they are noisy (and hot) making me glad I didn't get selected for Armoured Corps. All the time I was cooped up in that tin box, I was wondering what it would be like in there receiving A-T fire. Much more fun was the course on DUKW amphibians, which we did at Lake Nagambie. By the way, I had a letter from your sister, and she begs me to get you to write to your mother. Please, Andy, do the right (write?) thing, you ungrateful son, your Mum is a wonderful lady and misses you. Now, on another subject, ... >

Farewells: 1. Aleksi

On the phone, on receiving Jakob's explanation of his departure to Korea from Sydney, Jakob's grandfather sounded lighthearted. "Of course you will come stay here. Of course. This your home now. How long you got, 'Kuba?" "Just four days. My plane leaves for Darwin Sunday midday." Pause. "What means that, *meday*?" "Mid Day. You know, middle of the day, noon, twelve o'clock." "Yeah yeah, got that. How do you come – you still got the Beeza?" (BSA) "No, Dziadzia, sold that a while back. No problem, train to Richmond, and then I get a taxi the last bit home." "No, no you won't, I collect you." Which he did, the same old truck, seemingly in the same old condition (watch out for that dangerous back spring in the passenger side of the bench seat.) Dziadzu had also asked, "What about girl friend? She come with you?" (I had made the mistake of telling him I was seeing Claire in one of my early letters) "No, Dziadza. No girlfriend at the moment."

It was too long and complicated to explain. Claire and Jakob had spoken only once after that night at the nightclub in Melbourne while he was at the training school. Another meeting should have been just before his new posting, when full of hope, he had booked a room in Melbourne at the Kerry Family Hotel for the weekend, (instead of his regular monastic cell at the YMCA) imagining/hoping that maybe, he might be able to persuade Claire to spend at least one night with him, but it hadn't worked out like that. There was not a 'next time'. The week he was hoping to meet her, Claire phoned him at the school Officers' Mess to say that she had been called away home to help look after her father, who had had an accident on his tractor. She said "Like you, it is a call of duty. Looks like I will be a farm girl again for a little while, but I'll be thinking of you, and waiting for your letters." He tried to imagine her again, in that wheat town where the train ran up the main street, but the image faded.

When Jakob arrived at the station, Dziadzu grinned, embracing Jakob roughly. "You looking good, the army feeding you well." Jakob laughed, and his grandfather continued mischievously as they drove off in that noisy vehicle, full of rattles "Anyway, I got some surprise for you." Jakob guessed "A new annexe, a new room?" Aleksi laughed, "No, 'Kuba, same room like always; I show you surprise when we get there."

And what a surprise it was. As they pulled into the driveway (as usual scattered with odd building materials and two loose barking dogs (which didn't seem to belong to anyone), a somehow familiar smiling woman came out from the main house, and Jakob was stunned to remember Anja Nowak, the lady from his mother's funeral. Jakob asked his grandfather, as they pulled in "Are Anja and Victor visiting?" But Dziadziu grinned and elbowed Jakob in the ribs, "Not visit. Not Wictor. Just Anja. Anja and me" (he wagged his grizzled head) "arrangement. Is the right word? Arrangement?" Who knew what the right word was, for this situation? It was later that evening, that Jakob was able to ask, and get a proper answer. What about Victor? This time it was Anja who explained. "Wictor, he gone back Europe" she said happily, spreading her hands, "with girlfriend." And that was all Jakob was likely to get. He had vaguely thought, from his mother's funeral, that Anja and Victor might be contemporaries of his grandfather, but strangely, now, Anja appeared much younger. And maybe his grandfather had become younger, too. He was certainly acting that way. The 'arrangement' seemed to be positive. Was this 'love'? Although the old man's jumble of dwellings was as chaotic as always, Jakob noticed that the living accommodation was now much better organised and cleaner; less like an untidy bachelor pad. And the meals which Anja served up were wonderful. During his stay, Jakob noticed that his sweet grandmother's hand-coloured photo portrait (which used to hang above Dziadziu's bed), was now stacked with other spare materials in a side store room.

The four days went quickly, as Jakob helped his grandfather – both of them stripped to the waist and sweating - to extend a side wall and replace roofing over the new space, both of them working hard, and well as a team. They didn't discuss Jakob's imminent departure overseas at all. It was only on the last day, the

Sunday, when Dziadziu drove Jakob to Richmond railway station in the truck (with Anja on the bench seat between them) that his grandfather made any reference to the Korean War. "'Kuba" he said, "be careful out there, them Chinks; come back again one piece, hokay?" And he added "Write letters." "Yes", Jakob said, "I'll write, same as always." And the lady, Anja, smiling, hugging his arm, said "You be safe, Jakob, OK?. Don't worry Aleksi, I look after him, you know." Jakob sighed as he boarded the train. This was his family now.

Farewells: 2. Rita

Andrew's farewell to Rita went on during several days after the disembarkation warning order went up. It was complicated by Andrew being transferred to the battalion build-up at Ingleburn in New South Wales, so that much of their 'conversation' (if you could call it that) was conducted either by letters or over the phone. Andrew was puzzled by how their relationship had deteriorated, become so serious, from the light-hearted and passionate times they enjoyed when he was in camp at Seymour, visiting Melbourne. Suddenly, it seemed, Rita had become almost possessive. What had he missed, some signal in something he had said, or was it still the argument they had had about his posting – or his rejection of the routine National Service Instructor posting? He had laughed about it, mentioning it only in passing when it happened – "You won't credit this, but my bloody old man is still trying to meddle in my affairs. He tried to get me posted to a routine training battalion, but I got wind of it early and nipped that in the bud". "But why?" Rita asked, seemingly annoyed. "Wouldn't that mean you would stay here, and we'd get to see each other often?" "Rita," he tried to explain patiently, "There is no way I am going to let him control my life – that finished when I graduated." "But wouldn't you go along with it anyway, if it means we would see each other more often?" "Well, that's the disadvantage. Yeah, I know. But we always knew that some time, I would get a regimental posting and have to go away, didn't we? But it won't be forever. Besides, we can write and phone, and look forward to when we can be together again, even if it's only on leave." Rita had shaken her head sadly, as if he really didn't understand. Which he obviously didn't. She kept on coming back to the fact that he had an alternative to going away, and rejected it, purely because of this obsession he had about defying his father. Because rejecting that, meant, in effect, rejecting her, or the opportunity of being with her frequently. Couldn't he see that?

Their last time in Melbourne before he left, which should have been tender and poignant perhaps, became scrappy and unhappy. They went to an all-night cafe where they had been before, after her last show finished, and as usual he met her at the Stage Door, where both of them said goodnight to others from the show who knew them 'as a couple'. It wasn't cold, but Rita shivered and pulled her coat around her as they walked the two blocks and took a booth at the Hollywood in Little Bourke Street. Andrew ordered pizza with their coffee, but Rita didn't want anything to eat. She was morose, almost sulky, and when he reached across the table to enfold her hands with his, she didn't respond, moving her hands away. "Oh Rita, I'm so sorry. I don't want to go." "And I don't want you to go," she said softly, looking at his empty hands on the table. They had said it all before, with variations. Part of it was the separation, but there was always the significance of what the posting was. The War. "Listen," he had argued earnestly, "Don't worry. It's a foreign storm in a teacup. Police Action. It will probably be all over by the time we get up there. And I'll be back before you know it, really." She seemed to be waiting for something. "And?" Andy smiled, missing the point. "And - we'll be together again." Almost a shrug. It was so simple, according to him. But to Rita, it was all so vague, like: *I'm off to war for a year, and - if I don't get killed, We'll pick up where we left off, meeting you when I get time off duty (wherever I'm posted), and between your shifts. That's all right with you, isn't it?* She sighed, shaking her head wearily, sighing "Oh Andy" – meaning, You really don't understand, do you? He didn't. And so she didn't understand, either.

"What would you have me do,
Go to the wars?"

Shakespeare; Periclese

PART 3. STONE . . .

1952

Top Songs:
   You Belong To Me – Jo Stafford
   Blue Tango – Leroy Anderson
   Here In My Heart – Al Martino
   Wheel Of Fortune – Kay Starr
   Do Not Forsake Me (High Noon) - Frankie Lane

- King George VI of England dies, Princess Elizabeth returns from a royal tour of Africa to assume throne as Queen Elizabeth II

- Military Coup in Egypt ousts King Farouk

- Discovery of Uranium in Australia at Rum Jungle, Northern Territory

- ***Korean War: Stalemate on 38th Parallel - Armistice talks begin again at Kaesong***

- Lone Captain ('Stayput') Carlsen is rescued from the storm-damaged Flying Enterprise which sank after a two week battle to save the ship off Falmouth

- First contraceptive pill developed

- Dwight Eisenhower becomes President of USA

- Greece and Turkey join NATO

The first thing Jakob became aware of when he arrived at Pusan was the smell. Basically the place stank. A mixture of smells, none of them exactly pleasant; a lot of it vehicles and a different low octane fuel exhaust smell, plus woodsmoke, perhaps cooking smells – onion or garlic (Kimchi), everything overridden by the pungent smell of raw sewage – or was it just bad drains? Maybe that too. It was not until later that he was informed that human sewage was collected for farm and garden fertilisation from most home toilet pits, in man-drawn wagons filled with covered buckets, commonly known humorously as 'honey-carts'. Ridgeway, the British Lance-Corporal who picked Jakob up from the airstrip, explained laughing "You know what they say back home about 'muck is brass', sir, well here also, 'shit is brass'. Some of these coolies who collect the household shit are millionaires. They get paid by people to get rid of it, collect it, cart it, and paid again by the farmers who buy it for valuable fertiliser."

At least the barracks and officers' mess was plumbed for WC, and when you closed the doors you could avoid some of the stink which pervaded the downtown and port areas. Jakob was welcomed on arrival by a British Captain who was Mess secretary, and shown a basic vacant room across the yard which was one end of a semi-circular Nissen hut, next to others. The hut itself being partitioned into three rooms, with a door at each end and one in the centre, each of them heated by a dangerous-looking petrol heater with a chimney flue through the roof. The huts were surrounded by a high, secure-looking double barbed wire fence, on the other side of which were ramshackle Korean dwellings, seemingly constructed out of discarded and rescued materials. Because of the proximity, probably employees of the barracks. Jakob dumped his gear in the allocated room and went across to the mess with the secretary, who was welcoming. "You'll find we're quite a mixed bag here. Many in transit. Some regulars based here, mostly Brits, but you'll meet Peter and Jerry later, the other Aussies. Some chaps from PsyWar, the British Armed Forces Radio Station and Military Police, a few like

you from MSD, plus Movement Control. Nobody stays here long"
He laughed, adding "Nobody wants to stay here long."

Jake was already discovering that there is a point at which
arrival at a new unit Officers' Mess anywhere is generally
familiar and yet strange until after a few days it becomes the
norm. Pusan's Transit Mess was slightly different in that it was a
very mixed, and somewhat temporary membership, in a foreign
country in wartime, and even if remote from the actual fighting,
continually reminded of the war. The buildings were solid enough,
but their differing degrees of architecture showed evidence of
growth by additions rather than original planning. There was
the usual entrance and ante-room, serving as a waiting room
and cloakrooms, with the difference that inside the double doors
stood (and between duties, sat) a Royal Marines Sergeant behind
a wide table at which he politely and firmly relieved new arrivals
of their weapons in return for a register in which he wrote details.
The Sergeant himself was armed with a slung Sterling Gun (or
was it a Sten?) as protector of a growing arsenal of mainly pistols,
plus a couple of submachine-guns, together with their holsters
and belts, behind him. Around the walls were various framed
pictures of seated regimental groups grinning like sports teams,
plus one incongruous illustration of the Thames façade of British
Parliament House and Big Ben. Another table past the Marine
Sergeant's armoury contained the open pages of The Book, which
was the obligatory mess visitors' registry, and on the wall behind
that was a long row of hooks on which hung coats, parkas, and
a variety of military headgear representative of several nations'
armies. This was next to the door which led into the Mess proper,
a bar and clubroom midway along the side of which was a broad
open fireplace where a well-established log fire was contained
within a linked tank-track on its edge like a low picket fence.
Surprisingly, there were two Aircrew members sprawled asleep in
chairs, obviously exhausted, facing the fireplace despite the loud
conversation and sudden bursts of laughter. The room was heavy
with the smell of tobacco smoke and spilled liquor. Further doors

led to a civilised dining area consisting of two long tables joined at one end by a short table probably set for senior staff. As they entered the ante-room, the Captain who had introduced himself as Derek Wemyss (pronounced 'weems'), gestured to a side table with a ledger, and explained to Jakob that he was required to sign himself in. The Marine Sergeant asked Jakob if he had a weapon to check in "No," said Jakob looking around bemused, "I didn't think I needed a gun back here." Wemyss introduced Jakob to members of the mess as they passed. In particular, he pointed out Major Radwell, the deputy harbour-master, whom he assumed Jakob would be working with in a day or two.

Weeks later settling in on Pusan docks, crowded pierside berths were a visual tangle of ships masts, cranes, noise of rattling chains, ships' horns, motors, whistles, shouting orders and warnings, clanking winches, screaming seagulls. Olive-green army trucks with white stars lining up, reversing. Loading by Korean labourers under supervision of armed guards. Since taking up his duties, Jakob was always busy, striding this way and that supervising another consignment, checking tallies, controlling truck loading with the help of British NCOs. Suddenly, Jakob hesitated and called urgently over to the stevedore unloading a cargo net beside the rust-streaked hull of the Kohoro which is already closing hatches – "No," he shouted, "not finish". Since he had taken up his new duties, Jakob was now dressed typically in mixed uniform, wearing battledress protected by a sleeveless scratched British Army leather jerkin, loose canvas gloves on his big hands, with long GI gaiters over his boots and has a khaki woollen watch cap down to his ears. There was no sign of his rank insignia except for his obvious personal authority and the troops and labourers following his orders. As the swung crane cable released hook of the last cargo net, Jakob, shouting, took hold of the cable in his gloved hand and climbed onto the huge hook, putting one boot into the curve of the hook with the other foot on top, wrapping an arm around the cable and signalling up to the crane operator. The Korean stevedore supervisor protested, "No-no", but Jakob had already given the crane operator the raise signal, pointing with his free hand over towards the Kohoro deck and the aft hold, not yet covered, but where the Bosun or some senior crew member had already started ordering two seamen to haul the rasping hatch covers across and another seaman stood by to cast off springlines to get away and make room for another vessel. As the crane carried Jakob up and across over the ship's deck, he used his umpire's whistle which he wore on a lanyard around his neck, to attract the attention of the ship's crew, and it also attracted the attention of the assistant harbour master Major Radwell who came angrily to the short balcony overlooking the harbour outside his office. He shouted "That Man! That Man!" and automatically, more than one soldier working on the docks below stopped what he was doing, mistakenly assuming it was directed at him (which, so often it was). Frustrated at his lack of effect on the crane rider, Radwell shouted at the upturned faces of the nearer soldiers: "Who is that man! Him, Him on the crane. Take his name!" And then British Lance-Corporal McCormack below, hiding a smile at the incongruity of it, called up to Major Radwell: "Sir, that's the Australian, Lieutenant Blask, sir." "Who? I don't care who it is, get him down, and get him to report to me, immediately, here, in my office, is that clear?" "Yes sir." And for a minute, McCormack entertained the wicked thought of getting the crane to pick him up too (Jakob having now descended into the open aft hold of the Kohoro and released the hook swinging up and back onshore) but McCormack decided it was safer to head for the gangplank and work his way back along the deck to pass on the major's message to Lieutenant Blask even if it took five minutes. "Sorry sir, but the Rottweiler wants you straight away, in his office." "Who?" "The Rottweiler", he grinned, "Major Radwell, Guv. He's having a pink fit up there, about you riding the hook. Be prepared for a blast, sir."

"Why, what's the problem?" "Well Guv, he's a stickler for HRW certificates – have you got one?" And when Jakob looked at him blankly, he added "HRW – High Risk Work papers sir, like rigging or crane riding – dogmen."

When he eventually reported to Major Radwell's office, despite the cold wind, Jakob was flushed with perspiration and annoyance at this unnecessary interruption to his work. He didn't have time to get changed, but felt it appropriate to remove his scruffy watch cap, as he stood to attention in Radwell's doorway. "Lieutenant Blask. You wanted me, sir?" The major was irate, almost spluttering. "Well whatever your name is, Bass? Blask?; I won't have that behaviour – that showing-off playing on the equipment; not on my watch. Stupid. Dangerous, and poor example to the troops. I'll report it to your C.O., and I won't have any more of it here, is that clear?" "Sir, can I just say something?" "You might get away with that sort of thing where you come from, but there's no excuse for such behaviour, so don't try to fob me off." "Understood sir, but I need to explain something." "Well what is it, man? I've got work to do." "We just unloaded the Kohoro, which you gave clearance to leave, but we were short one pallet, so I had to urgently stop them closing their aft hatch and leaving – they were already casting off some lines – and I had no time to get back to the gangway which they were hauling up anyway. So I had to ride the hook to stop them. And I found 22 bags of our sugar in the aft hold – they were skimming." "What do you mean 'skimming'?" "Hiding part of the consignment they were supposed to have delivered; skimming some of the goods. Stealing. Sir", he added, thinking *How stupid is this man?* Radwell harrumphed "No excuse for your behaviour. And your dress. Not suitable for an officer. Don't want you here on my dock. Report back to your unit. That's all!" Major Radwell turned away ignoring Jakob in the door of the office, so he didn't see Jakob replace his watch cap, salute properly, but before turning to leave, smile and say - too softly for the Major to hear him against the harbour noise - *"And fuck you too, sir."*

Back at MSD, the Colonel laughed at Jakob when he reported back from the docks. "You too? Jeremy is a bit hard to get on with, I hear. No matter, Alan has asked me to send another officer up to 78 Coy for road patrols. Would you like a change of scene? Up past Seoul. Better than here."

Meanwhile at the other end of the dock area, two ships back, where the troopship Wo Sang had just tied up, a squad of new army reinforcements overnight from Japan were filing off down the gangplank in clean uniforms and shouldered arms while an American army brass band on the wharf in chromed helmet liners and bright-coloured cravats welcomed them, playing *"If I Knew You Were Coming, I'd have Baked A Cake"* to the troops' surprise and amusement. "Did you get a load of these blokes?" The American band members were all black soldiers, smart as a new pin and obviously proud of their outfit. They were also good musicians, enjoying their duty, grinning and swinging instruments. Their welcome to the disembarking troops was probably genuine.

As the reinforcements cleared the dockside end of the gangway, another squad of returning troops awaiting embarkation out (some of whom they were probably replacing) called laughing across to them, recognising friends: "Hey Smitty, where have you been? Did you miss the alarm?" someone answering "Hey there Higgins, when did they let you out?" or "Don't hurry boys, it's all over; we have finished it for you". A few of them breaking into rough song which they all seemed to know:

> *"I was workin back in Aussie, an havin lots of fun,*
> *when a war broke out in Ko-rea, an they handed me a gun*
> *just to fight for that bastard Syngman Rhee."*

And as the two squads approached, passing each other, and more men recognised old friends, despite NCOs trying to keep order and hurry them on, there was a lot of shouted repartee and insults back and forward: 'See you back at Ingleburn, Carter; save you a spot at the Wheatsheaf bar." "Chewy on ya boot." "G'day Willie, where ya been? Did ya miss the bus?" "Pull ya pants down Harris, ya voice is muffled." Another, familiar theme "You'll be sorree!" And always: "We've finished it, it's all over. You're too late Sheahan, didn't they tell you, the war's over mate, we've done it for you."

But it was not all over. As they were to find out.

The Platoon had enjoyed the short period in Japan, first at the Reinforcement Holding Unit (RHU) where they were reorganised, and then at the Haramura Battle School, where training suddenly became very serious, noisy, and dangerous with live ammunition, close deafening bombardment and real fear of danger at times as they followed different manoeuvres and tactics designed to simulate recent enemy attacks. The Commandant of the Battle School, an English Colonel, was inclined to be eccentric. His welcoming address was succinct: "Right, you Aussie cobbers, pay attention. This is a dangerous place. We do, sadly, have a recognised fatality rate in our training. But it doesn't have to be deadly. The way to avoid becoming one of the statistics is simple – follow orders, and keep your fucking heads down." The battle-hardened staff NCOs watching, and waiting to give the new trainees a hard time learning to stay alive, grinned.

At RHU, the Platoon had been reorganized into the unit which would go to Korea, and allocated a new OC, a Lieutenant, and a new Platoon Sergeant. The Lieutenant was a tall lanky young RMC graduate named Turner with a head of curly blond hair, which earned him the immediate nickname of 'Goldilocks'. The Sergeant was an experienced old-timer named Mason who had seen service in Charlie Green's scratched-together battalion during their push up to the Yalu River before the Chinese entered the war. It was hard to tell how old he was, but it must be at least 40. He was also big, but had a spare tyre which made him appear a few months pregnant. His nickname, 'Guts' came with him from previous units. 'Guts' usually meant bravery, as well as physical description. Michael had no complaints about his new management, and he got on well with both the other Section Corporals, making him comfortable with his new Platoon and Company.

Here at Pusan, at first glance a terrible place overflowing with poor Koreans who had fled the war, the men were re-equipped at the transit camp, and everyone laughed at the unfamiliar new-issue winter gear, especially the long-john underwear and mesh singlets, CWW boots and parkas, as well as two lots of gloves. But the dour British staff sergeant who equipped them warned them "You might laugh now sunshine, but when the Korean winter bites, you will be very grateful for every bit of this stuff, believe me." Even their new stiff boots were too big, but had nylon inserts and plenty of room for two pairs of socks. At the port and the transit camp, the section suddenly realized that they were a small part of a massive military machine. Japan had been busy, but this was almost frantic, masses of troops from so many armies, in different uniforms and with different equipment, coming, going, on foot and in unfamiliar vehicles, calling orders and responding in foreign languages, encamped in tent cities with strange signboards. A frisson of excitement went through the men as they recognized their inclusion in this international force – so different from their sheltered existence at home in their own familiar army surroundings. They also had a second feeling of almost inferiority, being unable to understand these foreign languages, while it seemed that many of the foreigners spoke English as well. It was also possible to think that some of the foreign uniforms and equipment seemed superior to the Australians'. And so many of the other armies had prior experience of this place, this war. The Australians were the new boys. At the transit camp, they were assembled again and addressed by another British Colonel, accompanied by an elderly South Korean officer whose badges of rank confused them – was he a Colonel too? – he smiled and nodded through the British Colonel's address, but didn't appear to speak much English. This British Colonel was austere and remote, automatically earning the nickname of 'Lord Haw-haw' because of his plum-in-the-mouth accent which some of the men later tried to copy. Most of them tuned out of the Colonel's boring monologue, which was along the lines of "We must be aware that we are guests in this country, and conduct ourselves accordingly; being respectful to its citizens, especially its womenfolk, and of their religion and customs...." Yeah, yeah yeah; *we we we*, when it is obvious from his attitude, he really means *'you bunch of uncouth colonials who don't know how to behave'*

As they were marched to the railway station for onward movement, they passed a miles-long road screen "fence" which they were told that Syngman Rhee had had built to hide the acres of Pusan slums which embarrassed him. Stupid – the cost of building the fence could have corrected at least some of the poverty it was meant to hide. Beyond the spread of the city, the countryside existed of rugged bare hills. A soldier commented "This place stinks like shit." And he was informed, laughing "Of course it does, because everyone's shit is collected here for the farms. The land is too barren to grow anything. It's the arsehole of the world."

The uncomfortable troop train, when they went aboard, consisted of mixed Canadian, Australian and British units going back after R&R plus reinforcements not knowing what to expect; young, keen and nervous. After a while at Taegu, they were pulled onto a siding away from the station to let an express through, and almost before their train came to a halt, armed redcaps travelling with the group were down and spread out both sides, forming a loose piquet guarding the train against pilferers, and maybe enterprising soldiers wanting to go for a wander, or escape what they were now headed for. A string of empty freight wagons stood rusting on an adjacent spur line (probably sheltering refugees), and a narrow verge nearby was cultivated with straight rows of vegetables, as if no fragment of spare earth could be wasted. There were a few beggars and vendors and pimps around the train in minutes, some of them kids. Sgt Mason had warned them about Korean kids. "You gotta watch them, the little buggers – cunning as a shit-house rat, they are. On the trains, they'll offer up dirty pictures, cheap as chips, at the windows, and if someone reaches down to get a closer shufti, the bloody kids will have your wristwatch off in a flash and scarper, I'm telling you."

God knows where they came from so quickly. One of them was a thin, sharp-eyed youth in some army's ragged combat fatigues who managed to dodge the MPs to call hoarsely up to the open carriage windows. "You wanna girl?" He got some whistling and encouragement from the next compartment back, so he moved there, sensing a more receptive market. "Hey Joe, wanna girl? Nice girl Joe. My sister, Joe, very clean." The troops laughed at the classic 'sister' routine, but the youth continued. "She number one, very *sukebi*, Joe." A discomforted padre major in the officers' compartment cleared his throat and said, to no-one in particular: "I keep on hearing this word 'Skibby' but I don't know what it means." While some of the others were trying to think of a suitable answer, a young English lieutenant with a spectacular broken nose, laughed and said: "Randy. It means Randy, father." He continued to grin at the padre, who tried not to look embarrassed, but you could see that he was. He had tried to draw attention away from the pitiful scene outside, by means of some intelligent discussion on linguistics, but it had, if anything, focused their minds on the possible randiness of the Korean's sister. As if that was what she was. Outside, the haggling had already begun. The Korean's voice was anxious. "No trouble MP, Joe. My sister very *sukebi*, jig-a-jig only one t'ousand *Won*." There was a chorus of laughter and some obscene abuse from the boisterous audience crowding the next carriage windows. "OK, how much you speak, Joe? One t'ousand *Won* very small you money, only t'ree dollar." One voice yelled "I'll give you one dollar, boy-san, go get your sister." But the Korean still argued for more, and then gave in. "OK but you give me one dollar greenback, no army scrip money, then I get sister." Another confusion of advice, and the same clear soldier's voice: "Go get your goddam sister first, buddy. Me give you the goddam greenback when I climb aboard." There were whistles and Yee-haws at this red-blooded challenge.

The padre stood up, distressed, climbing over everybody's knees to get to the corridor. "I must see if I can put a stop to this before it goes too far." As he manoeuvred past the duffels and kitbags and weapons stacked in the passageway, the Canadian Captain who had been trying to sleep by the window, grunted "Why don't you see if you can stop the whole fcking war while you're up." The padre probably didn't hear him. Outside, the Korean, looking both ways, was hurrying back from behind the next line of boxcars with the girl. She was slim and young, and dressed in the local high-waisted dress over long trousers – what did they call it? – *hanbok?* – or was that something else? She walked head-down, shy and reluctant, her hair shiny black down to her shoulders, and after a shocked second of silent disbelief at her apparent femininity, there was a rising chorus of yells and whistles which even the MP redcaps surely must hear. But suddenly the noise petered out as the girl lifted her head to look at the train and noise. Her young face was a pattern of purpled burn scars and mottled disfiguration hard to describe in its cruel ugliness.

The silence was broken by a cheerful shout: "Cancel all bets folks, cancel all bets." This signalled some laughter, while the Korean boy's face was showing urgent panic. One soldier's voice said: "Jesus, where did you get her from, the city dump?" While another laughed: "Come on, Miller, you can put a bag over her head." "If you're so hot, why don't you fck her," someone argued, and the Korean boy persisted: "Joe, only one dollar; she number one jig for you." "Never *hatchee* man, never happen." Then a different voice: "Hey boy-san, me give you a Hundred Won, you fck her, OK?" And another laughed: "Me too pal, make it two hundred, *ex-hi-bi-shi-on!*" Roars of laughter and ribaldry as this was relayed to those who couldn't hear. "Miller offered the Gook a hundred won to fck the chick, man. No, not Miller, the gook himself."

The girl showed no sign of understanding any of it. She stood, demure and very much alone in the midst of the male obscenity that flowed around her, because of her. She looked at her feet, and a breeze moved the hem of her dress. It tore at the heart.

The bidding increased. It had now reached 600 Won if the Korean had intercourse with his sister. "How I know you pay me? You pay now, then I do." Shouts and promises. Local money waved in hands out of train windows. The youth spoke urgently to the girl, who calmly, quickly, turned and removed the long trousers from beneath her dress. Even doing this, she somehow managed to remain modest and dignified. Amid more shouting and applause, the Korean boy pulled down his shabby khaki fatigue trousers, steadying himself with a hand on the girl's shoulder. His exposed legs were thin and bowed. The Canadian Captain, wide awake now, said: "My god, this is the sickest thing I've ever seen", but continued to look, as they all did, numbed by the scene, perhaps easier than looking at each other. Vaguely the sound of the other train, the express, its horn blowing hi-lo, approached on the other rail, but it seemed that nobody cared. The Korean boy was trying to stimulate himself enough sexually to earn the money, but apparently in vain. Soldiers were laughing and shouting encouragement to the bare-legged boy between the tracks, who was desperately working to awaken his cold and no doubt undernourished body. The sound of the express roared and clattered past behind, its near force making the troop train sway on its springs. The Canadian Captain said: "Oh no, just look at this will you, just lookit."

The shy demure girl had now gone berserk. At first she had crouched in front of the youth, fumbling with both hands at his private parts, talking fast; shouting at him with increasing anger at his failure. They watched, amazed, as she now stood, striking the boy with small clenched fists pounding, ignoring the whistle of the train, the returning running redcaps shouldering their arms and clambering back on board, the clanking carriage couplings jerking as the wheels began to turn. The boy now stood with his arms over his bent head as the girl rained blows upon him; a complete transformation from the cocky hustler of five minutes earlier, now naked-skinny-legged stumbling from his hobbled trousers around his ankles, vulnerable and ashamed as his "sister" attacked him, and the train moved slowly back to rejoin the main line towards Seoul, and their transport to the Commonwealth Division.

Letter from Vicky to Michael:

<Dearest Mikey, hoping and praying that you are safe and well. Thanks for your letters from Japan. Please be careful. Everything is fine here, but missing you so much, and counting the months until you can come back to me. Now, the big news. Remember I told you how disappointed Dad was, by not getting to Korea, he somehow felt cheated being made to stay home and train national servicemen. But now, suddenly a well-earned prize for being patient and good at his job – he has been selected for a special Australian contingent being sent to London as part of the new Queen's Coronation guard from all the Commonwealth. Of course there is massive preparation, and they will set sail in March next year by HMAS Sydney. You should see him, our dear Reg, like a dog with two tails. Mum is tickled pink too, and we will be dying to watch the newsreels when it happens, I'm sure they will be on the news; we are so proud. Life is much the same here, and you will be bored to hear about me collecting items for our bottom drawer. Every time I put something away for us, for our new life, I think about us being together as an old married couple. I can't wait!>

After a week of acclimatisation in board-sided tents at Camp Casey they were awed by the vastness of the encampments and organisation of hundreds, thousands of troops like them from different countries, different armies; able to relate to familiar barrack routines, tents, latrines and cookhouses, but always aware that the Real Thing was waiting for them not far away, the firing practise ranges within earshot, and they felt the butterfly stomach nerves of not knowing what was coming, and many of them did not sleep well that last night, from excitement, or something else. And the next day when they went forward – at first loaded onto GMCs a short distance, and then de-bussing and forming up to march in separate platoons as a company, along that churned-up track, making way for tracked armoured vehicles groaning their distinctive screeching way, as well as a succession of trucks and Jeeps going both ways, and ominously red-cross-painted khaki-green ambulance trucks obviously full of wounded (or bodies?) heading back. Even here, so close to the front, there were still Korean civilian refugees being herded back, some carrying loads on A-frames, occasionally being checked and channelled none too kindly by Field Provosts, all of the Koreans exhibiting shock to be caught up in the transit of armies of strange-looking foreigners, and it was obvious that there was fear in their faces. Maybe just fear of their total loss, fear of their unknown future, even fear of not knowing where they would spend this night, get another meal. Mainly old Koreans and women with children, children carrying other children, even one boy leading a cow with two other small children precarious on its back, going god knows where, just south, south, away from here which had possibly been their home before it became a war zone, but you knew from their meagre belongings, that they were already destitute. The few old men had typically-Korean high frames on their backs with bundles and household belongings; one A-frame even supporting a tiny frail old woman facing backwards.

As the company marched easy, rifles slung, along one side of the muddy road towards their new Company positions, a string of the refugees walked the other way down the other side of the track, and suddenly among them there was a small Korean girl, a toddler, who seemed to be alone between other groups, and without warning she dropped to sit down and cry as our unit was passing opposite. Crying mostly without a sound, just that terrible screwed-up infant face beyond crying, not aimed at anyone, just lost, hopeless. One of the digs – was it Walsh? – broke ranks, paused for a break in the traffic and hurried across the track towards the little girl, and Corporal Whan ordered him "Get back in the ranks! Walsh, come back, Now!" Walsh, who had almost reached the little girl, agonised, shouted back "But Corp, she's like... My little Suzy is the same age. .." And the corporal, his rifle slung over his shoulder, who had quickly reached Walsh and caught him by the arm, didn't shout now, both of them standing above the child, but 'Corp One' spoke to him as one friend to another "Dave, there's nothing you can do for her, we can't take her with us, mate. We all know how you feel, but there are just too many like her, we can't do anything, her own people will help," and fortunately, as if to confirm what he was saying, a middle-aged Korean woman with a baby strapped on her back, came quickly to the little girl and stooped to talk to her, and Corporal Whan shepherded Private Walsh (still looking back) across the track to join the outside file of the Platoon still marching forward, and Sergeant Mason, waiting, who had been watching without interfering, nodded to Whan that he had done the right thing. And as they marched on, their progress didn't stop Walsh from looking back, and his serious face still wore the distress he felt. But the rest of them were too nervously conscious of the rumble and flash and crack of heavy artillery gunfire in the distant direction they were marching.

RASC Corporal Rooney stopped Jakob's Jeep at the end of a South Korean village approaching Tokchong to give way to a convoy of ROK troop-carriers joining the road from a side-track. He switched off the engine, and Jakob got out the other side to stretch his legs and light a cigarette. The sun came and went as small gaps appeared in fast-moving low cloud, but there was no warmth in it and the steady wind was icy. There had already been two snowfalls and the frozen mud-crust crackled beneath their feet. It was a typical roadside village, with some of the squat tiled buildings in ruins, but the houses which remained were occupied and smoke rose from chimneys. The same old men in white with their tall traditional hats, the same vacant-faced women, the same old-young solemn children staring at the soldiers, the same hopeless refugees in the dirt road plodding on their way South with belongings on their backs, heads, and bundles in hands, going God knows where, anywhere, away from the front, the fighting, the destruction. In the ditch near the Jeep, two Korean men lay exhausted. Jakob looked again; there was something strange about the way they were lying. They were barefoot. Their hands were tied behind their backs and they were dead. The nearest one's neck was black with dried blood.

The last escorting ROK half-track towing a field gun was moving off down the road as Jakob turned to show Rooney the dead men in the ditch, but the Corporal was paying more attention to a Korean soldier at the far end of the village street, sing-song shouting as he approached, calling like a town crier, his carbine slung across his back, his hands hidden, probably in his baggy trouser pockets for warmth. None of the bystanders seemed to show any interest in what he was calling out. "Corporal?"

"Just a minute, Guv, I think he's talking to us." Corporal Rooney frowned, listening to the ROK soldier who had almost reached them, but it was, of course, in Korean. The soldier grinned, flicking them a jaunty salute before turning to face the way he had come. He was short, dark-skinned like a peasant farmer, solidly built, and smelled strongly of garlic as he waited a couple of paces from Jakob. "What's it all about?" "I couldn't make it out– something about Communists I think." And then they saw other figures coming towards them, one riding a pony followed by others walking. As they came closer, they saw that the horseman was a Korean policeman with a flak-jacket over his uniform, plus a bandolier and an elaborate shoulder-holster. Behind him, being led by a rope – no, it looked more like insulated wire – were three barefooted prisoners with their hands tied behind their backs. The policeman's wire went from neck to neck, allowing them no movement except to shuffle along at the pony's walking pace. Bringing up the rear was another soldier, his carbine held across his chest. A kind of tremor ran through Jakob and he looked at the Corporal, who had now seen the corpses in the ditch, and put two and two together, and started shaking his head slowly. The small procession kept coming towards them until the gendarme dismounted and barked out orders to the prisoners, who turned to the edge of the road where the other bodies were; then knelt, backs straight but heads bowed facing the field as the second soldier removed the wire from their necks. Meanwhile the policeman had drawn his pistol – an old-fashioned long barrelled 'broomstick' Mauser – and without warning, he shot the centre prisoner in the back of the head, making Jakob jerk as if it had been him. Almost simultaneously the rear soldier put his carbine against the farthest prisoner's neck and shot him in the same way. Both dead men fell forward, unmoving. The soldier nearest Jakob, the one who had spoken to them, had unslung his carbine and turned to Blask, grinning, offering Jakob the gun and gesturing towards the final waiting prisoner. At this delay in his execution, the prisoner turned and his eyes met Jakob's. There was nothing in his expression; no appeal, no fear, no anger, no defiance. Just the brown eyes of a man looking into Blask's soul. Jakob squeezed out the end of his cigarette and felt the burn in his trembling fingers, turning away to climb into the Jeep, not even looking up at the third shot, although that too, made him jerk at the sharp report. The last prisoner had fallen face down, and seemed to stiffen, slowly arch in some reflex then the body collapsed. The policeman remounted – with difficulty, the white-eyed pony shifting nervously around in a circle away from his swinging leg – and the two soldiers slung their carbines and sauntered off towards the far end of the street. A small boy ran to pick up the still-hot brass cartridge cases. The other villagers and refugees remained the same. No display of feeling. Not a word had been spoken since the horseman's order to the prisoners, no sound except the gunshots and the scuffling of the pony's hooves. Corporal Rooney, stunned, got in the driver's side, shaking his head slowly, staring out through the muddy windscreen, whispering "Oh, Sweet Jesus." He started the engine, still without looking at Jakob, who glanced out through the scratched yellowing side-curtain to where there were now five corpses in the ditch and the last three looked no different from the first two; bore no relation to the live men who had walked dully towards them a minute ago. They were, perhaps, infiltrators or enemies, spies or traitors, but it didn't make Blask feel any better. His mind kept on going back to the prisoner who had looked up at him, but what should he have done? What *could* he have done? Nothing. The phrase 'washed his hands of it' went through his mind. Over the rumble of their engine, Rooney grunted, as if to himself: "This is a shit of a country." "This is a shit of a war," Jakob added. The Corporal laughed: "Is there another kind?" as he put the Jeep into gear, and took off fast to try and catch up with their convoy.

I n the forward echelon, Andrew's OC called the newly-arrived Platoon Commanders together for 'a bit of a chat', as he called it, in Company HQ surrounded by sandbags, but still within hearing of the odd angry shot. There was a bank of field telephones on a trestle table, where survey maps were spread out" The Captain shook hands with each of them. He wore a heavy knitted khaki sweater with elbow and shoulder patches. He was a red-head with freckles and grin creases beside his eyes. "You all know your responsibilities and duties as platoon commanders, and you can always ask me if you are unsure about anything. Don't try to guess. This is war, and errors cost lives, so let's get things right first time, all work as a team, and make this the best Company in the Bn"

(He used the abbreviation for battalion, '***bn***', which is sort of pronounced 'bun' – no, shorter than that, more like b'n, get it?)

"I know your platoons are all new to you, and all of you are new to Korea, and to war. You will have to get to know your men in a short time. It's one of the most important tasks you have, to get to know them well, and to get them all on your side. Your success as fighting units, and all of your lives, depend on it. Write up your Platoon Book every chance you get, talk to each of your men and get their details into your book. Get to know names, nicknames, families, next of kin, kids, religion, where they went to school, what sports they play, what team they barrack for, what their grumbles are. You are going to live and play and fight so close to these men during this next year, you will get to know them better than their mothers do. OK, that's not original, that's what Bill Slim wrote, and he knows. But it is true, and so important – you are platoon commanders and closest officers to your men. I'm your Company OC, and I know <u>who</u> your men are, but I will never know them as well as you will, so get working on it. Get close to them. And," he grinned, "talk about getting to know them, one of the first tasks you have here in the Line, is to check them all for 'Japanese Souvenirs', which means a Short-Arm-Inspection (and don't groan, Vickery, it has to be done after every leave) so you will have a short-arm parade every day for a week, and weed out any drippy dick who might need a course of penicillin from the M.O. to get healthy again. Plus - no; you yourself will not escape, because you have also been in the land of the Rising-something (Oh, Sun, was it?" – they laughed) - "so you will inspect the wedding tackle of your Platoon Sergeant, and he will have the pleasure of checking yours. And let's not have any leisurely fondling, got it?" (More laughter) "Dunno what your sexual proclivities are, and I don't want to, but this is a serious medical inspection which has to be done, properly, like inspecting their feet, which you will also do. So listen; this is *my* Company, and your platoons (which are <u>my</u> platoons too, remember) will always be healthy, regimentally correct, clean shaven, punctual, obedient, happy, brave, and the best damn soldiers in the world, and you with them. Finally, you will need to manage water resources carefully – the only water you get will be the scarce amount brought up with hardship by the Korean supply columns, and terrific brave blokes that they are. So from here on, your washing arrangements will be minimal – an APC – armpit & crutch – but everyone still needs to keep clean and hygienic, and everyone will shave daily – no exceptions. Sometime you might find yourself close to one of the Korean rivers, but don't be tempted to push the dead animals and Chinese corpses aside and drink, OK? The rivers are badly contaminated. You have been warned. That's all for now. You're going to be here for a while, so there will be time to think up other questions. Fine, good luck and keep your f-ing heads down. Dismiss."

In their new position, Andrew scanned the hills in front, which seemed to go on forever. It seems inaccurate to describe them as hills. The word 'Hills' sounds nice. Hills should be rolling gentle elevations covered with grass and trees, even grazing sheep; not these – these effing rocky hostile crags which almost defy attempts to climb them, some of their rugged faces vertical (always the face you have to go up because the enemy thinks you won't be stupid enough to go that way) some, despite bombardment amazingly still covered with tangled scrubby growth and the remains of distorted trees which have been blasted and burnt. Their steepest approaches so difficult, you have to resort to hands and knees scrabbling with hand-holds for any upward progress as the hard gravel scree skids and rolls away from your boots trying to return you sliding to where you started. Using both hands prevents you from holding and using your personal weapon, or even shielding yourself in panic from some evil bastard above you, trying to kill you. Bloody hills. Yes, and sometimes *literally* bloody, fought over so many times changing ownership, and for what? Is it worth it? Who wants to own any of these god-forgotten pieces of real estate shit on which you could never plant anything, grow anything? And yet you are a soldier, and know well, in war, there is no victory unless men put feet on the ground to claim possession of land from the enemy. No use just bombing the living daylights out of a place from a great height, you've got to <u>be</u> there, <u>on</u> it, take it and hold it. So you fight for the hills. They become so familiar. Marked on orders talcs, maps and airphotos, identified by their metre height as Hill 355, 227, 210, 159, for example. And also given easy to remember nicknames like Betty Grable, Matthew, Mark, Luke, and John, or sometimes describing the shape of the feature like The Hinge, The Hook, The Mound, The Bowling Alley, The Slippery Dip. You get to know them so well, and the approaches to them. And now, because of anticipating an eventual ceasefire line, fierce battles are continually fought to secure another ridge, another hill, on which to base decisions of 'existing' territory and claims of occupation when the shooting stops. If it ever does.

(The armistice negotiations have been going on for nearly two years, what makes you think it will ever, <u>ever</u>, result in a ceasefire? Men are being killed, daily.)

Letter to Jakob at BAPO5 from Anja.

<Dear Jakob - or I call you Kuba, like Aleksi? Anyway, you know I'm writing from Aleksi and me both to answer your last letters which we got, and Aleksi got me read. Sometime he ask me question on your letter, which I am happy to give him explain. So, I am tell you, Aleksi is fine, good health, don't worry. He don't want you to know, he broke his arm a while ago, fell off build and broke it, but now it good as new. When he had it plasted up he was difficult, you know he is like, when I did too many thinks for him, mister independit, but after he always sorry. You know how. We understand him you and me? Everything OK here, no worries. You remember I have son Jakob too mining at Merbelbar well he got a girl, and they got a baby, so I am grandma but not see them, they now move down to Kalgoorlie mining area it too far for me. But maybe one day. You been there? Australia too big. You got to laugh Aleksi had to go again court for something against, and this time stupid complain neighber call him 'bloody Nieu Australian' and this time, Aleksi tell him – hey my grandson he a real Aussi digger in Korea, what about you? And this time magistrate maybe on Aleksi side, squash the case. Magistrate is a lady, and Aleksi told her thanks, she a nice chick. I think she get angry but no, she laugh too. We still worry you in that war, come back safe OK? And keep writing, Aleksi very proud on you. Me also. Love from us all both, Anja.>

ndrew began to write a letter in the confines of his
bunker, but his fountain-pen ran out of ink, and he
had to start again by finding the ink bottle in his kit
(always hoping it hadn't leaked) and going through the
rigmarole of unscrewing the pen case and inflating the ink bladder,
cleaning the excess ink off the nib and settling down to where he
left off. The sheets of supplied letter paper were headed 'Australian
Comforts Fund', obvious left-overs from the second world war,
bearing another crest of the Salvation Army. In the distance, he
could hear the Americans on the far hill firing short machine-gun
bursts on their fixed transits over their minefields – *pok-pok-pok-pok,
pok-pok, pok-pok-pok-pok*. After thinking for a moment, he began
writing: <*Gday Jakob you old B. Looks like we missed each other again.
We've got to stop* not-seeing *each other like this...*>

Corporal Abrams from Company HQ opened Andy's hootchie
by folding the rasping canvas sheet aside.

"Sorry Sir. Boss wants an O Group in fifteen minutes – I said
I'll tell you."

"OK Corp, I've been told. I'll be there."

Letter from Andrew to Jakob:

<*Gday Jake you old B. Looks like we missed each other again. (We've
got to stop* **not-seeing** *each other like this.) Worse than when I arrived
at Reinforcement Holding Unit expecting you to show us where all the
Japanese fleshpots were, and finding you were over at Pusan or somewhere
– are you trying to avoid us? Anyway you missed a good reunion with
Nicholson, Vickery and me, we managed a few cold ones somehow
without you. They are a mostly good bunch here, except would you
believe the Intelligence Officer is none other than that prick Holbrook?
Intelligence Officer? Now there's an oxymoron if ever there was. We are
now in bunkers after a few minor brushes with the real stuff, patrols etc
and I'll tell you all about it when we meet up. But I have to say that it is
nothing like we expected back at Clink, maybe war never is, after playing
at it. My new platoon is a good bunch, and I am really getting to know
them. I have finally landed with a great CO, who is freshly arrived too.*

What a change after that idiot Badger pretending to be a Colonel. Quite a few familiar faces here – Peters, Spencer & Clark are also up here with their own platoons, it's like a class reunion. we are suddenly discovering what that four years was supposed to have taught us, if only we had paid attention. Sorry we missed you. I guess the next time we might get together is when our unit gets R+R, but that might be Tokyo, do you ever get up there; we could really paint the town red. Watch out Ginza, here we come! Anyway, got to go, O-Group in a minute, maybe some action again. Drop us a line and let us know how you are doing. And you miserable B, if you ever get over near here again in this tourist paradise make sure you borrow a jeep and come up to see us. >

J acob looked around the small office space. It was neat and compact with a detail of small articles which hung, or lay, or stood, or were pinned to the walls. The desk was clean, with the inevitable "IN, OUT, and ON GUARD" labelled trays (yes, a dreary old army joke from bayonet practice, replacing In, Out and Pending). As if listed in an inventory, Jakob noted a chair office type swivel, stand ink, ashtray Bakelite, and telephone. A keyboard on the far wall was neatly marked with printed signs above each hook, and a double-ended ring spanner took the place of a missing key.

"By the way," Godfrey asked. "How do you like Japanese food?" "Never tried it," Jakob said. "Is it like Chinese?" "No, not really. Simple, but some different flavours. How about I introduce you to a sukiyaki dinner tomorrow night? You'll like it." "Sounds great. Is it expensive?" "No, mate, this one's on me."

It wasn't until the next day when Godfrey drove him back from Yoshiura QMPSD bulk fuel depot as part of the hand-over, that Jim enlarged on the subject. On the long drive back along the twisting coast road through tunnels, he explained: "Listen, Jake, you will probably hear – if you haven't already – that some of us who have been here for a while, are 'shacked up'. That is, we have a Japanese girlfriend *'up the yama'* as they say, up the hill, like a mistress, who we look after. Or who looks after us. In my case, she is Yukiko. Lovely girl, and as you will see, a terrific cook, so that's where we are going for our Sukiyaki dinner tonight, and so you will meet Yuki." Blask, cautious, paused before venturing to ask "Have you and.. you and Yuki, got any children?" Godfrey laughed, "Christ no. No room for complications like that. No, that would be too much trouble. I've already got two kids at school back home."

There was not much you could say to that, so Jakob didn't try. That evening, as arranged, Jakob was ready when Godfrey picked him up outside the mess. Jake thought he should take along a six-pack from the mess bar, and Godfrey said "You didn't have to do that, but good man, appreciate that." Godfrey was again driving one of the 119 Jeeps. They left the camp and joined the crowded Japanese traffic through a section of the city which was new to Blask, and as they progressed upwards towards the city's surrounding hills, the roads became narrower and climbed as they branched. Now and then they had to wait as pedestrians or unloading *Bata-batas* blocked their progress, but Godfrey was calm and friendly towards the Japanese, all of whom seemed to respond cheerfully at the intrusion of a foreign army vehicle. The bata-bata is a utility vehicle, generally three-wheeled and operated with motorcycle handlebars, but with a small truck-tray behind the rider for carrying merchandise. "What did you call them again?" "Bata-bata – it's supposed to be what they sound like. Most of them made by a bloke called Honda – clever bastard – he is alleged after the war, to have bought up all these 50cc two-stroke motors which had been military generators, and firstly converted them to run pushbikes. Then he redesigned a small pick-up truck like a motorbike which could go anywhere, particularly these narrow old streets, and cheap enough to appeal to one-man entrepreneurs, so he's making a fortune, and Japan's small business operators are flourishing. Typical; they're like ants, they're so bloody busy." The bata-bata in front of them finished hastily unloading and the driver and customer waved Godfrey through, saluting and bowing. He drove on up the hill until the narrow street became even too narrow for the Jeep, which he handbraked straddling a gutter inches from both adjoining buildings, with only a one-person squeeze space beside; from which he led Blask along a tiny meandering path between high houses. Jakob said "Is the Jeep safe there?" and Godfrey laughed "They all know me around here. The only problem would be if a rare MP patrol came way up here, but some of my Japanese neighbours would tip me off before the redcaps arrived, so that I could move it or prepare an official excuse. Listen, between us, I have disconnected the speedo, and I'll put in the petrol to make it up." He shrugged, "I'm not telling you what to do, just being honest about what I do. *Shikata ga nai.*" He stopped at a small footbridge across another chuckling creek or drain, and tapped on a wooden door. He called ahead "*Tadaima!*", and a female voice from inside cheerfully called back "*Okaerinasai*" while sliding the door open, to reveal a tiny entry space with a row of slippers. On the higher step of the small entry knelt a smiling Japanese woman dressed in kimono, bowing to Blask. "Boots off, I'm afraid" Godfrey said. "They're clean little buggers, the Japs, so no outside footwear inside a house." "Sounds fine to me," Jakob said. Godfrey grinned "It's Japanese, but you'll get used to it. By the way, this is Yukiko"; and to her, he said "*Kochira wa Blask-san desu.*" The Japanese woman, who was still on her knees, bowed very low – almost to the floor - and said "*Yoroshiku onegai itashimasu, Brask-san*" "Ah," added Godfrey, "The old Japanese 'L' – I'm afraid you'll have to get used to being called Brask everywhere here."

Jakob put down his six-pack of Kirin and accepted the pair of scuffs he was given to replace his boots, and followed Godfrey up into the house. Well, the room, really, because that is what the house was; a 2-room dwelling consisting of a tatami-mat floored 'front' room, next-door to an identical bedroom (he assumed), with a narrow passage leading to a minute galley kitchen on one side, and a toilet on the other. He could hear subdued radio music and canned laughter from an adjoining dwelling, and the sound of trickling water from a stream outside. He noticed that Godfrey had brought with him a small wrapped parcel which he handed over to Yukiko, who scuttled away with it. Tonight's dinner? The room bare of furnishings, just an ankle-low lacquered table in the middle, only one wall which was decorated with a recessed *tokonoma* alcove which displayed a vertical scroll of Japanese characters; the other three walls obviously made up of sliding storage doors or dividing screens between rooms. Godfrey indicated the table and said "Take a seat, Jake. 'Fraid you'll have to kneel or squat or spread yourself on the floor. Or lie. This is Japan…" "I know," Jakob anticipated laughing, "You'll get used to it." "Right, let's have one of your beers to start with", and he called easily to Yukiko "*Gurasu nihai kudasai*" to which she called back from the other room "*Haihai suguni!*"

When Yukiko returned, with two pilsner glasses and a tall bottle of Kirin beer, Jakob was able to notice more of this pleasant smiling woman. He had no way to gauge her age, but he guessed somewhere in her twenties, maybe even thirties. She was slim and her multicoloured, multi-layered kimono was wrapped tightly around her body from neck to white cotton two-toed socks (he discovered later were called 'Tabi'). Yukiko knelt at their table-side to expertly pour their glasses of beer, and as she laughed and smiled she revealed a glint of a gold tooth. Godfrey said, obviously for Jakob's benefit: "Yuki speak English", but the smiling woman, embarrassed, waved a small hand in front of her face and said:*"Dame, chigaimasu, Yuki no spik Inguris desho!"* And scuttled off back to the adjoining food preparation. Godfrey laughed, "She does actually speak quite a lot of English, or Australian, but she is shy of using it with someone she has just met. You'll see."   T h e Japanese meal was assembled in the kitchen, but cooked at the table in front of them, on a low electric grill called *Hibachi*, and it was a surprisingly quick mix of very thin sliced beef shreds cooked with vegetables and translucent noodles, tossed with soy sauce and *Mirin*, sprinkled with sugar. As the steam rose from the grill, the food smelled delicious. "What's this called again?" Jakob asked, and Godfrey replied "*Sukiyaki. Suku* meaning sliced thin, *Yaki* meaning grill. It's a very popular dish, and Yuki is an expert." But again, Yukiko had either understood or guessed, and waved her hand in front of her face again, "Yuki No Expert" she said carefully, and they laughed. She served two shallow bowls and a separate cupful of rice for both men, with delicate lacquered chopsticks which came to a fine point. Jakob waited, but there was no sign of Yukiko eating with them. He said "What about you?" And she answered haltingly "I cook, you eat" and giggled. Godfrey said, "Come on, dig in while it's hot. Don't mind Yuki, she wants to play hostess and waitress tonight. Can you manage chopsticks?" "Well, I'll give it a burl. Tell me if I do something wrong." Godfrey showed Jakob the basics of holding and using the chopsticks, and after a minute, Jakob got the gist of it.

After the meal, relaxing, they both lit up cigarettes, while Yukiko busied herself in the kitchen and Godfrey seemed to be nervously preparing himself for an announcement. "Listen, Jake, there's something I want to talk to you about." He paused, and Jake waited. Eventually, Godfrey launched into this subject he was hesitant about raising. "It's about Yuki. Obviously I can't take her home with me when I go, and I want to make sure she's looked after. I could send her money; I will anyway, but ... What I mean is ..." I mean, the ideal thing would be if someone decent takes her over... looks after her. The rent up here is cheap, she is a good housekeeper, and, not to put too fine a point on it, well, Japanese women know how to please a man ... Know what I mean? Plus, there's a risk with any new relationships you might make in town. But not with Yuki. She's ... Well, she's safe and clean, if you know what I mean."

Godfrey was obviously ill at ease, and Jake himself was uncomfortable with the subject. "Listen Jim, I understand. I appreciate everything you have said and done, but I'll have to give it a lot of thought. Anyway, wouldn't Yuki have a say in all this? Does she know what you are proposing?"

"Yes, she knows. And yes, we have talked about it. And yes, of course she has to agree with it all too. I just wanted to sound you out. Think about it, that's all, OK?"

Andrew cringed. Imagine the closest, LOUDEST lightning thunder crack you instinctively ducked your head from, and then imagine it happening not just once – but continuously, over and over again - right on top of you, right next to you, all around you. This is another incoming Chinese artillery bombardment. Shrieking, whistling, ear-piercing-cracking; the arrival of artillery shells and exploding mortar bombs around your deep bunker in a really deafening, blasting, roaring, non-stop series of metal explosions which not only belt your suffering eardrums, not only make the earth under your feet tremble, but actually subject your cowering body to thumps of pressure – physical air-pressure blasts, sometimes almost sucking the wind out of you, then buffeting you continually so that you cringe down low and try to make yourself smaller in the hopeful protection of the reinforced bunker, but knowing that not even its eight-foot depth and solidly engineered timber and rocky overhead covering would help you in the case of a very unlucky direct hit. You cower down down down against one of the rough vibrating rock walls instinctively (yet uselessly) holding your arms over your head, your mouth part-open as they taught you to equalise the pressure of the explosions to protect your eardrums, your heart double-thumping in overdrive, helpless against the screaming, tearing assault as the deadly rain of heavy metal erupts, together with a secondary lethal shower of sharp rock splinters and debris, clouds of dust, smoke and stinging gravel, the acrid stink of high explosive; sometimes wondering if praying ever did any good but wanting to plead with someone, anyone, any *thing*, to stop this; to save you from this. But it continues screaming, thudding, banging, ear-drum-belting. Another frighteningly close one, and dirt sifts down from where the explosion has loosened the deep overhead reinforcement, and your *hoochie* companions Corp Whan, Crowe, Cassidy and Calabria in the other half of the small deep pit which is your home, with the unintended decoration on the side wall where Crowe's overcooked C-Ration tin had exploded despite warnings. The men who share your hoochie and communication trench , who also instinctively cover their heads with both arms, sheepishly grin at you from their dirty faces in the dark dust and rotten stink of H-E smoke. Maybe they're thinking too, could this be our grave? A small piece of wayward ricocheting shrapnel trying to come in, the smoking remnant blackened tailfin of an expired enemy mortar shell, has bounced off the sandbags at the safe-angle zigzag entry, skidding in on the duckboard near your feet, and stupidly you make the mistake of reaching to move it, then drop it sharply because it is almost red-hot, making you flip your fingers and shout shit, but nobody else can hear you. You can't even hear yourself.

Your pulse is thumping fast, partly because of the continuing danger which the barrage itself presents, of immediate death or injury against which there is nothing you can do, nothing - but also because you know that this Chinese barrage like all of them is only a precursor, the softener-up, to the massed enemy attack which any minute now – maybe hundreds of them, wave after wave of them - as their keeping-you-down bombardment lifts marginally ahead of them and they will be coming at you – yes, you mate, **_you_**; with bugles, whistles, screams and a full-frontal mass uphill charge firing at you, accompanied by more mortars, stick grenades and burp-gun bullets, determined to kill you or drive you out of this precarious rocky strongpoint which they are under orders to take at any cost.

Scared? Nah.

Well, yeah; a bit. Of course. (_As in, privately, between you and me, effing terrified_). Not specifically about being shot, although there is that too, of course, the possibility of painful bloody wounds or even death, but more like the fear of the unknown, you understand? Maybe that's the worst part, not knowing how you will handle it. It's the common soldier's dilemma, isn't it? – of being afraid to be afraid. Of innocently believing that you are the only one being scared, hoping no-one else is aware of it. Hoping that you will pass the test. What test? Of being a soldier in action. In my case, of being an officer. A new Lieutenant, recently appointed to command this platoon which I am desperately getting to know.

Of course we have done all the drills, the endless training, the field rehearsals; after all this is our purpose, the thing we have practised for years, back home and here at rear echelon, including the just-over-your-head live firing and too-close explosive detonations back at the battle school, and on manoeuvres intended to give some small idea of what to expect going in, but this - what comes next - is the real McCoy, real bastard enemy soldiers firing live everything *at you*, trying to kill you; and you not knowing if you can handle it. Thank Christ there are some of us, our mob, my little platoon, who have done this before, that have been through it (we are not all greenhorns like me) - do you think they know how scared I am? Does it show? You know what they say: that an infantry soldier's Hour "is fifty-five minutes of bullshit and boredom, and five minutes of absolute terror" They're not wrong. <u>That</u> is bad enough, but worse still, here I am supposed to be in charge and full of confidence, a platoon commander, a bright squeaky-clean new boy fresh out of military college and infantry training; supposed to know what I am doing, trained to lead and inspire and motivate my 33 men, dutifully following the Company Commander's orders, based on the Colonel's tactics, in turn acting out his Divisional masters' strategic plans, hoping like hell that they all know what they are doing, not just stirring the Chinese possum. More importantly, hoping that I will not make mistakes, that my platoon will understand and respond to my orders, back me up, and that we will overcome the enemy and survive. Yeah. Most importantly, survive. All of us. Of course I have faith in my men. I know them. God, we have endlessly trained together, travelled together, lived together, rehearsed battle tactics together and played sport together (where you really get to know each other well), and – crossed fingers - I hope that they accept me as their leader. I think they do. Of course they know I am untested, have never fired a shot in anger, but then you have to start somewhere, don't you? Because I'm a professional soldier. A regular army man. So this is finally my battlefield initiation. Oh God, let me live up to it. Of course 'Guts', Sergeant Mason, who is our platoon sergeant and my invaluable 2 i/c in the next *hoochie* a few yards away, on whom I have come to rely so much, a 20-year man, has been through all of this heaps of times before – originally against Japs in New Guinea, and more recently chasing the North Koreans right up to the Yalu River in 1950 with the newly-formed and under-strength 3rd Battalion when this war first started, but now against the Chinese who have swarmed in fighting us, so I reckon Guts knows something about war and surviving; which is some consolation, so thank God for all the regular volunteers like him, the old timers, the K-Force men who re-enlisted when this war began. I know that he is here supporting me and helping me to become the leader I have to be, that I've signed on for, that everyone else expects me to be, that all my fellow RMC graduates are. He, Sergeant Mason, could easily ignore me and lead the platoon without me, but he is too much a professional soldier to do that. He knows how the army works, how our success is to operate as a total solid team, every man looking after every other man, and part of that is the unit automatically accepting me as their appointed platoon commander backed by all the NCOs as their go-betweens with the Company and Battalion commanders who direct our strategy. Back when we were digging in on this impossible rocky hill, Guts says to the gathered men; "Listen; when they come (and they will come), of course you'll be scared, I'd be worried about you if you weren't, but bear in mind you're a mile ahead of the gooks, you've got all the advantages. For one thing, you're securely dug in, well trained, fortified, well equipped, plenty of ammo, and Charlie has to attack you from out in the open, becoming bare-arsed targets running a long way uphill at you without cover – *uphill*, mind you, out of breath, and chancing their luck through our minefields and bombardment - knowing we are going to knock 'em down like ninepins. Second, we have practised this a thousand times, remember, and our platoon runs like a well-oiled machine, with everybody looking after his mates. That's what we do, back one another. Third, you can feel sorry for those poor buggers, the Chinese peasants who have been "volunteered" into this war, sorry for them because they have unluckily got placed directly opposite us - the best soldiers in the world - and we are going to wipe them off this mountain like ants off of a barbecue chop."

[Mind you. He didn't mention how these Chinese troops could be tough as nails, battle-hardened from their long war for years, against - first the occupying Japanese, then Kaichek's Nationalists, and now us, and they are well equipped by Russia; but then we didn't need to know that, did we?] Good old Guts. Well-oiled machine? Well, not too bad. I know a few of us like me are relative newcomers, but our platoon is seeded with K-Force men who are specially enlisted volunteers, experienced troops who have seen service in WWII and know what war is all about. And who you can rely on. Now, Corporal Whan waving his arms alerts me that I'm wanted on the skin and bone - the field telephone - but I'm deaf in one ear and can't hear out of the other; so jamming the receiver against one numb ear while trying to block the crashing bombardment on the other side of my head, I manage to hear Wally, our Company OC, shouting into his blower so that I can just hear him "Andy? The spotter says the Chinks are assembling, so stand by for their barrage to lift and their attack to start. Get ready, we're with you on all sides and in reserve. Mick's platoon on your left, Lou's on your right are ready too. Keep the mongrels back off the hill; it's ours! Good luck."

Here we are, we have got a thorough briefing by I.O. Holbrook with his talc overlays and air-photos which we share with every man in the platoon so we are all familiar with our backyard. Our Division is situated along the Jamestown Line, between the US Marines and the ROK positions, and opposite us is what they call the Nevada Complex, with hill features called Reno, Vegas, Detroit and Carson. Most of the hills look the same along the 38th – almost vertical, rocky, largely devoid of remaining timber but scrubby with undergrowth. Some of it has been fought over umpteen times with the burn and blast scars of artillery and phosphorus. And between, the valley of what used to be paddy fields with stubble and low scrub, hard to believe despite the fierce warfare – still inhabited by some remnants of birds and animals. Or, from time to time, invading hard men intent on occupation (ours or theirs).

So this is it; get ready, stack the spare loaded magazines and extra primed grenades near the forward firing step at the sandbagged rim of our pit facing downhill and the flanks where they will come from, together with the other sections of my platoon soon to emerge from their own pits next to us, and – thank God – our own battalion's zeroed-in mortar and artillery bombardment to be brought down on the attackers to stop them before they reach us.

Is it possible for my thudding heart to beat any faster...?

Letter from Elizabeth to Blask:
<Dear Jakob – I hope this reaches you, because it was not very clear where you were going to be, when you wrote last. But thanks for your letter and the little Japanese doll in its national dress – it is very elegant and sits on a shelf above the desk where I am writing, and where I do all my studying, which means a lot of the time. Did I tell you that I am going for Medicine? Some people think I am too young, but when I want a thing, I usually make the effort to achieve it, which is why I am working so hard. Mum was also delighted with the Japanese silk scarf by the way, and I know she is writing separately to thank you. We are glad to hear that you are safe and coming to terms with your new duties. Do you have comfortable quarters? From what I have heard, all army barracks are pretty ordinary wherever they build them, and I can't imagine places like Korea and Japan to be any better. Things here are not very happy, and poor Mum is at her wits' end with the lack of news from Andrew (only one letter in six months!), plus all the rows and Daddy moving into an apartment in Canberra. He tells everyone it is to be closer to the demands of the Department because of the involvement in Malaya and Korea, but we all know it is because of the fights over Andrew basically, because Andrew never wanted to be a soldier in the first place, and now he is in the front line so Mum is terrified for him. With all the fights I try to support Mum, but that hasn't always worked, and now I am sort of piggy in the middle. Anyway, I have really got a lot of study to keep up with, and I try to keep out of the family battlefield as much as I can, except I know Mum does a lot of crying in private, and I wish I could be more help to her. If you have any contact with Andrew, can you please persuade him to write to us.>

The Chinese assault began. Michael thought: this is it, the real thing, Christ. Now it starts. Suddenly, this is really **IT**, no way out. *(Don't tell me you somehow thought/ hoped that their attack was going to be called off? Wouldn't that be nice.)* The previous ten minutes' Chinese heavy artillery bombardment, just finished, was bad enough to test you while it lasted, ears still ringing, but at least that was sort of impersonal even if it frightened the bejesus out of you cowering in the bunker; but now, here is the actual enemy - here they come, the massed swarming yelling Chinese army charging up from the bottom of the hill – Look at them! – the valley is full of them, firing at you as they come, blowing bugles – millions of them emerging from their distant tunnels and joining the charge, is there no end to them? We won't be able to stop them, surely? Steady, boy. We are not alone, thank God. The action is being watched, measured, by Battalion, by Brigade, ready to reinforce us. And now our Battalions' zeroed-in defensive fire starts on cue; good-old New Zealand artillery whistling overhead as practised, as ordered, accurate as ever, supplemented by our mortar platoon's blasting cover, our flanking set heavy machine-gun platoon raking, the hull-down British Centurion tanks of the Hussars firing on fixed trajectory as planned to help us, plus direct sharp-shooting individual targets getting knocked down by our snipers. Remember Sgt Mason saying only yesterday "The great temptation when you are mass attacked is to automatic fire at the hordes, but don't give in to it, boys. That's useless hosing. Slow and steady wins the race. Make every shot count. Even though rapid fire is a natural instinct and makes you feel good, you don't want to blaze away and suddenly find yourself out of ammo, with your pants down."

The Chinese attack is already being blunted by our Battalion's defensive barrage, what a horrific sight in the midst of flashing bursting shells and clouds of smoke and dirt, their men being knocked down in droves, some poor bastards blown up, blown apart, from the Kiwi artillery shells and the tank H.E.; bodies and bits of men flying in the air. Soldiers tripping over the bodies of their depleted forward ranks, scuttling for a rocky foothold to maintain the momentum of their uphill charge in a courageous reaction to the loss of their mates in front of them. Some of them trying to take momentary cover where there is none. Surely no-one would want to be first. Are they mad, or brave? The still-advancing determined line of enemy troops scatters, falling to our raking Vickers, but some, incredibly, manage to escape the withering defensive fire and continue their attack, now coming up within our range. Which means us now in their range. We are all now engaging as a Company, firing furiously from our sandbagged Platoon pits. We have to, we have to stop them. In this same firing pit alongside me is our platoon commander Lieutenant Turner, Signalman Crowe, Privates Cassidy and Calabria. The rest of our platoon in firing pits either side of us. Now no difference in person or rank as we do what we are trained to do. All of us now frantically firing, reloading, our hot stinking weapons creating a din, and we hear the other sections also rattling fire down on the enemy. My heart is beating fast, all part of the body's natural reaction to fight or flight. (Well, flight's off the agenda here, isn't it? So it has to be fight.) Remember what they taught you, the body is supposedly getting a boost of adrenaline and sugar into the bloodstream, increasing production of red blood corpuscles, transferring blood from skin and gut to muscles and brain. Or so the theory goes. Everything working overtime. Heightened alertness, sharpened reactions, thumping pulses. And that's all of us. Probably even those Chink attackers, the bastards.

Quick now, Michael. Trembling. Aim at this man, steady, single shot, but already he has dropped, not from you, but from one of your mates. Aim again, yes, that other man, this time it's definitely your shot that dropped him. He fell, didn't get up again. And another. Moving targets on a range we are used to, but these are humans, firing at us as they run. Men, yes, but remember they want to kill you. It's no game. They have now reached where our minefield starts, where normally the wire and the red metal triangles warn friend and foe – but the recent bombardment has destroyed a lot of the boundary wire, and some of the flanking Chinese now set off mines as they cross. Poor buggers, losing a leg or two, maybe worse. Deafening. Magazine empty, flick it off, click in a new mag, don't fumble. Three more of their front soldiers getting too close, drop from our unrelenting shots. Someone in our sector is throwing grenades downhill which crack and bring down even more of the close enemy soldiers struggling up towards us. We are still well protected by our sandbags as we face them. You hear the whip zip of their wild bullets. (Too close) Their mass advancing bullets raise bursts of dirt, chips of rock around us, someone in the next bunker on the left screams in pain, one of my section hit, no time to check, of course I'm worried, but I can't get across there yet to help. Another zig-zagging enemy soldier nearly up to us has to be stopped. Did I hit him? Someone did. He went down. Sprawled face down, writhing. Here comes another, and another; both of them hit and fall, one of them going arse over backwards. Yet another, close enough to see his face, his yelling Chinese features shut down as his life switches off, his face a red mess. Another magazine. Have I got plenty? Me breathing faster open mouthed, like all of us, wild eyed; God my mouth's dry, no time yet to grab a swig from the water canteen while this panic battle for our lives is going on. Thank God, it looks like we have stopped them. We have torn them apart, no doubt their last ranks at the valley bottom falter while our moving artillery barrage halts them, then 'walks them back' to their trenches, they have given up, and then the finishing touch, no doubt called in by Battalion, an unexpected flight of American Corsairs come from behind us scream low over our heads scaring the hell out of us, so low above us you can count the rivets, fast into the fray, down the valley in front, cannons or wing guns blazing, cutting more enemy down, and before the planes zoom up again to avoid the next close jagged hill and away, they release those lazy tumbling napalm canisters which explode, spreading red black yellow liquid fire into the retreating Chinese still running in the valley. There is an instant blur-hazy image of some of the distant enemy soldiers totally ablaze, raised arms crumpling against the rolling balls of flame. And around here, a slower series of gunshots putting an end to any approaching enemy stragglers. The planes came and are gone in seconds. In a few minutes they will probably have landed safely on their heaving carrier on the Sea of Japan, laughing and joking in their briefing room over a coffee, the lucky bastards. While here in front of us, as the war continues, the valley and close hillside almost carpeted with enemy bodies, smoke rising from some of them where they lie. Some, a very few of them, move. And we know that in a few minutes Goldilocks – our platoon skipper - will check us for casualties, resupply ammunition, send up water, allocate duties and sentries and advise Company by radio that we are sending out a squad to check on the enemy lying in front of us, to separate them from their weapons so that we can collect any of their own wounded and stretcher them back with ours for treatment, and also check their close dead for any maps, orders or info that would be helpful to the I.O. and his team back at Battalion. Checking enemy dead is a job that nobody wants, because of the condition of some of those bodies, and the danger of one of them being a hero lying doggo with a live stick grenade. Nevertheless, it's another duty, and we treat their bodies like we hope they would treat ours, so we lay out their dead ready for them to collect later under white flag, and when we get back through our battered minefield gap past our sentries and report, we are sometimes covered in blood. Their blood. And now it is time to have that drink of water. God I'm dry. Still trembling from it all. We're all still trembling, bright-eyed, coming down.

So this is what Action is like? What the yanks called 'combat'. Killing, yes, killing. A first for many of us – most of our platoon. This is what all those old soldiers we knew from training, from family uncles, from those Anzac Day marches and reunions, knew but wouldn't or couldn't pass on to us. What our experienced instructors weren't able to tell us. And what we in turn won't be able to pass on to anyone else. You can't, can you? Maybe we were brave – if that is what bravery is – looking death in the face - being scared but standing firm doing what we were trained for. Holding the line. We have fought off a mass attack and survived (this time). We are still in this war, so we may not be so lucky next time, and we saw those others who were not lucky this time. The ones we killed. The ones who were going to kill us. We will never be the same again. It's just a fact of life; soldiers who experience war, can never ever be the same again. We have changed. We have become different. Not better, not worse, just different. As soldiers, this is what we were recruited for, even if we did not plan it. This is what we trained for. What was it, ten minutes? Fifteen? It seemed like a week. We did it, we survived this one, and we are now part of a brotherhood.

We are now Different.

Letter from Jake to Andrew:
<Dear Andy, thanks for your updates on winning the war all on your own, but make sure you tell the newsreels that I taught you all you know. Sorry I haven't managed to get up to your unit yet, my only Korean exploits being confined to Pusan and Seoul, although I am supposed to go to Tokchong next. At present I am coming to terms with running a transport platoon here in Kure, and don't laugh, but the guy I'm taking over from, has a Japanese mistress he wants me to take over as well. Ready-made comfort woman. He took me home, I suppose to get us to meet and 'consider' arrangements, but I had to disappoint him (and her? no, she was probably relieved) because I would prefer to make my own decisions in that regard. The lady was very nice, but not my type. Besides, we have got a good officers' mess here, plenty of sports, and it is a great town, but a lady up the yama is not on my immediate agenda. From what I hear, Korean ladies are not your first priority either. We hear very little here about your actions, and always hope that

the armistice will be ratified soon without any more losses – especially yours, you old b. I need you. Look after yourself, and keep your head down. And another reminder – did you write to your wonderful mother? Do it! >

"Ain't a-gonna work on the railroad,
Aint a-gonna work on the farm
Gonna lay around the shack,
till the mail train gets back,
Gonna roll in my sweet baby's arms"

This is Ginger on his guitar, singing hillbilly-style, which he is good at, he can even yodel, remember they said he used to go around the shows performing with Tex Morton's band; and we always like being entertained by him, often others pick it up and sing along with him if they know the words, beating time with an empty dixie, especially when we are a bit relaxed like today. You see, we are nearly due for leave rotation as a platoon. You got to admit, there was a different feeling throughout the platoon; I mean you don't really start counting *Weeks* to go, but when it gets down to *Days*, you can really see light at the end of the tunnel, know what I mean? Sure, we're still forward of the Company, still living in our reinforced bunkers here with our own B.O., rats, fleas and other infestations, and we still get random bombardments from Charlie when he wants to waste artillery, and we've still got some regular patrols to do in No Mans Land, but there's a recognition that we are on the short strokes, if you don't mind that expression. Because the OC has told Goldilocks (our Platoon Looie) that we are finally up for leave in five days, so that should mean that we will be relieved by another 'lucky' platoon any day now and sent back down to Camp Casey in preparation for re-entry to Civilisation – and all that means: Deloused, MLB (mobile laundry and bath), clean uniforms, proper food instead of ration packs, and transport to our plane out. I'll tell you my plans later, but I've got something special to look forward to. Anyway we are a bit relaxed at present on the reverse slope of our position, almost out of gunshot but ready to dive for shelter or action if we have to, enjoying the sunshine. Sure, we have sentries out, and even an FOP down front like an early warning, but we are mostly taking advantage of the beautiful weather. Some, like Sgt Mason writing letters, our Lieutenant writing up his report or his Stud Book (in which he keeps all our secrets), some playing cards, Rennie doing his usual Charles Atlas bodybuilding stuff, even unlucky Walshie with the latrine duty burning off the shit drum (being careful not to overdo the petrol and explode crap all over the sky – don't laugh, it has happened). People sleeping – yeah, quite a few catching some Zeds, because of daily dawn and dusk stand-to's and call-outs, none of us has had a proper sleep in years. Lazing around, even working on a tan with shirts off, but not far from our action stations and weapons if we need to. Get the picture?

Sgt Mason is one of those regular letter-writers, writes to his missus and kids at least once a week, and can I let you in on a secret? Once when we got a Stand-To and ran to our posts, he left a letter half-written which I picked up and gave back to him, I saw what he calls his missus: "Dear Chookie" he wrote. *Dear Chookie?* Yeah, OK. Well normally you'd tease the buggery out of someone with that, but we all have such a respect for Sgt Mason, I never mentioned it to anyone (except you this time, and you're not gonna tell anyone, right?). He is a great family man, three kids, and I imagine he is a wonderful Dad to them, just like he is a wonderful Sergeant to us all. Mother Hen is the phrase that comes to mind. We are all a bit subdued, because of the news that a Chinese attack on the Duke of Wellington's Regiment last night over-ran the British, and they had to call in the artillery on their own position to drive off the attackers. They suffered many casualties, including men buried by the counter-bombardment. Jesus. It could happen to any of us.

But anyway, here we are taking it easy, suddenly there is a panic series of _SHOUTS!_ which woke everybody up, and we thought it was a Stand-To, reaching for weapons and helmets; but then a laugh started up by the hootchies, and then it became clear – it was something up at the near communication trench. Both Lieutenant Turner, and Sergeant Mason had grabbed their guns and got to their feet running in case it was a Stand-To. There was more loud laughter. 'What's it all about?" "There's a snake in the dugout, and you should see Burnsie's mob falling over theirselves trying to climb out. Mack Sennett comedy." "Who's scared more, them or the snake?" Someone said. "Kill the bastard, shoot the bastard." "No leave it, maybe it will keep down the fcken rats." More laughter. "You can have it in your hootchie then, I'm not sleeping with a fcken snake near ours." "Is it poisonous?" "Fck knows, it's big enough. I'm not gonna find out." "Anybody know anything about Korean snakes?" "Who cares, the only good snake is a dead snake." "Get Cassidy." "What for?" "Hopalong is the bush-man, he'll kill it."

But it turned out Cassidy was down at Company HQ on an errand, and it was our Skipper who did for the snake. Nobody expected this. I mean, he is an officer, right? Everyone had vacated the trench and was milling about watching the reptile's progress, throwing things down at it, so that nobody seemed to notice Goldilocks stride across and jump down the far end of the trench away from the snake, which was probably trying to escape from the mob. Everyone was a bit surprised by this development, and because we all look the same in our combat gear, a couple of people even asked "Who is that?" "It's the skipper" "Who?" "It's Goldilocks." "Dinkum? What the fck is he doing?" And even then no-one had any expectation of what happened next. Lieutenant Turner, appearing bold and fearless (was he really, or only acting stupid?) threw something up ahead distracting the reptile, and seized the snake's long tail. While the reptile tried to double back along its length to what was holding it, Goldilocks quickly hauled it up, swung it out and around (everyone nearby ducking, even if they were well out of range), and he cracked the snake like a stockwhip to break its back, dropping it to leave it twisting and knotting itself on the floor of the dugout in its death throes. Cheers, roars, and clapping. "You're a fcken hero, boss." But someone also said, grudgingly, half admiringly "Mad as a two-bob watch, he is." Sgt Mason reached a hand down and helped the Lieutenant to clamber up from the dugout, laughing. "Jeez, skipper, I didn't know you could do that." Lt Turner answered, "Neither did I, Bruce. First time." He grinned "And the last."

(So it became a unit legend, as things like that did. It didn't do the platoon commander's reputation any harm. Word soon spread. Soon everyone in the Company knew. 'Bloody Tarzan'. 'Who?' 'Goldilocks - Lieutenant Turner – mad bastard - killed a fcken snake with his bare hands')

Michael shivered, and tried to turn side on to that Siberian wind. Freezing to death between energetic actions. By now, we understood and appreciated those gawky severe winter uniforms, long johns and snowproofs we were issued back when the climate was normal. But winter is almost over. Now, we can't wait to get out of this Siberian wind in a bunker up close and personal to one of the dangerous petrol heaters and their poisonous fumes. All of us are wearing every bit of uniform clothing we own. Now, we can't wait to be released from Goldilocks's warm-up exercise routines. No incentive to go out in the frozen paddy to wait for, and ambush, Chinese patrols when your hands are dropping off or sticking to anything metal, your fingers numb, even through the mittens with the separate trigger finger, and that icy wind cutting your eyes which are the only part of you not bundled up. Not only a reluctance to get out in the cold of an open country patrol, but already, because of the casualty lists, watching each patrol leave and return, wondering who of them are we not going to see come back in. And when it is our turn, my turn, thinking how many times? What if my luck runs out, will I make it another time?

Apart from the danger, we are all fed up with the (once novelty) ration packs and the discomforts of the dug-outs, the fleas, the bombardments, the lack of sleep as we are hauled out for stand-to's for dawn and dusk attack preparations, even the ones which don't happen. We are fed up with the lack of water and the inevitable lice and rats until the scheduled rotation and the luxury of a rear echelon mobile laundry and bath, with a change of uniform (even if it is the wrong size). We all yearn for the long-awaited leave across in Tokyo, where unimaginable civilised delights of bright lights, girls, drink, music, and real food, seem to last only a blink of the eye, before return to what has become the normality of war and someone's death. We are all too aware of the count-down to the end of tour, to getting out of here.

Anyway, this time we are safe, on exercise, one of the many rehearsals, practices, manoeuvers ordered by higher command.

Sometimes as a preparation for some big push to retrieve a piece of territory, an important hilltop, a dominating position. Maybe regaining a position that someone else lost. Here, there are troops as far as we can see, because we are in reserve and not actively engaged in this exercise, so we are freezing as we stand by awaiting orders. This is a huge exercise conducted in a rear echelon; battle rehearsal, wargames, whatever you call it, the whole bloody Brigade, with more important senior officers than you could poke with a stick; all of them trying to impress one another, to prove that they are God's answer to Alexander the Great. And they assemble endlessly changing their minds with different units forward flank and in reserve, and as luck would have it, our Company this time is tail-end Charlie with nothing to keep us warm while forward units charge and reconnoitre and reform until they get things done the way the brass-hats want. And eventually we get a welcome patch of sunshine – not enough to get warm, but enough to set everything steaming, and soon (thank God) we are allowed to stand down while forward units are given the benefit of further instruction and a repeat of their action. Goldilocks somehow has been smart enough to have liberated a couple of footballs, and while one platoon starts a small impromptu 5-man rugby game in limited space, another group begins a kick-to-kick, demonstrating their imagined VFL skill, encumbered by their cold winter gear and heavy boots.

The rest of us, when we hang around together warming up a bit again with a smoke, standing easy yakking and taking advantage of a steaming kindly brew which Goldilocks has organised and got delivered, we learn what some of our mates have got planned when this war's over – like Roy, who reckons when he gets out, he's identified some eroded unproductive part of his brother's farm on the main country road where nothing grows (except rabbits), and he's gonna start a business collecting old truck and machinery wrecks around the countryside which people, farmers, want to get rid of, and then charging people to come and buy spare parts off of him. The joke is, it might just work, and like as not the same people who might pay Roy to take away their junk, are the same people who would later come back to buy parts off of him – you know how that happens. Some other digs have long-term projects like Toxic, who hopes on applying for a soldiers' settlement allocation, to start a small farm (he wishes) in the Victorian Western District, a self-contained lifestyle with a few sheep, gradually building it up and extending it. Those of us who know the Western District tease him about having to stand on a slant because of the powerful prevailing winds there nearly blowing you base over apex. All the locals walk on an angle. Another, Fergie, reckons he is going to keep re-enlisting until he has saved enough to find and buy some small run-down country pub to fix up again; so that's why he is a bit of a tightwad, reluctant to let the moths out of his wallet, although to be fair he makes no bones about wanting to save his pennies. Even when they sling off at him with things like "Long pockets Short arms" "Still got the first quid he ever earned", "Wouldn't shout if a shark bit him"– you know how they go on. But you got to admire a man with a plan who doesn't let others bully him out of it. He's got an aim and sticks to it.

But me? No; no particular plans. Play it by ear, take it as it comes. Happy as I am. Maybe the eternal soldier. I'm a regular army man, aren't I? 30 years? Let's see what happens. I could end up a general. Vicky would love that. "What about you, boss?" Someone asks Goldilocks.

Peter chips in "No use asking him, officers are in the fkn army forever, right, skipper?" "Well, yes, we're permanent army. And it's a bit complicated to get out once you've signed up. I mean, they pay for us to qualify at university level for four years at RMC, so they are entitled to get a few years' service out of us, fair enough. But if I did get out – just saying – last leave, my girlfriend's father was at me to quit and join him in his business, so I reckon there could be a job for me there if I wanted it." "What sort of business is he in, boss?" "Building and concreting. Seems to have built half of Canberra. He's not a bad bloke. That's **if** we get married. If she wants to. If she's still there when I get back. There's a lot of ifs"

And then eventually we get relieved, and as a luxury out of the wind, get GMC'd forward again. In the back of the truck there is a bit of combined body warmth, but it also emphasizes our animal aromas, and The Professor wriggles aside a few inches from Nude Nut, who, without understanding, moves to take up the added space. The Prof whinges "Jeez Pete, don't get so close, you pong." And Nude Nut, who doesn't take it personal, says "you don't smell too sweet yourself, darling." It was the 'darling' that sends them off, roaring with laughter, but we all know that we stink — fact of life — we have lived in these clothes for so long they would stand up by themselves. In fact, somebody reckoned that our battle gear itself would deflect a burp-gun bullet. Skeeter says "One of the blokes from One Platoon managed to get a bottle of Aqua-Velva aftershave from the yank Ouijongbu PX, but before he could employ it as a deodorant, someone had stolen it to mix with canned juice as a cocktail." Hard to believe, but then again, some digs will do anything to get a hard drink. Skipper has warned us about Korean hooch, worse than Metho, guaranteed to send you blind. And yet, you gotta laugh; when we get an occasional issue of Japanese beer in the line, you'd be surprised how many of our mob don't drink. All the more for us real men. Back in the dug-outs there's Peachy telling jokes, always acting the goat, trying to be funny. "There's this officer, just fresh outa Duntroon," he says, and Goldilocks, sitting aside, writing up his Platoon Book, assuming he is going to get roasted, puts on a wearied look, slowly shaking his head, but not interfering. Peachy continues "He arrives at his first posting, bright eyed and bushy tailed, saluting everything that moves, okay? And a soldier passing throws him a salute, which the Looie returns, and the Looie says Good Morning, Private." Anyway, the digger says "Good Morning Sir, but just in case you didn't know, I'm in the Engineers, and we privates in the RAE are called Sapper, not Private." "Oh, thank you, er, Sapper. Thanks for telling me." Then comes another soldier and they exchange salutes, and the Lieutenant says, "Good Morning, Private." And the soldier corrects him and says,

"I'm in Artillery sir, and in the Arty we are not called Private, but Gunner." And the Lieutenant thanks him, takes it all in, and marches on. But then he is stumped, because the next one coming, is one of the new female soldiers, a WRAAC, who salutes him. And the officer says, "Good Morning Miss, but can I just ask you, what do you ladies in the army call your Privates?" And the WRAAC says, "Pussies, sir."

That gets a laugh, even though everyone has heard it before.

Undeterred, Peachy says "OK. This is Rome, back in the old Coliseum days, OK, and there's this giant African gladiator, black as the ace of spades, bald as a billiard ball, huge, nothing can beat him, OK? Kills all his opponents with one hand, slaughters the wild animals too, so the Emperor, Caesar or what-you-call- him, says, right, next time, handicap him a bit. So they dig a hole in the arena, and put this huge negro gladiator in up to his neck — that's it, up to the neck, only his bald head sticking out the only thing he can move, and then let the lion out. So the lion prowls around him, the gladiator twists and turns his head, and as the lion goes to attack, the negro bites the lion on the balls, and it goes off yelping. And the crowd boos, thumbs down, and shouts "Fight fair, you black bastard!"

That gets a good laugh too, and I am watching our platoon's only black soldier, Tommy Reilly, for his reaction, but he is roaring laughter with the rest of us, nodding, saying "Yeah. That'd be right." I've got to tell you about Tommy, he's the only Aborigine in our platoon — although there are a couple of others in the Company - and he's been with us since Pucka, way back. Tommy is a good soldier, and very popular, not only because he is a super sportsman — cricket, footy, can play anything, and boxer? Fights like a threshing machine, should be with Jimmy Sharman. But he is also popular because he is always good humoured, and would do anything for a mate. I remember asking him once, "Tommy, do you ever get any bad treatment from anyone because of your skin colour?" And he paused, and for a minute I thought I'd made a mistake, that he was going to say 'What skin colour?' Anyway

Tommy grins, "You got to be joking, Corp. The army is all my mates, they're my family. Anyone pick on me, and half the platoon would jump on 'em."

When you think about it, it's true. We are all one family here. Tommy's only colour problem would be when he is back in civilian life, when he would probably not get served in some bush pub, you know what some of those outback towns are like. But Tommy can also get some encouragement from the fact that our battalion has also got an Aborigine officer too, a popular infantry Captain, Company Commander.

Anyway, before I leave the subject, maybe it proves a point, a couple of days later, I overheard Tommy talking with some blokes from the Pioneer Platoon rewiring fences on Minefield duty, they're all laughing, and he says: "There's this giant African gladiator back in the Coliseum, black as the ace of spades..." His audience is smiling with him. And when he finished telling the joke: "*Fight fair you black bastard!*" they roared with laughter, Tommy too.

Letter from Elizabeth to Blask <Dear Jakob – it is a while since we heard from you, and even longer since we had a letter from Andrew. Have you seen him or heard from him? We know he is still with the Battalion in action, because Daddy manages to get news about him through his own sources, but I know they (Daddy and Andrew) had a really big final bust-up because Mum told me – it was about Daddy trying to get Andrew transferred to a special job back home, which he refused, and Andrew telling Daddy to stop interfering in his life. You will be surprised to hear that I am now 17 and starting University in Sydney, where I will be doing Medicine. Everyone said how I was too young, but my grades convinced them. Don't laugh, but when I first put my name down for Medicine, I had these childish fantasies of somehow treating a wounded soldier in a war zone (like you with a bandage around your head) – but that would have been Nursing, wouldn't it? I have grown up since then – a bit.

*Last I heard from you in that Korean port, (was it poo-san? Sounds terrible.) you were expecting to be posted back to Japan somewhere, so I now imagine you sitting under the cherry blossom with some beautiful Chocho-san, drinking Sake, and I am so jealous. Seriously, please, please write and tell me how you are, and particularly what you know about Andrew's situation, and if you do have any contact with him, please convince him to write to us - that is, Mum at least, and to answer our letters. And we miss you. (Well OK, that is, **I** miss you.) With love, Ellie.>*

1953

Top Songs:
'Moulin Rouge' Theme – Percy Faith
Vaya Con Dios – Les Paul & Mary Ford
That Doggie In The Window – Patti Page
I'm Walking Behind You – Eddie Fisher
Till I Waltz Again With You – Teresa Brewer
Don't Let The Stars Get In Your Eyes – Perry Como

- January – C+W singer Hank Williams dies

- March 5 – Stalin dies; (Soviet and China seem to lose desire to prolong fighting in Korea due to huge losses.)

- April - exchange of sick wounded POWs at Panmunjom - Armistice talks resume

- May – Tenzing Norgay & Hillary climb Everest

- June – UK Coronation of Queen Elizabeth

- 8 June – Korea POW repatriation agreed, but heavy Chinese & N Korean offensives increase.

- **24 – 26 July More Fierce Battles of Korean War**

- **27 July – armistice finally signed at Panmunjom.**

- SE Asia Treaty Organisation established.

- August – DeHavilland Comet flies London/Tokyo

- Atomic Weapons tested at Woomera, S. Australia

"Bless 'em all, bless em all – the long and the short and the tall
Bless all the sergeants and W.O. Ones,
Bless all the Corp'rals and their blinkin' sons.
Oh we're sayin' goodbye to them all. As
back to their billets they crawl.
You'll get no promotion this side of the ocean.
So cheer up my lads, bless 'em all."

But sometimes there <u>was</u> promotion, this side of the ocean, when you least expect it. RSM Anstey came up the hill from Battalion, greeting troops by name as he passed them in their dugouts. He seemed to know them all, which was another sign of his efficiency, because there were nearly a thousand of them. Certainly they all knew him. He was popular with the men even though he was strict, they knew him as a hard worker, as well as a fearless and welcome sight with resupply ammunition and water even when a fire-fight was raging. As he arrived still crouched from the communication trench into the line of bunkers where Sgt Mason was writing a letter to his wife, and Private Willett was cleaning the sergeant's Owen Gun, he greeted both of them, and told Willett he wanted to talk to Mason. Willett said "That's OK with me SarMajor, I don't mind." "But I do son, so take a hike." Willett, who is sometimes a bit thick, said "Where'll I go, SarMajor?" Maybe he was waiting for an instruction or something. Both of the NCOs laughed – there was an obvious, if rude, answer. Mason shook his head in wonder, and Anstey said kindly "Arthur, just piss off for a minute will you, I want a bit of privacy." Willett scuttled off, and Sgt Mason chuckled "Privacy, in the army, what's that?" They laughed, watching Willett sliding down the embankment clutching the Owen gun past where the toilet, situated over its temporary pit awaited non-private use. Anstey paused until Willett was well out of hearing, and then said: "Bruce, you've probably heard, I'll be movin' on soon. Time's nearly up. The Colonel's asked to me about a replacement. Wants to know if I got any ideas. Well, I have, and you're the top of them. How'd you feel about workin' for The Man, Bruce?" Sgt Mason was smiling, but shaking his head in pleased disbelief at the same time. "Jeez, Jack. I dunno. Don't forget I'm well into this third tour of duty too, you know." "I know that, Bruce, but you still got a while to go yet on your run. Would you be interested?" "Jeez Jack." He scratched his head "Do you think I could do it?" It was Anstey's turn to shake his head, in mild annoyance. "Mate, I wouldn't have asked you, if I didn't think you could do it. You got more experience than all the others put together." "But wouldn't the Old Man want a *Wo*?" (Warrant Officer) Anstey continued to shake his head "God you make things difficult. Listen, of course the job's a Wo. But you'd get the Crown and higher duties pay anyway until you could do the course and make it substantive. What I'm saying is, if I put your name forward, would you accept it readily and do it? The Old Man already has a high opinion of you. Just as important, have you got someone ready to take over from you, if you go?" Of course I was chuffed. I mean, a promotion is a promotion, even if it's only a temp, a fieldy. I was already thinking if I could mention the approach to Barbara in my letter; there was not much other news to tell her. I brought my mind back. "Yes; well there's young Whan of course, Michael Whan, you know him. He's a very good operator." "Yes, I know Mike. Good bloke. Think he could run the platoon if we gave him the job?" "Sure of it. He's well ready for Sergeant. Best of the bunch." "OK, then thinking a bit further, who could do Whan's position best? Calabria?" "Yes, that'd make sense. Tony would make a good Corporal, a good Section Leader." "All of it smooth? No noses out of joint if we do all that? "Not in the slightest. Those're good men, popular leaders." "Good. And talkin' about leaders, how's Goldilocks coming along himself?" "Oh he's fine, one of the best; he's done well, better than I thought he would; sometimes he can be a bit of a loose cannon, but the men really rate him. They'd do anything for him." "And would he and Whan continue managing the platoon well without any dramas?" "Not a worry in the world, Jack. I wouldn't leave my men with any no-hopers, you know that." Anstey smiled, looking at the sky, where a flight of Sabres scorched across in a blur heading North-East. Anstey started to get up, brushing dirt off. "Yes, I know that, Bruce. You've done a good job with them. Keep this to yourself for the moment, and I'll talk to the Old Man, and we'll get Goldilocks back for a chat to make sure he's OK with it all – it is, after all, his platoon - and then get you over for a briefing. It's a piece of cake, you'll take to it like the pro you are."

"Any idea where _you'll_ go, Jack?" "Well, don't laugh – and this is under your hat, mate. Sounds like I might get put up for RSM at Duntroon, the Military College." "Crikey, Jack, that's a great pat on the back. Congratulations!" "Hold on, back up, it's only smoke in the breeze at the moment. Might never happen. And I dunno on what terms. So, keep it between us, OK?" "Sure Jack."

A t the start of every patrol, Andrew experienced a sort of nervous excitement, something, he thought, like the charge you get when you run out onto the football field against a tough or unknown opposition, but in this case, the excitement is mixed with fear. Always fear of the unknown, fear of not knowing how you would perform, fear of letting your troops down – (but strangely never any thought of any of them letting you down; they were always going to be the true soldiers you could count on). The true soldiers you knew deep inside that you were not. Well, not yet, anyway. Gradually working on it...

At the briefing, Shep, the Major who replaced Wally as Company Commander, said "Just yours this time, Andy, take one section, a Night Recon Probe at 0130. You know where Charlie had his forward perimeter on Tuesday until we forced them back beyond 181. See the Talc. There's a suspicion they might be starting to move back up again, and we don't want them any closer; the valley is ours. Take Sergeant Whan and your best section, quiet as a mouse. Feel out where their front is, and their strength, listen for any new earthworks, but don't get into anything serious, because yours is not a fighting patrol, got it? Just Recon. Jerry here will be on hand with 3 Platoon on watch to reinforce if you need to extricate yourselves, in case things get sticky, and we'll be listening in to help if you need it. But you might be able to confirm their position without shots fired if we're lucky. You know the drill."

"But if we do make contact, what about prisoners?" Shep laughed at my question. "You should be that lucky, the way the Chinks have been ordered to die rather than surrender. But if someone taps you on the shoulder with a *Towchong* and begs to let him come over, the Colonel will probably give you a bonus leave in Tokyo and a bottle of Scotch if you bring one in with you. But that's not tonight's job. Just confirm Charlie's position and strength if you can gauge it, mark it on the map and come back with your section all in one piece is the name of today's game. If they are moving up, we'll organize a big bash to drive them back, but that's not tonight. It's too close to the siren to lose anyone, you know that. Good luck and be safe."

[Cassidy is on my far left, armed with Owen Gun and grenades, just this side of him is Peter (Nude-Nut) our Bren Gunner carrying the LMG and its ammo – all 25lbs of it plus several extra mags - as if it was light as a feather, then me and Crowe with his radio (turned off now, just available for calling in help if we need it), and close behind us, Sgt Whan and Bonsell, and on my right Fergie, the other side of him on the right flank is Mac, and then Corporal Calabria, all with an Owen or rifle and grenades. Everyone knows where everyone else is, and what we are doing, as I have explained it before we started. A formidable little army, able to handle anything if we have to. I almost said *Corporal* Whan, but Mike has been Platoon Sergeant for a while now, and it fits him like an old boot since Guts moved on to Battalion. We're used to this patrol routine by now. Piece of cake. But underneath, unspoken, there is the ever-present thought; we have been lucky so far, how long can our luck last? How many patrols is this? Nearly time for rotation home. Please Jesus, let us get out and back safe tonight, please, it's not much to ask.

So we creep along low like we had several times before, hoping Charlie is not venturing out tonight, and why would he? Maybe the enemy knows that the brass-hats, both theirs and ours along at Panmunjom are ready to sign the paper and blow the whistle, call it all off, so why risk it? Maybe the armistice has been signed at lunch time and they haven't told Brigade yet – the war might be already over. The I.O. had said there was rain forecast, low cloud and therefore no stars, we could be in for another routine night doing what we do best, staking out our territory while Charlie is home in their tunnels brewing up their green tea....

Then ***CRACK! CRACK! CRACK!*** Shit! Down, fire, move, fire, move. They must have been waiting for us, and the first thing we know is when they open fire on us. It is noisy. Thank god they're firing high. (I hope they're firing high). It is so dark, except for the muzzle flash of their weapons showing us where they are. I didn't hear any bugle, whistle, or command from them, just the sudden loud shots; fast-rasping burp-gun fire like ripping canvas, single rifle shots, and two close metallic bangs of stick grenades going off with the whistle of fragments. I tried to estimate our position for my report – (one of these days they'll invent something which will give you map coordinates at the push of a switch, but now, it's all guesswork, no features to go by in this black night, just instinct and number of paces.) Of course we reacted according to our training and experience, and I think Charlie wondered what a hornet's nest they had stirred up, because every one of us hit the ground and blazed back at them in between showering them with grenades, rolling aside to shift position and fire again. It was chaos, and although our training and rehearsals meant we're supposed to drop to the ground under fire, I was suddenly aware of bald Peter, silly bugger, but you can't tell him - standing crouched, blazing away with his trusty Bren from the hip, hosing them in short bursts, and a scream from away front which meant he had their measure. Comforted to hear Peter blazing away with his Bren at where the muzzle flashes had appeared; that solid .303 should give them something to think about. Should I call in extra help, artillery or mortars? Not at present, we can handle it, they seem to have hit and run. Luring us into an ambush? Well, not if we don't follow them. Check and consolidate, maintain our strong position, we have established their advanced front. Not more than ten of them by the look of their firing, maybe a patrol, probing, like us.

There was some shouting in Chinese, and then their attack stopped, and even in the dark I knew that their unit had pulled back, indicated by diminishing and distant muzzle flashes of the parting shots of their rearguard withdrawal from their patrol. Maybe Charlie had been on his way across to hassle us, and accidentally bumped into our patrol. Maybe the Chinese commander had instructions too, not to get bogged down in a battle only worth fifty feet of paddy field. I shouted 'Everyone Leapfrog Return – pass it on', and the platoon began the well-practised return to our lines, half-section by half-section, covering alert front and sides while the others passed back and in turn took up their own crouched defence and protection of the next withdrawing men, much of it instinctive, automatic movements in the night, their figures looming black against a less black background, hoarse-whispering progress to identify who was there and where they were. As usual it worked well. Closer to our lines and the expected challenge in the unit's controlled withdrawal, suddenly I became aware that my group was ragged – ahead of me, I counted off Doctor Mac, Crowe, Peachy, Peter, Calabria. Where the hell was Fergie, where was Cassidy? Sergeant Whan loomed up alongside, assisting Bonsell whose arm was over Mike's shoulder, limping, awkwardly swinging one foot and as they approached the minefield gap. Whan said "Bonza's got a foot injury. Is Fergie with you, Boss?" "No, he hasn't arrived yet" but at the same instant, Ferguson appeared out of the darkness, and I asked Whan "Have you seen Cassidy? He's not here yet." "Do you want me to go and look for him?" "No, I'll do it." And Sgt Whan said "Here, you take over Bonza, I'll go back and look for Cassidy." But I insisted it was my responsibility, and said "No, you carry on, it's my call; get Bonsell to treatment, look after the men, count them all in safely back, I'll find Cassidy. Warn them I'll be back with Cassidy in a minute, get a stretcher ready just in case I need help with him" and I turned and crept back from darkness into the other darkness we had just left. I knew which way we had come back and retraced that path back, estimating where the action had broken off, loudly whispering now after each twenty paces "Cassidy. Cassidy." My imagination felt sure there was at least a company of Chinese waiting to ambush and either kill or capture me, tensing at each pause ready for the expected sudden burst of fire, the blinding trip flare, the crack of a grenade and wild spray of deadly metal. My heart in my mouth. I continued on, keeping my silhouette low – hell, I must be soon tripping over Chinese corpses from the action, or an enemy stretcher party; I was halfway to Mongolia for fcks sake. I called again softly "Cassidy, Cassidy." And somewhere in the darkness over to my left, what was it – a response, or a groan? How did I know it wasn't a wounded Chinese? I didn't. And then an unmistakeable Australian-accented hoarse whisper "Over here mate, I'm down."

I moved to where I thought the voice came from, and almost tripped over Cassidy, who was lying on his side, one hand clamped against a field dressing on his thigh. Could I carry him? In the dark, I couldn't tell the seriousness of the wound, but said "If I can get you vertical, supporting you, can you hop along on one leg with me until we get back?" And surprisingly, Cassidy made a joke of it, laughing softly: "*Hop along?* HopalongCassidy? Yeah, nice one sir, not you too? Ha-ha, rightyo, let's give it a whirl." I packed another field dressing on Cassidy's sticky thigh wound and strapped it. I picked up Cassidy's weapon and slung both Owens over one shoulder by their slings and managed to haul Cassidy to his feet – or should that be 'foot'? Cassidy's hissed intake of breath and soft yelp "Yikes" was a signal of his pain, and I said "Sorry, mate", to which Cassidy answered "It's OK Skip, just me being a sissy." He put an arm over my shoulder and neck, and hobbled close alongside me like a Siamese twin footrace, through the rough stubble back towards our lines. Across to the East there was the *Dotdotdot* of someone's heavy machine-gun laying down a probable fixed range on their minefield gap, and even further away, there was a beautiful silent arc of coloured dashes from tracer across the sky like a firework. Cassidy husked something, and I stopped, whispering. "Are you OK, want to rest?" "No boss. No; just said; really appreciate it, you coming back. Thought I might be in for a Chinese holiday, and I don't fkn like rice." He grunted a laugh "Everybody else back OK?" "Yeah, far as I know. Bonsell has a foot wound, but everyone else is fine. We'll get you fixed up soon, just hang on." One of my arms around Cassidy's waist supporting him meant that the two weapons hanging by their slings kept getting in the way, and I knew that Cassidy was in some pain, but we were progressing well. And then suddenly out of nowhere there was Sgt Whan, returning, saying "Bonza's fixed up, let me take Cassidy off of you" but I replied "It's OK Mike thanks, got him, we're fine" but

Whan helped on Cassidy's other side, asking "Where you hit, Baz?" Cassidy answered "Just one slug I think, left thigh, hurts like a sonova bitch, but I think Skipper has stopped the bleeding." "Have you had morphine?" "No, butterfingers. Dropped the bastard and couldn't find it in the dark, anyway, they'll give me something down the RAP. Or a slug of rum would be nice." A sharp (maybe frightened?) young sentry voice in the dark called across their front as the forward post challenged, and Whan gave them the password, adding "Who's that, you Willie? There's three of us coming in, we need a stretcher, mate."

There were two medics waiting for us who expertly manoeuvred Cassidy from the Sergeant and me. Michael briefed them: "GSW left thigh, no happy juice yet" but one of the bearers said "Where's this other blood from? You got a head wound?" Cassidy said "Not as far as I know, can't feel anything" but Sgt Whan, sharp as a tack, said "Not yours Baz, it's come from Goldy... sorry sir, You. You're bleeding onto Cassidy from something." Having relieved myself of Cassidy and the weapons, I wiped the side of my head and felt a smear of wet blood, but shook my head "Nah, can't feel anything, must be a scratch." But the senior medic bearer wouldn't have it. "Not up to you sir, have to get it checked, come back in the other Jeep with us please." Firmly, like an order. And Sgt Whan added "He's right Skip, better get it looked at, we'll be right here; I'll tell the Major and do the Contact Report for Company. You go with them. See you back in a mo."

On the way steeply down the back of the ridge to the regimental aid post, Cassidy was taken away from me, and I found myself in the company of a private soldier from A Company named McLaren. Had they had engagement too? I asked him in the lurching downhill Jeep "Where are you hit?" And the digger held up one bloody bulky bandaged hand supported with the other hand. He must have sensed my hesitation and doubt. McLaren said indignantly – "What, did you think, I might have done this on purpose? That's a fucken laugh; this is my left hand mate, and I'm left-handed. That's my main hand what I do everything with. I eat with it, wipe my arse with it, scratch my balls with it; so I'm not going to put a bullet in it, am I? I'm not fucken stupid." And then, as if noticing my chest epaulette with my badges of rank, he added "Sir"

[We all knew, or heard of, men who had been evacuated because of 'accidental' bullet wounds in a foot or hand, (Accidental? Yeah, right), and the stigma which was attached to a GSW (gunshot wound) in an extremity, knowing that there was a possibility it was self-inflicted. Or so it was suspected. But then again, be reasonable; with the well-known ease with which anybody's Owen Gun could misfire, or the bolt get caught in clothing or equipment, who could be sure? Especially in the panic of reaction and sudden firing. Of course there would be an inquiry, maybe including a confidential unit report on the victim's behaviour or known (or suspected) mental attitude leading up to the incident; but this is war, and the demands of action, troop replacements, promotions, leave, etc. sometimes meant that such inquiries were incomplete or went astray; and anyway, men were constantly weapon testing, and weapon handling, and forever going out armed on hazardous patrols in which close-quarter firing took place, most often at night, sometimes in thick fog, always in limited visibility, on ground which was strewn with bits of barbed wire churned up by shellfire trying to ankle-trip you, who could tell how a GSW occurred? And after platoon or company medic first-aid and medevac back to Battalion or the Swedish MASH, you'd

231

have to consider the great temptation — which everybody knew but nobody ever really spoke about - of that dream smooth analgesic-assisted flight across to a clean sweet superior peacetime hospital in Japan with first-class nursing treatment, white sheets, and maybe even the 'hero' classification of WIA (wounded in action) to accompany a man's recovery and physio in Kure base before being shipped back home to Australia with a prestige maybe not completely earned. Wouldn't it be nice; what a temptation to get the hell out of here.]

At the regimental aid post, we were led into a busy bright-lit triage tent leading inside to the first emergency treatment zone with its stretchers and staff at tables in blood-spotted white gowns over their uniforms, but first they were confronted by a frowning stooped elderly Canadian army medical captain who was getting name and number, and giving every incoming wounded a preliminary inspection with his powerful torch and enquiry, partially removing field dressings to examine before replacing temporary wound covers as he continually spoke over his shoulder to an RAMC Corporal who was writing instructions to be labeled or handed on to each patient before registering them on. "GSW primary, low velocity to left tibia, Pantopon 22 ml., for wound debridement and transfusion, BP check." Then he examined Private McLaren, who was in front of me next: "GSW to hand – left hand?" he turned aside to the RAMC Corporal speaking very quietly, his eyebrows raised "Debridement and whole blood, Pantopon 22 mil. Query S.I?" But McLaren listening keenly spoke up hotly "What's that fucken S.I.? *SI?* Self-inflicted? No fear! It's not bloody self-inflicted I'm telling you." But the Captain didn't take it up. He was familiar dealing with shocked and stroppy patients before treatment, some under the influence of happy juice. "Keep moving son, we've got to clean you up first, stem that bleeding, get you a cup of tea, talk later." But McLaren continued arguing back as he was led away. And the Captain looked up and recognized me next in the line "Hullo; Danny

232

isn't it, from the Aussie battalion? You lot been in action again?" I was shaking my head at recognition of the serious purpose of the surgical tent "I'm Andy, not Danny. Look, mine's just a scratch, I'll be wasting your time, I'm fine." But the Captain saw the now crusted dry blood on my forehead and raised his bright torch beam, and said "No Andy, not just a scratch, might need a stitch when we clean it up, what caused it, do you know?" "Dunno, probably bit of grenade" and the Captain over his shoulder to his corporal "Shrapnel surface contusion, get Kelly to debride it, suture if necessary and patient on to One Twenty-First ." And I knew that '121st' meant the One Twenty-First Evac Hospital in Seoul, with the delays, observation, treatment, medication – probably two days at least. (Was this my temptation, a mini-holiday, a bit of a laugh? or was it a waste of time and a burden on Sgt Whan and the men in my platoon, and worse still -- possibly one of the spare subalterns at BHQ being moved in to take over my platoon so that I would be shovelled back to a supernumerary position with men I did not know? Never *hatchi*, It was not going to happen.) I dutifully took my 249 Triage sheet from the RAMC Corporal's clipboard, and when the Captain turned to the next incoming patient, I shoved the document inside my parka and walked briskly further into the next tent, telling the white-masked medico in the blood-stained apron who turned to look at me "I've just brought in a couple of my men, Private Cassidy, GSW left thigh, and Private Bonsell, right foot, just admitted." His orderly told me I was too late for Cassidy, he was already transferred to surgery at the Ouijongbu MASH, while Bonsell waved to me from a folding chair in which his raised foot was being freshly bandaged by a kneeling attendant. "Over here, Skip. They're sending me on leave. Tell Sarge I'll see youse all back in Kure, Japan, feet up with a drink in each hand, surrounded by girls" he laughed. Two stretcher bearers needed to get past me with a groaning patient, and another orderly needing the space fronted me "Are you waiting for treatment? Where's your 249?" And I knew I had to get out of there. "No, I'm finished here, just checking my men." And back to Bonsell "OK Bonza, we'll send your stuff on, good luck, take it easy." And he answered "Right, Skip. Baz has told everyone how you went back for him. Good on you." It was a busy thoroughfare and I was in everybody's way, so I ducked back out again past the guy ropes. As luck would have it, I appeared just as an RAR Signals Dispatch Rider was hauling on his gauntlets and kick-starting his thundering mud-caked Harley in the track outside. I tapped him and the rider unclipped the side ear-cover below his helmet. "I need a lift back to Battalion HQ, OK?" "OK by me sir, but there's no pillion and the rack will be hard on your arse." I swung my leg across. It seemed laughingly intimate to be hanging on like a lover around the DR's bulky parka-ed waist above his pistol holster, making me smile to myself as the rider skillfully wrestled that Harley like a rodeo bull-handler, skidding and sliding with and against traffic along that track of mud past endless unit signs, tents and dug-outs until we reached BHQ, where I tapped the DonR again and got down gingerly from my uncomfortable perch, thanking him. He was right about the sore backside. Familiar BHQ was a collection of sandbagged tents and hoochies on the reverse slope, plus the C.O.'s hidden caravan which was guarded by a sentry with a submachine-gun who was about to challenge me, when one of the HQ officers (Lt. Figgis) who was crossing, spotted me and said: "Andy? Are you OK? We heard you were medevac'ed out with a wound." But I just mumbled "Just a scratch; had to check on two of my wounded, I'm OK. Is the M.O. here?" And as it happened, he was, and I was able to get him to stick a plaster on the scratch, which is all I had wanted anyway. And while he was doing it, Major Shep the Company Commander came in and said "Andy! We heard you were hit. Thank goodness you're OK. Sgt. Whan told us about you going back for Cassidy, and the boss wants to put you up for a middy" (*an MID – mention in despatches*). And all I could say was "I just did what anybody would do." Shep asked the MO "Is he going to be all right?" To which David, the MO smiled "He'll live." But to me he added "Keep it covered, don't get dirt in it. And if you get any delayed pain from it, come and see me." So Shep said, "Whan gave me the contact report, but I'll need some more details for the I.O's War Diary. Come inside for a minute." That was when the Colonel came out of his command post caravan and saw me. "Young Turner! I hear you were wounded and went back for one of your men. Well done; is he alright? Come in and tell me all about it."

At Yong Dong Po, returning to Japan from Tokchong, Jakob waited patiently until the C47 was loaded with litters for patients followed by the nurse-supervised allocation of canvas seats for walking wounded up forward where they could be cared for. There was an RAAF one-striper with a clip-board marking off names as they boarded, and he read off Jakob's name and then added 'Sir' as he realised his rank. Blask's only badges – now faded khaki printed pips - were on the slide in the middle of his chest, where the parka was designed. The Leading Aircraftsman asked: "Have you got your seventeen thirty-five, sir?." "Whatever that is", Jakob answered. They laughed. "Your Movement Control order, sir." "Oh that. This." Jakob showed him his movement order from Comwel Div to BCFK." "That'll do nicely, sir. Welcome aboard."

An Australian Signals Corporal waiting next in line behind Jakob raised his chin at the North Eastern horizon where underclouds reflected a distant artillery barrage which flickered like summer lightning. "Some poor bastards are copping it again tonight," he said. "Thank Christ we're out of there."

Jakob boarded and secured his seat-strap ready for the usually not-very-comfortable 3 hour flight to Japan, during which he gratefully accepted a mug of tea and a slice of Red Cross fruitcake from the RAAF nurse. Maybe she thought that he was one of the repatriated wounded. Anyway, despite the cold and the noise, he managed, sitting, to doze off until the engines changed their pitch.

When he awoke (with a stiff neck), a patient strapped in the lower stretcher opposite seemed to be trying to get his attention, a bit agitated. Nobody could hear anything through the planes' throbbing engines, so Jakob unbuckled and crossed the short distance to the stretcher patient, bending down, asking "Say Again?" Despite the patient speaking again, Jakob still didn't understand, but by then the attending alert nursing sister intervened, but then she turned back to Jakob and said: "He needs to drink. Can you give him the tube for me? I'm looking after someone else up forward." So Jakob took the bottle from her and fed the tube to the patient's mouth, who nodded and sucked for a minute, until he terminated it by turning his mouth aside. "Cheers mate," he croaked. The medevac label on his chest indicated his name was Cassidy. So he was obviously talking, if not walking, wounded. Blask said "No problem. Are you all from the same action?" And the soldier said "No, only me, caught in an ambush of our patrol – the others here are from an earlier stoush, they're from MASH or 121st – I think." Jakob waited until the soldier dozed off again, and then resumed his seat. He was tempted to ask if the soldier knew Andy, but decided it would be too much of a coincidence.

After the long cold flight, the plane taxied in at Iwakuni past parked fighter planes and disembarkation began, supervised by the medical staff carefully transferring wounded on stretchers for their overnight treatment or observation until the hospital train to Kure BCGH next day. Jakob was checked off the disembarkation list, and ran in the light rain across the wet tarmac down to the jetty where the workboat was waiting for him and the half-dozen non-medical passengers. A canvas-wet Jeep and trailer soon followed them with their greatcoats and kitbags, which the Japanese crewman stowed for them.

Then motoring slowly out through the marker buoys in a steady drizzle past the Sunderland flying boats moored by the slipway. Once outside the harbour's protection, the army sergeant coxswain gunned the engines to a roar which cancelled any possibility of conversation onboard. Waves broke on the bow sending long sprays back on the foredeck and windscreen, while the wind drove scuds of rain in intermittent dashes across the glass. Already it was night, and below the dark starless sky, grey island shapes merged into the gloom, allowing occasional distant light pinpoints to penetrate the steady rain. The travel-weary troops sat along each side of the workboat with their backs against the gunwales, their heads close to the vibrating sidecovers. Some slept (or tried to), some tried to talk (and quickly gave up), some smoked, staring dully at the wet planking deck beneath their feet.

All of their kitbags, like Blask's, wet from the transfer from plane to boat, were stacked aft, and for a time, forgotten. The men were damp, tired, and silent. This was just another episode in a volunteer soldier's life – it was served up to you, and you put up with it. But relieved to be out of that war zone, looking forward to a leave pass in the small city full of bright noisy beer halls and bars – and girls. Not to mention far away from deep defence pits and dugouts infested with rats and - just by the way – enemy maniacs charging, shooting at you and blasting you with mortars and artillery. OK, so the troops' future was, what? Reassignment, drill, retraining, route marches, live-ammunition exercises at the Haramura Battle School, and reallocation before going back all too soon to face bugle-blowing mass attacks of Chinese Peoples' Volunteers who really wanted to kill them, and putting up with this all for a pittance you can't spend and sleeping rough when you could get a chance, between stand-to's and patrols. But meanwhile, this, this dream was real – leave, comfortable clean beds, good food, beer, and maybe if you were lucky, a friendly female.

The Japanese crewman in the workboat sat on a fixed highstool next to the coxswain, as if for companionship, but his eyes were not forward on the course or the occasional approaching navigation lights; he seemed fascinated by the soldiers' uniforms and badges. Maybe it was the slouch hats with their upturned sides. From time to time the wind blew a curtain of rain aside, now to reveal the glow of city lights indicating Hiroshima on the port bow and the sacred island of Miyajima almost opposite, and the coxswain announced – if anyone was interested, and able to hear him above the engines' roar – "We're about half-way".

It had been the same on Jakob's first arrival from Australia. The rain had eased when AM1488 slowed and pulled into Kure harbour half an hour later. The city beyond was still lit up, bright coloured advertising neons glaring on and off, and every light was reflected on the wet buildings and concrete paving dockside as the workboat glided on reduced engine power through the breakwater to the terminal, halting beneath the pier light, where the Japanese crewman leapt ashore and took the bow line to a sturdy bollard, making fast, before dropping fenders alongside and running aft to take the stern line in hand. There were a few NCOs from the receiving reinforcement camps in glistening wet ponchos protecting their documents from the rain, no doubt to 'take delivery' of their allocated personnel in transit from the workboat, and behind them, a 2½ ton GMC and two Jeeps waited for passengers. The rain glistened on the iron pontoon which see-sawed up and down on the hinged ramp, rocked by the boat's returning waves, water slap-slapping against the pier.]

When the duty jeep finally dropped Jakob off in Cassels Camp at the mess entrance after midnight, the building was all but closed; only a couple of lights on, and 'Happy' the Japanese barman at the door waiting to meet him with a waxed paper Japanese umbrella on a bamboo frame. The pattern on it was large hibiscus flowers. "Werrcome back, sir."

"Hello Happy. Good to see you again. Where is everybody?"

"All gone bed or in town sir, rate-rate. (Late-late) Captain Kelly-san gave me your key, same-same room like before. You want eat, sir? Drink, sir?"

"No thanks, Happy. Eat drink tomorrow. Thanks for waiting to meet me." The barman wanted to take his kitbag and duffle, but Jakob dismissed him and went in and up the familiar stairs carrying his luggage. There was a muffled sound of Armed Forces radio music from behind a couple of doors along the passage, and someone singing tunelessly from the shared shower cubicles at the end. There always seemed to be someone doing that. He made a toilet visit and then found his way to the familiar room.

The same loose window glass rattling in the wind, the same bare electric globe swinging on its frowsy cord sending shadows dodging each way. As expected, his blankets and sheets folded regimentally correct with a bare pillow on the bare mattress waiting for him to assemble. Ah well, no big deal. At least it was away from Korea. Better than the tents of Camp Casey, better than the Seoul bombed-out school floor, better than the half-Nissan hut with its dangerous petrol heater.

And then in the morning, back in his room after a shower and shave, the door suddenly opened and 'Smiler', the old (as in former) shared Kure 'housegirl' came in, not bothering to knock, or worrying about Jakob being naked, not smiling, (never smiling, hence the nickname), waving her finger at him. "You number one bad boy; *damé desu!*, you no tell me you come back." For a moment he entertained the thought of having to notify Smiler each of his detailed movement orders to Kure. She was bossing him about (as she did everyone), crossly hauling the bedclothes off 'Who do this bed? No good. Where you kit? You give *Smyra* you kit now, all washy-washy.' And pulling things out of his duffel 'Why all wet?' And recoiling from finding his service revolver heavy in its holster, flapping her hands '*Ajiapaa!* Take away, take away!'

Back at the familiar old barrack room at the end of the day, in his absence Smiler had made a neat home again, somewhere finding a square piece of matting for the bedside floor, and the bed was neatly remade – of course much better than he could do it, his pyjamas already washed, dried, ironed and folded on the pillow. The room was warm; so she must have galvanised Miyonamae the janitor into action. All he needed to do now was to rescue his foot-locker and spare clothes from the depot, and report for what duty they have for him this time in the familiar transport depot. He unloaded his books from the carton the porter had delivered from the store, plugged in his record-player, and put on the first record of Dvorak's 9th; *Sinfonie aus der neuen Welt*. The familiar room almost felt like coming home.

"Someone to see you, sir." Driver Cullen at the door of Jakob's Kure transport office, and as he rose from his chair, a strange but familiar figure in battledress took Cullen's place. "Bloody Blask" he said, entering, holding out his hand, and Jakob reflected his broad smile. "Bloody Vickery" he replied, as they shook hands. "My God, Vickery, what are you doing here?" Jakob had not seen Vickery since their graduation all that long time ago. "I hope you haven't brought your friend Thunderbum up with you." They shook hands warmly, loosely embracing, patting shoulders. "No"

Vickery said laughing, "Our mate Thunderbum. Last seen a year ago terrorizing a new batch of young sirs north of the Molonglo River." He looked around him. "Hey, this is a nice cushy set-up, Jake, what a sweet cop. How did you manage it?" "Come in, sit down, tell me what you've been up to." "Well, I've just left Andy on leave up in Tokyo, and promised to pass on his regards and insults. I'm posted to the Battle School down at Haramura, so I imagine I'll be in and out of Kure a bit." "That's wonderful, and how is my old mate Andy?" "Complaining that you never answer his letters." "What letters?" "Andy was fine when I left him in Tokyo. We were on R&R at Ebisu, and he should be back at Battalion by now, after a bit of bother."

A knock on the door frame, and Muriel intruded politely "Would you like a cup of tea, sir?" Blask already had one on his desk. "Yes please," Vickery said, and Jakob introduced them, so that Muriel came across to shake Vickery's hand, before going for the tea. As she left, Vickery made a face of approval behind her back, being impressed. "Wow." And Blask shook his head warningly "No, mate, off limits."

Blask now said "What was the bother was Andy in?" "Well, one of his platoon shot through, went AWOL, deserted. They still haven't located him. Poor old Andy would have to front the Colonel when he got back. Fortunately, he's in pretty good with the CO. You know he got a MID?" "No, really? What did he get that for? He never told me." "Well Andy's been getting a bit Gung-ho lately, volunteering for anything. He got the Middy for refusing treatment after being hit, going back for one of his wounded after a patrol. He's very popular with his men. They call him Tarzan, would go anywhere with him. *For* him. You know once, he used to be pretty quiet; well now he'll try anything." Muriel interrupted them, bringing Vickery his mug of tea, and he thanked her. When she left, he continued. "About Andy. You know his old man is a politician in the Defence Department? Well, he apparently wangled Andy a job back home as *aide-de-camp* to the State Governor, but Andy turned it down, wouldn't leave his troops, argued with the Colonel who said it was a privilege and not to be rejected, but Andy dug in his heels and insisted he wanted to be a real soldier, not a poodle-faker." "God no," Jakob said, "I didn't hear any of this. Bloody Andrew, never tells me anything. Sounds like he's got the bit between his teeth. What's it been like, over there?" "Well, to be honest, I'm glad I'm out of it. Some people are getting a bit toey going on every patrol with the uncertainty of the armistice talks. The yank brass are always pressuring for prisoners, but every time it just means more casualties, and no prisoners anyway. The bloody Chinese would rather die than surrender." "Yeah, I heard that from some of the Brits. Have you been amongst it yourself?" "A bit. We all got our share of patrols and action. Did you know two of our class got killed? Peters, and Spencer. Peters was shot dead on patrol, but Spencer was very unlucky; misread his compass we think, and led his men into their own minefield, where the fences had been blasted by Chinese artillery. Poor Toby, he and two of his men were blown apart." "God, poor Spencer. And his men."

The phone on Jakob's desk rang, and it was Muriel. "Major Blackheath for you, sir." Jakob grimaced to Vickery, and took the call. "Sir. What can I do for you?" "Hello, Jake. I've had Sub-area Seoul on the line again today.

They want to borrow you for a few weeks back at Tokchong Advance Supply Depot. Captain Davis from Tokyo is going to come and take over from you here, on his way home. He'll be on tomorrow morning's train – can you meet him and arrange a hand-over?"

When he hung up, Blask shook his head at Vickery. "So much for the nice cushy set-up. That was another posting, back to the Queer Country again – I only arrived back last week. Vickery laughed. "I must have put the Mozz on you. Sorry about that. Will you be coming back here, again?" "Anybody's guess. Until just now, I didn't know I was leaving. This is the army." They laughed.

242

"Hear the blowing of bugles, hear the patter of feet
The ROK Seventh* is in full retreat
'Cause they're movin' on, and they'll soon be gone,
They're travellin' far, down the MSR** Yes they're movin' on.
The Chows are comin' up 3.5.5,
The Yanks are buggin' out the other side
'Cause they're movin' on, and they'll soon be gone
They won't stop to boast, till they reach the coast,
Cause they're movin' on."

*(Insert preferred insulted unit here)   **(MSR = Main Supply Route)
[Original song by Hank Snow 1950]

Peachy is yakking as usual. "There's this man and woman in an upstairs bedroom, going at it like a couple of rabbits, but down outside suddenly a car door slams, and the woman panics and goes to the window. 'Quick' she says, 'it's my husband, I'll distract him downstairs. You hide in the wardrobe.' So this guy bundles up his clothes and gets into the wardrobe and pulls the door shut. But there's a little squeaky kid's voice that says 'It's dark in here, innit?' Shhh. The man gets the kid to be quiet. Persuades the kid it is a game, a big secret, don't tell anyone. But the little kid is smart, and says he hasn't got a bike, but he'd like one. 'OK, but you can't tell anyone, promise.' So the next day, this kid is riding a new bike, and his dad says 'where did you get the bike?' And the kid says 'It's a secret.' 'You stole it, didn't you?' 'No, someone gave it to me.' 'Who?' 'I can't tell you.' So the dad grabs the kid and marches him off to the local church, saying 'you will go to confession, and you will tell the truth.' Anyway, the kid gets inside the confession box, and he squeaks 'It's dark in here, innit?' And the priest says 'Oh no, not you again!'

Peachy's listeners laugh. As usual.

Exciting to realise that this is maybe getting near the end of our year in this stupid war for us, and looking back, we are not the same people who came here. For example, the platoon has changed in composition; well, all units change don't they, people come and go with leave and promotions and special duties and sickness. And death. Yeah, there is that too - we don't talk about death very much. I was going to say it's a fact of life, but that would be a wrong word, wouldn't it? A fact of death. There were four more fatal casualties in Dog Company a few days ago, and some poor Korean water-boy got shot through the head by a sniper as he was coming up to our lines. Poor kid. Just crack thud, down he went, a couple of metres from delivering to us in our position. They called him Kim, but then every Korean seems to be called Kim. He had tried teaching us a few words in his language, but we knew nothing about him. We do talk about our mates we've lost, KIA, in the same way we talk about the ones who have just transferred out, after all we have a group history together, and various things remind us of those who are no longer here, the things they did or said. And we are generally only too well aware when one of us is killed in action if it happens while we are together. But then some people also die later as a result of wounds, and that usually happens out of sight, en route to treatment at Casualty Clearing, or M.A.S.H, or at a surgical hospital in Japan or even at home, and it takes a while for that news to get back to us. But if one of us is killed ***I.A.*** (in action), there is no opportunity to make a proper farewell, because everything's happening right there and then, you know, the war goes on around you, you have to keep fighting, and you might not even hear about it until the action is over and you withdraw or consolidate, when you are told 'by the way so-and-so got hit', and by then his body is already taken away, and we don't have any part in the formal processes and that's it, except later, when we're back in Echelon or on leave, that's when we get to talk about our mate who is no longer with us; or no longer with anyone. And it's then that we have a sort of wake over a few drinks, talking about him, remembering the things he said or did, laughing about some good times, even taking the mickey about some of the things he did or said, drinking his health (well not his health obviously if he's dead, but you know what I mean). Even dead, he is still part of us. One of our Band of Brothers. We never forget one of our own.

Letter from Elizabeth to Jakob from Sydney:
<Dear Jakob – thanks for getting Andrew to finally write to us – well, to Mum. Not only writing once, but several times? Wow. Don't know what has happened to him, but he has really changed. I mean a year ago, it was you who were the serious professional soldier and Andrew was just sort of passing time – but suddenly he seems to have stopped drifting and started enjoying what he is doing. Soldiering, fighting a war? In his letters he talks about the men in his unit as though they are really his mates. Perhaps they are, and it's them who have changed him. I can't help feeling that you helped change him too. But enough about my dopey brother, how are you? You seem to have been moving about, one minute you were in Japan, next in Korea, but maybe it is all the same zone anyway. You asked me how I was managing all the study, and the answer is, just putting my nose to the grindstone and working, instead of playing-up like many of the students do, either socializing or getting involved with politics. Oh well, here I am writing to you and studying all the hours that God gave, while everyone else seems to be out partying. I really have changed from the idiot teenager I was. Seriously. Picture me at Sydney Uni's Old Med School in a team of seven of us around our own dedicated cadaver gradually dissecting him before sitting on the lawns eating our sandwiches as if it was the most normal thing in the world. (We sit on the lawns below the National Standards building, listening to the university carillon playing Gaudeamus Igitur, which is a sort of student hymn). You might be surprised to hear that Mum and Dad finally got divorced and sold the Belconnen house. I am in digs here at college, while Mum has a nice flat at Rose Bay where I also have a room for weekends. Mum has discovered life afresh in all sorts of voluntary activities. The last time I saw Dad (who came to my school graduation), he mentioned that he was going to leave the public service and stand for parliament. I don't know how that

will go. I sense that he has a few enemies. I sometimes wonder about your family, you don't mention them - is it only your wonderful grandfather I met at your graduation? He was great. Is he here in Sydney? I could visit him for you if you'd like. I'd love that.

You mentioned leave in your last letter, but I suppose that is only local. Do you have any idea when you would be coming back to Australia? And where they might send you next? Will that war ever end? Wherever you go, my fingers are crossed that we might meet again, but I suppose that is also a fantasy, although I hope not. I really hope not.>

----

hat day is it? Skeeter asked no-one in particular, vaguely. "I haven't got the faintest," Someone answered. "Search me," said Corporal Calabria, "must be about 25th." And Specs chimes in, the man who knows everything, "Sunday. Sunday the 26th of July, 1953, to be exact." Which is probably accurate, but then again, Specs ("The Professor") isn't always right. Remember that business about him supposed to be helpful to Battalion HQ because he was learning Chinese? It didn't happen. It turned out that Specs had picked up a Teach Yourself Chinese book in transit at Hong Kong, and was only just starting to learn Chapter One, practicing on everyone; and anyway that was Cantonese, not Mandarin which is apparently quite different, and what our enemy here in Korea is supposed to speak. But then Specs is always a bit different, isn't he?

Anyway, we know that this could be our last patrol. Shep said the platoon is due for rotation again, and after a spell in reserve tomorrow, it looks like we'll then be on our way back home via Japan like I wrote to Rita. Whoop-de-do. No big deal today, patrols like this are becoming almost routine. On the airphotos there were the same old diggings forward of the hill they called Marilyn, which the Chinese had used two weeks ago until the battalion operation had driven them off with the Kiwis bombarding the hell out of them, destroying their earthworks, so that no-one thought they'd ever try to occupy them again. Except everyone was aware Charlie was getting desperate to push their front forward again so as to claim 'existing territory' when the armistice is finally agreed. If and when. And now, the I.O. reports activity at that old site again, maybe they are sending out an observation post, maybe they left something behind, or maybe it's just a feeler to check the condition of their old bunkers before a new push to re-occupy. At the Orders Group, Shep says "Don't get involved in any big stoush, just observe and report. If it's just a Chinese scout group, take them on, see if you can snatch one of them for interrogation. You know the drill, Andy. But if they are already back occupying in strength, don't try to take them on, we will organize another heavy action to choof them out. So a small patrol this time. Just a section, have a shufti and report." *Shufti*, (a look) in the middle of the night, that's a joke. We'd done a daylight recce – we knew where we would go, no sign of activity through the field glasses, so probably nothing happening. Not far to go really, the valley NML is only about 300 metres wide, so you can almost count your paces and know where you are in the dark. Should be a piece of cake again. Put the kettle on, we'll be back in a minute.

So, only a handful of us, and seeing how I got the feeling that some of my men were getting nervous about getting into another battle this late in their tour, their time nearly over, how their luck has lasted so far, and why push your chances; I made it a volunteer squad. Usually no shortage of volunteers from which to get a hand-picked group. I looked around them, laughing, teasing them, "You lot. What a bunch of fking no-hopers. Have we got a white flag?" They laugh with me, or at me too. Peachy says "I've always got my leaflet, Boss, just in case" – meaning the Chinese leaflets the enemy leave for us, inviting us to surrender; the leaflets made a great souvenir. But everyone knows Peachy is the last person you'd imagine surrendering, he is a barrack-room clown, but he loves a battle. Tough as nails. Always a few other guys up for it, ready to have a go, and this is no exception. Peachy is one of them, Peter of course, our Bren man, loves his gun and fighting, and always Fergie. Fergie's in the middle of a poker game with some others, and says "Take over my hand, Macka, too good to fold, I'm on a run of luck." Which he shouldn't say; you never tempt fate by saying you're feeling lucky. Even young Timmy puts his hand up this time, hasn't yet been in a proper battle, and I don't want to include him this time either – it could be one of the last patrols for the platoon, and I don't want to risk him. "I need you on minefield gap look-out this time, Timmy." As a platoon leader, you are always aware that the decisions you make might be life or death, even amongst volunteers. Crowe is nervous, doesn't really want to go on this one, but I had to disappoint him: "Sorry, Richie, but I need you and your radio with me - just this last one, OK?" Sergeant Whan of course, and Corporal Calabria, both reliable members of any patrol. That should be more than enough. Walshy and Skeeter and Timmy on reserve duty at the wired minefield gap. We had an OG (orders group) in the afternoon and sussed out the lie of the land together through binoculars before weapon testing. Then when it was getting near time, when we were blacking-up in the communication trench from the shared tube, Peachy dropped on one knee and did an Al Jolson, singing "Mammy", so that some others joined him, *"The sun shines East, the sun shines West"* which is an old joke. But why not. Crowe complained that we were short one flak-jacket, so I sent Timmy back down to Company HQ to get another, but he hadn't returned in time, maybe he got sidetracked, and it's already H-hour on the dot and timing is always everything, Time Out, Time In, we can't wait, so I gave Richie my jacket, seeing he was nervous about it. It's not that long since we started to wear them — at the beginning of this war nobody wore flak-jackets, they were a novelty and they're always being improved. Remember one of our newly commissioned officers got chest-shot with burp-gun bullets penetrating the front join of his vest a while back, and as a result, the jackets were redesigned to provide a bulletproof flap over the fastening. Some flak jackets are uncomfortable. I had gone without one before, and there were never enough of the bloody things available. I know, going on patrol without one is a bit of a risk, but the whole fucking war is a risk, isn't it? You could say that about everything we were doing, from surviving the deafening Chinese artillery bombardment in our fortified hutchies; from creeping about at night in abandoned paddyfields possibly landmined or tripflared since our last patrol; from the fact we don't wear helmets on patrol; Yeah, everyone knows there is that recent order about always having to wear helmets forward of Battalion HQ, but Shep doesn't enforce that on patrols. No-one did. I mean everyone understood about the poor chances of recovery from direct head wounds, but then they also knew from experience that helmets are noisy and restrict hearing and visibility and are a damn nuisance when we were trying to creep up on Charlie. Mind you, don't tell anyone, but when we went out on patrol blackfaced in just a Caps Comforter or bandanna wrapped around our head, we knew between ourselves that we looked a bit piratical and dangerous, a bunch of tough guys, which is part of the morale thing, and it helped to counteract the, (you know, *f. e. a. r.*) which nobody talks about. Because we're soldiers, right?

Our usual practiced formation, so that we know where everybody is, so we were not likely to shoot one of our own in error. Nobody can see anything, not even the enemy in this pitch black. We creep low across the stubble, trying not to sound like a mob of cattle, eyes and ears pricked. Same as usual. You can hear your own loud breathing, staring into the darkness sure that everything is an enemy figure. Slow, slow. We are a long way across now. Nearly there. And the next thing we know, making everyone jump out of our skin, is when a Charlie ambush opens fire on us, just past halfway, and I get hit.

Yes, I got hit. This is not part of the plan. Suddenly I am not able to give any more orders myself, because I am knocked down. Copped a burst, chest and belly. Oddly, I don't feel any pain of bullets piercing me, just the physical whack, as if someone had hit me with a cricket bat across the midriff, and two things happen – I lose all power and fall arse over tip backwards like a sack of spuds, and can't fetch any breath. Can't do anything. Fuck. I hear my patrol return fire (good men, take the initiative, that's the way, taking the fight to the enemy like we practised, I'm out of this for a minute, but they don't need me, Michael Whan easily in charge like I knew he would, like we rehearsed so often – how to react to an ambush and loss of the leader), and in the scattered orange-yellow flickering light of stinking deafening gunfire I see good old Peter, typically not retiring but advancing at them, bracing himself with his heavy slung Bren-gun at the waist, blazing away in controlled short bursts left and right at the enemy muzzle flashes like some movie hero, and I also hear Crowe's high voice call out "The skipper's hit, the skipper's hit", and he is already kneeling at my side shrugging off his radio, feeling for where he might apply a field dressing to stop bleeding, and I am smiling, really, because I can't do anything, and can't even tell him about it, and feel useless, wanting to laugh; this isn't fair. And then a fleeting professional worry that — apart from me, who else copped it? But Sgt Whan quickly comes and kneels by my side saying "Hang on Skip, we'll get you back out in a minute, all the other boys are OK" before checking Ritchie's wound dressing, giving me the relief needle and joining the firefight as we all know the drill — control the situation first, achieve our aim, a strategic withdrawal if we have to, but nobody left behind — then keeping low they will haul me one each side still holding and firing their weapons to get out of this bad patch shouting unit identity at the standing patrol at the minefield passage - And as so often arguing; fck your stupid password, just get the medic, bring a stretcher quick, it's Goldilocks, he's hit bad.

(and then get me back into our lines where the precarious flying fox on the back of the hill can carry me down to a waiting Jeep and fast away for medical treatment at the Swedish MASH and a nice long holiday in Tokyo with sheets and pretty nurses...)

Wouldn't that be nice? But I already know that isn't going to happen. Not this time. And I am smiling to myself because this really is it, the end of Goldilocks the great war hero, who never wanted to be a soldier anyway, never <u>was</u> a soldier really, such a disappointment to the old man — (but you can be proud of me now, Daddy, your brave officer son — KIA, Killed In Action; you can't get a better referral than that for your colleagues in the Department to say about you, giving you vicarious kudos you don't deserve, you who never wore a uniform but thought you knew all about soldiering). But here I am, Goldilocks the dying MID hero, not even able to give directions, drowning choking on my own blood — I wish I could tell you about it, Jake, you'd see the funny side of it, me lying here useless as a concrete parachute, with rain gently falling on my face, and me even unable to wipe it away. Poor Sig Richie Crowe, having tried to stem some of my wounds with field dressings; in a flicker of gunfire I can see he is actually crying, the idiot, his face all screwed up like a kid who's lost his lollypop, probably because I gave him my flak jacket. Sergeant Whan well in control, shouting orders against the crack and spatter of grenades and Peter's solid rolling Bren bursts, the stink of gunsmoke. Choking, coughing, I hear Peachy calling back "I got two, Sarge, I got two of the bastards - the rest've scarpered back to their lines." And maybe I am going in and out of consciousness, because the next thing I know, I am being dragged roughly by my upper arms, bumping low along the uneven ricefield stubble on my backside with Sergeant Whan saying "Sorry Boss, it won't be long now, we've got you. Hang on. You'll be right, mate." I should remind him I dropped my gun, but it would be too late for that housekeeping. And as I fade in and out, still lying on my back and choking coughing spitting metallic tasting blood, I see that distant vertical searchlight hitting low cloud, the searchlight which marks the artificial 'Peace' village where the generals, ours and theirs, are still arguing about how and when to stop the war; sometime, next week, or maybe it already happened an hour ago unknown to us; but it doesn't matter any more. Not to me. Nothing matters any more.

Dammit, there are so many things I still meant to do, things I need to say. No time now. It's all too late; Sorry, Mum, Liz... I wish... Sorry Rita... Sorry... Now despite the happy juice, the pain starts. Oh. Christ...

The *Next* War

1962

Top Songs:
  Stranger On The Shore – Acker Bilk
  I Can't Stop Loving You – Ray Charles
  Roses Are Red, My Love – Bobby Vinton
  The Twist – Chubby Checker
  Breaking Up Is Hard To Do – Neil Sedaka

International Tension as President Kennedy blockades Cuba after USSR plan to build Missile Base there. Russia backs down. Everyone breathes again.

* Marilyn Monroe dies of drug overdose.

* New Pop band 'The Beatles' issue "Love Me Do"

* America's space probe Mariner II reaches Venus.

* Jamaica, Uganda, Samoa & Burundi gain Independence. Algeria gains independence from France amid bloodshed.

* Wimbledon: Rod laver def. M. Mulligan.

Oh, and just a few more wars meanwhile...

* The Burmese coup d'etat

* The civil war in North Yemen

* El Porteñazo, in Venezuela (Cuba threatening to invade)

* The Brunei Revolt

* The Communist Insurgence in Sarawak

* And the border war between China and India....

At the end of the day at Holsworthy Barracks near Sydney, the rain became heavier, if that were possible, ankle deep in the gutters, drenching the guards in their slickers checking vehicles entering or leaving the army base, and pedestrians hurrying to the civilian bus stops outside the gate, most in raincoats or ponchos, a few smart ones wielding umbrellas. Michael had already put up the roof canopy on his MG TF1500 inside the battalion car-port shelter, glad to be snug inside, and now as he neared the sentry posts with rain spattering on the canvas, the sports car's wipers were going full pelt, flicking water off the glass at both sides. He had to wait in the line of leaving vehicles being checked through, and a tall Captain in a gabardine raincoat nodded to him as he passed the MG's open window. Michael knew him from somewhere. He saw the Captain return the sentry's salute and didn't know why he did it, but he called from his side window panel "Would you like a lift, sir?" "Great, if you're going into town. I'm heading for the Station." "OK, hop in." For a second, a burst of rain came into the car with the new passenger, but then the sentry waved him through the raised boom gate, and the MG growled as he entered the main road traffic. The Captain said "Thanks, Sar-Major, appreciate it." "No worries." There was a stream of home-going vehicles entering the main road, and a string of municipal buses crowded with commuters behind fogged-up windows. Michael said "I'm just heading for Married Quarters, but it's no trouble to drop you off near the pedestrian tunnel, if that's OK" "Are you sure? I don't mind if you drop me near the roundabout." "Nah, you'll get soaked." The Captain laughed, "Once you're wet, you're wet. Wouldn't be the first time." Michael couldn't remember where he had met the Captain before. "No, no problem." A motorcycle with a pillion passenger hugging the rider tight, both of them in heavy wet army greatcoats, roared past the low sports car, laughing faces shining rain-wet and stringy hair, and the motorbike had to immediately brake to get in behind the car in front. "Bloody cowboys," Michael grumbled. "They'll be another

statistic if they don't watch out. Are you going into Sydney?"
"No, only Bankstown. My wife is on the staff at St. George's, and
we've got a flat nearby."

The Captain looked around him "Nice car. I'd forgotten how
close to the ground they are." "Yes, she's my pride and joy. But
really better in the sunshine with the roof down." They laughed.
They drove without speaking for a minute, and then Michael asked
"Are you part of this new training team going to French Indo-
China?" "Yes. You too?" "Yes. Just told me today. Do you think it
will become a full-size involvement?" "Doubt it. Probably not.
I don't think Australia will go for another Asian war just to suck
up to the Yanks." *(But then he knew that there was a national price
to pay for treaty obligations. He sighed.)* "Still, we do what we have
to do, don't we?" (What was it the Commandant said, way back
at Duntroon: 'We take the King's shilling...'? But now it was the
Queen's shilling wasn't it, and yet another Government?) It is what
it is as Jakob would have said.

Michael said "I think we met before somewhere, didn't we, was
it up in Korea?" "Probably. Or maybe Japan. You were with 3Bn?"
"Yes, also 2Bn." "I was with Supply and Transport with the Brits
at Seoul and Tokchong. But also at Kure Base." Michael had to
wipe the fogging concentration on the inside of the screen, and the
Captain, noticing, apologised "Sorry, that's due to me getting into
your car, wet." The Sergeant-Major changed gear deftly, and safely
avoided another bus pulling out. "I reckon you would have been
at Duntroon about the same time as my Korean skipper, Andy
Turner?" "Yes, same class, and Andy was my best mate. More than
that – he was family - I married his sister." Michael, remembering,
smiling, said: "He was one of our most popular officers; we missed
him after he was killed. Goldilocks, we called him." And then it was
like an angry outburst as he thumped the wheel with the heel of
his hand "He was killed on the last day of the war, the last *hours*
of the war; it's not fucking fair!" And then he collected himself,
shaking his head. "What a waste. He died at the 38th parallel, where
it all started. And never finished. I sometimes wondered what we

achieved." The Captain spoke quietly. "Oh, there's no doubt about what we – what you – what all of us, achieved. We rescued South Korea. You can be proud of that."

When the Captain spoke next, his voice had lowered. "I made a special trip back to visit Andy's grave at the war cemetery in Pusan, before I left. Desolate bloody place."

THE END

The Korean War

Military Deaths:

Australia	339	Belgium	101
Canada	516	Colombia	163
China	183,108	Ethiopia	121
France	262	Greece	192
N.Korea	294,151	S.Korea	137,899
Luxembourg	2	Netherlands	122
New Zealand	34	Philippines	92
South Africa	34	Thailand	129
Turkey	741	United Kingdom	1,109
United States	33,686		

Civilian Deaths:

South Korea	2,730,000 (est.)

GLOSSARY

Barrack, (verb)= to cheer, support a team

BCGH (abbrev.) = British Commonwealth General Hospital (Kure, Japan)

Blanco = Paste used to dress army webbing straps and equipment, khaki, white or black

Blue Light Outfit = Army issue anti-VD prophylactic kit

Bonza: Slang = Very good.

Bookfook: BCFK = British Commonwealth Forces, Korea

Bowser = Service Station Petrol Pump.

Bodgie = Member of youthful subculture, similar Rocker, Greaser. ('Widgie' = female equivalent)

Brahms & Liszt - rhyming slang = Pissed (drunk)

Bricosat = (Abbrev.) Brit Com Sub-Area Tokyo

BVDs = Underpants, from Commercial Brand of men's underwear

Bumf = Short for bum-fodder, red-tape, useless paperwork

Burl: Slang = Attempt, Trial "Give it a burl"

Cactus = Slang, meaning broken, useless, dead

Calwell – Arthur Calwell, Minister for Immigration in Australia's postwar Labor Government

Chewy On Your Boot = Australian football slang : intended to deter player accuracy

Chifley = Joseph 'Ben' Chifley, Australian postwar prime Minister. Labor Party leader

CPV (abbrev.) Chinese Peoples Volunteers

Daijobu (Japanese) = OK

Damé-desu (Japanese) = Bad, No good.

Dinkum = Real, True – also <u>Fair</u> Dinkum = Honest

Dig (abbrev.), **Digger** = Australian soldier

DR, DonR = Despatch Rider, Army Motorcycle messenger

Drongo = idiot (slang). (Actually, a drongo is an Australian bird, not stupid at all)

Dunny = Toilet, esp. Outdoor version. See also 'thunderbox', 'pissaphone'

Duntroon = Australia's Royal Military College, named from an original country property.

Dziadzia (Polish) = Grandad (pronounced Jaja)

Dziadziu (Polish) = Grandfather (pronounced Jajo)

Fang Farrier (Slang) = Dentist

Frangers = 'French Letters', condoms.

Galah : (Slang) = Idiot; also a pink & grey cockatoo (not an idiot)

Grouse : (slang) = good, great

GSW = Gunshot Wound

Hootchie /Hutchi/hoochy = Military shelter, bunker, tent (Possibly from Japanese Uchi = house)

Hubba Hubba = 1. Appreciation of beautiful girl, 2. Japanese slang = Hurry hurry (also 'chop-chop')

Jankers = Military Punishment or imprisonment (Unknown origin)

Jimmy Sharman = An Australian Travelling Boxing Troupe

Josonghamnida = (Korean) Sorry

K16 = Seoul Airbase (all airports were given numbers during the war)

Katcom = initials, '**K**orean **A**ugmentation **T**o **Com**monwealth' soldiers,

Khyber - rhyming slang, 'Khyber pass' = arse.

Kimshi= (Kimchi / Gimchi) Korean pungent fermented spicy vegetable dish

Kiwi = New Zealander (from national flightless bird)

Lair , **Mug Lair** = flashily dressed young man, show-off

Looie = Lieutenant (slang abbrev.)

Mallee = A hot dry region of North Western Victoria

Marsden Mat = Perforated steel plates as temporary runway surface or track

Metho = Methylated Spirit – denatured alcohol

Mo (Slang, abbrev.) = Moment (as in, 'Wait a mo')

Molly the Monk : rhyming slang = Drunk

Mozz (Slang) = Jinx

Musumé = (Japanese) Young Woman

Mutt & Jeff - rhyming slang = Deaf (Mutt & Jeff – comic strip)

Never hatchi (English/Japanese slang) = Never Happen *('nevahachi tomodachi '*= no way, mate)

OC = Officer Commanding

Okaerinasai = (Japanese) 'Welcome home'

Ort = vulgar slang = backside

Pierogi = Unleavened savoury dumplings

Pissaphone = Field Urinal – shell-case or other receptacle

Poodle-Faker = Brit army slang - Ladies'Man, woman-chaser, show-pony

Poof/Poofter = Male homosexual (derogatory)

Pucka (abbrev.) = Puckapunyal, Major Aust. Army base in Victoria.

PX = Post Exchange, US Forces Canteen & Stores

QMPSD = (US) Quarter Master Petroleum Supply Depot

Quid = Slang, Pound (Currency of 20 Shillings) Full Quid = Top Rate. (Not the Full Quid = Stupid)

QStore = Quartermaster Store

RAP = Regimental Aid Post, Fwd medical treatment

Rasky = **RAASC**, Royal Australian Army Service Corps (Supply & Transport)

RAEME = Royal Australian Electrical & Mechanical Engineers, 'Ray-me'

RAMC = Royal Army medical Corps (British)

RASC – Royal Army Service Corps (British) Supply & Transport

Recce (also Recon) = reconnaissance

Redcaps = Military Police (from wearing red caps/berets) – also 'Meat-Heads'

Repat. (abbrev.) = Repatriation General Hospital

Resch's = A brand of Sydney beer

RMC = Royal Military College (Duntroon)

Rollins = The makings for a rolled cigarette

Roneo = commercial brand of duplicator system

Scarper = run away, escape

Sheila (Slang) = any girl or woman (From Irish name)

Shikata ga nai = (Japanese) = 'C'est la vie', It is what it is

Shinpai nai (Japanese) = no worries

Short-Arm Inspection = Penis inspection for signs of venereal infection after leave

Shufti = Look – from Middle East Service, corruption of Arabic (šaf – 'to see')

Skin and Bone - rhyming slang = Phone (also 'Dog & Bone')

Solvol= Commercial Brand of Abrasive soap

Sook = Babyish person, coward (Derogatory)

Stoush = fight, argument (Unknown origin)

Tadaima (Japanese) = 'I'm home'

Technicolour Yodel (Slang) = Vomit

Thunderbox = Field Toilet – pit or drum receptacle

Toey = Edgy, nervous

Tomodachi = (Japanese) Friend, mate

Tucker – Slang= Food, meals.

Tui-san (Japanese) = Lieutenant

Up The Duff = Pregnant. (Also 'Bun in the oven')

Up There, Cazaly = Australian football slang, (Call of encouragement)

UXB (abbrev.) = Unexploded Bomb

VFL (abbrev.) = Victorian Football League – Australian Rules Football Code

Vandoos = (Vingt-deuzième) Royal Canadian 22nd Regiment

Waddy = Club, baton.

WRAAC = Womens Royal Australian Army Corps

WVS = Women's Voluntary Service (UK civilian aid workers)

Yama = (Japanese) Mountain, Hill

Yangnom (Korean) = Foreigner (derogatory)

R.N. (Ron) Callander is an award-winning Queensland Playwright, Author, and Freelance Journalist. He is a former State Secretary of The Australian Radio, Television and Screen Writers' Guild (AWG), and Member of the Fellowship of Australian Writers (FAW).

By the same author:

'Third Witness' (Screenplay)

'MacArthur's Pyjamas & Other Stories' (Seaview Press)

'One Beat of a Butterfly's Heart' (30° South Publ.)

www.ingramcontent.com/pod-product-compliance
Lightning Source LLC
Chambersburg PA
CBHW020435030726
47495CB00006B/1822